DEATH'S DARK WINGS

DEATH'S DARK WINGS

Raven Dane

Published in the UK by Telos Moonrise: Dark Endeavours
(An imprint of Telos Publishing Ltd)
5A Church Road, Shortlands, Bromley BR2 0HP, UK

Telos Publishing Ltd values feedback. Please e-mail us with any comments
you may have about this book to: feedback@telos.co.uk

Cover Design: David J Howe
Cover Art: Sessha Batto

First Edition

ISBN: 978-1-84583-895-9

British Library Cataloguing in Publication Data. A catalogue record for this
book is available from the British Library.

AUTHOR'S NOTE

This book is a work of alternative history, a total fabrication. There are some allusions to actual historic facts and figures but distorted through the warped lens of fiction and unrepentant personal bias.

My gratitude to Jonathan Ward and Adam Greenwood for their wise advice and having faith in a book with such an unusual plot.

PART ONE

From deep within a dark dimension beyond all that is known by the world of men, the soul of a great raven broke free, tearing through the Veil between worlds. The brutal rent in the Veil gave out a scream of warning resonating through the minds of humans and Sidhe alike. The eerie sound tainted all souls though only a few could hear it, even fewer understood its meaning.

The raven's cold, jet eyes took in the world of the living beneath the steady beat of its great wings. Its time was near.

1

Ireland, 1064

What had happened to the summer? The warrior Brandan mused as he rode alone for the first time since the season of many battles. Solitude allowed him to drop his customary air of bravado and nonchalance in the company of his fellow mercenaries. Now with only birds and hares to hear him, he could groan out loud at aching, weary back muscles during the long ride through a darkening landscape. He could openly wince at the sharp sting from healing sword slashes and the pain of deep bruises caused by axe blows and fists.

Bruised and battered, at least he was alive; many of his companions among the mercenary caste, known as Na Fianna, were not, a loss he bore with his usual pragmatic resignation. What choice did he have? He was a young man gifted with fighting skills but no noble blood or inheritance. At least life as a wandering mercenary paid well. It gave him the protection of a king or high-born lord during the summer months and payment of enough gold to survive the harsh winter. At least, it should have: the nobility were not above treachery and cheating the warriors from their just reward, especially if they lost one of their endless blood feuds with other tribal leaders. Brandan smiled and patted the heavy purse tied to his belt beneath his plaid cloak. This summer he had battled hard for an honourable master. The king's victory had helped swell Brandan's purse and added to the warrior's fearsome reputation.

Brandan was a risk-taker and not just on the battlefield. If he should arrive seeking winter shelter at the hearth of a powerful noble to discover he had bedded the man's wife in the past, then his winter would be a short one, his body left to rot from some high tree. But he courted danger as he courted pleasure, the memories of each amorous encounter merging into a blur of soft sighs and willing, scented bodies.

Pushing aside a stray lock of black hair from his equally dark eyes, he searched the woodland trail ahead for signs of hidden threat. There was always danger as winter approached with relentless, frost-edged stealth. The long, hazy days between Bealtaine and Samhain he had spent in battle were as fleet as swifts darting across summer skies. And like the birds, the days of warmth and plenty were gone. It was time to plan for the harsh time of *Cailleach Beara,* the Dark Mother, where survival through the winter months was at the forefront of all minds, especially the desperate and hungry man or beast.

He steered his grey mare along a narrow path beside a wide meandering river, choked at its banks with fallen boughs and rotting leaves from a recent late autumn storm. He disliked the smell of the choked river, too close to the stench of ruin and decay. He had dealt enough death and bloodshed that year and it was time now to dwell on the finer things in life: strong mead, his harp music that brought so much pleasure to noble and peasant alike and the warm bodies of the beautiful women he would charm. An allure aided by his lean good looks and rumours of his legendary expertise in bed.

A branch broke ahead of him. Throwing up her head, the horse baulked and snorted. *Danger.* Settling her with a soothing caress down her neck, Brandan's hand reached down behind his thigh to the sword strapped to his saddle. Furtive but clumsy rustling warned the warrior this was an ambush by humans; no wolf pack would give so much warning.

As one, armed men pushed through the undergrowth and stood around him. They were desperate men, runaway slaves by their apparel and predatory eyes deep set in lean, hungry faces. Men now cast beyond the tiers of Irish society as punishment for criminal acts or as prisoners of war. Despite the fact that slavery bought them food, shelter and the opportunity to work toward an honourable freedom, some men cherished liberty beyond any yoke. This sort ran, and with every hearth barred to them, became bandits. They were as dangerous as outcast wolves.

Brandan with his quality warhorse, fine sword and gilded harp was a prize worth killing for. Even his cloak of finest grey lamb's wool lined with fox fur and held in place with a gold and garnet pin was a prize that would keep a man from starving and freezing come winter. The warrior sighed; there would be no charming or reasoning with this pack of human killers.

One stepped forward, a broad-faced man with Pictish blood from the bright orange hue of his hair and beard.

'You know what we want. Hand over everything and we will leave you with your life.'

The warrior's hand tightened around his sword hilt. 'It is long past Bealtaine, my friends. I told Fiacre, my sword, it was time he had a well-earned rest after months of taking heads. You wouldn't want me to break my word to him, would you?'

Brandan's lack of fear and light-hearted tone sent a ripple of hesitation among some of the bandits., Perhaps they were no more fearsome than swineherd who had stolen their master's prize sow before ending up in such desperation. But the Pictish one had his eyes on the bag of coin at the Fiann warrior's belt. Nothing would stand in his way of the gold, even though reason would have warned him only a man of great arrogance and fighting skill would ride alone with his wealth on such obvious display.

Raising a large wooden club, Orange Beard rushed forward with a roar, to be sent sprawling by the warhorse as she spun around on her quarters. Brandan spurred her forward as the Pict struggled back onto his feet, decapitating the man in one slash. With a gush of hot blood, the head rolled toward the other bandits, open-mouthed shock frozen forever on the ruddy face. Screaming, one of the men fled in a panicked headlong rush through the tangle of trees. Three remained, standing together to take on the warrior, cursing and brandishing their makeshift weaponry of brutish clubs and hay-making scythes.

Brandan was not a fool – even the scratch from a farm implement could fester and take his life – but he was damned if he was going to allow these men to live, raid and murder innocent farmers and their families during the hard times to come.

'Come on lads, it's just one rich prick on a nag,' shouted one. 'Aengus was a fool to rush him alone.'

These men had no honour and would attack as a frenzied mob. Again Brandan spurred forward at a controlled pace. Highly trained in warfare, his mare balanced her weight down on her hindquarters, enabling her to spin on her back legs and lash out at her attackers with her front hooves, stoving in the skull of the nearest man. Indifferent to their screams of pain and terror, Brandan hacked and slashed with no clemency, killing the other two in a ferocious display of merciless slaughter. The remaining man had already fled, but the warrior was giving no quarter. He released the horse into a gallop to pursue the bandit through a sodden grove of willow saplings.

The ground was hard-going and it slowed down the hunted man but hardly hindered Brandan's agile mare, who dodged or trampled the young trees in her way. Lithe as a deer, she swerved and twisted, leaping fallen logs and streams. As horse and rider closed in, the warrior reined her in hard, giving him the balance he needed to run his victim through the back, impaling the man to the hilt of his sword. With no more thought than a terrier slaughtering a nest of rats, Brandan dismounted to put one foot on the body and pull out his sword, washing the weapon in the river before continuing his journey. He left the bodies to the crows, kites and foxes. The heads of the slain men were not worth taking, too contemptible to be considered trophies.

Shadows lengthened in through the willow grove in the wan sunlight. .

A dangerous time to travel, even though wolves would not yet be winter starved enough to be bold. No, other things would immerge in the cover of darkness, evil spirits and creatures of dread and fear.

Alone again, Brandan caressed the well-muscled neck of his precious warhorse and remounted, pushing her onto a brisk canter, determined to be clear of the woodland before dark. His thoughts went back to his fellow warriors. All had to fend for themselves through the winter. Some without good enough reward hunted for food and skins to sell to keep themselves alive during the cold months of peace. All Fiann had to be poets; he was much more, a harpist so gifted, it was said his music could summon Morrigu - the Goddess of life, death and war herself - and move the fearsome deity to tears. It was not something he intended on trying.

This year he hoped he would not starve or freeze to death. Brandan had the promise of a destination where he had been welcome in the past, one where a warm bed and plentiful food would be provided without question. The warrior smiled to himself as his mind filled with thoughts of the pleasant short days and even more pleasurable long, dark nights to come.

'Not long now, my lovely,' he murmured, patting his warhorse again on her snow-white shoulder. 'You will lie in a thick bed of soft clean straw and dream of your great courage in battle.'

As if in answer, the mare snorted and tossed her head, her ears pricked forward with enthusiasm as she quickened her pace. How could he think he was ever alone, not with such a good, brave mare, a sharp sword and an enchanted harp that sang to him softly as he rode beneath the awakening stars?

2

Five days of quiet travelling brought Brandan away from gentle landscape and dense forests to the wilder, open country of Soghain. Shelter was harder to find here and the population scared and scattered. The rough moorland tracts covered hidden treacherous bogs and were strewn with outcrops of granite and green marble; all these hazards slowed his progress.

With no wish to endanger himself or his mare Lia, Brandan had travelled across this difficult landscape at a leisurely pace. With no other choice, he had been forced to take shelter overnight in open ground where he could. That night, there were no spinneys of windbreak woodland and he was forced to rest with only a large block of green marble to stave off the bitter wind straight from the western ocean. Wrapped tightly in his cloak, sword in hand, he dozed off to the sound of a hobbled Lia cropping the tough, dry grass around him.

Hot breath on his face awoke the warrior with a start. The mare was anxious, nuzzling him to stir, and for good reason. From its protective cover tied on his saddle, harp strings stirred in a warning crescendo that he had slumbered through, unheard. During the night an intense frost had clenched the land into frozen stillness. In a state of shock, Brandan got to his feet with difficulty, his limbs pain-wracked from stiffness, his head spinning in near delirium. He realised that had it not been for his horse, he might never have woken up, drifting into the deep sleep, then death, of exposure and hypothermia. He needed to eat, but his supplies had gone three days before and he had seen no sight of game to shoot or habitation on his journey.

Muttering his gratitude to horse and harp, he saddled his mare, fumbling with the metal buckles with fingers frozen into gnarled claws. Brandan wondered about this sudden, unseasonal bitter cold. Unusual in late winter, it was unheard of in autumn. It appeared to bewilder everything around him in this white landscape. No birds flitted from the ice-glazed gorse bushes still in flower, no deer or hares bounded across his path. An eerie silence had fallen over Soghain, broken only by Lia's hoof beats as she crunched across the moorland, her breath sending out plumes of frozen air.

For the first time, hunger and thirst distracted Brandan, and the solid ice caused him concern for his horse. She would attempt to eat frozen grass but it could lead to potentially dangerous ailments like colic. Water was their main priority, but in open moorland, finding dry timber to start a fire and melt ice would be difficult. He decided to press on toward his destination and prayed to the gods that the strength and endurance of horse and rider would be enough to survive the journey.

By the third day's slow traverse, the frost had deepened its iron grip on an unprepared landscape, and rivers that had never frozen in living memory were now solid, the cold bringing death to the aquatic dwellers and those who depended on them to survive. His competition for game, the local scavengers and predators, were too quick, as the warrior searched the riverbanks in vain for ducks and other victims of the cold. Brandan and his mare now added thirst to their troubles; as he had feared, there was no dry timber to make a fire to melt the frozen river, nor was it easy to collect any. Uttering many violent oaths, he had fought to get the ice to yield to his knife. Frustration made him short-tempered, not helped when he arrived at a collection of crude mud and straw dwellings, too squalid in nature to be called a village. At first there was no sign of habitation beyond the impatient grunt of a penned sow with a late litter of runty piglets. A common thief with the same desperate hunger would have risked making off with a squealing piglet or two, but the warrior reined in his horse and waited for the inhabitants to show themselves.

Realising the visitor had no intention of moving, a man pushed aside a leather door cover and stepped out of his hovel, brandishing an old, well worn axe … a farm tool rather than weapon of war but just as lethal in the right hands. Despite the cold the man was clad only in ragged plaid, and his shivering body was thin with malnutrition.

'There is nothing for you here, rider … we do not have enough to feed our children and the winter not fully upon us yet.' He spat with dangerous contempt, 'Be on your way before we take your horse to feed us.'

Such ill manners were born of desperation. Brandan took no offence at the man's attitude but remained in the saddle. He had no desire to bring further misery to this doomed hamlet by defending himself against any attack … weakened men wielding peasant staves and billhooks were no match against his sword.

'I can pay … well …'

The villager's laugh was bitter, laced with contempt.

'What use is coin when there is nothing to buy or those who have food are unwilling to part with it?'

He gestured to the surrounding bleak landscape. 'Did you see any prosperous villages or busy towns within a man's walking distance on your journey across the bog lands?'

Brandan searched the man's brown eyes for a flicker of despair-driven avarice at the sight of a quality horse before him, but there was nothing but bleak resignation in the peasant's mind. By now, others had grown bolder and emerged from their meagre dwellings, and the warrior's gorge rose at the outpouring odours of rancid, unwashed flesh, the stench of hastily-dampened peat fires. None of the shivering, naked children looked sick or hungry, all still summer fat, but that would follow as surely as night follows day. Like Brandan, these people had no idea how long the early, harsh winter would last. The ever-present threat of starvation had already kicked down the flimsy doors of their huts and gripped them by the throat. He could not blame them for their refusal to provide food and shelter.

A woman, despite being heavily pregnant, ignored the headman's curses and offered Brandan's grateful horse a full bucket of water. Another gave the warrior a crudely-carved wooden mug also filled with clean water, thankfully freshly melted from a nearby iron-hard stream. Such hospitality impressed Brandan; it was all they could risk giving a stranger, but it meant their hearts had not been turned to stone like the landscape. Yet. There could well come a time later in the year if the winter remained so hard, that he and his horse would have been attacked … perhaps both destined to feed the starving villagers.

Shuddering at the thought, he took some coins from his purse and gave them to the pregnant woman … not too much to make her a target but enough to buy bread if she could find any. He gave out more to the outstretched hands that then surrounded him.

If they had any hidden supplies, he could have taken what he wanted from the peasants, but that would have made Brandan no better than the curs he had despatched at the start of his journey. He would rather starve.

His forbearance and generosity toward the peasants must have pleased the gods. As twilight hushed the landscape and he prepared to make camp in the shelterless open, a flight of ducks rose from a small lake that had been stilled by the ice into a mirror. One well-aimed arrow brought him a fat drake. Somehow he managed to scrape together enough dead bulrushes at the edge of the frozen water to make a decent fire.

That night he rested, warmed by a merry blaze and stuffed full of roasted meat. Nothing in his life had ever tasted as good.

3

Normandy

As dawn's wan light made low sparkling mist rise to their horses' knees, the hunters turned their swift hounds. Excited by the scent of their prey, the dogs ran before them, pouring through the undergrowth in a river of bounding energy. The rising of the pale sun did little to melt the rock-hard frost. The hunters sat in silence, eager to hear the first hound toll sight of prey as their fidgety mounts snorted plumes of dragon breath and stamped, as eager for action as their riders.

No less keen was a young man, distinct from his companions by his waist-length flaxen hair. Though rising early from the warmth of a blazing hearth and comfortable bed of clean furs had been difficult, it was still good to get the morning smoke fug from the keep at Caen Castle out of his lungs. The young Saxon thrilled at the chance to go hunting, loving the feel of a good swift horse beneath him and the sting of fresh ice-laden air on his face.

'Hereward.'

He glanced up as Duke Guillaume's gruff voice called to him across the forest glade.

'*Mon ami,*' the Duke continued, 'my Master of Hounds has spoken of a magnificent 12-pointer in this woodland. The antlers will make a fine trophy to take back on your return home. You could mount them on the mud walls of your hovel in the fens.'

Inwardly grimacing, the Saxon nobleman grinned in reply at the jesting banter and spurred his bay stallion on to be closer to the Duke's mount.

'Indeed so, my Lord, it would be a vast improvement on our native trophies – swamp rat and beaver skulls.'

Home, the last place Hereward wanted to be right then. Home was a pestilential, flyblown primitive manor in the middle of the arsehole of England. The Fenlands. Home was always bone-numbingly cold from the damp of the marshes and the biting east wind direct from the North Sea. The lazy wind, the peasants called it, one that went straight through rather than around you. A life spent day and night on guard, protecting his father's lands and people from attacks by raiding parties of ruthless Norsemen.

His English homeland was a peaceful realm on the surface at least for peasants, clergy and merchants, but beneath the tranquillity roiled raw ambition for power between the noble houses, fuelled by a pious, Norman-loving weakling as a King. One who had avowed celibacy and had produced no heir. Hereward wanted no part of this turmoil. He was 16, a man … and yet still a youth pining for a time with no responsibility. Time to chase comely wenches, fine stags and drink too much ale.

Life in the Norman stronghold was good. For once, Hereward could relax and enjoy things other than warfare and survival. The company of beautiful women garbed in finery. Plentiful fresh meat from the well-stocked farms and forests. The pleasure of music, gaming and hunting. He could thrive in such a place, had he been a Norman by birth, serving such a leader as the Duke, whose stern authority brooked no argument. Unlike the English King, Hereward had no great affection for the Normans as a people. As a Saxon patriot, he feared them, their organisation and growing might under Guillaume's iron rule. He puzzled at their rejection of their Nordic roots, their slavish adoption of French names, language and manners when they despised the French themselves.

But what else could he do? The English King had sent him as an envoy to further the peace pact with Normandy, the Godwin family had given him their own orders to spy for them and see for himself whether the rumours were true of foul witchcraft, unnatural dabbling in the dark arts, including alchemy and necromancy. The Godwins trusted him. The King trusted him. But Hereward had no burning desire to return across the channel with the problems of future succession bubbling over like a fetid brew. He did not want to pick sides, for in that lay great danger.

'Ha … Thia Hilaud!' The Duke cried out as the serf beaters startled a pair of hinds from the undergrowth, followed by a stag. Not the sought-for 12-pointer but still a fine beast. Fury darkened Guilaume's features, his lips a thin grim line. 'Call off the hounds,' he roared at his attendants. He had promised his guest an exceptional stag; nothing less would do.

Glaring with murderous intent at the hapless Master of Hounds, he hauled on his stallion's mouth, causing it to rear in distress, and spurred it away in a reckless gallop across the iron-hard ground. Bemused, Hereward followed his host at a more sensible pace; he had no intention of ruining a good horse to keep up with the notoriously short-tempered Duke.

On his return to the fortress, Hereward returned to his guest quarters to change into indoor garb. Back home, he would have removed only his waxed wool, squirrel fur lined cloak, but the Duke's household kept the nobles' living quarters warm and dry, allowing the luxury of courtly clothes to be worn inside. To his acute embarrassment, Hereward had arrived at Caen without any finery to match that of the Norman aristocracy. He had felt as shabby as a peasant and no doubt smelled like one too. This had soon been remedied by Guillaume, who had personally taken considerable time and pleasure providing the young Saxon with a new wardrobe of splendid garments, even to the point of helping him with the fitting and dressing of the new garb. So fine were the garments, Hereward had decided to leave them there in Normandy when he returned to the Fens for fear of mockery from his family and the huscarls as a weakling and popinjay.

Once dressed and refreshed by some warmed wine, smoky in taste from the poker used to heat it, he strolled down to the main hall, immediately noticing a more relaxed air among the courtiers and household servants. The Duke had left Caen immediately on return from hunting, taking a small party of his closest barons, and had told no-one where his destination was. Again.

Though he was accustomed to wielding heavy swords, the weight of the new weapon placed in the Duke's hands by the smith caused him to gasp, and he struggled to keep both his stern composure in front of the barons and the object firmly balanced. Their loyalty to him had been bought and paid for in bloodshed and expensive favours in lands and titles. Descendants of pillaging Viking raiders, they were French-speaking barons and lords now.

As the onlookers saw the strangeness of the new weapon, Duke Guillaume could feel their curiosity turn to acute anxiety. It hung like a pall above them as they gathered in a stretch of open pasture, well hidden from any village or road by bordering acres of dense forest. Ducal hunting land, anyone from serf to nobleman caught wandering there would be killed on the spot for trespass, their bodies hung from trees at the forest edge as a warning to other poachers.

Guillaume sensed an almost tangible hunger festering within the survivors of past crushed rebellions. They watched him all the time, impatient gore crows waiting for the first sign of weakness. They would not see any that day. This occasion would be another demonstration of the might and ruthlessness that kept him ruler of these lands. They wanted him to fail.

Already set up ready, wood and straw effigies of a stag, a wild boar, a bear and a Saxon warrior stood propped up in the clearing. The last target did not amuse the Duke: he had sought good relationships with these people, soon they would be his to rule. At least there were no Saxons there in his company that morning. No serfs or servants either, just his closest barons and the understandably nervous master smith who had forged the new weapon.

'I see fear in your eyes, gentlemen. Why? Are you so cowed by priests that you see witchcraft and devilry everywhere?'

No-one answered, but the Duke knew exactly what was haunting their thoughts: fear for their immortal souls. How had this religious weakness from England crossed the channel? Was it influence from that sanctimonious milksop King Edward? What good was his lifetime of prayer now, with no lusty male heirs and powerful families like the Godwins waiting to grab the throne for themselves? They were in for a rude awakening.

Lifting the metal weapon above his head, a feat of brute strength, his only protection against anything life could send his way, the Duke yelled back at them, 'All nonsense, a devious ploy to keep you on your knees obeying tonsured weaklings. There is nothing of the devil in this honest work of skilled men, hardworking smiths like this good fellow here, good men with vision and determination. It is a construct of wood and metal, copper, iron and brass. Nothing more.'

The Duke examined the object closely. A round barrel of beaten copper held some hidden mechanism that hissed steam like a small caged dragon. It had a steel protrusion loaded with five shortened pikes. Longer than arrows, shorter than spears, they awaited release to do their deadly duty.

'This, gentlemen, will make us the masters of the world, should we wish that. I am content to protect what is rightly mine.'

The Duke's eyes bore into those of the barons; the disputed legitimacy of his reign was the root cause of all those past rebellions, all successfully and bloodily crushed. He strode across to Guy, Baron de Pas de Caux, inwardly delighted as the big man buckled at the knees as the weapon was thrust into his hands.

'You have ridden by my side since I was a lad, you deserve to be the first man to operate it.'

The Duke ignored the hesitation, the paling of the man's ruddy, weather tanned face, the tremble in his battle-callused hands as he readied the weapon to aim at the stag target, the biggest and easiest to hit.

'What must I do, my Lord?'

'Balance the thing with your left hand, aim for the target. There is a small lever beneath it that you must pull back on with your right finger to release the pike.'

With no choice but to obey. The baron took aim and engaged the mechanism. Hissing like some monstrous snake, the weapon spat out a pike with much force, knocking Baron Guy to the ground, his shoulder badly bruised by the recoil. As he staggered to his feet, he heard the cheers around him. How dare they make such jest as his fall? Yet none was looking at his discomfort; they were gawping not at him, but at the target – cleaved cleanly in two by the projectile.

Elated, the big man picked up the weapon again and aimed at the boar, ignoring the horrified smith's shout and raised arms of warning. As his finger pulled back on the lever, the barrel exploded in a frenzy of torn metal and scalding steam. Baron Guy died instantly, a wedge of knife-sharp copper blown deep into his forehead.

'Impetuous idiot, he should have learned how to re-arm the weapon before firing it,' snarled the Duke, openly furious at the destruction of the first prototype from such folly. Within him was a glow of satisfaction. Pas de Caux was a filthy traitor. Scheming, ambition-fuelled missives had been intercepted between him and Guillaume's enemy, the French King. Now the Duke knew how not to operate the weapon and had saved the expense of a trial and execution. A successful morning.

He clapped his broad arms around the smith's quivering shoulders, silenced the man's urgent prayers with a laugh. 'Fear not, Master Robert, there is nothing flawed in your invention, just the fool who fired it.'

4

England

The figure looked as still as the dead, an exquisitely carved statue, with only his frosted breath rising to hover above him in a narrow cloud betraying his status as a living being.

Bathed in multicoloured light streaming from high windows, King Edward smiled, allowing his inner rapture to colour his outward expression. He did not feel the blood freezing cold, his bruised knees from the long hours knelt on the cold unyielding flagstones, or the sharp muscle cramps in his back, neck and arms. Surrounded by the serenity and beauty of the, as yet unfinished, cathedral, the glory of the stained glass in this chapel was sublime. Edward had sensed the presence of Heaven, a foretaste of the eternal joys to come in the next world. One he had dedicated his life to achieving after his death. One he looked forward too, content his soul was sin-free and ready for judgement.

Reluctant to leave this sanctuary of peace and serenity, Edward knew what awaited him beyond the Abbey's walls. Anger and bitterness and the bloodthirsty talk of ambitious and powerful men. Harold, the Godwin heir, was back. His success against rebellious Northumberland at least overshadowed his past defeat by the heinous, pagan Welsh. This recent victory would not be enough for Harold; nothing could. The King knew nothing would stop the Earl from attacking Wales again, and his revenge would be brutal.

A powerful man from a formidable family, his strength kept England safe. Had not Edward believed he was King by God's command, he would have joyfully given the young warlord the crown, then retreated to a life of piety and contemplation in a monastery.

But such choice was not open to Edward. Nor could his conscience allow the foul stench of pagan worship to be carried in the wind to English shores from Ireland or across the troubled borders from Wales, Cumbria or Cornwall. No peaceful missionary returned alive from these lands, and

Edward had decided with some reluctance and trepidation during his many hours of meditation, that if they could not be converted to the true faith by reason and prayer, then it must be by the sword.

Sighing, he struggled to his feet, the pain and stiffness snatching him away from the state of grace to one of an aging mortal man with responsibility for an entire nation lying heavily on his narrow shoulders. Much as he desired it, Edward could no longer dwell within these sacred walls that he had so joyfully caused to be built as a symbol of his devotion. The real world, bleak and blood-stained, lay beyond the doors. The real world represented by the imposing form of Harold Godwin, who awaited him at court.

As the King's carriage bumped and jarred over the ice-bound roads to his palace, Edward huddled, wrapped in his furs. So deep in prayer, he had not noticed the cold within the Abbey, but there was no escaping it now. He glanced briefly through the heavy tapestry curtains across the carriage windows. He saw that the people were struggling in the long freeze. They gathered around communal braziers, pausing from their gossip to lustily cheer his passage through their midst. He had given them peace, and food was not a problem; good summers uninterrupted by Norse raids had led to a bumper harvest. England was indeed a blessed Isle, and that made it a target, a juicy meat-laden bone surrounded by starving curs. The sea-borne raiders would be back, in force.

The pagan Celtic lands were a threat too. But strong enough to try to retake their old kingdoms? Only if they stopped fighting among themselves and became united. This had been proved impossible in the past; they were a fiery people, easily provoked, who never forgot slights and wrongs, carrying blood feuds through many generations. This belligerent nature weakened them, kept them at bay for many centuries. Now, Edward had heard worrying rumours about one of the Welsh princes, a charismatic leader called Llewellyn ap Grufyyd. If anyone could galvanise his people into unity, this man would be that leader. Many of his people already called him King of Cymru, and a stronger Wales would foment trouble in the twilight lands of Cornwall, or Kernow as the sullen Celtic inhabitants insisted on calling it.

England needed strong allies, and who stronger than Normandy, whose people had protected him in exile? One ruled by Edward's blood relation, Duke Guillaume, an ally and friend. The only fear stemmed from the implausible rumours of unholy machinations surrounding the Duke's court. Tales of Devil-spawned weapons and heresy. And no word from the young Mercian nobleman Edward had sent as an envoy. If these rumours were true, then England was in dire peril, for there was no way a devout Christian King would make an ally with the minions of the Devil. All nonsense, of course. Edward greatly admired the Norman Duke's piety, the wealth of monasteries and cathedrals he'd had built in soaring stone. An inspiration to Edward to do the same in England.

As the King entered the palace, Harold was waiting for him in a private chamber. He was an imposing figure with natural charisma. The best of the Godwin brood. Edward sighed. How easy it would be to hand him the crown and walk away. Yet how impossible. The younger man bowed with suitable respect then spoke first, a brazen move born from the strength of his position in court and his devotion to England's fate.

'Your Majesty, I have spoken with other noblemen and we grow concerned at the lack of word from Normandy. My contacts tell me the young fen lord is well treated at Guillaume's court. Is it possible, too well?'

Edward did not answer but sought a seat by the hearth. The long vigil in the Abbey had taken a toll on him; his blood felt watery and ice-cold in his veins. He was not long for this troubled world, if God had any mercy for his flawed servant on Earth. He accepted a goblet of hot mead from the Godwin lord and shrugged. 'Hereward is safe and winter is upon us early. I do not expect him to return until spring.'

Edward's answer triggered an angry sigh from the younger man.

'If we have anything to fear from the Normans,' Harold muttered, 'then spring may be too late. You must recall him.'

It was close to a direct command, but Edward chose to ignore it. As he had ignored so much of the arrogance bred into Harold with the blood of the ambitious Godwin lineage in his veins. This Wessex earl was one of the large and troublesome brood – intelligent, brave and thankfully devoted to England. Edward ignored his many breaches of protocol, because though Harold was known to his enemies at court as a Wessex wolf, at least he was the English King's loyal protector. His own wolf.

'I agree with you. I too see the wisdom of recalling Hereward from Normandy,' the King admitted, weary of the machinations of power, 'though I cannot believe a word of these far-fetched rumours concerning Duke Guillaume. It would settle our fears to hear from the young man in person.

'We will bring the lad home to celebrate the birth of Christ with his family.'

5

Pulling a fox fur cloak tightly around her shoulders, Seren followed the path along a once tumbling stream. Sure footed, she knew every raised tree root, every curve and jink along her way. A long willow staff protected her from fallen branches and stones. October's early hard frost had turned the land to iron, halting the singing water and turning it into a glass memory of its lively self. It was all as it should be; this was time of the Dark Mother, of Ceridwen, the crone aspect of the triple Goddess. Ceridwen was the giver of ancient wisdom, she knew the land must slumber, to recover from the bountiful harvests of autumn. To sleep beneath blankets of soft snow and be washed clean by the rain. Lives would be lost during the winter and this was part of the Dark Mother's plan; the sick and weak must pass on to the Summerlands to make room for the new born of spring. That She had brought this blessing so early was not to be questioned.

With confidence, Seren easily found the sacred grove in the forest, a natural alcove of thickly intertwined hawthorn and holly bushes interwoven by ivy beneath a rowan, the grove surrounded by majestic, protective oak and ash trees. A precious, private place where Seren could revere the Mother and her Consort Cerunnos protected by the five elemental spirits. But a portal opened to benevolence could also allow in dark forces. She passed her right hand over an empty crucible to represent air, put in some ice to melt for water. She patiently scraped away the frost and placed some forest soil to symbolise the earth. Her own breath symbolised spirit. Then, for fire, she lit a fat tallow candle with two flint stones and waited for moonrise to journey with the ancient ones.

Seren was slender as a reed, with shining black hair and a ready, happy laugh and compassionate nature. Her large green eyes were flecked with magical gold light and shimmered so much with joy and life, it was difficult for anyone to comprehend they were sightless. For what the girl could see went beyond this realm, beyond the outward words and actions of men but straight into their souls.

Now, although Seren was warmly wrapped in thick furs, darkness brought the sharpness of night to sting her face. The candle's flickering warmth could not ward off the cold, and she was forced to use her will power to rise above the distraction and concentrate on her meditation. All sense of time blurred into a frozen now, all movement stopped in the surrounding darkness and the hushed forest. No night beast stirred, no hunting owl flitted ghost-like through the trees.

She was not alone. The beat of powerful wings encircled her. A mighty hawk, one not born of this Earth, filled her mind with images as it descended to fly around her head. Seren could not halt the scream rising from her soul at the horror of the visions. Blood on snow. The agonised cries of mortally wounded men and horses. Many kingdoms crushed beneath monstrous weapons that hissed and steamed like dragons. And above the carnage flew a huge black bird. As the vision became clearer, she realised it was not just a raven. It too was more than a mortal bird. A mysterious creature from beyond the Veil between worlds. Every wing beat resonated with primal power from the dawn of time, when the gods and goddesses made the world and all that lived on it. Seren became aware this was a shadow, a glimpse of its full form and strength. She never wanted to be in the presence of the raven-being and witness its curse of death.

What does this mean? Seren pleaded with Ceridwen's hawk messenger, but it left her with only the strong echoes of the horrific vision in her mind.

Once more she was alone in the forest as it returned to life. She heard the pant of a fox padding past her in the frost-stilled undergrowth, the call of a hunting owl. All was back to normal, if anything could ever be for Seren after what she had seen.

Fully awake from her trance, Seren could feel the faint fingers of dawn's slight warmth on her face and, whispering her thanks to the Dark Mother, she made her way back along the forest track to return to the settlement of the wise women. Recklessly, she broke into a run, anxiety behind each swift step. There was not a minute to lose. The spirit message spoke of a great and overwhelming force sweeping first through the stolen lands then on to threaten the exile homelands of Kernow, Cymru and Eire. She had to reach her guardian and use his power and influence to warn the Welsh King and the Princes, though how any army could defend against what was coming had not been shown to her by the spirit hawk.

As she left the forest, two other young women on horseback waited for her in the clearing, one holding the reins of Seren's sturdy mountain pony, Olwyn, a blue roan mare. Ceinwen and Delyth were novice wise women like herself, though without her abundant and ever-growing abilities. The girls were also Seren's closest friends, any anxiety on their faces dissolved into smiles of delight at her arrival.

'*Cariad*. We were so worried.'

Delyth leapt from her pony and ran to hug her friend. 'I will never understand why you insisted on going alone into a dark forest. Promise me you will never do that again.'

Returning the hug, Seren attempted a smile, though her heart was laden with fear and sorrow for what might befall their land.

'We have waited all night for you to return,' continued Delyth. 'All we could think of was the frights that might harm you.'

Joining them, leading the other ponies, Ceinwen's face was pale with fatigue and concern. 'Marauding Saxons, bears, wolves and the terrible gwiber, who knows what other horrors could be lurking. Seren? You are brave but not invincible.'

Seren shuddered at the mention of the gwiber, a monstrous flying snake that could live in water. The fearsome beast but a month before had eaten a farmer in nearby Penmachno. Her friends were right: she did her best to be fearless. All the more reason for those who cared for her to worry about her safety. Whirling around in a carefree dance, one that was just for show to reassure her friends, Seren laughed. 'I am fine, look … nothing has eaten me.'

'This time,' Delyth muttered dourly, 'we must get a move on. That old biddy Cafell will make us scrub cauldrons all week if we are late for her lesson this morning.'

Seren laughed, this time genuinely, '*Mistress* Cafell will be delighted to sleep in an extra hour or two.'

'I am not going to risk it,' returned Ceinwen, urging her pony into a sharp trot, eager to be away from the forest and its lurking dangers.

On return to the nearby fortified settlement of thatched and stone homes, Seren hastily took her leave of her friends and sought out the wise counsel of the head witch, Rhan. She passed with confidence through the crowds of local villagers and farmers awaiting the freely-given medicine and advice. This was a place of sanctuary and guidance, a spiritual beacon to all who needed it. Seren was happy there and had been content to continue with her training among the gentle wise women. But this was not her true home. That was an austere stronghold in Nercwys, a place of men, toughened warriors honed from birth to defend their lands.

She sought out a building in the centre of the settlement, finding the right portal by the sound of tinkling from an entrance hung with ash and oak branches and bright with dangling gifts – carved wooden and beaten metal talismans of stars, moons, hares and ravens. Once in Rhan's serene presence, the girl dipped her head in respect to her mentor, then raised her faced in the direction of the woman's calm, grey eyes. 'Mother, I must go home, back to the company of warriors.'

The older woman stepped forward. Seren took in her scent of summer flowers, sweet meadow herbs and incense, her aura of eons of passed down ancient wisdom, as Rhan held her hands in a firm, affectionate embrace. 'Of course you must, my dear child. I too have received warning from the Dark Mother. Sad as I am to see you leave us so soon, this warning cannot be ignored. You should have been free to enjoy your youth here in the company of your sisters, learning more, gaining strength and power. This has come too soon.'

Rhan dropped her hands with a sigh, one born of deep sorrow and regret. She moved to the portal entrance and gazed to the east, to the borders with the enemy English. 'I can sense only a shadow of what you must have seen and heard, *cariad*. But it is enough to chill me to the depths of my being. Go home, Seren, go home and save our people.'

6

Ruddy-bellied clouds scudded across the brightening sky as Seren's escort cleared a forest pass to take their first view of their destination. The fortress stood on a hill, a brute statement of might surrounded by a valley littered with granite boulders and populated by grazing sheep. Lyn, the witches' village headman, lightly touched her hand … 'You are home, Lady Seren, we have arrived at the fortress.'

Urging her tired pony to begin the ascent, Seren was relieved that the journey had ended safely, with no attacks by bandits, Norsemen or Saxons. No delay caused by peasants seeking her aid, which of course she could not refuse. The hungry wolves of winter had not slunk down from the mountains to harry their horses. Thoughts of the warm welcome and blazing hearth awaiting her in the fortress brought a smile of anticipation to brighten the fatigue etched into her features.

She could also feel the excitement building in the horses as their hooves touched soft pasture. Ahead lay warm, dry stables, rest and plentiful fodder. Seren's staid pony was no less caught up in the eager pace. It would take little to trigger the horses into an excited bolt, and she was grateful when the headman clipped a lead onto Olwyn's bit and led the pony from his staid horse.

The low rumble of approaching hooves reverberated across the valley; the little party had been spotted. As the riders neared, Seren recognised familiar voices rising in the morning air. Her smile broadened to a grin of delight. It was Idris and Medyr, the young men she had been raised with, whom she loved and considered her brothers, no less close to her heart than any of shared blood.

After gaining her consent, Medyr took over control of her pony, and together they cantered across the valley, familiarity with the rough terrain allowing them to avoid the boulders and roughest ground. Seren's laughter rang out in the grey light. For a few moments of exhilaration, all her burden of grim knowledge fell away and she was a child again. Carefree and loved.

The Prince awaited his family in the inner courtyard, his craggy, battle-scarred features softened with a broad grin of delight. He waited while his youngest son helped the girl off her pony before striding across the frost-glistened cobbles to greet her.

'Seren, my beautiful little star, how it gladdens my old warrior's heart to see you back in my home.' Lord Gwion stretched out his arms to embrace the young woman, his ward, with genuine affection. 'We were not expecting you before the spring celebrations of *Calan Haf,* but you will hear no complaint from me or your family.'

That was how she had been raised by the Prince and his household – with equal love. Her father, Cynan ap Yorath, had been the lord's favourite warrior, and had valiantly lost his life defending their lands from the yellow-haired barbarians. The invader race from mainland Europe who now wore the grisly talisman of a dead man around their necks for protection. Cynan had been a member of the *Teulu*, which meant 'family', the strongly armed and mounted retainers of a powerful Prince's household. Seren was considered family too, a beloved daughter, as if of Gwion's own bloodline. No greater tribute could he pay to his fallen friend.

Seren's mother had passed to the Summer Lands 12 springs before, and with her passing, her gift of divination had been reborn in her daughter. The girl had blossomed into a beauty, and at 14, it was overdue time to find a suitable match to protect her future. One from a good family, for the blood of many princely houses ran in her veins; maybe even fairy blood from the distant times when the Veil between the realms was gossamer thin. It would have to be the best match Lord Gwion could find, a strong, brave man but one with a kind and gentle soul, for nothing less would do for the fey and vulnerable blind girl that he loved as his own daughter. Sadly, he had long dismissed partnering her with one of his fine, strong and brave sons. They had been raised together as one litter despite the difference in blood. They loved each other as brothers and sister. Any more intimate union would be wrong.

Returning the embrace, Seren was relieved to be safely back in Lord Gwion's stronghold, her beloved home, but her news was grim and could no longer wait. Sensing her sombre and anxious mood, the Prince beckoned over his sons to join them and, placing Seren's hand on his arm, guided her to a private chamber. Seren didn't need a guide, however, as despite her blindness she knew the interior of the keep well. Now her anxious expression conveyed to the Prince that the months of relative peace across his lands might soon be over.

7

Ireland

Wisps of blue-grey wood smoke rose from behind a range of low hills clad in frosted grass. Slumped in his saddle, one hand twisted tightly in Lia's mane for greater security in the saddle, Brandan somehow found a smile of relief. At last the endless sea of frozen bog was at an end and the warmth and shelter of Lismore was within a day's ride. Though exhausted and weak from lack of food, he dismounted and led Lia across the last of the peat moss and sedges toward the more sustaining sward of the higher land.

The mare raised her head for the first time in many days, her nostrils flared at the muted scent of grass and she found the resolve to travel at a quicker pace, stepping out beyond the peat and up into the hills. Before long, they walked into a well-built and busy small town, made wealthy by trading peat cut from the bogs, dried and sold as fuel throughout the land. No doubt the heavy slabs of peat were cut by wretched peasants like the ones he'd encountered on his long ride. It was an arduous task.

Brandan had no trouble finding a comfortable inn with stabling and good feed for his mare. He decided to remain there, recuperating until his energy and good looks were restored. The mare certainly needed to recuperate. Brandan knew he looked haggard and his garb filthy and travel-worn. This time of year, it was not his sword that rich patrons wanted, it was his good looks and enchanted music. It would not do to disappoint, with winter coming and space by noble hearths growing scarce.

Brandan placed a gold coin in the innkeeper's hand as he showed him to the finest room.

'I'll need a tub and hot water,' Brandan said.

The innkeeper's smile widened as his hand closed around the coin.

'And some wine, bread and cheese ...' Brandan said.

As the innkeeper left, Brandan surveyed the room. It was poor compared with the room he expected to have when he reached his final destination, but it would do for now. And after the trials of his journey, even this place, with its threadbare tapestries, and undoubtedly lumpy bed, was nothing short of luxury.

The days and nights of rest passed swiftly, and when he awoke one morning in a lithe tangle of limbs, from sharing his bed with two pert local girls, Brandan knew he was strong enough to ride. He pushed the girls aside and hurriedly dressed. Once packed, he shooed the girls from his bed, and his room, placing a coin in each of their hands as something of a callous goodbye. The girls, one blonde, one red, giggled and hurried away as he closed the door.

Brandan turned to survey the room for the last time, then he picked up his meagre possessions and left the inn.

Beyond the walls of the town, the glacial landscape had not softened, but a wan sun brightened his mood as it sparkled off the frost diamonds. His mare had recovered her jaunty pace, her head high, ears pricked, and was now ready once more to be free of the stable and journey on. Still in its leather pouch, Brandan's harp accompanied their journey with many merry airs and reels, falling silent only when they passed another traveller along the well-trodden road. The harp's magic was such that it sensed others long before he did.

By the time he arrived at the drawbridge at the Lismore stronghold, his long hair shone like a raven's wing and his excited mare danced beneath him to the gilded harp's lively gig. Lookouts on the stronghold's wooden battlements had already spread word of the lone warrior's approach, and the courtyard beyond the gates would be filling with the curious of Lismore's household. He reached down to pat the mare's neck and caress the harp.

'Steady now Lia … Time to behave like the lady you are. Hush now. And Thaisce, save your strings for the long night ahead. These people will expect to be entertained.'

Few warnings of danger came in such a delicate manner, a waft of roses rising above the smell of wet hounds, damp rushes and peat smoke. *Lady Grainne?* The warrior bard, Brandan swore colourfully to himself. *Why is she here? And why now?* Last time he had encountered this lady, it was at her home in Fermanagh, where he enjoyed a furtive tumble with her in her husband Lord Fineen's bed when he was away feuding with an upstart cousin. Yet another blood feud, always guaranteed at some time from the quarrelsome Delaneys. Grainne was the last person Brandan wanted to encounter at King Donal's stronghold at Lismore. Their brief affair had ended badly, and it was a complication he could do without.

Ducking into a side corridor, Brandan waited to see if his suspicions were founded in reality. Three young women giggled past in a swish of fine linen. The bard sighed with relief; none was the Lady Grainne. Yet the distinctive and very personal scent of her rose perfume lingered in the air. Perhaps he was being punished for some slight unwittingly done to the Sidhe? His mind raced, trying to think of anything he could have done to upset the powerful *Other* folk. Had he ridden over a fairy mound or snapped a branch off a sacred tree? Not praised them enough in a song? Apologies and restitution must be made – as soon as possible – or the taunting would continue. There was nothing he could do for the time being; an all-too-human King had summoned him to court, and as a warrior he had no choice but to obey.

As he approached the audience hall, he was stopped by the King's personal guard and waited to be summoned. He was relaxed, confident he had done nothing to upset the King and had been always warmly welcomed at Donal's hearth. Brandan was an exceptionally good-looking young man who could transform the winter-bound fortress's cold stone great hall into a fragrant fairy bower in the warm light of spring with the magic of his music. That gift gave him a reasonably safe passage through this land, but maybe not in Fermanagh for a while.

His entrance with a sword and a gilded harp slung across his broad shoulders sent another quiver of excitement through the Lismore stronghold. He represented a welcome diversion for the ladies of the court and the battle-hardened warriors alike. He sensed the collective intake of breath from the womenfolk and smiled to himself. No fear of a cold bed alone that night. Not after the beauty of his music had wrung many a tear from any blood-stained warlord or reduced a maiden to hopeless, unrequited love for him. That he was equally at home wielding a sword against the heathen Viking raiders was as important a part of his appeal as his easy charm. Brandan briefly paused before approaching the throne, assessing the atmosphere, alert for any telltale tension that spoke of brooding mistrust and treachery, but there was none.

Donal's delight at seeing his friend was genuine. No more than a couple of winters older than him, the King leapt from his throne, clearing the brindled heads of his dozing wolfhounds and pulling Brandan to him in a fierce embrace.

'Now this old heap of cold stone will have some life! Welcome back to Lismore.'

The young bard tried to bow in respect but Donal was having none of it, calling for mead and guiding him to a finely-carved and gilded seat next to the throne. It was the Queen's chair, but any breach of protocol was overlooked, such was the warrior bard's popularity. Everyone knew young Queen Liadan was in the last stages of her confinement with the imminent birth of her first child and would not enter the great hall that night.

'See the flushed faces of the ladies of the court,' laughed the King. 'Brandan, your reputation as ever arrives before you, carried on the north wind.'

Donal turned to address the crowded court. 'What is the matter with you people? Has that vile monster, the *Fear Dearg* stolen your tongues? Let us express our hearty appreciation at the arrival of Ireland's bravest warrior, greatest bard and most skilful lover to our midst again.'

Grinning ruefully, Brandan glanced down the ranks of applauding and cheering nobles. Again, he sought the telltale bright auburn tresses of Lady Grainne, but she was not there, nor could he ask the King about her without betraying their indiscretion. Once more, thoughts of mischief against him by the Sidhe filled his mind. Despite the dangers, he decided he must make contact with the Shining Ones as soon as he could. The deep willow groves of Lismore were a sacred site for them, making a meeting easier to fulfil.

An excited clamour from the crowd calling out for his music pulled Brandan back to the present. Feigning a humble smile of acquiescence, he unslung from his back his most precious possession, the gilded, ornately inlaid harp, and after stretching and warming his long fingers, began to play. First a few beautiful old laments, then a series of wild gigs and reels, until the audience-hall was a blur of dancing figures, bright colours from swirling gowns and cloaks, the gleam of gold and gems in the flickering torchlight. The tapping rhythm of many feet and laughter ringing to the oak rafters gave witness to Brandan's talent at lifting moods, but he himself was immune to the merriment. His mind still dwelled on the scent of roses and what it foretold for his future.

Brandan awoke with a groan, head pounding with the surfeit of merriment from his revels of the night before. What was in the Lismore mead? It was strong enough to intoxicate an ox. As he slowly arose, his long black hair was intertwined with the rich russet locks of his bedmate, still slumbering from a night of energetic love making. Brandan shook his head and grinned as vivid erotic memories returned through the fug of his mead hangover. What a wild night.

Not wishing to disturb his lover's hard-earned slumbers, he left the bed quietly and began to dress.. As he threw his fine lamb's wool surcoat over his head, he gasped in pain. Something sharp cut into the skin above his high cheekbone. Swearing, he examined the garment, to find a long rose stem embedded in the fabric by its large, cruel barbs. One now red with his blood. A rose in winter? Brandan shuddered. This was a worse taunt than the scent of roses. It was downright malicious. His cussing woke up the King.

'Back to bed – I haven't finished with you yet.' Donal's voice was slurred with sleep and desire. 'That is a royal command.'

Badly shaken, Brandan wiped away the blood with a kerchief and attempted a smile as he rejoined his lover. He sat on the edge of the bed, eager to be gone before the household awoke. He had no wish to distress Donal's young Queen so close to her due time with servant rumours and court gossip. The King's hand reached up to the bard's face and gently touched the still-bleeding injury.

'Ouch. Did I do that?'

Brandan reached down and kissed him with genuine affection bordering on love, a dangerous, unruly emotion he had deliberately shunned all his life. 'Of course not, you give me nothing but the greatest pleasure. I cut myself just now on my dagger while dressing, a clumsy victim of your people's strong mead.'

'In that case I definitely will not take no for an answer,' laughed Donal as he pulled him back onto the bed.' Being a monarch has some advantages.'

Brandan gave in. Why not? He enjoyed his time alone with the King and it might distract from the ice tendrils of dread creeping into his soul. Unwittingly, he glanced across to the floor, where he had dropped the rose. It was not there. If it had not been for the fresh cut along his cheekbone, his encounter might have been no more than a waking dream.

But dreams did not maim. Dreams did not bleed.

His mind in turmoil, Brandan arose as soon as the King gave in to a deep, contented and sated slumber after the latest exertion. The warrior dressed quickly and quietly, first double-checking his garb for any more unwelcome additions, then sought out the stables. He found Lia dozing, head down, one hind leg resting. Ignoring her display of righteous equine displeasure at being saddled before breakfast, he led her out into the yard. None of the equally half-asleep guards challenged the King's favoured visitor and bed warmer as he rode out of Lismore, and Brandan soon found himself alone on a track with only the company of his horse and scurrying night creatures returning to their homes, including the ghost-like form of a barn owl sweeping low over his head.

Brandan's journey through a dazzling, frost-diamond-coated landscape to seek out a location with the right mystical ambience was soon rewarded. Since the most ancient of times, those from behind the Veil had favoured the land around Lismore, and by some deep old instinct he found a place musical with the sound of water running down time-polished stones.

This had to be the ideal place, a natural conjunction of a tumbling clear spring, miraculously not frozen to stillness, slender willows still graceful despite their winter-bare branches, and a surrounding collection of attendant oak, ash and rowan trees. The still air and lack of birdsong all pointed to a portal between two worlds. A meeting place with a race who were sometimes beautiful, generous and noble but never harmless or benign.

There had never been a time when human and Sidhe had lived in harmony; their shared history was of mistrust and betrayal. There were those who told of a time when the fairy folk were defeated by the first humans to step onto Irish soil when the Great Ice retreated. They said that the Sidhe had chosen to retreat to Tir Na Nog, the Land of Eternal Youth. Brandan had no time for such a tale; the Sidhe were powerful, too powerful to be defeated by a rabble of land-hungry humans.

In his opinion, the Sidhe had never left Ireland, but dwelt alongside humans behind the gossamer veil of perceived reality. Eternal beings that chose what form they presented to humans; sometimes beautiful, often horrific, but always unpredictable and enigmatic. And always dangerous. They did not share human emotions or desires, nor did they seek to understand them. This was what made dealing with them so precarious. History and legend were full of tales of those who failed.

As he settled on a frost-glittered oak trunk to unwrap his harp from its protective cover of soft green leather, Brandan could not stop his fingers trembling, not just from the cold but also from his anxiety. Who, if any, of the Sidhe would step through the portal? There was one he did not want to encounter, a lovely but deadly Sidhe Queen, whose jealousy was inevitably lethal. It was she who trapped the soul of a female Fae, imprisoned her within the golden harp for eternity as punishment for falling in love with Brandan. After this outrage, he had fled the Queen's company, stealing the harp, one of very few human musicians that had survived an encounter with Leanan. She preferred her young male human songbirds to live out their whole lives in servitude to entertain her - and not just with music.

Fearing her, he prayed fervently to the Blessed Mother Danu and the Great Father Dagda: those deities whom both human and Sidhe must respect and revere. Any of the Shining Ones, even the hideous Sluagh Sidhe, would be better than that fairy queen. Even the thought of encountering her again turned his blood colder than the thick ice on the nearby lake.

It was a risk he had to take. His stay at Lismore was so full of portent and warning. These increasingly unsubtle messages were for a reason, and here he hoped to find the answers.

Blowing on his fingers in an effort to warm them up, Brandan prepared to risk his life and play. There were many tunes he would not perform now, for risk of summoning *her.* He chose lilting but human-composed melodies but played in a key that would have sounded strange and discordant to anyone but those of the fairy folk. Time ceased to have meaning, the sun continued its swift low passage over the autumn sky, shadows lengthened, but the bard played on until his frozen fingers lost all feeling, unaware that they had begun to bleed.

It began with the incongruous sound of humming, low and faint like summer afternoons, the sleep-inducing buzz of bees gathering pollen. The noise grew in intensity until the air was wild with the sound of thousands of invisible bees, enough to send most men fleeing the grove in terror, but not the bard. He continued to play, blood running freely down his whitened elegant fingers as he coaxed more unearthly music from his harp. The air became more agitated as the buzzing gave way to a furious whirlwind, snapping branches and hurling them around the musician's body, some glancing off him with bruising force. But still he played on.

Stillness fell, arrow-strike sudden, and all the grove's life seemed to hold its breath as the last echoing chords of Brandan's music faded to silence and anticipation. The still, icy air filled with sweet perfume, an exotic fragrance born of no earthly flower or spice. He had company.

The grey light of an early October morning gave way to a shimmering brightness with no warmth but a golden hue building up within a vortex in the clearing. Brandan dropped to his knees, knowing the Sidhe brooked no signs of disrespect or arrogance in those that summoned them. Nor would he use a word of their language, the Sidhea Bruidin, a curious mixture of lyrical and harsh tones. He was fluent in their tongue but wanted to appear a lowly and ignorant human; this was the safest option in the company of such capricious and unpredictable beings.

Blurring beams of gold and purple hues coalesced into the shape of a tall young man, causing Brandan to sigh quietly in relief; it could so easily have been something monstrous – not that the human-like form made the Sidhe any less dangerous. He lowered his head and waited to be addressed by the apparition, who to Brandan's relief spoke to him in Irish.

'A human songbird. What possible purpose could you have to summon me to your cold, dreary realm?'

Keeping his head low, Brandan spoke softly, reverentially. 'I have been haunted these past days by the scent of roses, my Lord. I fear I may have caused offence to the Shining Ones by some unknown, clumsy slight, and for that inadvertent folly I apologise with all my heart and soul.'

'Raise your head and repeat those words,' the being commanded. Brandan knew the Sidhe would study his eyes for signs of deception. Compared with them, humans were clumsy at duplicity and easily exposed. The bard did what he was told and bore the scrutiny with calm confidence. He had not lied. The Sidhe's own eyes were wondrous, a constantly changing whirl of many hues, some not of this world; but their beauty was cold, indifferent and unfathomable.

'That golden harp of yours … a great prize. How came you by it?'

Brandan swore to himself. Now he did have to lie. At least the soul of the haunted harp would not betray him but remain mute in the presence of the

Sidhe.

'My Lord, it was a gift from the King Donal of Lismore, much pleased by my playing at his wedding feast.'

'It looks of our design.'

'Indeed, but only as a clumsy homage to the beautiful harps of your people. Mine is of purely human crafting.'

To Brandan's relief, the Sidhe seemed content with the explanation and began to retreat through the portal. The notion of a mere human possessing a Sidhe harp was too preposterous to take seriously.

'Whatever is causing your haunting, it is not of our making. You have caused no offence to us. For an answer, I suggest you look closer to home. Much closer ...'

With the suddenness of a snuffed-out candle the Sidhe was gone, Brandan was once more alone in the stillness of a winter morning. Initially he was relieved that he was not to be eternally tormented by the Lady of the spun silver hair, lilting hypnotic voice and infinite jealousy to all that spurned her love. A jealousy from which even death was no release. Then realisation sank in: something else was haunting him, and if that something was not of the Sidhe, by all the gods, what was it?

8

Rhuddlan, Wales

The birds were silent. That was wrong. A bright dawn and rising temperatures should have had them carolling their joy at surviving another freezing night. Though none of the other riders of Prince Gwion's Teulu was aware of this warning, Seren's fingers tightened on her pony's reins; a bad move, causing the little mare to fret and skitter. She forced herself to relax, to calm the pony and concentrate. Though she could hear nothing amiss beyond the eerie silence, there was an odour building up in the still air, fetid, cloying like rotting meat. Ice touched her face and hands as if the sun had suddenly disappeared from the sky. Something large moved through the thick undergrowth of frosted ferns, something fast, sinuous, following the travellers. That it was silent meant it was not of this world.

'My Lord,' Seren's mind raced, 'we are in great danger …'

'Wolves? Gwiber?'

'If only.'

In rising desperation, Seren turned her head, trying to track the movement of their pursuer as the warriors unsheathed their swords in a clatter of metal. Would their weapons be of any use? She was certain it was not a gwiber, a large vicious creature but one of flesh and blood and vulnerable to cold steel. Whatever was now circling round them was of magic origin, a being created with intense malevolent energy. One that might be invisible to the Teulu. How could they fight something a blind girl could only sense?

It was closer now, and she had a better feeling for the creature's dimensions. It was a snake. A monstrous serpent long enough to trap them within the coils of its invisible body. The horses were aware of it now, snorting and throwing up their heads, their panic dangerous to both rider and mount. Maybe this was the intent of whatever had summoned the snake. The warriors' mounts, steadfast in the heat of battle, were whirling, rearing and bucking in their terror. No rider, whether Prince, warrior or witch, was immune to being thrown and trampled in the chaos of thrashing hooves. Could they outrun it? Could letting the animals have their head and bolt be the safest option? Seren thought so.

'We must flee, my Lord … let the horses run.'

She shoved her feet deep into the stirrups and with one hand, grabbed a handful of her pony's long, shaggy mane. With the other hand she wove a symbol in the air, and in a loud, confident voice evoked Ceridwen in a powerful plea for the Dark Mother's aid. Prince Gwion did not argue but roared a command to give the horses their heads. Seren dropped low to her pony's neck, clinging on tightly, giving in to fear and anguish as the horses surged forward and galloped flat out along the path, oblivious to the rough ground and tree roots.

Panic blurred her senses; this was folly. She must concentrate on awareness of the threat, somehow clear her mind of fear and reach out to the ghost snake. This time she could smell it, a strong taint of corruption, rotting flesh left to the sun. A horrified cry rose in her throat. It was ahead of them! How could that be? So … it could not be outrun or fought with cold steel. There was no need to warn the Prince to halt his troops; the horses abruptly sat back on their haunches, balked and swerved from their flat-out run, terrified and unwilling to move forward, snorting in alarm. There was only one hope to defeat this threat, and that lay with her.

With difficulty, she dismounted from her frantic pony, somehow avoiding Olwyn's dangerously whirling body and trampling hooves, and ignoring the horrified warnings from her escort. Gathering her strength, she stood tall and proud, holding out both hands before her. In a loud, clear voice she incanted all the sacred names of the Mother Goddess Modron and the Father God Cerunnos, desperately building up an invisible wall of protection to shield her from the seething malevolence that writhed before her. Coils of hatred surrounded the troop, ever tightening, preparing to crush them. But could it actually harm them physically? Seren's mind raced. This was emotional energy – powerful but not made of bone and sinew.

She turned back to the warriors and shouted, her voice stronger and more compelling than how she really felt. 'Stand your ground but do not feel anger or fear. You must *not* fear it. This is nothing, a thing of shadow.'

She turned to face the head of the monstrous snake; she could not see it but was aware of cold, glaring eyes fixing on her, the focus of its malicious intent.

'I am not afraid of you. You are smoke, you are a puff of poisoned air. The softest breath of wind could disperse you to nothing.'

Her mind echoed with a deafening hiss of contempt and vile curses in a woman's sharp voice. Waves of morale-sapping whispers followed; foul lies about her parents, her friends, about herself. She ignored them as she gathered up her willpower to summon the wind, using incantations used by witches from the dawn of time. Concentrating the rising power from deep within her soul into one purpose, harnessing the wind to do her will.

It began as the lightest breeze whispering through the bare branches of the surrounding woodland. The hissing in her mind changed to mocking laughter. 'Is that all you can do? You are but a girl with a child witch's pathetic and weak power.'

Again Seren ignored the taunts, allowing the breeze to build into a blustery gale that snapped branches and howled along the valley floor. She sensed doubt in her adversary; clearly her unknown enemy had underestimated her power. Before it could gather its thoughts and fight back, Seren concentrated the wind into an intense hammer blow of nature's energy, and sent it blasting into the head of the serpent.

It was gone, dissipated instantly, only a howl of fury and defeat echoing briefly in her mind from the shadow beast's creator.

As the riders raced over to her side, Seren struggled to stay on her feet, drained emotionally and physically by her battle with the snake and its summoner. Prince Gwion leapt off his horse and caught her in his arms as her legs failed her. She looked up into his face, wracked with anxiety.

'We must say nothing of this, my Lord. Not until I know who sent this thing to attack us.'

She took in his stern nod of assent before sinking into the welcome oblivion of a faint.

Still shaken from their encounter in the forest, Seren tightened her hand on her guardian's arm as he led her into Rhuddlan fortress's great hall, into the presence of the many wealthy, powerful men gathered there to listen to her words. Shaking with trepidation, she took in the smell of their sweat, armour, leather and fine fur as it blended with the smoke from a blazing oak trunk on the hearth ... and their curiosity about her arrival with Prince Gwion. An interest as sharp and tangible as the overpowering wood smoke.

Seren steeled herself to address an extraordinary, charismatic man, Gruffydd ap Llewelyn, who had overcome great adversity to unite the warring principalities of this land under one banner. The man now proclaimed King of Wales had defeated and humiliated Earl Harold's English army. Seren had heard many tales of his feats of valour as visitors gathered around the hearths back at the witches' village. Now she stood trembling before the great man as he greeted her guardian.

'I welcome my brother Gwion to my court. Your company as ever gladdens my heart. But I fear bad tidings have caused you to cross the ice-bound landscape with no warrior sons but only the bright star of your court and some brave followers of your Teulu for company.'

So, no-one at the court knew of their encounter with danger in the woods. Maybe that was a good thing. Seren smiled shyly at his affectionate use of the meaning of her name, but she could detect stress and fatigue in the King's voice. The endless battles to keep the Welsh Princes from tearing apart the fragile unity from endless feuds as well as keeping the English and Norse at bay were etched deeply into his voice. These were uneasy times for the new King; his fledgling kingdom had reeled when he survived an assassination attempt the year before from Cynan ap Iago, the son of a man he had executed for treason. Friends and enemies must seem sides of the same coin. Seren knew the King had no cause to distrust Prince Gwion, but that meant nothing in these times when loyalty was as firm as wave-lashed sand.

A slight draught and the sound of fine fabric swishing against the flagstones announced the arrival of a new female to the company, one that made Seren shiver with unease. There was considerable power here, old magic but tainted with hostility and arrogance. In other words, trouble. Something not helped by the change in the King's voice; his tone was terse as he introduced the newcomer.

'Ah, as ever, your timing is perfect, my dear.' He paused to let the woman move to stand at his side, a position of considerable status and influence, then turned back to Prince Gwion. 'May I introduce you to my seer, the Lady Vanora of Rumenea. Her wisdom and insight into the spirit world and the nature of our deities have been a source of great strength to my court.' He spoke then to the Vanora. 'My honoured guest, Prince Gwion, has brought his ward to court to bring us warning of great danger. A vision sent directly to her by the Dark Mother herself.'

Seren bowed low as more hostility washed over her. Her ability to pick up other peoples' emotions had never felt more of a curse than now. The other woman's inner contempt for her was so strong that it caused Seren tight pain in her chest and throat.

'The fevered dreams of a novice witch, little more than a child? A blind child at that. And for this, all the Princes of Cymru have been summoned to Rhuddlan?'

Shocked by the open scorn and disrespectful manner of the lady, Seren felt her resolve began to falter, and she shrank back. An angry Gwion supported her by placing his arm around her waist before replying, his voice strong and full of pride.

'My King, this girl is destined to be the most powerful wise woman ever born. She is under the tutelage of Rhan of the Golden Dove. No greater seer exists anywhere in these lands, and Rhan has affirmed this is so.'

He paused to allow the slight to Vanora to sink in before continuing.

'I bring a letter from that great lady, attesting to the accuracy of all Seren's visions, for though the girl cannot see our everyday world, she can gaze deeply into other realms, both past and future.'

Jealousy ... that was the emotion now seething from the older seer; jealousy and fear that this slender reed of a girl with the power to summon every great leader of the kingdom under one roof would usurp her position in court. Something Seren had no desire for. It was time to reassure the woman; this was not a time to make powerful enemies. Struggling to control the betraying weakness in a tremble in her voice, she addressed Vanora directly.

'My lady ... I want nothing but a swift return to my studies with my sister witches, but first I must do my duty in giving this warning. One given to me by a great spirit hawk, a messenger of Ceridwen herself.'

Mention of the Dark Mother's name, rarely spoken aloud, caused the already hushed crowd to take a sharp intake of breath. She was never invoked lightly, especially in her sacred season. Seren's spirits sank lower. The seer's contempt had deepened, and Seren detected a faint odour insinuate across the court; the same taint of corruption that had emanated from the monstrous ghost snake. Now Seren knew the source of the attack in the forest, and the knowledge made her blood run with ice at the implications. This woman was powerful and malevolent, and no amount of appeasement and humility would make her any less an enemy.

'Our guests have travelled for long and across a difficult land,' the King announced, to lessen the tension in the court; defusing a clearly angry Vanora would be a more difficult task. 'We must allow them the grace of time to rest before discussing this important matter in more detail. I call for an audience for all when tomorrow's sun reaches the blessed stones.'

Later, curled up at the feet of her guardian, Seren rested her head against his legs, the cheery warmth from a crackling hearth fire on her face.

'You will do your best, *cariad*,' Prince Gwion murmured, stroking her hair. 'Then we must wait for the great and good of the land to decide what to do.'

Seren sighed. She had faced the intense scrutiny of the most powerful men and women in Wales, the Princes, warlords and druids and wise women. Their unease fuelled by the presence of that damned snake witch whose unseen eyes still managed to gleam like shards of river ice into her mind, trying to intimidate her and nearly succeeding. Only the calm, resolute company of Prince Gwion by her side prevented her from turning and running from the court.

Denied peace and rest by the Goddess, Seren found her light, troubled sleep invaded by another vision. She awoke from blindness to the same horrific battlefield, the same sensation of a disaster yet to happen. With a shock of reality, the stench of the brutal slaughter assaulted her. With tears rolling down her face, Seren stumbled through the tangle of burnt and broken bodies and weapons. She could reach down and touch the dead and dying warriors, the brave sons of Cymru and Kernow, as they lay at her feet. Worst of all, the few still alive could see her, and were beseeching her for the aid she was unable to give them. And all the time, above her head circled the monstrous raven, revelling in the slaughter.

Awaking to her blindness was no curse but a mercy. She welcomed the blackness, it was comfort, it was her reality, a respite from the terrible vision. Seren knew she had been brought there for a reason and that her duty was far from fulfilled. Could she prevent that future battle from ever happening? It had to be so, why else was she given these warnings?

Forcing her heart to slow from its fearful pounding, Seren lay back on the bed. But sleep would not return. The vision of destruction reared behind her closed lids until all she could do was wait until the castle stirred.

Soon it would be time for the sun to touch the great stones. Trepidation making her heart race and flutter, Seren allowed her attendants to dress her, giving her the time to gather her thoughts and control her nerves. The gown was special, made for. her by the village craftswomen, every stitch woven with love and magic. Seren knew what the dress looked like; her friends had described it as they made it. They had used the finest spun lambs' wool mixed with ultra-fine linen, dyed to a shade of silver green. The gown was so light, it fell around her slender body like a second skin. It had no decorations or embroidery, allowing her youth and beauty to be its only adornment.

They fastened a simple cloak of deep blue across her shoulders with a silver pin topped with a carefully-worked five-pointed star and a moon. A parting gift from Rhan. Seren touched the pin lightly and her throat constricted with homesickness for the witches' village, her friends and the simple life she loved.

As if its makers knew her sadness, the magic in the dress began to work; the warmth of their friendship, hope and support enveloped her, lifting her spirits and making her smile. She whispered a fervent 'Thank you' to them, promising she would see them soon.

Her newly-washed dark hair shone, fragrant with flower-scented soap, and tumbled free down her back, as befitted a maiden. They gently placed on her head her silver circlet with a central motif of the triple moon, the symbol of the Mother Goddess and of Seren's role in life, to be a wise woman, a witch.

Seren smiled and thanked the attendants, held her hand out for her stick. Took in a deep breath, and raised her head. She was ready.

She sought out her guardian, who had also suffered a difficult night. Still dressed in his travelling clothes, he sat at a newly-lit hearth and broke his fast early with cold mutton and fresh bread.

'I have never seen you look so lovely,' Gwion murmured, his voice brim-full of paternal pride, strengthening his resolve to make sure he made an exceptional marriage arrangement for the girl. Nothing but the very best for Seren.

'I hope we can go back soon,' Seren whispered. 'This place is difficult for me. I cannot move around freely like at home, where I know the position of every chair, the resting place of all the castle hounds. I have tripped up over several here already. One tried to bite me.'

'Ill-bred cur. I'll have it soundly whipped.'

Seren laughed. 'First you will have to find out which one. Remember I couldn't actually see the culprit hound.'

Gwion hugged her. 'I will need to get out soon, sir,' she went on, 'to feel the living earth beneath my feet, to speak to the Goddess amid the beauty of her sacred groves ...' Her voice trailed away, the terrifying memories of the spectral snake still alive in both their minds. 'I will never understand how the Christians must be encased in stone walls to worship their one dead god.'

'A mystery to us all, my little star,' Gwion replied. 'As is their overwhelming need to force us to do the same, which has caused so much bloodshed.' There must be somewhere close to the fortress where you can find comfort. You will be safe with an escort.'

Seren heard the uncertainty in his voice. She had not shared her discovery of the enemy within the Llewellyn's court, but Gwion was no fool. Vanora's power and open hostility made her an obvious suspect in malice.

'But first,' added Gwion, 'we must do our duty and deliver the Dark Mother's message.' He rose heavily to his feet to prepare for the meeting. 'It would not do to keep such a gathering of princes waiting for one battered old war horse and his beloved ward.'

The raucous sound of the sentries sounding horns, followed by the howling of the fortress hounds, announced unexpected new arrivals to the fortress. Not enemies, for Seren heard no call to arms, but the alarm still roused the entire household and sent servants rushing in a frenzy to make the newcomers welcome. Curious, Seren pulled on a wool cloak and, with her long stick tapping out the unfamiliar route, cautiously wandered alone into the courtyard.

Avoiding the confused mêlée of riders and horses as best she could, Seren heard voices speaking in a language close to hers yet subtly different in tone and pronunciation. Bretons? Cumbrians? She concentrated on their speech pattern. No, they were Cornish. To the surprise of all at Rhuddlan, a deputation from King Cadoc had arrived. They had travelled fast and hard. Seren could feel the heat mist rise from their horses and smell the animals' dripping sweat.

She thought she had found a good place in the shadows to listen unobserved, but she was spotted by one of the visitors. The power of his presence enveloped her across the courtyard. She realised he was a man of magic and great wisdom, and as he took and held her hand with great tenderness, a man of compassion too.

'My name is Adwen of Men an Tol … The connection between those who truly serve to protect our people with the Sight is strong. I believe we share a terrible vision of the future, sent by the Dark Mother to warn us.'

Seren's heart beat faster in gratitude. She had found someone else with the same burden and possibly, by his tone of voice; a friend at last at Llewellyn's court?

'To have seen such horrors in your visions must have been hard for one so young,' the druid continued. 'The future carnage I witnessed haunts my every waking moment and has purged my soul of all serenity.'

Seren sighed, recognising her own unpleasant experiences since that fateful tryst in the woods back home. She looked up in the direction of his strong voice and gave a sad smile, 'We that are gifted with the Sight were warned for a reason. To be given time to prevent this nightmare. To weave the thread of fate into a different pattern.'

He bowed his head. 'I agree. We must not fail.' And after kissing her hand, he moved off with the rest of the Cornish deputation, leaving her feeling strangely bereft by his absence.

As the household stirred into the morning's preparations for the summit meeting, Seren found herself eager to spend more time with the Cornish druid. She enlisted Prince Gwion to describe his appearance in detail to her; Adwen's inner being she could discover for herself.

Sensing Seren's need for a respected and much-needed ally, the Prince was happy to help her. As the newcomers gathered for the meeting in Llewellyn's audience hall, Gwion took her arm and guided her to a comfortable place by the hearth, which was already ablaze with a whole oak log. He could feel her tremble and had assumed she was cold, as were many, with a peevish ice-laden wind whining through the window slits. The welcome short truce with the early winter was coming to an end.

In truth, it was Seren's anxiety that made her shiver. What if Adwen had merely humoured her during their brief meeting that morning? What if he sided with the snake witch? Seren's cause here would be truly lost and she would return home in defeat and disgrace; yet the message remained as strident as ever and would come to pass.

'The Cornishman is not much in stature but he has the presence of a man who stands tall in the minds of all who behold him,' began Prince Gwion. 'He is in his late twenties but already there is a streak of silver in his dark hair.'

Seren nodded, trying to form a picture of the druid in the darkness, hoping she could see him in her dreams. Her guardian continued, 'His features are of noble aspect. His eyes are grey, piercing. Almost silver in hue.'

Gwion leant down to whisper, 'And he is smiling at you most favourably ... I think you may have an ally in this court.'

Seren needed someone beyond her own family on her side. That morning, the mood at court was more hostile than curious, all due to Vanora's open scorn. The woman must have spent her night poisoning minds against her, for those without seers sharing the vision chafed at the summons to the King's court in winter, when travel was difficult and dangerous. Their anger reached her in a wave of negative energy, draining her resolve. Seren felt all of her mere 14 years on this side of the Veil. Could she do the Dark Mother's bidding and convince these hardened warlords and princes of the truth? That terrible danger threatened them all?

As the King arrived into the great hall, Seren's guardian informed her that he had the witch Vanora already at his side, resplendent in a sweeping gown of dark green, brown and yellow ... the colours of a viper. Seren did not need to be told; the malign waves of the woman's hatred and jealousy had already swept over her. This time, Seren was ready, putting up a defensive shield against the assault of negative, weakening emotions. The resulting fury from Vanora at being thwarted gave the younger witch great satisfaction. The seer was not going to have everything her own way at court – at least not that day.

Once the crowds had assembled and settled, Vanora stepped forward, using her dramatic presence and feared reputation to great effect. All were hushed; even the fortress hounds lay still and quiet on the rush-strewn floor and the ever present crows and kites ceased to circle above.

'I have spent the night within the circle of stones, in deep meditation and in communion with many powerful spirits from beyond the Veil. I can reassure you, there is no terrible conflagration to come. There will always be war and bloody battles, but no catastrophe, no monstrous raven.'

The crowd erupted into confused clamour, expressions of relief clashed with pitched arguments among those who believed in Seren's vision. The King demanded silence, then with the tension tangible and expectation of more drama hanging in the air, summoned Seren and the Cornish druid to address the assembly.

Vanora was furious. 'My Lord King, there is no need to prolong this. I have spoken to the gods, there is no more to say.'

'But there is, my lady of the serpents.' Adwen's voice held great authority as he strode forward, holding out his hand for the blind witch and sending a thrill of hope through her. 'How can you so easily dismiss our testimony to the contrary?'

He waited until the mumbles of dissent and anger quietened down. At least the King was allowing him to continue; Llewellyn could so easily have accepted the word of his own seer and dismissed the court.

'I am here to represent every druid, witch and seer in Kernow, and many ordinary folk too. All have shared the same vision in its horrific entirety. You also have a great treasure here. Though still a fledgling, this girl will become the most gifted wise woman in the whole of Cymru. Her gifts already bypass those of her elder sisters of the Craft.'

He deflected a mystic lance of hatred from Vanora with the ease of a man swatting away a noisome fly.

'So I ask you good people of this wise and ancient realm: do you listen to the many who warn you, or to the one the gods have chosen not to confide in?'

The affront was too great for Vanora's vanity to ignore. She turned to the King, her face blanched white with fury.

'How can you allow such a heinous slur from a foreigner? Nothing more than a primitive teller of fortunes rummaging through animal entrails, drunk on mistletoe and spurious power.'

'No more than I can allow my honoured guests to be insulted,' the King replied, controlling his embarrassment and fury with great skill. 'Please leave the court, lady, and return to your quarters until summoned.'

Clearly unsettled by the behaviour of a long-trusted advisor, the King dismissed the court. 'This matter needs more deliberation and greater study. I am certain none of our noble princes will endure the expense and difficulty of raising a big army on the evidence of a dream, however strange that it is a vision shared. Likewise, we cannot allow our future to be jeopardised by ignoring a direct warning from the Dark Mother.'

He held out his arms toward the court.

'Those lords who need to return to your domains are free to leave with my full blessing and gratitude. I have welcomed your wise counsel over this issue. But I command that our honoured guest Adwen of Kernow and Seren of Nercwys remain.'

Seren, previously so desperate to return home, now felt a tremor of joy. The prospect of spending more time with Adwen in the warmth and security of Rhuddlan over the winter months felt more blessing than a curse. The druid reached across and gave her hand a supportive squeeze. Seren knew he felt the same.

9

England

'Did you not use the coming Christmas as an excuse to summon the fellow home?' Harold's patience with both the King and their spy in the Norman bastard's court had evaporated into a cold fury. 'Or simply demand as his King that Hereward return to his lands and duties?'

Edward sighed and pulled his robes closer, as if the gesture could shut out both the bone-numbing cold and the heat of the Godwin Earl's anger.

'We need to know,' Harold persisted. 'He has been in the Norman court long enough to hear rumours, learn some truths … however distracted by hunting, feasting and the lure of foreign maidens he may be,'

They walked through the grounds of Westminster Palace, between trees and bushes frozen into a petrified, glittering extravaganza, and found a place out of sight and sound of the court. The King paused, let his gaze wander to the Thames and the craft stilled and trapped in the river ice. A gathering of daring urchins had ventured onto the motionless river, and the sound of their bravado and laughter carried far on the still air. Edward prayed to the Holy Mother that their voices would not turn to screams if the ice gave way beneath them. A distraction: he forced himself to return to the politically awkward matter in hand.

'Were it that simple! It appears Guillaume thinks highly of the boy, and to drag him back home now would be seen as a slight to the Duke's generous hospitality.'

Harold resisted the urge to spit in disgust at the French version of the man's name. His mind churned with resentment. He too had spent time at the Duke's court, as a guest, or more accurately a hostage after being shipwrecked off the coast of Normandy. It had not enamoured him to William, and had made him suspicious of the man's ambitions. One drunken night, the Duke had even tried to force Harold into swearing allegiance to him and his spurious claim to the English throne. Was he doing the same to Hereward? The Mercians were nearly as powerful as his own

Wessex family. They would make a useful ally to further the Duke's ambition.

It was obvious to Harold and the other earls that the King's own, much longer exile in the past, enjoying Norman hospitality, had turned his mind from l*oyalty to his own people to those upstart Norsemen. Though the English court had been purged of the King's Norman hangers-on, his attitude of dog-like devotion to 'William the Bastard' was still a cause of great concern to the Witan, the Saxon parliament. These were the men who would decide the succession, for only the strongest and most able nobleman would be chosen as the next King of the English.

A rare glimmer of enthusiasm lit up Edward's wan, aesthetic features. 'I have a plan forming in my mind, given to me by God during my prayer vigils.'

The Earl did his best not to sigh openly with a mixture of trepidation and concern. The less Edward thought, the better. Beyond, that was, building abbeys and cathedrals throughout his realm. He folded his arms, head slightly to one side, and waited to hear the King's latest celestial revelation.

'Let us rid these Isles of the scourge of paganism once and for all. God is calling on me to organise a mighty, righteous Crusade against Wales and Ireland and those renegades in Cornwall. Before you interject, I know we cannot do this alone, Harold.'

Grabbing the Earl by the shoulder, Edward's eyes gleamed with a manic fervour. It has the most animated he had been for years, since first declaring his desire to build Westminster Abbey. 'We must call in our allies from overseas and Scotland. Good, brave Christian nations who will do their duty to the one true God.'

Greatly alarmed, Harold fought to stay calm. Wealthy, settled England was too much of a prize to allow foreign armies on her soil for whatever purpose, however noble. 'What of Normandy, what of the rumours of ungodliness festering there now seeping across the Channel?'

The King smiled, another sight so rare it was unnerving. 'I am inclined to dismiss it as no more than foolish prattle, the fireside gossip of old women. If there was truth to these stories, our young fen tiger would have found it by now and got word back to us.'

Doubting the youth could find his own sword unless handed to him by a servant, Harold grunted his displeasure. No matter how secret Guillaume's plans were, enough information had already filtered from Normandy to cause great anxiety. Wild, unbelievable tales of the Duke's ability to harness small dragons to create powerful weapons. Total nonsense of course; but something worrying was brewing across the Channel. Never had that stormy strip of seawater seemed so slight a barrier to England's many enemies.

'Your Grace, send for Hereward.' The Earl's request sounded closer to a threat. 'Let us hear the truth directly from someone loyal to England, one entertained in the heart of William's household.'

Edward felt cornered again. No matter how many nobles bowed in respect for him, he felt their impatience, saw the cold light of contempt in their power-greedy eyes. A knife-stab of old guilt twisted in his heart, one no amount of prayer or painful penance would erase. By God's Holy Mercy, he would leave this Earth soon and hopefully be granted a place in Heaven, leaving the festering sore of succession for others to fight over. Nothing Edward could do in this life could change what he had done …

10

Normandy

The Spaniard waited, anxiety triggered sweat pooling in his palms and running down his back. He ignored the deerhounds rifling through the fresh rushes on the stone slabs in futile hope of finding any scraps of food. The Keep was spotless, with all signs of the feast night before cleaned away. This Norman Duke kept a tight run household, with the same military precision as his army. Ferro of Jerez had made the long perilous journey to the fortress at Falaise by sea. Maybe this would be the last time he would have to endure the humiliation of sea sickness and bone jarring fatigue from the travel overland by mule cart. At least his precious cargo was safe, undamaged by the brutal frost hardened ruts along what passed for roads both in his home country and France from this coldest of autumns in living memory.

What manner of man was this Duke? A hard man, a battle scarred warlord with a short fuse, that was common knowledge and obvious from his success in the battlefield and ruthless treatment of the defeated. One who overcame the Norman barons' loathing of him for being the old Duke's by-blow, the bastard son born of a lowborn tanner's daughter. By his skill at statesmanship and brutal defeat of all rebellion. But not a man cowed by superstition and religion. Otherwise men like Ferro himself would not be racing to Falaise in search of his patronage. The wheezing, rhythmic sound of bellows and the clash of hammer on anvils would not be reverberating around the hidden stronghold. Nor would the air be heavy with the stench of molten metal and thick smoke. All this fevered industry was heaven to Ferro, a place where he could work and thrive if only Guillaume the Bastard, Duke of Normandy would give him patronage. And sponsor his beloved creation still hidden beneath heavy leather covers tied down with thick chains.

A burly Norman baron, his Viking heritage apparent in his piercing blue eyes and short-cropped white blond hair, interrupted Ferro's musing. Without the courtesy of addressing him, the warrior signalled for Ferro to follow him into an inner chamber. Duke Guillaume paced behind a large oak table.. Tall, heavy set with receding dark hair and cold eyes, the Duke was as formidable as his reputation. Ferro was relieved he was there to be of great use to this man and not an enemy.

'Were you stopped on route to this fortress?'

The Duke's manner was abrupt, shorn at any pretence of noble born civility. Nobility? The Spaniard sneered inwardly, what nonsense. That was a flimsy veneer all these Norman warlords affected. Just beneath the surface lurked the blood of predatory sea wolves that burnt, raped and marauded through so many peaceful lands. They were infidel, barbarians.

Ferro bin Abzuleiman bin Zaid came from Al Andalus, he was a Moor by birth and from beautiful Jerez, raised in a civilised society rightly proud of its learning and scientific progress. He was also very poor and in dangerously bad grace with a Caliphate besieged by invading Christian armies. It was time to flee and make his peril-ridden journey to seek out Duke Guillaume. A man who paid for advancement in solid gold. A man who would appreciate his intellect and skills.

'No, my Lord Duke', Ferro bowed low before continuing, 'the documents you sent me were believed at every border, none challenged that I was carting untanned goat skins to trade.' He risked a smile. 'The stench from the skins I used to disguise it was proof enough.'

Guillaume did not answer, a curt gesture dismissed his attendants and when alone, he strode over to the whippet lean Spaniard and gripped his shoulder. 'Does it work, Moor?'

This time Ferro's smile was genuine, full of pride, 'It works, my Lord Duke, better than in your wildest imagination.'

Guillaume's eyes flashed with excited anticipation and, hauling the Spaniard with him, left the inner chamber and strode down into the castle courtyard. There indeed was a large cart hauled by sturdy mules and laden high with reeking, bloodied goatskins. No sign of the wonder concealed by the hides. The Duke paced around the wagon, wondering if the Moor's pride was justified. Could such a thing exist? Something that would give him mastery of the skies? A tremor of excitement shivered through him, stronger than the one that had arisen when he watched the prototype pike launcher explode and kill an enemy in front of him.

'Can there be more?'

Bowing low again, Ferro was delighted to announce to his new master that there could, as many as the Duke commanded to be created. All he needed was an army of master craftsmen and smiths and the raw materials.

'You speak not of payment,' remarked Guillaume as he patted the wagon as if confirming his ownership of its contents.

'I am yours to serve, My Lord Duke,' replied Ferro calmly. 'I will give you many marvels and in return I wish only for your written assurance that I will not have to worry about my next meal or a roof over my head.'

He wanted to add protection from his enemies but decided to keep that to himself. By the time the Caliphate discovered where he had fled to Europe with his priceless knowledge, Ferro would be safely secure within the Duke's patronage.

His stern features breaking into a thin smile, the Duke patted Ferro's shoulder with the same gesture of ownership, 'You drive a hard bargain, Moor, one I am forced to accept.'

Guillaume turned on his heel and strode away, 'Make many marvels for me and you will dine off plates of gold and dwell beneath a gilded roof.'

11

Ireland

Brandan could hear the cheers and merriment rising from Lismore's stern walls long before his horse's hooves clattered back into the central courtyard. It had to be good news. Though it did not lift his own spirits, anything agreeable was an excuse for celebrations, prolonging his reason to stay at the fortress. The icy grip on the land had not faltered and he was unwilling to pass over a warm bed and a full belly. And the stolen hours alone with Donal.

A groom ran to take Brandan's horse from him, a broad smile on the man's ruddy features.

'It is a boy, My Lord. Danu has blessed this household. Our lovely Queen Liadan is safely delivered of a healthy boy.'

Good news indeed. There had been much quietly-whispered concern over the young Queen's health in her first pregnancy. She was a slender reed of a girl, 13 summers old and seemingly delicate of constitution. Donal would be jubilant and in need of celebration. Brandan suspected another discreet summons to the King's bed later that night. A grin of pleasurable anticipation flitted briefly across his features, but nothing could lift his mood completely. Not with the encounter with the Sidhe male still filling his thoughts with foreboding. Who else could he turn to? Who else would know who or what was taunting him?

Such thoughts were soon pushed aside as he entered the fortress, swept up by the infectious jubilation. Ruefully he glanced down at his fingers, cut and raw from summoning the Sidhe. They would expect him to play at the celebrations, and he would not disappoint. Nothing binding his fingers with balm and tight cloth couldn't solve. The injuries to his fingertips were trivial in comparison with others he had suffered. He was a warrior, his body scarred with old battle wounds, many nearly fatal.

He had nothing to give to the baby and his mother as a gift, and decided to retire to his quarters and compose a song full of love and hope dedicated to the child. As he passed through the fortress, a servant told him the infant was strong and feeding well, healthy enough to risk naming him early. Donal had called his first son Aralt, meaning a leader of men. Brandan would reflect that in his song for the future king of Lismore.

As the bard had suspected, he was in great demand to play for the festivities, and to his surprise found himself enjoying the evening. How could he not, when all around him were so happy? King Donal's pride and joy shone from his eyes. and a smile that never left his face all evening turning to free-flowing tears as Brandan performed the new song to honour the baby.

Much later that night, when the fortress was slumbering away its revelries, the King arrived at Brandan's room, gathering him into his arms in a fierce embrace. He looked into the bard's near-black eyes, more tears gathering in his own.

'Can any man be so blessed by the gods as me? My beautiful wife has survived her first childbirth in fine health and our son feeds contentedly at her breast. My people rejoice as one at our good fortune.'

He reached out to caress Brandan's face. 'And I have you.'

The following morning, Lismore's nobles gathered in the courtyard for a celebratory morning's hunting. The iron grip of the frost had finally loosened and the fleeting warmth of the waning sun graced the landscape with a silver mist. As grooms led horses out and released a brindled sea of hounds, the already hearty mood became as excited as the milling, eager bitch pack. The scent would be good and the ground safe for many sharp, swift gallops across country with a hoped-for reward of fresh meat for the banquet tables that night.

'She is a bit fractious this morning, My Lord,' muttered a dour-faced groom, grumpy from the arm-wrenching antics of Brandan's grey mare. Other horses in the courtyard, all eager for the chase, had picked up her skittering about and head tossing. The bard took away the reins from the grateful servant and tried to sooth her before attempting to jump into the saddle.

'Lia, please. Be a lady ...'

The mare was having none of it. Her agitation grew worse, causing some ribald banter from the nobles and a concerned look on the King's face as she reared and bucked frantically. With every other rider now mounted and the hunting party ready to leave, Brandan had no choice but to ignore the stirrup iron and leap straight up into the saddle. The normally compliant and reliable Lia turned into a squealing fury of plunging equine mayhem, bucking wildly before bolting back to the stable block. Brandan kept his seat at first, struggling to control her with his body weight and reins. As she reached the sanctuary of the stables, she swerved violently and bucked with her head between her knees, catapulting her rider into the wall, where he crumpled, knocked clean out.

A few moments later Brandan came back to consciousness, still on the ground, cradled by a distraught Donal.

'By Dagda, I thought I had lost you, a punishment for being so happy. I will have that crazy bitch dealt with.'

Brandan struggled to rise to his feet, but sank back down, his gorge rising with nausea, an imaginary axe embedded in his head, such was the brute force of the pain. 'No, please. Lia is a good mare. There must be something wrong with her. She is a tough and fearless war horse; it is unlike her to play up like that.'

The King summoned grooms to check the mare over as Brandan struggled back to his feet, a trickle of blood running from his forehead down his cheek from the injury. As they removed the mare's saddle, the gasps of shock told their own story. Her back was a mass of lacerations, thin but deep and bleeding, although they found nothing sharp embedded in her saddlecloth. The poor animal must have been in torment. Brandan closely examined her injuries but already knew what had caused them – rose barbs.

'You have an enemy,' murmured the King as he helped support the still unsteady Brandan. 'It appears to be someone here at Lismore. You didn't really cut your cheek on your dagger while dressing, did you?'

Shaking his head, Brandan forced himself to stand tall, though the world was whirling and his legs were wobbling as if he was drunk. 'I have a tormenter, My Lord King. But not one of this world.'

With every incident escalating in threat, Brandan knew now it would not stop until he was dead.

He had crossed the line, ignored self-made rules that he had sworn never to break. Pacing the room, Brandan prepared himself for the difficult task ahead. Leaving Lismore.

How could he have been so stupid? He glanced back at Donal, thankfully slumbering with a wide smile of contentment as he sprawled out on the wolf fur covering his bed. It had happened as they had enjoyed another wild night of mutual passion. It should have meant nothing more to him than the pleasure of a night of laughter and song, or sharing good mead or riding together on a fast hunt. But at some point during the fierce, fevered tumble of bodies, against his nature, Brendan had opened not just his body but his heart, his soul, his mind to Donal. A terrible mistake. Brandan had always kept his heart locked securely in a place no-one could reach it. It belonged only to him.

So why prise it open now? Keeping his back turned from the King, Brandan wiped away a tear. A tear? He gazed in dismay at the single drop of salt water on the back of his hand. He had never cried, not even as an orphan foundling raised by a brutal, tyrannical musician who had taught him to play by beating him until there was no more skin left to bruise on his back. Never harming the boy's gifted fingers or his face. He had needed Brandan's dark-eyed beauty and skill as a harpist to earn gold to keep him in a luxury not passed down to the boy. The child that was Brandan had not wept, but had stored each thrashing, each winter spent cold and starving, each insult and humiliation, deep in his heart, festering.

It was a grievance that had remained until he was a scrawny 12-year-old, grown enough to stand tall, to take a sword and release all the anger in one devastating blow against his guardian's scrawny neck. He had ignored the one brief scream, the sound of metal crunch against bone, the blood. The severed head bouncing and rolling across the filthy rush floor, with a last expression of shock on its face. He had walked away without a backward glance at the body, taking only his ash wood harp, the sword and a bag of his hard-earned gold. He'd taken many heads since then, none as satisfying as that first.

'It is happening again, just like last time.' A saddened Donal spoke softly, now fully awake and sat on the edge of the bed. 'Every time there is the smallest risk of real emotion touching your life, you leave.'

Brandan shrugged. What was there to say? It was true.

'It is time for me to go, my King,' he replied, head down. 'You have Liadan and your son. I am a distraction to your reign and a potential source of heartache for the Queen. That I cannot allow.'

The King leapt from the bed and held Brandan's face in a firm grip. 'I have the greatest respect and affection for Liadan,' said. 'No man could ask for a gentler, more supportive wife. Or a more dutiful Queen. Despite our arranged match, for dynastic reasons, by some miracle we have become firm and affectionate friends. My son is now the centre of my world, I would lay my life down for him.'

His eyes blinded by tears, Donal gently pushed aside a stray lock of jet hair and kissed the warrior bard's forehead. 'But you, Brandan of the Golden Harp, are my heart's choice. I love you.'

For the sake of the King's dignity and respectful of his emotional declaration, Brandan lingered, statue-still and unresponsive. Someone had to stay in control.

'I say again, my continued presence in your court and in your bed will damage your reign. The Queen's confinement is over, she will be at your side again, as it should be.'

Donal's fingers entwined into the bard's tangled hair. 'This is insane, there is no reason for you to leave. Eire still belongs to us and our gods, and all are free to follow their hearts in matters of love. The foreigners with their dead man on a wooden cross, guilt-ridden laws and brutal punishments for being human, have no place here.'

Deep within his own heart, Donal knew the real reason why his lover wanted to flee the sanctuary of Lismore to an uncertain fate, with winter deepening. Was Brandan's fear of experiencing emotions greater than the dread of what unknown horror stalked him? It appeared so. The King stepped away, unable to curb his exasperation. He strode over to the narrow slit of a window and looked out over the night-cloaked landscape, the dark woods that held hungry wolf packs, lurking *puca* and gangs of verminous bandits.

'How can you leave now? Your life is in grave danger from this haunting. Where can you go and be safe?' I can protect you here at Lismore. I can send for the best *druidecht* and *faithe*, the wisest seers and sorcerers in the land to conjure up and fight this unseen enemy. I will not allow you to leave.'

Brandan was a mercenary, a warrior at liberty to choose what lord he served. A sword-for-hire and a free man. Common sense told him not to be foolish, that he was in greater danger riding alone until this unknown peril was defeated. If it could be. The King was wrong to command him to stay, yet there was wisdom in his words. The torment was from something not of this earth and not of the Sidhe. It had to be defeated by someone skilled in the ways of the darkness beyond the Veil of the mortal world.

He sighed assent and allowed the King to enfold him in a tight embrace, grateful for his strength, his love. With no other solution, Brandan had to stay at Lismore.

12

Normandy

Grim-faced, Guillaume tossed a parchment scroll into the hearth, watching with satisfaction as the flames eagerly devoured it. He took great pleasure as the English King's red wax seal melted last, his pious features contorting then dripping to nothing. The Duke ignored the loud intake of breath from the hapless Saxon messenger, one whose party had all fallen to bandits before reaching Caen – or so the reports would say that filtered back to their leader's master, King Edward. The truth was rather different. The man and his escort would simply disappear – forever. As would the news he brought to Normandy, that Edward wanted his envoy to return to England. Delaying tactics that Guillaume could not employ too often without creating suspicion, but that bought him more time with Hereward.

The Duke had tormented himself over his preoccupation with the young man. He had suffered many days and nights of fasting, wearing hair shirts beneath his fine garb, self scourging until the tortured flesh on his torn back ran with streams of blood. Everything he could think of to try to drive this insanity from his mind – including hours of prayer in his private chapel, kneeling on cold, rough stone floors until his knees bled. Everything except Holy Confession. He would rather be damned to an eternity of hellfire then speak of this to any human being. If God was truly omnipotent, He would know already and forgive him, for Guillaume was repentant. Yet although ashamed and guilt-ridden, he remained unwilling to allow Hereward to return to his fenland home. Guillaume most definitely did not desire the youth's body. In truth the thought of any intimacy filled him with intense revulsion and loathing. But still he could not bear to be without his company. Why? The pain-filled vigils gave him no answer.

The Duke had tried to purge his strange obsession by regularly visiting his wife, the elfin Matilda, in her chambers, despite her pregnancy. He had also sampled the delights of comely maidens brought to him by discreet household aides. His ability to make love to his wife had not changed, nor had his great love for her faded. His ability to lustily deflower virgins was as potent as ever. This should have reassured him, but it did not. Witchcraft? Had some vile spell been cast to weaken him as a man? Not superstitious by nature, he had never had such foolish thoughts before. What answer could there be but a curse?

Allowing the Saxon youth to return home would make sense, be an instant cure, but the enchantment, if that was what had infected his reason, bound him too tightly. Enough to murder King Edward's messengers. But enough to risk eternal damnation? Under this terrible spell, it seemed so. Determined that nothing should control his life – no man, beast or devil's curse – Guillaume raged to himself, sending his knowing hounds skulking from his reach, with no other candidates for their master to purge his fury on. A drastic situation such as this required blood to alleviate it, but with no target for his sword and no means to obtain counsel without exposing his shame, Guillaume felt a sharp snare of frustration closing around him.

Something had to be done before the noose pulled to a lethal tightness.

England

Edward's visions had always been full of angelic light, dazzling his eyes but with no pain, of celestial song descending from the clouds to bathe the earth with holy grace. Sometimes he heard messages, like the one urging him to build the Abbey – and what a triumph that was proving, arising as praise to God perfected in stone that would last for centuries, maybe even to Judgement Day. How eagerly he looked forward to his time alone with his Maker and His angels and saints. Time where the daily tension and strife of mortal life could be forgotten as he transcended into a place of purity and heavenly bliss.

It had seemed an age since his last time of prayer alone in his private chapel in the Abbey. He had been trapped, snowbound, in the palace at Winchester, becoming mired down by the politics of his realm. Talk among his nobles of dire omens and portents of ill-boding enraged him. This foolish talk had unseemly pagan undertones, and he had warned the Witan that anyone caught consulting witches would be executed as a heretic and traitor to the realm. There was always the threat of invasion from the Celtic lands, too much to allow any residual taint of paganism to remain festering beneath the surface in his Christian England. Nothing must ruin his vision of England as a shining beacon of righteousness, lighting up Northern Europe all the way to Rome.

Over the past week, a temporary thaw had opened the roads again, though the resulting thick mud and slush made for difficult and dangerous travelling. King Edward was determined to return to London and the

Abbey, to the open dismay of his court. He ignored the sullenness of their compliance: nowhere on this earthly plain was closer to Heaven than his light-drenched chapel with its miracle of colours beaming from the glorious stained glass.

For the first time in many months, his entourage did not include Earl Harold. A mixed blessing. Though he admired the young nobleman, his intensity and rabid anti-Norman sentiments could rankle. The Danes had increased their raids against Wessex, and there was no-one better to fend off the barbarians from his lands than Harold.

There would never be a meeting of minds with the Earl; though devout, Harold had the sound of metal against bone in his soul and not heavenly choirs.

At last he was alone. Edward sunk to his knees in a prayer of gratitude, welcoming the cold, rough stone beneath him as a friend. He prayed for many hours, one full recital of the rosary after another until his mind began to lift from the drudgery of mortal life and soar into the sublime. Bright yet soft colours bathed him in beauty, and he sighed in delight as he heard the first shimmering sound of music from the heavenly spheres, angelic music … A shadow flickered at the periphery of his vision. That was wrong. There was no darkness in this exalted realm. It did not belong. The song of the spheres was drowned out by a rhythmic beat, wings … Something approached him on huge wings, but it could not be one of the angelic host. Not with the increasing darkness that came before it.

Edward could not stay there, not in a place contaminated by some nameless evil. He fought to snap out of his deep trance, crying for help from any source. He was dimly aware of strong arms grabbing him, pulling him to his feet. He began to lose consciousness, but not before seeing a large raven encircle him. Words filled his mind in a language he didn't understand. Then there was darkness.

A badly shaken Edward awoke back in his bed, surrounded by his closest inner court, the monks who cared for his health, the protective ranks of his house carls and his wife in name only, Queen Edith - one of the Godwin clan from a political alliance. Servants had gone before and darkened the room for his comfort, but it alarmed him greatly, reminding him of the spectre of the raven. He sat bolt upright, eyes huge and haunted, and called to his household: 'Pull open those tapestries blocking the window, light all the candles. Stoke up the hearth until it blazes bright. Now.'

Only when his chambers were warm and bright did he relax. His mind sought to rationalise what he had seen. Was it possible that he had drifted asleep during his meditation? That the raven had been nothing more than a nightmare? That had to be the answer, the only one that could sooth his troubled mind. How else could he bear to meditate in his chapel again, how could he dare sleep again for fear of that devil-spawned bird invading his dreams?

His eyes distracted, haunted, King Edward hardly heard the petition from the visiting thegns from Wessex. Their gruff voices filled his ears but not his mind. Lack of sleep and acute anxiety had replaced all serenity in his heart, which no amount of prayer and penance could lift. He was so weary of life now and prayed every day and night for the Lord to take him up to paradise.

A painfully firm grip on his arm pulled him back to the reality he so despised. His wife, Edith, whispered that the deputation from Wessex wanted an answer. It was rare for her to make an appearance at court, for everyday mundane matters she found tedious, but she was a Godwin and always favoured matters concerning her kin.

'You are troubled, my lord and King, and in need of rest, but these good men have fought hard and travelled far, they deserve a fair hearing.'

Edward removed her hand from his arm, loathing her touch as intrusive and controlling. Did all Godwin spawn suckle fierce ambition at their mother's breast?

'Our good friend Earl Harold,' she continued, 'sends word that the skirmish with the Danish raiders was brief and easily overcome.'

Edward nodded, doing his best to focus on the deputation before him. 'And for that blessing of a swift victory, I will have the city bells rung and a Mass said tonight in the Abbey.'

The leader of the thegns stepped forward and bowed down on one knee. Edward signalled his assent and allowed the man to address him, overcoming a wave of revulsion as the thegn's stench of human and horse sweat, metal and blood drifted his way. The same stench of battle and death from his nightmarish vision.

'Your Majesty, the men of Wessex fought with great valour and took many prisoners. Among them we discovered not just Danish sea dogs but many Cornish curs fighting alongside them.'

The King knew what was coming next, another call for him to sanction an English war against the pagans. This time from Earl Harold, still furious and humiliated at his defeat by the Welsh. Edward also wanted that with all his heart, but England was not ready. His people thrived on the long peace, a time that had lasted all his reign. A prolonged war with Cornwall and no doubt her allies, the Welsh, would be costly in men and taxes. A holy crusade sanctioned by the Holy Father in Rome against the pagans was the only sane solution; how could those depraved, Godless barbarians hold out against the combined might of Christian Europe? That would take much time and political manoeuvring to set in motion, if at all possible. But as the King knew to his cost, Harold Godwin was not only impatient but also a hard man to refuse. If he wanted to punish the Cornish now, the King would have to find an iron-tight reason to restrain the Earl's sword arm – and there was none.

Unscrolling a parchment from the Earl, Edward studied the missive. It was typical of Harold: terse and direct. He wanted Edward to send men at arms and totally crush the Cornish in order to weaken the morale of their cousins across the Severn. The King grew dismayed at the tone of the letter. It read more like a command than a request. He gave a heavy sigh at the man's impudence. Unable to escape the image of the carnage with the raven's flight above the broken English bodies, Edward was reluctant to make any rash moves. Was it a portent? An omen of what was to come?

Edward shivered despite the warmth of his garb and the heat of his crowded court, dropping the parchment as he sought to keep from fainting. There was never a good time for a King to show weakness, and his increasing frailty was already sharpening the claws of the ambitious amongst his nobility.

'Our household will take care of your needs.' Edward rose to leave the audience chamber, gritting his teeth as he took Edith's cold, bony hand. 'We must retire to consider this request from the Earl of Wessex.'

When the petitioners from the West Country had left, Edward dismissed his entourage and braced himself for a furious onslaught from his wife, fearing that the harridan would demand an army raised to support her kinsman. Instead she fixed him with a spite-laden glare, her contempt seeming to fill the audience hall with a tangible malignancy.

'I have not given an answer yet, madam.'

The King's words did not change her stance and she rose from her throne slowly to take her leave.

'You do not need to, my lord and King. This realm needs a warrior king with fire in his belly and potent loins to sire an heir. It does not need a saint.'

13

Normandy

Hereward sat at a table in a small anteroom, attempting to study French under the tutelage of Frere Herve, a patient, elderly monk. The Saxon found all studies tiresome and strove to stay awake as old Herve droned on and on with one verb declension after another. Even so, Hereward understood the need to be able to communicate with his Norman hosts, that he was isolated by his language. He accepted he would be of more use back home at King Edward's court if he spoke their ally's tongue.

But by God's holy teeth, it was so boring. The crackle and heat of the hearth fire added to the stupor overcoming him. He bit his tongue, dug his fingernails into his palm, hoping the pain would keep him awake. Down in the courtyard he could hear a serving girl break into song.

The monk paused., 'My young friend, if you pay attention to me, you will soon be able to understand that songbird's pretty *chanson.*'

Muttering an apology, Hereward did his best to concentrate on the lesson, but within minutes the same heavy-lidded daze had returned. He could still hear the monk's wavering voice, make out the words clearly, but he was no longer in the chamber at Caen. He was on a battlefield, surrounded by terrible carnage, agonised screams, broken bodies, rivulets of blood, a deafening thunder that rumbled, shaking the ground beneath his feet and not from the air. Hereward spun in horror. How could this be a dream? He could smell the copper tang of spilt blood and the stench of steaming guts. He could *feel* the ground beneath his feet reverberate and a hot wind burn his face.

He stumbled forward, seeking survivors, seeking answers, shocked to the depths of his soul. As he passed the piles of bodies, he recognised those of his own people, and a cry of despair rose in his throat.

The sound of wing-beats rose above the thunder, and Hereward looked up to see a huge raven, its size far beyond that of any natural bird. The baleful creature circled above him, the downdraught from its wings like a mighty gale forcing him to crouch low to the ground. Its eyes glittered like black diamonds, and words filled Hereward's mind, strange words in a language unknown to him.

With an abrupt wrench in reality, he was back in the stuffy anteroom in Caen. The monk was clearly unaware of what had happened; the old man's voice was still incanting a list of verbs as if his pupil had never left the room.

A dream, that was all it had been. A horrific day dream triggered by boredom and too much red wine and cheese for breakfast. But his face still burned and the stench of death was in his nostrils. There was no time to dwell on this, for his lesson received the welcome interruption of a household messenger.

'My Lord Hereward, the Duchess wishes you to visit her at her court at this hour.'

Hereward ignored the tut-tutting and fussing of the monk, who was clearly irritated at the disturbance, and thanking him in faltering French, prepared himself to speak to Guillaume's wife. This was a rare occurrence; Matilda, whether from the fatigue of her latest pregnancy or a desire not to be seen in the company of a Saxon, had barely spoken to Hereward. Duke Guillaume was away again on one of his mysterious journeys and Caen had settled back into a more relaxed regime away from the grim stare of its formidable master. Matilda had been an elusive

figure at the court during Hereward's stay. She was a diminutive woman, barely four foot tall, but strong in body and, Hereward was told, indomitable in will too. The Duke was devoted to her, and though theirs was a political match, it was clearly a happy and fruitful one, with six children already born including three healthy boys.

Matilda welcomed the Saxon into her audience chamber. Though child-like in stature, she was clearly a formidable woman, handsome rather than a beauty, with dark eyes that glinted with shrewd intelligence.

'Forgive me for being less than forthcoming in my time with our honoured guest,' she said. Her voice was assured, commanding yet feminine, speaking fluent Saxon with a pronounced French accent. 'I am under great scrutiny from the barons, because though I am from the royal line of France, I also have Saxon blood in my ancestry, from the old Royal house of Wessex.'

Hereward marvelled at how such a high-born lady, descended from the legendary Saxon King Alfred, had ended up with Guillaume, descended from a Norse sea wolf, Hrolf the Ganger.

'So you must appreciate that any private discourse between us will be conceived as plotting by our enemies.'

Nodding his understanding, Hereward was relieved the Duchess had so many attendants within hearing distance, many witnesses to their conversation.

'Pardon my frankness,' continued Matilda, 'but why are you still here? The weather is holding fair, and your family will want you home for the celebrations of Christ's birth.'

'I have received no summons to return from my King,' Hereward answered, careful not to cause any unwitting offence to his hostess. 'I am therefore still honoured and duty bound to be King Edward's envoy to the Norman court.'

'Indeed.'

The Duchess moved to a window, moving with grace despite her swollen belly.

'Have you had the dream, Hereward?'

She spoke without turning round, keeping her gaze fixed on the nearby woodlands. 'The battlefield, the brutality, the slaughter?'

'A dream? Have *you*, My Lady?'

Still without looking round, Matilda sighed. 'Thank the Sacred Virgin, no. I have not. The Abbess at the convent I had built at Caen has though. The haunted look in your eyes tells me you have had the dream too, and not that long ago. So many Norman dead.' She shuddered and pulled her cloak closer and her. 'So much death. And above it all, flies the terrible raven.'

Hereward's mind reeled. Norman dead? He had seen only Saxon casualties in his terrible vision.

'Go home, Hereward of the Saxons.' Matilda turned her head and fixed him with her direct, sharp stare. 'Go home and do what you can to prevent this vision of hell from befalling us all.'

'I am but one man,' Hereward answered, bewildered at the implication of her words. 'There is little I can do, especially on the strength of a nun's bad dream.'

'What you must understand, Saxon,' Matilda replied, her voice hardening, 'is that I love my husband. The match between us was considered an outrage by the rest of France, but we wed for love. My loyalty is to him, my sons and the people of Normandy.

'There will come a time soon when your King Edward will pass to the heavenly kingdom he so yearns for. England will have no leader. Go back to your Godwin masters, remind them that Edward himself gave our Duke assurances of the English succession. Warn them that the Duke is a proud and ambitious man and will not brook opposition.'

Anger threatened to surface, but Hereward fought it. Did this woman expect him to help pave the way for a Norman Duke to sit on the English throne just to prevent a bloodbath? The comfort of Guillaume's court felt less welcome now; any wine would taste sour, tainted. He wanted to go home; even leaving now would not be soon enough, but aware the Duchess had not finished addressing him, Hereward forced himself to listen.

'The only way to preserve the peace is for Earl Harold to accept his

King's wishes without challenge and accept the righteous Norman succession. One that will be blessed by the Holy Father in Rome.'

Bowing low, Hereward sought to leave the Duchess's claustrophobic chambers, a place of her cloistered ambition frustrated by the restrictions on her gender in Norman society and her many pregnancies.

He feigned sincerity as he replied. 'There is nothing I desire more than the continued friendship and a lasting peace between our two realms.'

He added with a slight shrug, 'As for the battlefield and the raven? My Lady, I have had no such dream.'

14

Normandy

Steam, smoke and molten metal … the new smells of victory. Guillaume breathed in the acrid air of his secret forges and workshops beyond Falaise, striding through the newly-created streets with great satisfaction. Around him clashed the sound of industry, men's raised voices, hammering and the rhythmic woof of bellows. The enthusiasm and skill brought to Normandy by the Spanish Moor was infectious. Thanks to his organisation, skilled artisans and smiths from all over France had been recruited in secret and were now flourishing. Paid and housed well, respected, with their creativity allowed a free rein, their innovations and improvements were in full flow.

Keeping this place of wonders and innovation secret would soon be impossible, but the Duke no longer cared. Let them fear what he had created deep in this forest. Let them spare many of their warriors' lives by surrendering to the greater Norman might without a costly battle.

He sought out Ferro. The Duke had given him a purpose-built barn as large as a well-appointed manor house, and it was kept locked and heavily guarded around the clock. Guillaume was not yet ready to reveal the secret behind the solid oak plank and iron doors. As the guards bowed to him and opened the doors, anticipation welled up in Guillaume at the prospect of what he would find inside the building. -. The first thing he noticed was he saw a billowing cloud floating in the roof beams. He gasped with surprise. Ferro had captured a cloud? He was a magician!

As the shock subsided, he realised the cloud was not God-made but created by man. He could see now it was made of grey fabric and tethered by ropes. It had beneath it a brazier of smouldering coals, the purpose of which was lost on the Duke.

The Spaniard stepped out from behind a boat made from woven wicker and, on seeing Guillaume, bowed low.

'Explain this thing to me,' the Duke commanded. 'I do not understand what you are building. You promised me flight.'

'And I have given you the means to fly, my Lord Duke. I will show you ...'

He beckoned the Norman over to a large piece of parchment nailed to the barn's wall. It was covered in drawings, diagrams and sets of numbers.

'See how the fabric is inflated and stays in the air ... The hot air from the brazier lifts the canopy and keeps it afloat. If we attach a lightweight boat with its own central brazier, we can fly. We *will* fly.'

The Duke shook his head in astonishment. 'Can such a flimsy canopy carry the weight of men ... and their weapons?'

'With ease, My Lord Duke ... with consummate ease. Look at the flight of storks and swans ... great birds yet held aloft by the wind as if as light as a sparrow's feather. You will have the very air itself at your command.'

Guillaume was in buoyant spirits as he re-entered the familiar inner courtyard back at Caen. His journey to his secret testing ground had been a considerable success. As well as the astonishing flying vessel, adjustments to the steam-powered harpoon had worked well and there had been no more casualties to the new weapon – at least, not human ones. Many pigs and cattle had been slain as targets, their flesh readily devoured later in a celebratory feast. Guillaume hated waste.

Struggling to halt his tall stallion with reins slick from a persistent cold sleet that had hampered every mile of his journey home, Guillaume was disappointed not to see Hereward in the welcoming party. His good mood rapidly dissipating, he dismounted stiffly from the soaking leather saddle onto the slippery cobbles, a stab of cramp shooting up from his insteps into his legs from the long hours in the saddle.

His harsh gaze sought out any sign of his guest in the windows of the inner keep, but there were only the ladies of the court, including Matilda. He managed a smile and a wave to his wife and children before striding inside. Where in God's holy name was the Saxon?

Hereward was a stranger to prayer. Attendance at Mass was a duty and a time to daydream, his mind wandering free as the priest droned on in monosyllabic Latin, his lips automatically forming the responses. In fact he often enjoyed this captive time, when he could plan and think things through uninterrupted by day-to-day distractions.

Now though he prayed fervently and sincerely as he knelt beneath a gilded statue of the Virgin, beseeching her to speak to God on his behalf. He did not feel worthy of a direct approach to his Creator. He wanted to go home straight way, that day. Queen Matilda's revelations were shocking. His people needed to be warned about the threat from across the Channel, but he doubted the Duke would allow him to leave Normandy should the

Queen's indiscretion to him become known. Would Guillaume even allow him to live?

His mind became increasingly distressed. The need to flee was so strong. Could he slip from the Abbey while Guillaume was away? Forget his belongings at the castle, just walk out of the nearby side doors and ride away, even run from there on foot, not pausing until he found a ship to take him home? He reached for his purse, feeling guilty for resenting the generous amount he had just left for the poor on entering the Abbey, even wondering if he could retrieve it before any of the holy sisters noticed his largess. The Virgin would forgive him, wouldn't she? He was trying to save a whole country from destruction, not just his own life.

Hereward's heart hammered as he bowed low and kissed the Virgin's sculptured stone sandaled feet and stood up. He stared across at the poor box and the door nearby, so close, so easy. There was no-one around. Who beyond Heaven would know?

The main door flung open and a familiar heavy stride marched down the central aisle. Guillaume.

Hereward feigned a warm smile of surprise and allowed the Duke to embrace him, too tightly and for longer than seemed appropriate.

'I did not take you for a man of piety, my young friend,' laughed the Duke as he grabbed Hereward by the shoulder and strode with him out of the Abbey.

The Saxon did his best to echo Guillaume's heavy-handed banter. 'Everyone needs a little extra spiritual help in this life, my Lord Duke. Especially with a night of sinning to look forward to now you are home.'

Guillaume grinned with lascivious glee. 'A wise move indeed. The kitchens have taken on two new maidens from the country, creamy of breast and white of smile. Tender rustic blooms ripe to be plucked!'

15

Ireland

A ripple of excitement overcame the Lismore household at the announcement of important visitors, setting the servants into a frenzy of preparation. The warrior princess, Kellan, daughter of King Loman of Dal Cais, was seeking audience, bringing urgent news.

On the day of her arrival, Brandan joined the other warriors on the battlements for the first sight of Kellan's entourage approaching from the west. His eyes had grown shadowed with fatigue. He was wary of the next move by his unseen, unknown tormentor; one that might well be fatal. He was no coward; there was no enemy he would not fearlessly meet face to face in battle. This furtive, craven assault was shredding his nerves and stealing his rest. But he had spurned all offers of sleeping draughts and strong mead to help him slumber. He wanted to be fully alert to the next attack. A fitful, nightmare-ridden sleep came only when he was resting in Donal's arms. When alone, he stayed awake, pacing his chambers, seeking answers that did not come. Music was his only release from the tension, his heart soothed by the ancient songs of his people and the fairy songs from the loving heart of the harp.

Beyond the fortress's walls, mild, mercifully dry days continued, allowing travellers to cross the land without the curse of the earlier intense cold or driving rain and mud. It was not long before word reached Lismore of a worrying vision affecting many of those with the Sight throughout Eire. Despite the blessing of the unseasonal fine weather, a pall of dread fell across the land. The wise ones were besieged, answers sought but not forthcoming. All this passed Brandan by. He was too consumed with his own problems.

The afternoon's rare mildness brought a whirling minuet of six red kites above the midden and a less welcome haze of dancing midges. It was good to feel the light touch of the winter sun on his face, but Brandan had heard that morning that a local village crone had declared the unseasonal weather a bad omen. She had spoken of dreams of terrible bloodshed, a battleground with so many valiant Fianna slain, a catastrophic defeat of the Irish, and flying over the carnage a monstrous raven.

On such a fine, sunny afternoon, with the whirl of the kites above and the first sighting of Kellan's banners cresting the horizon in a flurry of red and gold, it would have been easy to dismiss these as the ravings of a demented old woman. Brandan stayed on the battlements as the Princess's party rode through the valley. As a mercenary, he was not part of this household's militia and did not wish to intrude on the formalities. He had never seen Kellan before, and watched, fascinated, as her party drew up at the front of Lismore's stronghold. Tall, slim, Kellan sat proudly straight in her saddle on a high stepping chestnut stallion. She led another well-bred horse carrying her armour. The skilfully-crafted breastplate, in bronze and copper, was inlaid with garnets that caught the sun with their inner fire.

Brandan watched as the King tactfully stood by while she dismounted in one lithe movement; a warrior princess needed no help from her tall horse, unlike the more timid ladies of Donal's court. He then greeted her warmly with a kiss on each cheek. The party gave their tired horses to the Lismore servants and walked on stiff, aching legs into the fortress, no doubt relieved to be at their destination after their long ride.

One paused and looked up directly at the watching warrior. An elderly man, *druidecht* by his garb. His piercing blue eyes, undimmed by age, stared up at Brandan, and Brandan saw his gnarled face blanch and his body shudder. The man grabbed a talisman from his belt, passing his hand in front of his body in an ancient and powerful symbol of protection. But against what? Certainly not against him; Brandan was nothing more than a hired sword and a bard. He spun around: maybe the old man had seen Brandan's invisible enemy? But there was nothing but empty battlements and the circling kites above. Brandan looked back down, but the druid was gone.

In the grand hall, Brandan's place at Donal's side had gone, as was expected. At the King's right hand sat a smiling Liadan, proudly showing off her trim post-partum figure in a pale blue linen gown and ermine stole. The left-hand throne was for the visiting princess, resplendent in a sweeping cape of tawny fox fur over her gold-embossed warrior garb.

Brandan found himself a spot well away from the main action; anything else would have been provocative and disrespectful. He ranked far below the nobles and warriors of the court. He was not concerned; he knew his place and had the King's love, which was worth far more than the fleeting trappings of status.

As he settled to listen to Kellan's druid talking of a terrifying premonition among the wise ones of the realm, a woman's voice distracted him, close by, whispering his name. He turned, seeking who was addressing him, but all around him remained silent, focused on the visiting holy man's words.

'Brandan of the golden harp … your days on this Earth are over …'

The venom in the unseen woman's voice seeped from every word. Such hatred, such malice, but why? Deeply unsettled, he pushed his way out of the crowded main hall, certain his phantom enemy would follow his every step.

'Run, cruel breaker of hearts, run … but you cannot escape your death …'

His mind raced, trying to recognise the woman's voice. Was it a past conquest taunting him from the other side of the Veil between life and death? No, there was nothing familiar, nor could he think of any woman he had slighted so badly as to warrant such a haunting from beyond the grave. He had promised nothing to the women he bedded. Made sure they always knew what he was, that their encounters would always be short-lived, brief affairs of the willing flesh, not the heart.

'Who are you?' Brandan felt ridiculous and vulnerable, facing up to thin air. 'Name yourself and your purpose with me.'

'I want your death, slow and in agony. Nothing less than to watch your beauty disappear as your corpse slowly rots. You can run, warrior bard, but you are nothing more than walking crow bait …'

The voice faded with a peal of humourless laughter more chilling than the spoken threat. Brandan's throat constricted with tension. Had it not been for the physical nature of this torment, he could have shaken off the voice with a show of bravado and contempt. What harm could a mere voice do to him, however malevolent? Much harm: his face still bore the mark of this ghost's ability to cause physical pain. Donal being preoccupied with his visitors, Brandan was alone. With nowhere else to go, he sought out his bedchamber.

The gallows noose he found hanging above his bed from an overhead beam was all too real.

It was still there when the King sought him out later, anxious at not seeing him in the grand hall. The warrior was slumped by the window in a posture of defeat. His head cradled in his hands. Without looking up, he murmured to Donal, 'I cannot fight this … A flesh and blood enemy, yes, but not the unseen.'

Donal hauled down the noose and, with a growl of disgust, threw it onto the blazing hearth, then walked across to the distraught Brandan and held him tightly.

'There must be someone you have enraged to cause so much hatred.'

'The thought has not left my mind. It drives away all sleep. Haunts every moment of my day.'

He looked up at the King. 'I am certain there is no-one. One reason women desire me is that I give them what they want with no complications of the heart. I have never pledged loyalty or love to any of them. Nor have I ever disappointed them, left them aching in dissatisfaction at pleasure denied.'

Stepping away, Donal paced the floor. He had a solution, albeit a temporary one, and one that would break his own heart. He explained about Princess Killan's visit and the visions rippling like a stream of poison through the minds of all visionaries in Ireland. Visions that also had infected their counterparts in Cornwall and Wales, possibly the distant Cumbrians.

'There is a call for representatives of all the Irish Kings and our religious leaders to join those of the Welsh Princes and King Cadoc of Cornwall and meet in Wales to discuss what this means to us all.

'The Princess has kindly agreed to speak for me and her father. You will accompany Kellan as part of her armed escort. We must pray to the Mother and Father that this evil curse cannot cross the Irish Sea.'

16

Normandy

Noxious plumes of marsh gas rose in the dank murkiness, obscuring the Duke's route through treacherous terrain.. A fetid stench of decay and stagnant water from the mire invaded his body. He had no choice but to breathe it in but he was convinced it seeped through the pores of his exposed skin. He felt contaminated by the evil, putrid air. Unclean. As did this desperate journey, heavily in disguise, deep into the vast Marais region, to seek one of the last remaining wise women in Normandy. There were many to be found in neighbouring pagan Brittany, but travel there was out of the question with a violent blood feud simmering between him and its King Blaez.

For all its unpleasantness, this was an area rich in life: some pleasing like the storks and herons appearing out of the mist and swooping overhead like small benign dragons; some far less pleasant like the midges that did their best to eat him alive. Rank meant nothing to these maddening denizens of the swamplands. Their attacks helped reinforce his confusion of thoughts. He should not be there, but with the madness consuming him, Guillaume needed to know if he was bewitched. What other answer could there be? He had ordered the Saxon to remain at Caen for the Christmas celebrations, and with no letter of recall to England, Hereward had been forced to agree. How much easier it would have been simply to let him go home.

Now, dressed as a poor merchant, alone and on foot, the Duke followed the instructions from local peasants and sought out Madame Cecilie, a wise crone of reputed great power, who was much respected by the superstitious locals. He found her home built on an island in the wetlands, approachable only by a narrow swing bridge on her side of the water. It was a tidy, cultivated haven from the mire. Neat rows of vegetables grew in the fertile soil, around which scratched well kept, plump chickens. Though the midday sun had tried and failed to break through the haze, a tallow lamp flickered through the gloom as if it were night. Someone was home.

'Hau,' he called. 'Hau there, I seek the wise council of Madame Cecilie.'

At first there was no answer. Guillaume, never a patient man, swore to himself, angry at his own folly for being there as well as the woman's tardiness in reply. Then a heavily-cloaked, tall figure left the humble dwelling.

'Such a commanding stance and manner for one so low in station.'

The Duke cursed at his poor attempt at deception, and in revealing she knew he was not a merchant but nobility, the woman had sealed her doom.

'I will only allow those who mean me no harm across the bridge,' Cecilie continued. 'A lie is not a good start in winning my favour.'

Guillaume did his best to soften his tone. 'Forgive my folly, Madame. But you must receive many high-born petitioners who need great discretion in seeking your wisdom. I am unarmed and quite alone.'

There was a long silence punctuated only by the chirrup of frogs and the call of birds, then the woman pushed the wood and rope bridge across the stretch of treacherous water. The bridge could barely cope with Guillaume's height and weight, swaying alarmingly with his every tentative step. Locals had warned him that the still water in the marshland hid quicksand; a man falling from the bridge could disappear forever within seconds.

As she threw back her hood to reveal her face, she wasn't what the Duke had expected. No filthy, rheumy-eyed hag but a still-handsome woman in her forties with strong, gaunt features and bright, intelligent green eyes that clearly brooked no nonsense from man or beast. Once blonde, her hair was now more silver than gold. Her garb was simple, clean and well cared for. She could have been a prosperous farmer's wife if not for the remote and hostile location of her calling. She beckoned Guillaume to enter her home, a conical building of stacked stone slabs, ancient in design and sturdy against the worst weather.

Inside there were no weird potions or shamanic symbols, not even bunches of healing herbs. Nothing that gave a clue to her profession. A wise move in a Christian realm. There were two robust chairs covered in clean sheepskins by a hearth over which a cauldron bubbled not with some foul concoction but with an aromatic rabbit broth.

Once he was seated, the woman ladled a bowl of the broth into a bowl and handed it to her visitor. Despite the circumstances, Guillaume found himself relaxing, perhaps helped by her no-nonsense attitude and the lack of occult accoutrements. To the outside world, she was just a widow living in the Marais du Bessin, giving charitable aid to a traveller lost in the marsh.

She sat in the other chair and did not speak, fixing him with eyes that saw more than the mortal world, understood far more than a man's words. To Guillaume, she was the most dangerous woman in the world at this moment, yet he willingly unburdened his soul to her, telling her all beyond his true identity. The relief was instant, far better than any time spent on his knees in Holy Confession. It was as if she could strip the guilt from his soul by the power of her intense gaze alone.

'Tell me, chevalier, does it give you pleasure when you enter a woman?'

Despite himself, the Duke smiled readily. 'A great deal of pleasure, Madame. So much so, I "enter" as many women as possible every day.'

Madame Cecilie did not return his smile; she knew that this was a man who frequently slaked his considerable desire by force, by rape, and insistence on his rights of *droit de seigneur*.

'And would doing the same to a young man give you the same pleasure?'

Guillaume understood he could give nothing but a totally honest answer to this forthright woman. He lowered his head and groaned.

'It would fill me with abhorrence and loathing. I could not do it. Even to save my life or that of my beloved sons.'

Madame Cecilie took both his hands in a firm grip and closed her eyes. The moment seemed to last an eternity but Guillaume did not pull away as he felt his soul gradually lighten.

'This feeling you have is not for the Saxon himself but for all he represents. His freedom from responsibility, that he was raised in the love of a caring family, his youth. Most importantly … his country.'

Now Guillaume was shocked: he had never mentioned the nationality of his obsession. He tried to pull away, but the woman tightened her grip with surprising strength.

'You had a childhood tormented by fear and humiliation. It has made you ruthless, driven to succeed. To thwart all who have harmed you. This lad has the warmth of love and genuine respect of his tribe as son of one of the oldest, most powerful noble Saxon families. Nobody questions his place in their society. Everything you could never have as a child and still strive in vain for now.'

The woman released his hands and sat back in her chair. Her eyes fixed on the crackling hearth, watching the blue smoke rise from the flames. She sighed. 'It is obvious by now that I know who you are and that you intend to kill me after this meeting. But I hope you will not. You will need my advice again in the future.'

She turned to look directly into her visitor's stern features. 'I will tell you what you need to know now. The truth under God. There is nothing wrong with you, Duke Guillaume. You are not bewitched, nor have you any sexual urges towards the Saxon.' She paused as a visible wave of relief passed through the man. 'It is England itself you crave.'

'It is already mine, Madame. Promised me by their pious fool of a King.'

'A promise written by a weakling in shifting sand. You will still have to take it by force, and you will succeed but only if your ambition remains just for the lands of the Saxons. Though you will command awesome and overwhelming power, make one move against the pagan lands and you will meet the Prince of Ravens at your peril.'

Guillaume tried to rise. 'What irrational nonsense is this? An empty threat from a pagan witch?'

The woman pulled aside the top of her gown to reveal a gem-encrusted silver crucifix, an ornate and beautiful object. 'I was once a lady from an old noble family, attendant to the Queen of France at her court. A devout Christian, then as now. But my God-given gift of prophesy was wrongly considered witchcraft. Once betrayed by someone I tried to help, my life was in danger. I fled alone to the sanctuary of the Marais.'

Shocked, Guillaume sat back into the chair, placing the broth bowl onto the floor. What bloody fools. To let superstition rob them of one so useful. He would never let that happen. In the same way, he cultivated the brilliant minds of the Arabs and Moors, unshackled by Europe's primitive beliefs.

'This place is not fit for a woman of noble blood. I can give you hospitality and sanctuary in my fortress at Falaise,' began the Duke, but she silenced him by one raised hand.

'And trigger harmful gossip? No, my place is here, where you can always find me.'

For the first time she smiled, wreathing her face with a sad beauty. 'That is if you haven't killed me.'

Guillaume rose to leave and returned the smile., 'But, my lady, you already know the answer to that …'

17

Wessex, England

Battle. The only sane solution to protecting his lands. Earl Harold sat relaxed on his horse, unafraid of the next few hours of combat. His thegns and warriors far outnumbered the painted rabble gathering in the Tamar valley below his army. With no answer from that pious milksop of a King, an impatient Harold had waited for more overt provocation. He had not had long to linger: a band of Cornish raiders had pillaged and torched a Wessex border village. He needed no permission to protect his boundary from the accursed Cornish. He'd received word that the thieving bastards had also colluded with his Danish enemies. They needed another bloody reminder of Saxon might.

A wide, meandering snake, slate grey beneath the sullen sky, the eastern bank of the Tamar was a natural barrier between the Godless Celts and the settled, prosperous lands of the western Saxons - but it was being breached with alarming regularity recently. Harold accepted the only solution was the King's Holy Crusade, to march into Cornwall with a force powerful enough to drive the unruly natives into the sea. What was harder to accept was the presence of any foreign troops on English soil. They didn't always leave. The morning air was still, the smell of the river rose with the warming air, a distinct blend of fetid silt, weeds and fresh water. Aedric, his second in command, rode over to halt his horse next to the Earl's.

'These Cornish rats must be eager for a brawl or just plain stupid.'

Shaking his head, Harold smiled, 'These hag worshippers are many things but never stupid. But they are unprepared and undisciplined. We will win the day with ease.'

There was no more time. The discordant howl of a Cornish battle horn rent the morning, an unnerving sound designed to sap the morale of their enemies. The Saxons dismounted from their spooked horses, handing the reins to waiting slaves, and prepared to silence the noisome droning once and for all. Harold looked out for the banners of King Cadoc but there was no sign of the white chough on a black background, just those of local chieftains. The Earl was disappointed. Cadoc's head would be a fine trophy to take to the King, and his death a crushing blow to the Cornish.

The enemy were in high spirits now, banging on their oval shields with their swords and hurling insults in their infernal language. The Tamar was at its most benign there, slow and shallow; the legendary turbulence and fury lay further down its course to the sea. The Cornish normally expected a stalemate on either side of its banks, a display of brandishing weapons and insults designed to consolidate the boundary between Wessex and their kingdom. The Saxons had the advantage of the higher ground and would not be foolish enough to move down from their defendable stand. Nor would the men of Kernow cross the Tamar in a suicidal charge against their enemy. A perfect scenario for a standoff.

But not today.

Ignoring the bloodcurdling war cries and raucous battle horns, the Earl made a subtle signal that triggered a series of messages passed from thegn to thegn in a coordinated movement. As the Saxon foot soldiers swept across the river in a massive fleet of coracles, many skilled archers, hidden in scrubland by the river bank, released volley after volley of arrows deep into the Cornish ranks. The site and manner of attack had been planned for weeks.

Using their descent of the hill to add impetus to their charge, the disciplined ranks of the Saxons crashed into the enemy like an iron fist, slashing and flailing with sword and axe, like men possessed.

Wrong-footed, the Cornish warriors were disorganised, some scrambling away from the death rain of arrows, some standing their ground in confused small groups easily overcome in the mêlée. With no-one strong enough to regroup the native warriors, the Saxon attack was swift and brutally decisive. Within two hours, Earl Harold stood on the rich Cornish soil, that was now drenched red with pagan blood. He knelt, head bowed in prayer, as Alban, a Wessex bishop, arrived to plant a large crucifix in the ruddy earth.

'This is now just one small area of Christian land, but I will not rest until every inch of these Isles is under God's holy rule.'

Words deliberately spoken aloud in front of the pious spy Alban. Words Harold knew would get back to the King. In Harold's ambitious heart, he meant Saxon rule, but wasn't that the same thing?

He called for a Cornish prisoner to be brought to him, one with a chance of surviving from his wounds. His warriors brought a youth of little more than 15 summers, dragging him by his long dark hair and throwing him at Harold's feet. Heavily tattooed, near naked but for a leather kilt and a wool plaid cloak, he was unafraid to die, his dark eyes full of defiant fire.

'Do you speak English, heathen?'

'Enough to send the curse of *Bucca Dhu* to you and all bastard yellow-haired thieves.'

A thegn raised his hand to strike the Cornish youth across the face, but Harold growled his dissent. 'We are not the savages, Godfric. Let him be.'

Removing a gold cross from his neck, Harold handed it over to the youth.

'Take this to King Cadoc. It is my guarantee no more Cornish blood will be spilled if your people convert to the one true faith.'

The young Cornish warrior refused to touch the crucifix, letting it fall onto the ground and spitting on it. 'The people of Kernow will never live under your yoke or bow to the image of a dead man. Our gods and goddesses are alive and all around us.'

Harold sighed as he picked up and cleaned the cross. 'Kill him and find me another more cooperative. There must be one willing to live to see another dawn.'

18

Wales

His mood as bleak at the weather, Brandan rode at the back of the Princess's escort. Shivering as driving sleet whipped his face, he struggled to keep control of his fractious mare with reins and saddle slippery and his hands frozen within sodden gauntlets. As he had feared, Lia had not travelled well on a rough crossing of the Irish Sea to Wales, but the thought of leaving her behind at Lismore with that malevolent spirit had been intolerable. With him out of reach, the fiend could well take out her malice on his innocent mare. That was unbearable. As was leaving Donal. There. He had it. For the first time in his life he had allowed the cruel curse of love to enter his heart.

This was a love story that could have no happy ending. How could it?

The journey had been hard from the moment they set foot on Welsh soil at Pwlheli. Used to the worst the great ocean could hurl at Ireland, Princess Kellan's entourage seemed doomed also to suffer the worst weather possible in Wales. Howling winds shrieked like Ban Sidhe, buffeting the horses, who struggled to keep their balance along muddy and rock-strewn narrow tracks. Icy rain turned to hail then sheets of driving sleet, sapping energy and morale. The dropping temperature and brooding sky foretold of heavy snow to come before the night was over.

Brandan's mood was at an all time low. He had obeyed the King without question; it had made sense to leave Lismore after Donal's decision was backed up by the wise ones he had summoned to give advice. The warrior accepted his place as a lowly sword for hire. He didn't need the princess to rub salt in the wounds as they rode out of Lismore's fortifications. Once out of sight of the stronghold lookouts, she had tugged her horse to an abrupt halt and ridden to Brandan's side, fixing him with an imperious glare, her voice cutting and dismissive.

'Listen to me well, Fianna … You may warm King Donal's bed at night, but that gives you no privileges on my mission. You can forget your harp and honeyed words too. None of that nonsense will work on me.'

So, he and Donal were common knowledge. Brandan was beyond caring. He rode in silence at the back of the party, slept where he could, usually with the horses, as the lords and warriors took shelter in warmth and comfort. He ignored the occasional unkind ribald jibe aimed at him and the strange, hostile glares from the druid. All this he could endure, for to be free of the spectral enemy was a blessing that was giving him time to work out who she was and how to fight her.

Exhausted, hungry and cold, Brandan viewed the distant lights from Rhuddlan piercing the gloom as a gift from the gods. In a few hours, he would have done his duty and helped deliver Kellan safely to the meeting. He could now look forward to collapsing in a pile of straw in the stables and sleeping until it was time for her to return to Ireland. He risked taking one hand off the reins, caressed the mare's cold, sodden neck. 'Not long now my darlin'. We'll soon be away from this dour land, back to the sweet meadows of Erin.'

Lia rewarded his affection by laying back her ears, snorting and hunching her back, attempting a bad-tempered buck. Good horseman that he was, Brandan was too tired and cold to correct her bad manners and sat out the explosion of equine temper in silence. How could he blame her? This was a long, horrible journey in the worst weather possible, and she was right to complain.

Morning dawned with the glare of unseen fresh snow brightening the stone walls of Seren's chamber. With no fire lit, Seren slipped quickly from the warmth of her bed and dressed. As she pulled back the wooden shutters across the window, she felt the outside air tingling cold on her face. A unique smell told her the world had been transformed overnight: the land slumbered beneath Ceridwen's blanket of purest white. Fat, lazy flakes spiralled slowly from a granite sky; she reached out and caught one on her hand, marvelling in its fragility before it dissolved to cold nothing.

As if the morning wasn't magical enough, the lilting sound of a harp rose from the courtyard as if the notes were dancing with the snowflakes. It was the most beautiful, sad music she had ever heard. It was mesmerising, enough to impel her to leave the safety of her room and seek out the harpist.

Seren walked slowly. The wet snow was thick and icy; it could hide things her guide-stick could miss, and she did not relish the prospect of a heavy fall in an unfamiliar courtyard. When she reached the location of the music, she picked up the aroma of the player ... A man wearing dank and muddy woollen garb, a cloak of sodden fur. A traveller, and one with an aura of dejection and misery.

On noticing he had an audience, the musician stopped playing.

'Please, I would love to hear more.'

Silence. Had she upset the man? Then realisation dawned. Perhaps he was one of the visitors from Ireland and would not understand her language? She was such an idiot. Seren shrugged with an apologetic smile and began to move away.

'I am so sorry, my lady, that was ill mannered of me.' The man spoke her language with a pronounced Irish accent that she found attractive. 'Of course I will play more for you, but something more suitable than that doleful lament.'

He ran his fingers down the harp with a flourish and began a joyous reel that made Seren want to whirl and dance across the snowy courtyard. A wild and dangerous impulse that warned her there was more than a touch of magic in this Irish man's music. She was glad when he stopped playing.

'My name is Brandan, also known by the nickname Brandan of the Golden Harp. I am of Na Fianna and, as you have probably guessed by now, also a bard.'

Ah, Seren thought, so he was one of Ireland's caste of wandering warriors; a man of courage, but maybe as a sword for hire he would have no regret for his victims in battle. His lack of rank or title would explain why the haughty Irish Princess did not include him in her party; they enjoyed Llewellyn's lavish hospitality while Brandan remained sleeping in the stables – the pungent aroma of horse dung and straw told her much about his situation. Perhaps he was even forced to charm the kitchen maids for scraps of food. She would do her best to see he was given hot food that morning and a warmer place to slumber that night; a corner of the Great Hall like the visiting Welsh warriors of the Teulu.

'I am Seren, daughter of Lord Cynan ap Yorath and now ward of Prince Gwion.'

She could sense that he had bowed to her, low and courtly.

'In case no-one has told you already this morning,' he said, 'you are very beautiful. As lovely as the stars you were named after. No, that is wrong … you are more lovely than those cold, distant diamonds.'

She was right, he was indeed a charmer, but it would take more than this Irishman's honeyed tongue to turn her head. The village of the witches did not produce girls with empty heads easily swayed by flattery. So why did her wretched cheeks flush at his words? Her lips curved into a shy smile - the traitors!

Aware she was blind, Brandan asked her permission to take her hands and place them on his face. Happy to agree, for this mixture of poet and warrior fascinated her, Seren gently traced the chiselled contours. She discovered through her finely attuned fingertips that he was young, handsome – exceptionally so, with a strong, lean face, high cheekbones, a noble brow and wide smile. Without touching him, her right hand moved down to pause above his heart, wanting to delve behind the good-looking façade and into his soul.

A shock-wave coursed through her and she drew back with a shiver of unease. Even without touching him, Seren could sense darkness there beyond that gained from a life spent with much blood on his hands. It was as if he was more than an Irish warrior, more than human. Whatever that other thing was, it was hidden from all, perhaps even from himself. She did not want to know more, not now. The black shadow within him was cold, unworldly, unlike the comforting velvet darkness of her life. Seren stepped back, greatly alarmed at the encounter.

'Have I done something wrong?' Brandan questioned, puzzled by her now pale face, wide eyes and the way she shrank away from him in fear.

'No, nothing …' she muttered, embarrassed by her startled reaction in front of the warrior. 'I was carried away by your music and it made me forget the cold. Now I am freezing.'

Seren turned away in haste, pushing her stick in front of her. 'I must get back. Thank you for playing for me. It was beautiful.'

The warrior watched as she hurried away through the swirling snow. There was something about her dignified bearing as she crossed the courtyard that made him decide not to help her. The Welsh girl was clearly proud of her independence. But she had lied about the cold. Blind as she was, Seren had become afraid of him in such a short time, and for the life of him Brandan could not understand why.

19

Unseen by Seren, the snow stopped, the clouds faded away in deference to a low sun with no warmth. Her turbulent thoughts of the mysterious Irishman were thankfully pushed aside by an unexpected visit from Adwen, his calm demeanour a welcome relief. They sat together by the Great Hall's wide hearth and shared goblets of cider warmed by fire irons. Winter smoke mingled with the taste of the past summer's apples in their mouths. The Cornish druid took one of her hands in his. Gave it a gentle squeeze.

'My heart is heavy this morning for I wish you could see the beauty of the landscape.'

Seren smiled. 'You will have to describe it to me. I can see in my visions and trance dreams. My mind will make pictures of your words.'

'The sky is an unbroken ceiling of a deep, bright blue. The sun has covered the virgin white of the new snow with more diamonds than there are stars in the night sky.'

Sighing with pleasure as the images formed, Seren laughed, 'You have the wrong calling, Adwen of Kernow, you should be a poet not a priest.'

'Are they not the same thing in your country?'

Seren thought of some of the grumpy elderly druids that visited her village seeking rest and free hospitality; men more concerned with the comforts on offer and the herbal infusions to ease the aches and pains of old age. 'Not always.'

'Are you up to a short walk from the castle, Seren? We must prepare for the great meeting today.'

Alarmed, Seren dropped the goblet. Warm wine spilled down her gown like blood. She hardly knew the druid, and the thought of facing down Lady Vanora again alarmed her. Adwen called for an attendant to help the girl, taking her hand again to calm her down.

'I am no fool, Seren. News passes freely between the druids of Cymru and Kernow. The Lady Vanora has held great influence and authority in this land for many years. She will not take kindly to a young novice witch attracting so much attention from the good and the great here.'

He stood up as the servants cleared up the spilt wine and did their best to dry Seren's gown. He waited until they had finished and had scurried away before continuing, 'I am furious at my tardiness. I could not reach Nercwys in time to escort you to the stronghold myself.'

The druid's talk alarmed Seren. The aura of that creature's malice tainted the air of Rhuddlan. She was powerful, her fury was amplified by jealousy and fear. If Vanora could send that serpent, she could have ways of listening to their conversation. Adwen could see her anxiety rising and guessed the cause. When trapped in a viper's nest, it did no good to poke the snake with a stick.

'Seren, your fear is understandable. The woman is afraid of your latent abilities, powers you have no idea you possess. I must tell you something that may calm you. She is absolutely terrified of me.

'Come with me, little star,' he continued. 'There is a place nearby where we can speak in peace and tranquillity to the gods that rule our destinies. There is nothing she can conjure there that can harm us.'

His words had not convinced her. Adwen knew that the hag must have already threatened her and that she was frightened. Adwen had one way of showing her the truth. 'Place your hand over my heart, Seren of Nercwys. Only then will you truly know me.'

For the second time that morning, she prepared to discover what dwelled behind a man's voice and pleasant manner, but this time there was no troubling turbulence. Seren found someone of great honour, valour and compassion. There was nothing sinister, hidden or duplicitous. She would be safe with this man.

As warmly wrapped against the cold as she could be, and discreetly attended by three servant girls and two of Gwion's warriors sent with the Prince's full blessing, Seren walked beyond the fortress gates on the arm of the Cornish druid. Gwion remained at court, using the excuse of preparation for the hours of debate to come. In truth he was keeping an eye out for any attempt to follow the pair on their short sacred pilgrimage. Seren had not spoken openly about the incident in the woods, but Gwion was no fool. The girl had an enemy at Rhuddlan. One who could summon spectral serpents.

Seren breathed in the sharp air, as fresh and pure as the world's first morning, deeply exhaling to force out the fug of smoke and the odour of too many humans and hounds cooped up in the fortress. The cold pinched her face, but Seren did not mind, she was enjoying being outside too much, and if she was truly honest with herself, she liked being with Adwen. Not exactly alone with the druid, but as nearly as she could be in this place where so many eyes watched her every move. Not all human.

When she had placed her hand over the druid's heart she had discovered courage and honesty. Someone dedicated to his faith and his people. A genuinely good man. Seren felt safe with him in a way no other person could. She knew he carried a sword, she could hear the rasp of metal against his clothing, but it was his inner power that would protect her. Adwen had so much energy and wisdom drawn from study of thousands of years of druidic knowledge, he made the magic wielded by Vanora seem like that of an infant.

It did not take long to reach their destination, a standing stone set on a hill in an area kept clear of bushes and obscuring undergrowth. The attendants remained at the foot of the slight incline while Adwen's guiding hand helped Seren to climb. The thick snow made the short ascent more arduous, but it was worth each crunching trudge through the crystalline blanket. Even from afar, Seren could hear the ancient stone singing to her, a song of welcome from her ancestors of the past thousands of years. With her left hand on the stone, her right in Adwen's, Seren allowed her mind its freedom.

At first there was a time of greeting. Her vision returned and the snow was replaced by a sun-drenched summer meadow fragrant with a tapestry of bright coloured blooms, dancing with butterflies. Birds sang and soared across a cloudless blue sky. It was so beautiful, a privileged glimpse into the Summerlands, the world beyond mortal life. One by one, her family from all the past ages arrived to greet her. She recognised only her parents, tears of love pouring unchecked down her cheeks as she was with them once more.

'Do not be in a hurry to join us, Seren,' her mother Briallan murmured, kissing her forehead. 'There is much work for you to be done in the mortal vale.'

Before she could reply, Seren was in a new place, one of a featureless sparkling silver mist. The unsettling feeling of floating provoked a sense of rising panic, but an unseen strong hand gripped hers – Adwen's – and she knew she was safe.

This was a portal to the world of powerful spirits, the deities of their peoples. The gods might not come in person but their message would, through an elemental form. Seren wondered who would visit them, what words they would bring. The Divine Mother, Modron? Or a warlike deity in this time of coming strife: Agrona, Goddess of slaughter and battle; or Bran, the Raven God of prophesy and war? A curious sensation began to build within her body, an agitation spreading through her nerves and veins that was both thrilling and unnerving, one that grew in intensity to become almost unbearable. Seren wanted to cry out and flee, but the druid's hand held her firm, giving her comfort from his strength.

A shimmering before her eyes transformed to a faint outline of a beautiful woman sparkling as if made of diamonds. The woman addressed them, and her voice was not human but as the sound of stars singing across the heavens.

'Both your peoples know me as Aerfen, one who watches over the fates of men.'

Seren tried to bow, but the mist held her upright, unable to move. At least she had tried to show respect, as the Goddess continued.

'All that will be has not been carved in the world's stones, only what has passed before. The outcome of the future is in the hands of mortals. We can guide you but not alter the fate of your own choices.

'This day will be a momentous one, one in which the future of your race is decided. The Dark Mother has sent many visions of what may be. It is up to you to change the outcome to what *should* be ...'

Cold. Seren shivered as another reality returned without warning. Snow froze her feet through her sheepskin boots, one hand was like ice held against the stone, the other warm within Adwen's strong grip. She broke all contact with a gasp, thrilled by the changes within her. The Goddess had done more than speak to her, she had filled her with strength and courage. Vanora no longer felt like a threat, but a sad, aging woman desperate to hold on to her youth and position. Seren pitied her.

Druid and witch walked back down together, elated by the blessing of Aerfen, pushing aside for now the great responsibility they faced. The sense of renewed purpose and energy was too exhilarating.

'Right, little star, let us give that snake in the grass a taste of what she is up against if she dares to cross you again!'

Seren laughed. 'Thank you, my friend, but I am certain I can handle that fangless old adder on my own now.'

20

'On behalf of my noble warriors and druidecht, I strongly object to the presence of King Donal's whore at this meeting. What reason is there to include a mere Na Fianna bard at this meeting?'

Certain that Princess Killan's fury distorted the stern beauty of her features, Seren sensed that the woman's anger was fuelled by fear. What had that cunning old weasel druid said to her about Brandan? Had he too picked up that curious inner wall of darkness deep within the otherwise affable and charming Irishman? A stunned silence stilled the meeting at Killan's unexpected outburst. So much anger directed at a warrior bard, low in rank but still a respected visitor from Ireland. What could possibly have caused her to do this? The breach of good manners before their host caused a ripple of anger through the crowded audience hall, and Seren could feel the tension rising to a dangerous level.

Brandan stood up and bowed to the assembly. 'The King of Lismore sent me here to help protect the Princess on her journey to attend the meeting, but if my presence offends, I am perfectly content to leave. I can smell a fine venison broth simmering in the kitchens. And I know there will be lovely Welsh lasses to serve it to me in return for a merry tune on my harp.'

His self-deprecating humour and mock humility were disarming; a practised manner, thought Seren, and one that must have served him well in the past. Relieved murmurs rippled through the crowded hall, followed by silence as King Llewellyn rose to give judgement.

'I see no reason for this warrior to attend. I bow to Princess Killan's wisdom in raising her druid's objection. This meeting concerns a spiritual matter. Sadly I believe there will be time for warriors later.'

Seren could hear an undertone of embarrassment and apology in the King's voice. Deference to the wishes of a visiting princess overrode any loss of face to an untitled warrior.

'Brandan,' he continued, 'I release you to the more congenial company and hospitality of the kitchens for now. I beg that you will grace us later with your legendary skills on the harp.'

'It would be my greatest honour and pleasure, Your Grace.'

Brandan left a puzzled assembly, and some intuitive part of Seren's mind was relieved he was no longer in the hall, yet she did not know why.

Brandan had no intention of lurking like a whipped cur in the fortress kitchens. The only person whose company at Rhuddlan he might have enjoyed was the sylph-like Welsh girl Seren ... now the centre of attention at the assembly. He wandered down to the stables and tacked up Lia. His mare was stiff from the sea crossing and journey, a gentle walk around the fortress would do her good.

Leaving the fortress with a cheery wave to the curious sentries, he kept the reins loose, encouraging the mare to lower her head and amble, so she would know this was just a leg-stretching walk rather than the start of another arduous trek. To Brandan's relief, the grey horse did not jog or fidget but strolled along with her ears pricked but her body relaxed. He was too troubled to have to control a fractious horse today.

As he rode along a wide, well used track, following churned-up hoof and wheel prints in the deep snow, a shadow flitted across the sun. With no clouds in the sky, the sudden movement made him lift his head to see a huge raven fly above him. A common enough bird, though this one was unusually large. Maybe they grew that big in Wales? Unconcerned, Brandan rode on. The raven had other ideas. It flew above him, following his route, occasionally alighting on a tree stump or branch, its head to one side as it watched him with its glassy black eyes.

There was something unnerving about this bird. Already ill at ease after the haunting at Lismore, Brandan hoped this was not the start of another incident. He tried startling the thing, urging it to fly away with a loud shout and hand claps, but its only reaction was to give a disdainful caw and flourish of its wings. Brandan had a hunting bow strapped to the saddle but did not want to harm a raven. It was sacred to Morrigu, whose goodwill he so needed in battle.

'What do you want with me?' Brandan called. 'Have you a message from the Goddess?'

If the bird had anything to pass on, it was interrupted by the sound of approaching horses galloping under duress. Their stumbling gait and wheezing, laboured breath sent the raven spiralling high to disappear into the blue sky. A group of warriors tumbled toward Brandan, their mounts on the verge of collapse. He blocked their path with his horse and raised his arm in greeting. His interruption of their mission was not well received, but their animals were too fatigued to push past Lia without protest.

'In the blessed name of Rhiannon, let these brave beasts rest,' declared Brandan, 'or you will kill them long before reaching your destination.'

'Out of our way, Irish fool. We have urgent business at Rhuddlan,' shouted their leader, brandishing his sword with the courage only a man with so many armed supporters could command.

'I am a guest of the King and have a fresh, swift horse. Let me carry the message on to the fortress.'

'How can we trust a foreigner? One riding away from our destination.'

Brandan shrugged. 'You can't. But carry on and your message will be delayed as, one by one, your horses collapse beneath you.'

This seemed to sew dissent among the riders, weakening the threat to Brandan from the angry swordsman. There was a curt exchange of Cornish between them and a consensus reached. Now halted, their horses had no energy left to carry on; they had been running on instinct and courage for some miles. With their sides heaving, their heads dropped low, nostrils flaring as they fought to breathe with painful lungs.

Bowing to the inevitable, the swordsman crossed to Brandan's side and handed him a scroll. 'We were sent by our King to tell the Welsh that the yellow-haired bastards have crossed the Tamar. Earl Harold has breached our borders with the Wessex army and waits for their King to raise and send the Saxon fyrd to conquer Kernow.'

Without wasting another word, Brandan raised a hand in salute to the riders, then turned his mare back toward the fortress and spurred her on to a gallop. Delighted to be heading back toward shelter and food, Lia gave a little squeal of pleasure and took off at full speed.

The assembly had reached a showdown. All debate among the nobility had finished, and all that was left was to decide who to believe and what to do with the information. To Seren's relief, she was no longer the centre of attention. An attendant led her away from her position stood before Llewellyn's throne, and she sat again by Prince Gwion, grateful for his hug of support. Her legs felt weak, her throat dry and her spirits low as the enormity of what they all faced hit again.

In her place in the centre of the hall were two opposing mystics – Lady Vanora and the druid Adwen. The hostility between them crackled like the air before a lightning strike, an anticipatory silence adding to the tension throughout the Great Hall. Vanora stepped forward, using her authority at the fortress as advantage over a visiting foreigner. Her voice dripped with heavy sarcasm.

'We have heard some "interesting" interpretations of dreams, but is this enough to act on? I think not. There has been not one instance of solid proof that we face some future destruction.'

She walked slowly past the ranks of Welsh nobility, making full use of her dramatic appearance, her floor-sweeping robes of multi-hued green and yellow silks decorated by arcane symbols embroidered in gold thread. Her long, green-painted wooden staff was topped with intertwined gold snakes with polished green marble eyes.

'Would you waste your precious resources of men and weapons preparing for a child's bad dream? If this was truly a message from the gods, I, Lady Vanora of the Rumenea, would have received it first.'

She turned to glare at Seren and Adwen.

'There was no message.'

Wisely waiting for the resultant furore to die down, Adwen stepped forward, no less a commanding figure. His presence was naturally charismatic, aided by his height, his waist-length black hair with a single dramatic streak of silver and his simple garb of dove-grey robes. He held an oak staff unadorned with any carving or gems.

'Your sheltered tenure at this fine stronghold has deafened you to the truth. This message reached many more seers throughout our realms. I do not know why you did not receive it. This has clearly distressed you. That is understandable. But for the sake of all our peoples, we must move past personal pride.'

Adwen paused as his words fell on hostile ears. Seren was no longer alone in having a dangerous enemy.

'You have a difficult choice,' he told the assembled throng. 'To believe a vision shared by many trusted mystics from across three nations. Or the word of the only one who has not received it.'

Vanora's amber eyes flashed a spear of pure hatred toward the druid's heart, but he turned it into nothing with a slight wave of his right hand, sending back a broad smile in return.

'What we should be concentrating on,' Adwen continued 'is how to prevent this catastrophe. This could be perilous. The wrong choice could be the very trigger of events that leads to this terrible outcome.'

Adwen waited until the magnitude of his words sank in. King Llewellyn stood up from his throne and walked over to the two mystics, his brow furrowed in thought. 'I believe this vision is real and given to us by the Dark Mother as a warning,' he said.

Ignoring his witch's fury, the King halted in the centre of his great hall and addressed the packed assembly.

'Unless we get another message, we must treat every situation with caution and great consideration before reacting. But most of all, for once in our long history, we must think as one people.'

Llewellyn paused, knowing what he would say next would be contentious. 'We must push aside the futile centuries-old blood feuds, the origins of which are often lost in time. The squabbles over land boundaries or water. Quarrels triggered by lust or love. Forget whether we are of Eire, Kernow or Cymru. We are all children of the God and Goddess.

'If we are threatened, we must fight as one.'

The loud rumbles of open discontent began at once, as Llewellyn had expected. To seek any unity amongst such belligerent peoples was well-nigh impossible. His voice rang out again across the assembly.

'This constant division is what has kept the Saxons sleeping in peace and contentment every night. They laugh at us, call us barbarians ready to slaughter each other over a stolen cow.'

'So, under whose banner would we march?' called a hostile voice from the crowd.

'Must we all now bow our heads to the King of Wales?' yelled another.

The quarrelsome ways of the Celtic tribes had resurfaced, and any dream of unity was fading.

Seren leapt to her feet and, in a reckless move, pushed her way to the floor. Breaking all protocol, she called out to the assembly:

'We will march under the same banner … not one of Kings, Queens and Princes, but of the Great Mother whom we all revere.'

A shock of cold air rushed through the hall, causing overhead pennants to stir and candle flames to flicker or blow out. One woman shrieked, no doubt expecting the arrival of something supernatural. Seren recognised the dark aura of the man striding through the assembly. Perhaps the startled woman was right. It was the warrior, Brandan. At that moment, a small, unworthy part of her hated him for interrupting the assembly at such a crucial moment.

'We may have urgent use of that new banner,' Brandan announced to the assembly, then knelt before the King and handed him the message scroll from Cadoc's riders.

Seren's blood turned to ice water in her veins as she felt Llewellyn's emotions turn from surprise to anger as he read the message, then cast aside the scroll with a snarl of contempt.

It had started.

21

Normandy

Hereward avoided his reflection at every opportunity, shunning sight of his face in the water of the morning or in the polished gleam of pewter goblets or sword blades. He knew he wouldn't like the person staring back. The strain of keeping a relaxed manner and normal behaviour around Guillaume was showing on him. He had lost weight, dark shadows had spread beneath his eyes. Fear and now guilt lay heavily on his soul. Whatever kindness the Blessed Virgin may have wished upon him was gone, driven away by the screams and pain of violated young women.

Meanwhile his mind sought every possible way of escaping what now was a prison. Warm, comfortable, but a prison all the same, one with invisible but very real chains.

The Duke had changed toward him since the last mysterious foray. For once he hadn't returned with his garb stinking of smoke, charcoal and metal. His banter had become more raucous and demeaning toward Hereward, the roistering more aggressively sexual. Playful bouts of swordplay were increasingly dangerous, with bruising and bloodshed now a common practice. It was as if Guillaume was trying to prove he was the better man, that Normans were superior to Saxons in all ways, out-drinking, out-whoring and out-battling. Even proving Normans were more pious, with Hereward made to endure several interminable Masses every Sunday, hours of kneeling on cold stone floors alongside Guillaume and his family.

It was the misuse of the women that affected Hereward the most, yet he was unable to offend his host for fear of his own life. Though sickened to his soul, the Saxon took part in Guillaume's favourite sport of ravishing young virgins. Frightened country girls wrenched straight from their families were brought to court by the Duke's minions and left in a private chamber for Guillaume to rape and debauch at his leisure. Once it had been a lone blood sport, now he expected Hereward to take part. The Duke would sit by the bed, watching intently as the Saxon took the first girl. Hereward did his best to be gentle with his victim, finishing as quickly as he could as he tried not to look at the terror and tears in her eyes, shutting his ears to her pleading for mercy for fear of his manhood failing through pity and guilt.

Laughing and mocking Hereward's lack of manliness, Guillaume would throw the other girl onto the bed and enter her in an assault of brutal thrusts. He was indefatigable, pounding away for what must have been an eternity at the unfortunate pinned helpless beneath his weight.

What was going on? Why was the Duke behaving this way toward him? What had Matilda told Guillaume about her conversation with him?

It was with these nerve-wracking thoughts that Hereward reluctantly agreed to accompany the Duke on a journey to the border lands with neighbouring pagan Brittany - though there was in any case no question of refusing what had been a command laden with threat dressed up as a request.

The Saxon soon realised this was far from a good idea, but with the Duke's worrying attitude toward him, he really had no choice but to comply. As he joined the Duke at the stable yard, it was apparent this was not to be a diplomatic mission. Hereward noted with alarm the large number of barons arriving with their heavily-armed troops to rally just beyond the castle. This was to be a war party.

Hereward wanted no part of this, and he was barely able to disguise his fury as he mounted an over-fresh horse, using the time spent controlling its skittering on the cobble stones to get his feelings under wraps. England had no current quarrel with the Bretons, he was a guest at Caen … how dare Guillaume drag him into a war? Unless the Duke did not want him to survive and return to England.

Two days riding toward the Breton border brought Hereward little peace. Throughout the journey, the Duke had been taciturn and sullen, ignoring his guest. Hereward watched a leisurely heron fly overhead and envied the big bird its freedom. The bird could turn now and fly across the Channel, leave this land forever if it wanted. He had never thought he would envy a heron.

He shifted in the saddle to ease stiffness in his lower back, still suffering the after-effects of the shameful night of debauchery laid on by the duke to celebrate their departure. Would the Blessed Virgin ever forgive him? Hereward doubted it. Now there would be more to atone for: the spilling of innocent blood. Hereward eavesdropped on the banter among the Norman soldiers riding close by; this was no skirmish against another army. This was to be a rout, a punishment for some petty slight against some Norman traders. Guillaume was merciless to his enemies, killing women and children with no remorse. Hereward's prayer that the engagement would be against only warriors had fallen on deaf ears in Heaven.

Hereward was now convinced the Duke's insistence that he accompanied him on an attack on the neighbouring pagan land was bad news for his survival prospects. Anything could happen in the heat of battle; a sword thrust to the heart or stomach was fatal, whether from friend or foe. Head down and uneasy, the Saxon rode in silence as they trekked across a flat, windswept landscape of salt marshes and many stone circles. The Norman raiding party followed a blustery route along a rugged coastline with trees contorted by the near constant Atlantic winds to fantastical shapes. Indeed it was difficult for the men to ride without crouching low, close to their horses' necks, the animals themselves buffeted and irritated by the wind and becoming difficult to control.

Tension deepened as they reached the far edge of an area of cultivated fields, created by hard toil from the harsh marshland and protected from the salt-laden winds by high stone walls. Guillaume called for his troops to pause and rest but not make camp, waiting for the cowardly cover of night to attack. There was no sign of any local opposition, of a waiting Breton army. Hereward's trepidation grew, as did his fear for his own survival, but he played the game well, returning Guillaume's mocking banter with a show of relaxed good humour while dreading what the next hours would bring.

He did not have long to find out as he was surrounded by a vision of hell. Sheer bloody hell. Hereward let tears of shame mingle with blood and smoke grime on his face, creating a mask as horrific as his soul as he rode through smouldering ruins. There was no honour in this night, nothing but the grisly aftermath of a bloody slaughter.

Hereward should have feared the worst as they arrived at the outskirts of a small town. Barely guarded, surrounded by cultivated fields and grazing livestock, the settlement was no threat to anyone, let alone the most powerful warlord in France. No emissaries were sent ahead to ask for terms. Guillaume's troops simply ran riot, looting, setting fire to every building without warning to those trapped within, slaughtering the old folk, the men, the livestock. Raping the women and capturing the young girls to use later in celebration of their great victory. Hereward kept well clear of the Duke, using the confusion and smoke as allies.

Why had Guillaume dragged an outsider into this act of barbarity? There could be only one answer: to demonstrate the ruthless might of the Normans, what they had done to this town a mere foretaste of what they would do in England if the Duke's claim on the throne was disputed. So many innocent lives lost to prove a point, bile rose unchecked in Hereward's throat. He wanted to dismount and vomit but could not risk making himself vulnerable.

Everyone was now a potential enemy, the few Breton townsfolk able to fight back, the Normans … Hereward could not take anymore. He leapt off his horse, smeared as much blood from a minor knife wound as he could on its neck and saddle and with a wallop on its rump sent it back to join its stable mates still circling the stricken town, their riders drunk with bloodlust and victory. Let them assume he had been killed in the conflict. By the time they realised they couldn't find his body, Hereward would have run as far into Brittany as he could, heading for the nearest port. And home.

At least, that was the panic-driven and reckless plan. Once the horse bolted away, he ran blindly, legs pumping, heart pounding, vaguely aware he was heading away from the route back to Normandy. At first he was not alone. He was aware of crashing branches, frightened sobs, women calling for their children as the Breton survivors fled. With a yelp of surprise he fell over a body … a young lad, too young … who had succumbed to his wounds. Scrambling to his feet, Hereward ran on, driven on by the horror of capture. Guillaume's vengeance at his desertion would be terrible, cruel and prolonged.

He lost track of time, running and resting, keeping to the marsh, grateful for the cover of the high Marais grass and undulating dunes. Just before dawn, he tripped into a shallow stream of freshwater that ran through the edge of the marsh toward the sea. Hereward drank deeply, the cold liquid now more precious to him than the finest French wine. With visions of the slaughter still so vivid, he swore to the Holy Mother that he would never drink wine again, accepting the freezing water as part of the penance he would do for the rest of his life. He stripped off his clothing and bathed in the river, watching the grime and blood wash away from him and head down to the sea. Would that the sins he had committed trying to stay in Guillaume's favour for his own survival, wash from his soul so easily.

22

Seren stood on a grassy bank outside Rhuddlan supported by three handmaidens given to her by the King during her stay at the castle. Sun warmed her face but she wished it was raining, better to hide the tears she struggled not to shed. Below her, warriors and their supporters were gathering, ready to ride to Cornwall. She could hear the whinnies and squeals of excited horses as they jostled, eager to be moving, the banter of the fighters taking their leave. It was a day of departures, and the beginning of something they had all hoped to avoid.

The young women at her side were sniffling into their kerchiefs. Llewelyn had donated some of his own Teulu to the Cornish cause, no doubt favourites among the household females in the gathering below. Seren had no right to weep; these warriors were someone's loved ones, their brothers, husbands, sons, and not known to her. What was she to Adwen that she should mourn his departure to battle? Her own journey would start later that morning, returning first to her home with Prince Gwion, then back to the village with her sister witches and kindly mentor Rhan. It was what she wanted yet here she was, a total idiot, snivelling like the women beside her. At least they could see their men depart, Adwen was somewhere in the noisy, milling throng; but she being without sight, he was already lost to her.

A now familiar scent of venom and the swishing sound of heavily embroidered linen announced an unwelcome arrival on the hillside. Vanora, accompanied by her many servants and heavily armed guards. Safety in numbers or an open threat? Seren steeled herself to stay calm. There was nothing the older witch could do to her under the protection of the King and her own magic.

'Greetings, lady,' murmured Seren with a slight bow. 'No doubt you will be relieved that the vexations I cause you will soon be over. I leave just after noon, never to disturb the peace of Rhuddlan again.'

The woman came close, too close. Seren could feel the chill of her barely curbed hatred.. Before Seren could stop her, the woman grabbed her face, sinking in her talon-long nails into the girl's cheeks.

'You stupid, naïve little cripple, do you honestly believe the King will allow you to be lost to him, to the future of Cymru? Your Cornish sweetheart made sure Gruffydd ap Llewellyn knows what a powerful witch you will become, too important to waste birthing peasant brats and curing warts in some distant valley.'

Below her the army of Cornish, Welsh and mercenary warriors were moving off, the rumble of many hooves drumming out a song of sorrow to all left behind. How many would survive to return? Would the English finally have the ancient lands of Kernow defeated and conquered, to inhabit and mould to their own culture and faith like they had across the once British isles? These were the thoughts she wanted to dwell on, not the poisonous rancour of Lady Vanora.

'You should listen to your own words, lady. The powerful witch I *will* become. I am not ready yet, and need to return to my studies at the village.'

'Such a foolish little girl,' Vanora jeered. 'The King wants only the best seer in the land at his side. If he wants you to replace me now, are you going to defy the supreme monarch of Cymru?'

'Maybe …' Seren became frightened and confused. She was too young for such a responsibility, she had so much more to learn.

Vanora continued, enjoying the distress on the young witch's face. 'It is so easy for you. Born of an old noble house and raised by a Prince as his daughter. Maybe you could say no and actually get away with it.'

The woman began to pace, her anger manifested in more strong waves of negative emotion that Seren fought hard to dissipate before they entered and hurt her soul.

'I was born to a poor hill shepherd and his fertile bitch of a wife,' Vanora went on, 'the tenth child of 14, all of which sadly survived, leaving us always hungry, always cold and dirty. Luckily the local wise woman spotted my abilities and made me her apprentice. A cold, hard woman, prone to random beatings and verbal cruelty.'

Seren felt sympathy course through her for the young witch of Vanora's past, but said nothing. The woman had not finished. 'I was also blessed with beauty, far more than your homely looks. I grew into a wildly alluring siren who could entrance any man she wanted. And I wanted many. Eventually I found a nobleman mad enough in lust to marry me, and through him, I was given a chance to become who I am today.'

Vanora grabbed a lock of the young witch's hair and twisted it with sadistic malice. 'So no simpering chit is going to take that away from me … do you hear?'

All sympathy evaporated at Vanora's open threat and spite. Seren pulled away and held out her stick to the ground to find a way past the woman.

'We are both servants of the Goddess. It is She who decides our fate, not some mortal be it King, Prince or witch. I believe now I have fulfilled

Ceridwen's wishes and my part in this nightmare is over. It is time for me to return to my studies.'

'Thank you for pointing that out to me, sweet sister of the Craft.' Contempt contorted Vanora's speech, more serpent than human. 'Such a lonely, remote village can be a dangerous place, the countryside filled with poisonous snakes; and the huge gwiber dwelling in the valley lakes are always hungry for tender young human flesh.'

Catching the older woman unawares, Seren raised her staff and held it close to Vanora's throat. She heard the ominous slide of metal against leather as Vanora's men at arms prepared to defend her. She ignored them.

'Do not make threats against the village of the witches, against Rhan of the Golden Dove. We may be young, our skills raw and untested, but there are many of us. Harm one of my sisters and you will incur the revenge of us all.'

Vanora laughed, the sound scornful and arrogant. 'Sweet child, I made no threat, as all these good people around us will verify. I said nothing beyond a sisterly warning. With your future importance to the King, I have nothing but concern for your wellbeing and safety.'

The woman stroked Seren's face and then, surrounded by her supporters, turned away, leaving Seren in no doubt the sanctuary of her village and the safety of friends would be in grave peril.

With the war party bound for Cornwall now beyond earshot, Seren steeled herself to put all thoughts of Adwen behind her. She was now in the throes of a nightmarish dilemma. Should she go home and risk bringing Vanora's wrath on innocents, people she loved? Or take her chances and battle the witch on Vanora's home ground at Rhuddlan?

23

Cornwall

'They are a cheerful bunch, those Irish …' remarked Berwin, King Cadoc's youngest son, his voice laden with sarcasm. They rode across a wind-blighted stretch of open moorland, with local horsemen going in front of the King and his elite guard to guide the army through a complex network of streams, gorse thickets and treacherous bogs. Behind the Cornish knights were the Fianna mercenaries, their behaviour in stark contrast with that of the local foot soldiers trudging behind. Ordinary men of Kernow whose minds were full of memories of their farewells to loved ones and families. Of leaving the warm hearths where they belonged, to face a fearsome enemy.

'How can they sing and joke around like that?' Berwin continued. 'It is unseemly.'

Smiling, the druid Adwen, a warrior as well as holy man, rode up to join the young Prince. 'They are a race apart, my lord. Men and women who live to fight and die.'

'For money …' Berwin's face showed his open contempt. 'They will kill anyone for a handful of coin.'

Adwen shrugged. This was a beardless lad of 14 summers, he had much to learn of the world – if he survived the conflict to come.

'Everyone has to survive. The shepherd tends his flocks, the smith forges iron. Na Fianna fight.'

'There is dignity and honour in the toil of shepherds and smiths,' the Prince continued. Adwen warmed to the lad; such insight was good in one so young and highborn.

'I shall tell you what I know about our guests. No ordinary man or woman could survive their initiation. Could you stand in a waist high hole in the ground armed only with a shield and fend off nine warriors throwing spears at you?'

Adwen enjoyed watching the boy's eyes widen in surprise, not sure if he believed this, yet still fascinated. The Irish mercenaries were the stuff of future legends; this campaign would be one for Berwin to bore his future grandchildren with tales of on long winter nights.

'If the candidate was wounded, he had failed.,' added Adwen.

'Even more so if he was killed!' Berwin laughed.

Nodding in agreement, the druid continued, 'Another test involved braiding the warrior's hair and sending him into a deeply-wooded forest. He would fail if a branch cracked under his feet or the braids in his hair were disturbed by twigs.'

'That is impossible!'

'Why not ask them yourself? I can translate for you. No?'

Prince Berwin frowned and shook his head. The Irish warriors, with their tattoos, brutal array of weaponry and swagger alarmed him.

'What is more, the prospective Fiann, male or female, would need to be able to leap over a branch the height of their forehead, pass under one as low as their knee and pull a thorn from their foot without slowing down.'

Shaking his head in grudging respect, Berwin added, 'And be able to kill without mercy or conscience.'

'Of course. That would be expected from the start. But do you know what the strangest requirement is to join the Fianna?'

Berwin shrugged, not sure he wanted to know the grisly details. He had to sleep in a makeshift shelter every night with these savages within sight. Not one would he trust. He would feel safer resting amid a pack of wolves.

Glancing back at the Irish riders, in particular the handsome devil his compatriots called Brandan of the Golden Harp, Adwen announced to the astonished young prince:

'Every one of them must also be a skilled poet.'

Brandan made himself as comfortable as possible, using a slab of granite as a back-rest as he huddled wrapped in his cloak, sharing the natural windbreak of scattered stones with the other Irish warriors. There could be no campfires, no morale-boosting songs or bawdy tall tales. Not with Earl Harold's entrenched troops less than an hour's march away. The night would be infested with his scouts; the bastard was no fool and would be expecting the Cornish to fight back.

After the assembly broke up, the Princess had returned home to Ireland with her entourage. Brandan remained in Wales. What had he to go back to? He had answered the Cornish call to arms against Earl Harold's outrage without hesitation, as had the stray Na Fianna with him now, enduring another bleak night in the open. Unable to adapt to a normal life during the winter months, some of them preferred to fight than starve to death.

So they had ridden together, a Cornish force of foot soldiers and mounted warriors strengthened by these Irish professionals and volunteer warriors from Cymru. Also among the war party crossing the wild Cornish countryside were a gathering of Bretons and Manxmen, all visitors to Kernow who wanted their chance to hit back at the Saxon invaders. The mood through the ranks was solemn; no-one underestimated the strength and efficiency of Earl Harold's thegns. This would be a hard and protracted campaign against a determined force.

Brandan finished the last of his only meal in two days, a lump of bitter bread as hard as the surrounding rock, washed down with freezing brackish water that tasted of peat. Pulling his hood down, the warrior prepared to rest. He did not fear losing control to sleep; he never dreamed, nor had his tormenter sent anything across the sea to harm him. A light but determined tug on his arm changed his plan. With nothing else to do to pass the hours, someone else had an idea how to spend what could be their last night this side of the Veil.

'I am cold …'

It was Tailte, one of the young female warriors. Slender as an ash bow, tough as a forged iron blade, she was always recklessly brave. He was surprised to feel tears on her face as his hand stroked it with a gentle touch, giving her permission to progress further. She snuggled up next to him, letting her thigh rub against his, making clear her intention toward him. Brandan ran his hand down her back in a firm caress, triggering a quiver of excitement within her. She grinned an assent for him to continue, biting her lower lip to prevent herself from crying out. With the enemy so close, they would have to take this journey of discovery in near silence. As his fingers increased the erotic pressure on her lower back, moving to her stomach and inner thighs, Tailte shuddered and gasped, her eyes widening and shining with desire.

There was no shelter in this wind-blasted, rock-strewn moorland, or any possibility of privacy. With Death's whispered invite carried on the wind, they were beyond caring. The girl straddled his legs, throwing her cloak over them both. Her fingers began undoing his breeches, hesitant as if expecting him to halt her advances. When he did not object but caressed her thick mane of dark brown hair with his long fingers, the tears began to flow again.

'I know now that I am going to die in the morning … why else would the gods give you to me? The last man to enjoy my body is already a legend of the Na Fianna.'

Brandan lifted her face and brushed away the tears. 'I am no legend, just a man, Tailte, flawed and all too mortal.'

The girl shook her head sadly. 'You would not have chosen me, handsome Brandan of the Golden Harp, unless a god intervened.'

The warrior bard smiled with sorrow and compassion. 'By all that I hold dear, there is no-one I would rather spend this night with than you.'

His fine words were said in truth. Tailte was a kindred soul, an equal bonded by shared experiences, of spilled blood and the joyous celebration of survival. Now they shared the sensual celebration of being human. Or would have, if he could have overcome his weariness of life. Indifference to his own fate had even spread down to his normally reliable loins. Lie back and think of his lover King Donal? The thought did not raise a smile … or anything else. An unwanted sigh of yearning did not help the situation. His opinion that love was a curse had not changed.

He leant back against the stone and allowed Tailte to free him and take him deep into her mouth, her slender tongue agile and eager. She pausing only to smile in triumph at his first groan of pleasure and stirring.

He lifted her face up to meet his own mouth, kissing her with quiet desperation. She tasted so sweet, so young. Her eagerness to enjoy him, to give him pleasure in return, was heartrending. This could indeed be her last night alive, and it was an honour she chose him to make it memorable. He took hold of her waist and positioned her beneath him, freeing her from the restriction of her own lower garb without ceasing to kiss her eyes, her throat, moving down to seek out her small breasts with his tongue. She whimpered and moaned with delight, her hips rising to meet him, desire making her impatient.

One slender hand sought him, held him, eager to take him deep inside her, but he pulled back, shaking his head with a wicked grin. Instead he put her down onto the ground, knelt between her legs and burrowed down to her moist soft mound, loving her stifled cry of surprise and writhing, bucking reaction to the skilled probing of his tongue. A reaction that worked its magic on him too, making him hard and ready.

'Forget the battle, I will die here and now if you don't fuck me,' Tailte gasped, on the brink of her climax. Brandan pushed her thighs back wider and entered her in one powerful movement. Her legs wrapped around his waist, tight, tighter, pushing up her hips to grind into his, wanting to take all of him inside her as deeply as she could. They moved together with an urgency born of the fragility of their warrior lives, a powerful collision of two hard, muscled young bodies. Brandan drove into her with strong, hard strokes, confident she could take them, rewarded with her meeting him with equal power and passion. Danger smothered the cries from their shared climax, the repression adding to the exquisite intensity coursing through them.

Shuddering with the pleasure aftershocks, Brandan slowly pulled away and, lying back, gathered her in his arms, ignoring the inevitable mocking banter from the rest of the Na Fianna.

'Jealous bastards!' he returned good naturedly. 'There's nothing stopping you from amusing each other. An eager cock is not fussy what type of lips give it pleasure.'

Brandan woke up as the war party began to stir. A camp of dark shadows moving through a dense freezing fog. Cold from the damp ground had worked its way into his back and legs, making them stiff and aching. Only his chest was warm with Tailte lying across it, one arm lightly around his waist, a content smile on her pale, freckled face. He hoped he had answered the desperate need within her to connect with another human being, to soar above their perilous situation for brief moments of joyous escape. His own mood had not changed; the bleakness of his soul echoed the desolation of the landscape slowly revealing itself as the fog lifted in the grey light of a winter dawn. He wriggled from beneath her, waking her with a firm kiss on the forehead.

'Time to ride, Princess …'

An hour before dawn, the war party moved on in near silence with only the muffled rumble of hooves, snort of horses, tramp of marching feet, occasional chink and clash of metal to mark their passage to confrontation with the Saxon. As an act of diplomacy, King Cadoc ordered that the new flag of unity be flown above the army, deep blue with the three silver spirals of the Goddess. No other pennants were displayed. The flag would send a message back to the English King, that the living gods of the pagans would no longer tolerate persecution from the followers of their single dead one. Crossing the Tamar was a breach of the only treaty that had held firm. There would be no more treaties.

Other than a raffish smile and wink of greeting, Brandan avoided Tailte as they rode with the other Na Fianna, not to reject her after the last night's tryst but to help them concentrate on the conflict to come. Death awaited them at the end of this short journey. He was not concerned for himself, but he wanted the girl to live. With a peevish wind tangling through her hair where his hands had been just an hour before, her eyes glinting ruddy light from the rising sun, a secret smile no doubt in reminiscence of their coupling, Tailte was the essence of life itself to Brandan.

Their route took them through a settlement, little more than an untidy collection of circular mud and thatch hovels through which thin hens scratched and a few bony pigs rooted listlessly. As the leading riders approached, the villagers ran out to greet them along the track. Brandan recognised their poverty; he had ridden through enough such villages in Ireland in hard winters. The same too large, haunted eyes staring from grey, pinched faces, near naked children with famine and worm-distended bellies.

All signs of a bad harvest the last summer. He had known such bitter hunger many times in his own life.

The villagers stood by the side of the track. To Brandan's astonishment, none of them held out their hands to beg, none pleaded for help. Instead, they watched the warriors with what looked like pride. Maybe hope was a stronger emotion than despair to these people?

'Why are they still here,' he wondered out loud, 'with the accursed Saxons so close?'

The war party had passed many locals fleeing the area, taking what little they had, often just their lives, yet *these* people had stayed. Two children ran up to him, maybe drawn by his mare's white coat with its pretty star dapples. Her magical appearance always entranced the young. Confident that Lia adored children and would behave, Brandan first scooped up the girl to ride in front of him, then swung her brother behind and rode toward the hamlet with his passengers giggling in delight. As one hand steadied the girl, Brandan was shocked by the feel of her bones sticking through the grimy scraps of clothing. He doubted she would survive until spring.

As the riders reached their homes, he answered his own question. They did not fear a foraging raid from the Saxons because they had nothing left to lose. Nor had he anything to give them to ease their suffering; the warriors' food supply was gone. Would the handful of small coins left in his purse do anything to help, or cause them further suffering as they fought over the money? How far would one cloak go to clothe a whole village?

His eyes were drawn to a circle of ancient standing stones on a hill above the village. Could these hold the answer? That these people remained, guarding their sacred site of worship, ready to die before allowing the Christian Saxons to defile them? It would explain their pride and resolve in the face or war and famine.

The swoop of wings above his head interrupted any further sorrowful musings. Another huge raven circled above them. Or was it the same eldritch bird from Wales? Surely impossible, and yet something about its manner and unusual size suggested it was. The warriors raised their weapons in joyous salute to the raven ... greeting it as a good omen of victory in the battle to come. To the Irish warriors, it was a symbol of their war goddess Morrigu. To the Cornish and Welsh, the bird represented their war deity Bran. The raven was theirs and they prayed it would fly high, well out of arrow range above the enemy encampment. The Saxons would see the bird as a portent of doom and defeat. They would be right.

Brandan made a silent promise to these people, that if he survived the conflict with the Saxons, he would bring back as many supplies as he could from the enemy encampment. England was a prosperous realm, the men of Wessex would be well stocked with provisions from their side of the Tamar. He heard the raven's harsh call from a nearby circle of tall stones. It sat on the tallest of the ancient symbols and with its head cocked to one side, appeared to be looking directly at him.

'What do you want of me, Morrigu? I am here, ready to fight to defend the children of the Goddess. I have vowed to help these people … what more can I do to serve you?'

24

Cornwall

Without support from the fyrd of other earldoms, Harold had moved into Cornwall as far as he could justify. To his disappointment, it wasn't nearly far enough into this godforsaken bleak land to count as a victory. Unbidden, the thought of being held at bay like a cornered stag crept like a traitor into his mind, as did the idea of retreating back across the Tamar while the river was relatively low and benign. Any prolonged snowfall or heavy rain could turn its lazy meander into a dangerous torrent.

What was holding that old fool Edward back? He wanted his Christian Crusade to eliminate the scourge of paganism, so why hadn't he grabbed this opportunity to bring the Cornish to their miserable knees? A question he could see echoed in the eyes of his men. This was no place to spend the winter. Their closeness to their homes and families was a constant source of rumbling discontent and increasingly frequent desertion.

His eyes caught sight of a beacon lit from a hill in the west. The Cornish were coming! Harold's heart beat faster. At last, action, the best way to shake off this melancholy and push further into Cornwall. He watched with pride as his troops readied for battle. There was no panic, no confusion, but the disciplined, organised preparation of skilled fighting men. The Cornish had proved they were a rabble, easily routed. Again he cursed King Edward for his weakness and indecision. With a strong English army, Cornwall could easily be theirs.

Cadoc's army halted on a ridge close to but out of sight of the Saxon camp. Beneath them, the sun glinted on pewter waves rippling along the Tamar. The river was slow, lazy, wandering through a broad, verdant valley still wreathed in the trailing remnants of the night's fog. Swans and geese dipped their heads into the water and fed, oblivious to the threat of violence hanging in the air like a falling sword. From his place in the mounted ranks,

Brandan noticed the Cornish King turning to some riders to his right, signalling to his chief druid, Adwen. Clearly acting out some pre-arranged plan, the druid lead a group of warriors to break away and ride toward the valley in a brisk gallop. They headed in an opposite direction to Earl Harold's force of occupation.

Brandan had to accept and trust Cadoc's strategy, but there were murmurings of puzzlement and discontent among the ranks. Surely every fighting man and woman was needed to take on the formidable force of the Wessex Saxons? The King made no attempt at explanation, and the remaining warriors moved off at his signal, following the banks of the river. Within an hour, they spotted a line of lit beacons on hilltops on the opposite side of the Tamar. The enemy knew they were close.

Brandan was calm, relaxed. Doing battle was his reason to exist, once he had chosen the life of the Na Fianna, and not caring if he lived or died made preparation for the assault to come easy. He could see the rising fear and tension spread among the Cornish and Welsh, see it transmit to their horses, who became skittish and fractious, throwing up their heads and fighting their bits. All in stark contrast to the Irish. Brandan dropped the reins onto his mare's neck, cocked one leg over the pommel of his saddle and rode with a nonchalant swagger. The mood among the rest of the Na Fianna was also calm, their fatalistic banter laced with dark humour.

As expected, they found the Saxons on full battle alert behind their earth ramparts studded with bristling rows of sharpened poles aimed at both horse and man height. The enemy were clearly ready and prepared for a long siege, expecting the Cornish forces to become depleted and demoralised with wave after wave of futile attacks. Now fully alert with sword in hand and reins taut, Brandan carefully studied the terrain. As a paid warrior, he acted on orders, but his mind considered the options – what little there were; Earl Harold was no fool and a seasoned campaigner. Brandan noted every hazard to his mare on the ground leading to the Saxon ramparts, each hummock, ditch and steep drop in the terrain, checking for any cover from the deadly rain of arrows to come.

As one, the Fianna spoke aloud their treasured mottos, the words that bound them as one family in life and death: *Glaine ár g-croí* (Purity of our hearts), *Neart ár n-géag* (Strength of our limbs), *Beart de réir ár m-briathar* (Action to match our speech).

As they paused on the edge of death or glory, Cadoc, mounted on a golden-hued stallion flanked by his banner holders, rode closer to the Saxons, wisely halting out of arrow range. He waited in the open for signs of an answering deputation from the Earl, but at first none appeared. Cadoc showed no sign of impatience, sitting relaxed on his horse, chatting to his outriders. Back in the waiting army, Brandan wondered at this. It was as if the arrogant and disrespectful delay from the enemy was somehow playing into the Cornish King's plans, for Cadoc was clearly in no hurry to return to his army. Finally a small group of riders emerged from the Saxon defences. With no banners, they were low-ranking free men. Further insult. Whatever was said between them was lost to the wind, but the Saxon gestures were dismissive. Then both parties turned and galloped briskly back to their respective ranks.

Cadoc himself rode down the ranks of mounted warriors, singling some out to form a separate group. He arrived at the Na Fianna and addressed them in their own tongue: 'Brave cousins of Eire, it seems Earl Harold refuses to talk to "mere crow and kite bait". I call on your valour and swift steeds to harry and attack the Saxons head-on. Try to lure them out if you can, but most of all I need their full attention focused on us on this side of the ramparts for as long as possible. Can you do this?'

A suicidal mission. Brandan urged his mare forward and bowed his head in respect to the King. 'Let me show this Saxon braggart how much carnage "crow bait" can do to his thegns.'

As one, all the Na Fianna rode to join him. Cadoc gave a sad, apologetic smile. 'I knew I could rely on the fighting Irish. I am sorry to have to pitch you head-on into death's maw, but my people are desperate; their men folk are not warriors but are here out of desperation and courage, fighting for survival.'

Brandan patted his mare, then whispered a prayer to Morrigu. Kissed his sword and looked down at the enemy's defences.

'It is about time my sword Fiacre tasted Saxon blood.'

He urged Lia into a gallop and began his attack, yelling out the Na Fianna battle cry, *'Diord Fionn!'*

As Brandan rode, he took in a deep breath of the sharp morning air, tinged with the silt smell of the river. If he lived, he would soon choke on the stench of blood, ordure, smoke and spilt guts, the familiar acrid tang of battle. His mare galloped downhill, swift and balanced beneath him, allowing him to focus on his foes. Brandan heard the twang of released arrows aimed at the riders. As one, fleet and agile as a flock of starlings, the Na Fianna jinked their horses sharply to the right, barely losing a stride of speed, hearing the satisfying clatter of spent arrows landing harmlessly on the ground alongside.

A forest edge in their path gave easy cover, but it was also a trap, for the Saxons would know where the next attack was coming from. Brandan whirled his mare away from the sanctuary of trees, but the temptation was too much for some of the others. Broken branches snapped and crashed as riders forced their way through the tangle of undergrowth.

Reining in his mare to an abrupt halt, Brandan heard the roar of fighting men at the other side of the valley; Cadoc had launched another assault using a mixture of foot soldiers and mounted warriors. With a possible three-pronged attack splitting the rain of arrows, the odds were better, and with a group of mainly Na Fianna, he spurred on for another head-on assault on the Saxon ramparts.

No fools, the Saxons ignored the mounted warriors armed with swords and axes and trained their arrows on the Cornish archers on foot. Brandan swore: this would be a massacre with few if any enemy casualties unless Cadoc had hatched a miraculous master plan with his druid. If he had nothing in reserve, this assault was doomed to fail, and the day would belong to the invading English. Was Cadoc just a reckless fool, or a master tactician? Much blood would be spilled before the answer was known.

Roaring insults, Brandan circled the ramparts, defying the Saxons to engage him in battle. He left himself deliberately exposed, an easy target, but his suicidal bravado was also mesmerising. Many eyes turned to stare at the young rider on a dappled grey mare. Brave or foolish, the Irish warrior seemed oblivious to the danger. Brandan's brief moments of charmed life ended when more riders joined him to goad the Saxon. The spell broken, a flurry of arrows found targets. Horses and men crumpled to the ground, mortally wounded. For the sake of the others, Brandan reluctantly withdrew again to regroup out of range.

Tailte rode up beside him, the gleam of battle flaring in her eyes. 'I do not care for this. We are nothing but defenceless targets for those bastards' arrows.'

Another Irish warrior snarled as he pulled an arrow from his saddle; luckily it had not penetrated the tough leather to harm his horse. 'Can we trust this Cornish King? He wants us to buy him time, but for what?'

Shrugging in stern agreement, Brandan wheeled his horse around in a tight circle to face the enemy ramparts again. 'We are a long way from home, my friends, and we've got nothing better to do today. I suggest we waste some more Saxon arrows!'

With that, he urged Lia on to another flat-out gallop as he stood in the stirrups roaring with defiance and violent oaths.

25

Stood on his high vantage point on the ramparts, Earl Harold tightened his fingers around his sword. He had expected an unruly but brave army attacking his defences head-on but instead was presented with a series of brief skirmishes, resulting in enemy dead but frustration that he could not rout the Cornish army in one decisive battle.

One moment from the long morning still lingered. Harold recalled the Irish rider on the star-dappled horse, one of the Na Fianna, glorious in his courage and folly. A man who would gallop into the maw of hell and brazenly defy Satan himself. Only this warrior was a pagan and did not believe in Hell or the devil. The Irishman would find out for himself soon enough when faced with the terrifying reality after his death. As the Na Fianna had galloped his swift mare beneath the Saxon ramparts, Harold had called off the archers from such an easy target. There was something about the man that fascinated him. Such courage, madness or even a harboured death wish deserved a better death than an anonymous chance arrow. Harold wanted to take him on, sword against sword. Defeat him and make the Irish warrior yield, then graciously offer the man his life if he would convert to Christianity. Despatch him with honour when he inevitably refused.

That could happen only if the Earl's army left the defences and took the battle out to the Cornish, but why jeopardise such a strategic advantage as these strong battlements made of the local red earth? An earth that would be stained redder with enemy blood, if only the bastards would make a serious assault. Did that fool Cadoc plan a siege? The locals were starving, unable to feed the Cornish King's army, while Harold and his men were well stocked in food, water and weapons with a supply route established back into Wessex. A siege would break the Cornish and their rag tag of allies.

Something was happening. The harrying had finished and Harold could see the Cornish army had swelled their numbers and were preparing to make their move on the Saxon defences. That explained the time-consuming but pointless assaults; Cadoc had been stalling as he waited for reinforcements. Harold sent word to his thegns and fighting free men to remain behind the ramparts for as long as possible, wear down and kill as many of the enemy as they could from their position of advantage.

And leave the Irish warrior on the grey horse for him.

The horses felt it first, some deep disturbance in the balance of reality. Already fractious at being held in check for so long, the animals began to whirl and rear, dropping less competent riders to the ground. Brandan felt a curious vibration through his body, uncomfortable but not painful, but there was no time to ponder on the mystery. King Cadoc had ordered an advance on the Saxons.

'Steady, slow and noisy … Let them know they are on the way to their feeble heaven …'

This was it at last, no more running and feigning. Brandan struggled with Lia; , the mare, always so brave in battle, was snatching at the bit and fighting for her head, desperate to turn and bolt away. He had to clamp his legs hard against her sides and drive her forward with voice and spur. The reluctance of the horses to move down the valley slowed the advance and could have spelled disaster for the Cornish army. It certainly amused their enemy; the jeering and laughter of the invaders echoed across the vale. Only the King seemed unperturbed, sitting out his stallion's cavorting with an expression of calm resolution.

All eyes shot upward at a thunderous roar, but the sky was as clear and blue as the first day of creation. The tumultuous crashing noise continued growing louder and louder in volume, something monstrous was howling down the valley. It was the river, a tidal wave of dammed-up water, released as a weapon against the Saxon defences, the sheer brute force of the water impossible for the earthen ramparts to resist. Battered by the weight and velocity of the water, they turned instantly to red mud that crumbled and fell into the raging torrent.

Men tumbled from the ramparts, howling in shock to be lost to the flood. Others, the strong swimmers or the lucky, made it to higher ground. By the time the Tamar's great surge had flowed through and a silent calm returned over the flooded valley, there was nothing left of the defensive wall. Cadoc's men cheered as the sodden remnants of Harold's army fled back toward England in disarray.

Adwen. It had to have been the druid's work. Brandan was torn. One part of him was sorely tempted to ride on and harry the Saxons all the way back to the border; he had promised his sword some English blood. The other part was inclined to seek out the druid. There had been no time or enough manpower to dam the Tamar by natural means, so Adwen had to have used magic – a great deal of magic, maybe too much for one man. He could be in urgent need of help.

A group of the Na Fianna including Tailte joined him, eager for some action. They galloped toward the place where Cadoc's army had parted company with the druid and encountered many fleeing Saxons. Within minutes Brandan was able to keep his promise to his sword as they attacked the fleeing invaders. Most were on foot; they were not a natural race of horsemen like the Irish. Demoralised and badly shaken, they still fought back with the vicious desperation of cornered wounded wolves.

The air sung with his sword's joy as the weapon cleaved its way through living flesh and bone. Brandan turned to hear Tailte's chilling war cry as she decapitated a second enemy warrior, then tied the head by its long blond hair to the pommel of her saddle. Her face was gore-splashed, her horse's bay coat ran bright red with enemy blood, her eyes glittered with the joy of victory. Brandan shook his head and smiled at her in admiration of her determined ferocity. The old dark ways were far stronger in her. Tailte was a primal force, an earthly embodiment of all the fierce war goddesses – Morrigu, Macha and Babdh. She echoed Morrigu's dual aspect of life and death, for the female warrior had the ability to create new life within her. Brandan grinned again. Maybe it would be with his child, after the last night's enjoyable coupling.

26

Wales

At last, Seren was sure she could smell ribbons of smoke rising above the forest from the village hearths, and her heart swelled with relief and love. Within the hour, she would be among the friends and mentors she'd left behind so reluctantly. She had hoped all the memories from her stay in Rhuddlan would seem no more than a bad dream, but for one thing. A constant reminder followed her: the warrior bard's gilded harp tied to a pack pony's saddle. Even in its protective cover, the wind seemed to stir its strings into what sounded like weeping, a curious and eerie sound. The man with a dark, hidden soul had left it in her safekeeping during the dawn hours before he rode to battle. Unknown to her, this was a momentous gesture, as it had never left his side before.

Seren had taken the instrument with a heavy heart. Keeping it close meant she would have to meet the warrior bard again, should he survive and return. Or have it as a permanent reminder if he was lost to the battle. A battle that would also be fought by the Cornish druid Adwen, as much a warrior as a holy man.

Seren wiped away tears of anxiety and fear for Adwen. Why had the druid become so important to her? A first love? Maybe. Even the memory of his voice, strong yet gentle, made her heart beat faster. She accepted it might be just an infatuation born of his protection against the monstrous hatred of Lady Vanora. Yet she was certain there had been a spark of something more when they had parted. He had taken her hands in his, held them as he murmured he would see her again.

'This is but a skirmish, Seren. Brief and bloody but not the vision we shared come to fruition.'

Adwen had kissed her forehead and, as she lifted her head to seek his, had kissed her lips. 'I will return to Cymru and to you,' he had said. 'Someone has to make sure that damned Irishman stays alive to gets his harp back.'

She had made a brave attempt at a smile, her heart already breaking, as he had climbed into the saddle and ridden away from her life. Maybe that eerie harp would not be such a burden after all if it brought Adwen back to her.

Inevitably, her thoughts also went back to her last encounter with Llewelyn's seer. Ironically, the Welsh King had made no command that Seren should remain in his household. Indeed, he had apparently forgotten her in the turmoil to prepare to defend his realm against the possibility of a Saxon invasion. The young witch had ridden away with her family without hindrance, but her heart had remained heavy with anxiety throughout every long mile of travel home.

Maybe her return would not be so welcomed when they knew the truth of Vanora's thinly-veiled threats? Prince Gwion insisted she was safer away from Rhuddlan, protected by the collective magic of the village. He also made sure a company of warriors would remain camped close by ... not in the village itself, for it was forbidden to carry weapons of death within its confines. Their presence was of little comfort. Vanora's attack, if it came, would be supernatural in origin.

Familiar voices snapped her out of her unhappy reverie. Her closest friends, Ceinwen and Delyth, ran along the forest track to greet her, crying out her name in delight. Seren should have felt safe now, surrounded by familiar places and beloved friends, with the powerful witch Rhan and the other tutors to protect her. But she could not. There was only one who could give her that feeling, and he was hundreds of miles away, about to face a ruthless foe. It was time to learn as much as she could, to grow wiser and stronger. For in the end, the best person to protect her from the threat of the snake witch Vanora, was herself.

'Come back to me, Adwen,' she whispered, 'Return safe and strong. I miss you so much.'

Shrill screams suddenly rent the peace like knife slashes. Seren held on tight to her frightened pony as the Prince's guard drew their swords and formed a protective shield around her. Hoof beats echoed along the forest track from an approaching pony, in a flat-out gallop of terror, but it was riderless, its rich bay sides splashed with fresh blood. The girls cried out in shock as they recognised it as belonging to one of the new novices; it was young Ffion's mountain pony, Myfi ...

The pony's panic-driven bolt lessened as it saw the approaching group of warriors' horses, veering into them at breakneck speed. Riders pushed their mounts to form an even closer protective circle around Seren and her pony to prevent the chestnut gelding crashing into them. Seren whimpered in horror as she recognised the scent of human blood on the pony, but she was unable to tell the others as the trees around them swayed and flattened from the onslaught of a powerful wind. The downbeat of huge, leathery and veined red wings as a vast dragon, a gwiber, rose above the valley.

Seren's blindness spared her the sight of the broken body of a young girl clamped in the dragon's long, slavering jaws, impaled on curving yellow fangs, each as long as a warhorse. Ffion's blood dripped down, gleaming on the bronze iridescent scales of its neck and breast. The dragon gave a deafening roar, part bellow, part screech, bolting all the horses below and allowing gobbets of the girl's flesh to fall from its jaws. With no choice but to allow their distressed horses their heads, the warriors could do nothing to protect the young witches on the path. Seren hauled on the reins of her pony with all her strength but to no avail; the monstrous beast had reduced their well-trained mounts to a mindless stampede. Against such a monster, only flight offered any chance of survival.

Finally, only sheer exhaustion brought the animals back under their riders' control, far from the valley and the gwiber's attack. Seren sobbed for the child lost to its hunger for human flesh and in fear of the fate of the rest of the village. She was also aware that the dragon had not followed to attack her and the warriors, despite them being beneath its great wings. Which meant that like all predators, it had taken its fill – but of what?

The gwiber was not a supernatural beast, nor a predatory animal like the bears and wolves that dwelled in the forests. A well-aimed spear or arrow could bring down one of those threats, but it seemed nothing could get through the gwiber's armoured body of red scales. As the story of a valiant but doomed local hero Owen Ap Gruffydd confirmed. His perhaps foolish lone attempt at ridding the Wibernant valley of one of the beasts had ended in his three-fold death, being bitten on the neck by the gwiber, falling and breaking his neck from a high vantage point and finally drowning in the river below.

Attacks from the lake-dwelling gwiber were rare if they had a plentiful supply of fish; and if not, they rested for years after a good feast of livestock. Was this attack a normal occurrence of nature or was it Vanora's threat come to chilling fruition? Magic could not harm a gwiber but could it summon one?

Answers had to wait. The captain of the escort rallied his warriors and turned their horses along the path back toward the safety of Prince Gwion's stronghold. His ward was not to be put in harm's way. Seren, realising what was happening, knew it was pointless to argue with the warrior; he had his orders, and men of the Teulu always obeyed them. All she had was the element of surprise, the endurance of her tough little mountain pony and the hope that it had enough courage to leave the rest and find her way home to the village.

Seren wheeled Olwyn around sharply and dug her heels into the pony's sides harder than she had ever needed to. Shocked at the rough treatment, the pony reared for the first time carrying Seren, then surged forward into a sharp-paced canter down the track toward the village. Seren could do nothing but hold on tight and continue to drive the pony on, ignoring the shocked shouts of her bodyguards. They would follow her, honour bound to do so, and Seren gambled she was right about the dragon, that it had feasted well and flown back to its lair in the lake near Penmachno.

27

Brittany

Was he crazy? Maybe Hereward's desperate flight from his Norman hosts was one of survival over reason. Why else would he be smearing black silt from the depth of the marsh into his hair, hoping it would dry and darken its flaxen strands into a less give-away hue? The Bretons were a dark-haired people of the ancient blood of the Pretani, a race as old as the ancient stones that stood in lonely defiance on hilltops on both sides of the Channel. Such resilience against waves of conquerors must mean a fierce people, suspicious of strangers.

His route through the Marais had brought him to the edge of a bustling coastal town. He sat down on a log in a spinney of wind-twisted pines, his body on the edge of exhaustion. For the first time since fleeing the massacre, he was able to think about his plight. Hereward had no idea what he was going do next, but his spirits rose at the sight of ship masts bobbing and dipping above the quayside houses and taverns. He still had some gold coin, but who could he trust to give him safe passage to England?

Hereward froze at the sound of voices, a group of children approaching the spinney. There was little cover to hide in but he crouched low behind a holly bush, hardly daring to breathe. To his dismay, they lingered in the clearing, sitting on the log. One lad had a brace of duck tied to a pole. Another unpacked some bread from a bag over his shoulder. A little girl, perhaps their younger sister, made herself busy gathering wood for a fire. Hereward swore under his breath; the young hunters were preparing to stay and cook a meal. There was nothing he could do but stay crouched until they moved away.

'*Salud?*'

A small voice addressed him, and Hereward glanced to his left to see another girl child gazing at him with fearless but curious eyes. '*Enebor?*'

Not knowing a word of Breton, he was forced to smile and shrug. This was not going to end well. The child dropped her armful of kindling and ran back to the others, shouting, '*Klask. Gwaz. Gwaz.*'

He had no choice but to make a run for it, heading for the town with their shrill cries ringing in his ears. Hereward cursed his lack of skill at being furtive. He had been raised an earl's son, well versed in swordplay and horsemanship, not skulking about trying not to be seen. There was no cover of darkness, indeed the clouds had cleared, the winter sun was bright and blindingly low in the sky. Hereward could not have been more obvious if he jumped up and down and screamed, 'I am a Saxon.'

Hereward sloped head down toward the town, hoping his pace would look relaxed yet purposeful, just another peasant on lawful business. The cobbled streets of the town were busy, people thronging a market set up along the main streets. His senses assaulted by the smell of raw meat, chicken and duck shit and vegetables trodden underfoot. Many voices raised in a muddle of unknown words. Hereward was glad of the purposeful confusion; it would make reaching the dock easier than if he was standing out as a stranger in an empty street.

A winding side street, as narrow as a grave, appeared to be the quickest route through to the ships. He could see yellow sails, hear them billowing with the wind of freedom. So close now … Hereward quickened his pace, trying hard not to break into a run. So focused was he on the ships that he did not spot a burly man push his way out of a doorway, fastening his breeches.

'*Beulke!*'

He did hear the man swear before blackness overcame him.

Hereward awoke in a world of pain, face down on sodden straw reeking of stale urine. He struggled to his feet but was pulled back to the ground by tight manacles around his ankles, chained to the dank cell wall. He was a prisoner, beaten black and blue. The more awareness dawned, the more bruises made their presence known. A gash above his eye seeped blood down his face. Hereward moaned in frustration. He had had freedom within his grasp, now this!

Where was he? The dungeon was gloomy, cramped, with only a narrow chink of light above him illuminating iron and heavy oak doors, firmly shut. Apart from the scampering presence of large, damp-coated rats, he was the cell's only guest. Chained up in Brittany or back with the Normans? Hereward strained his ears for any clues. There was nothing but the chittering of the rats and the scrabble of cockroaches. He had been left with no food or water. Clearly whoever had captured him wanted him alive, but only just. With no means of escape, Hereward had to bide his time and pray.

Time became measured by the dimming of the faint light above him, and Hereward fought hard against the idea he had been left there to die of starvation and thirst. Or to be eaten alive by the rats. The creatures had become bold, daring to approach and bite him, but he doubted he would live long enough for sickness from their bites to kill him. Already weakened, he had to use precious energy to kick away at the hungry vermin, his thirst-parched throat now raw from roaring threats at them. Need overcame his shame as he urinated and relieved himself as far away as he could from his place chained to the wall. It was not far enough. If he could not have freedom, he prayed to God for the mercy of a quick death.

Nobody came before nightfall, and with the threat of attack from the rats growing, Hereward prepared to spend the night awake, defending his torn flesh against their needle-sharp teeth.

The iron door slammed open, and light from flaring torches seared his eyes as three heavy-set figures entered Hereward's cell. Two were armed, one dumped a leather flagon of water and a lump of hard rye bread in front of their prisoner.

'Where am I?' Hereward gasped, his throat raw and dry. His answer was a blow to the side of his head from a guard's pike staff. The men left without addressing him, but before they locked the cell door, one spoke to the others in the unmistakably Breton language. That was one question answered: he was still in Brittany. Uncertain whether or not this was the better alternative, Hereward dived on the water and bread, weeping as the brackish liquid flooded his painful, parched throat. At least they wanted him to live a little longer.

It became a routine. The narrow sliver of light, becoming his focus, bestowed almost deity-like hope into his wretched existence, measured his days and nights. The jailors visited only once a day, and they made no attempt to clear up the ordure, so Hereward added clouds of flies to his unwelcome companions. He made a pact with the rats, sharing his food with them in return for being left alone to sleep for an hour or two.

'I see Ankou, our God of Death has spared you, Saxon.'

Hereward must have dozed off just before dawn; he shook his head to clear the confusing fug of brief, troubled sleep and focus on whoever had addressed him in heavily accented English.

'I will not insult you by welcoming you to my home, so do not insult me by refusing to tell me the truth. What are you doing in Brittany?'

He struggled to his feet to address his captor – a pampered nobleman judging from his fine garb and fastidious reaction to the reeking dungeon. So squeamish was the man that he had clamped a cloth pad stuffed with dried lavender to his nose. His corpulent frame strained to escape from its enclosure of fabric; clearly no warrior now, this was a man rich enough not to have to fight – he could pay others to die on his behalf. His florid face and fleshy lips were glistening, covered in meat grease from a recent meal, as were his bead and short, fat fingers. Fatty old mutton, judging from the smell, which caused even the starving Saxon's gorge to rise. Hereward prayed the nobleman would keep his distance, preferring a heavy blow from the guards to the touch of those slimy hands.

'Your enemy is also mine, my lord.' Hereward struggled to speak; his throat was parched, his lips swollen and bruised from the daily beatings. Haltingly, he told the Breton about his stay with William the Bastard and his flight into Brittany.

'There is nothing in your words that makes me change my mind,' returned the nobleman with a sneer. 'You are a spy; your life ends at dawn.'

'I am Hereward, son of Earl Leofric of Mercia, who is a man of great wealth and power. My brother, the new Earl, will pay well to have me returned safely.'

'And I am the King of France!' His captor laughed, looking Hereward up and down, taking in his filthy garb and battered body.

'Isn't it worth finding out the truth? A corpse has no value except to the devourers of carrion.' Hereward reached into his clothing and tore out the hem of his under tunic to produce a gold ring set with a carved agate symbol. The Breton snatched the ring off Hereward, tossing it in the air before holding it in a tight grip.

'A spy and a thief.'

With all the dignity he could muster, Hereward stood tall, his pale blue eyes flaring with defiance and pride. 'My fate is in your hands, but nothing will take away the truth. I am Hereward of Mercia.'

His captor turned to leave, waving aside the guards eagerly waiting to give Hereward another beating.

'I am Lord Hoel. I will be merciful and give you enough time in this world to learn if you are indeed the son of an English earl. One wealthy enough to reward me for your safe return. But if you have lied to me, I promise your death will be slow and agonising.'

He swept out of the cell but muttered something in rapid Breton to the guards. Something that did not please them. Minutes later, the filth in his cell was removed, fresh straw lain down as a bed and clean water and fresh bread brought. Hereward was still chained in a cold, wet cell with rats as company, but it was an improvement.

28

Normandy

'What did you say to him?'

Guillaume's features contorted with rage, with lips pulled back in a rictus sneer, face red, eyes bulging. He pinned his wife up against a wall, one hand gripping her neck. Around him, the braver of his children shouted, trying to pull him off their mother, while the little ones trembled whimpering behind a tapestry arras. They had seen their father angry before but never with their *maman* and were rightly terrified. Matilda was so petite, her neck so fragile. The sight of the thickset Duke towering over her, his warrior grip around her throat, was a vision from the darkest nightmare.

Despite the danger, Matilda kept calm, her arms protectively folded over her belly and the child growing within, her thoughts with her children – especially Robert, her eldest boy, who had produced a dagger to defend her. Unmoved by the lad's courageous action, Guillaume brutally kicked the boy away.

'Not yet man enough to take me on, *"brevis-ocrea"*. Your "short boots" cannot yet step in place of mine,' he sneered at Robert, using a much-despised nickname. 'Try again when you have grown a beard.'

He turned his attention back to his wife. 'The Saxon fled like a hunted hare from the campaign, preferring the company of hostile savages to that of his friends and allies. I know he was here, having an audience with you in this room, while I was away. There was no shortage of witnesses.'

He shook his wife as if to release the truth from her by force.

'So I say again, what did you say to him?'

Matilda's eyes glared with the pride of her aristocratic blood. She loved the Duke but nothing he could do would make her beg or cower. At least there were no dangerous accusations of infidelity.

'Our conversation was brief, my husband. We spoke of nothing that wasn't common knowledge in this court.'

He did not believe her, but Guillaume knew his wife. Knew he had already gone too far. There was something Matilda was not telling him, but the woman would die before admitting it. The Duke's own stubborn pride, born of arrogance and the self-belief he had needed to survive, would never allow him to apologise to her. He released his hold and stormed out of her chambers, indifferent to his wife's and children's' distress and the fire of hatred blazing from Robert's eyes.

At least he had *her* to speak to, *she* would not deceive him. The only human being in the world he could ever fully trust. Despite his short time back at Caen, the Duke returned immediately to the sanctuary he'd created for Lady Cecilie at Falaise. Taking only an escort of the most trustworthy of his elite guard, he pushed on hard and fast to the castle, his mind too troubled to accept any delay.

The troop arrived at Falaise in a furious clatter of iron-clad hooves striking sparks on the cobbles, the whirling horses scattering startled serfs who'd run into the courtyard to take their reins. Ignoring his retainers, Guillaume leapt out of the saddle and immediately sought out her quarters in a sealed-off section of the castle. Waiting patiently behind the guarded outer doors, the Duke growled with impatience as the lady's old maidservant, Avis, grovelled at his feet.

'My lord, all is well with my mistress. She has had no visitors, just as you ordered.'

Ignoring the woman, Guillaume continued up a narrow winding staircase to the turret rooms that were the seer's private quarters. With haste causing his hands to falter, he took a key off his belt and let himself into Lady Cecilie's rooms. She sat by the window, head resting lightly on the stone surround, her hands folded elegantly on her lap. She did not turn to address him, she never did, but gazed over the misty winter landscape. Her face was serene, never giving away her true emotions. He wasted no time with pleasantries; she would not mind, knowing him for the brusque warlord he had to be to survive in power against a hostile world.

'Tell me, lady, does the Saxon Hereward live? We found no sign of his body in the ruins of that Breton town.'

Guillaume gave no further explanation about the assault; Cecilie would already know.

'The Saxon fled in horror, appalled by your callous murders of innocents. He escaped further into the land of the Bretons …'

Standing abruptly, the Duke paced the room as the implications of this desertion sank in.

'I need to know what knowledge he is taking back to England.'

The lady did not answer straight away; her gift required time and patience, neither of which were easy for Guillaume. He sat down at a nearby table and poured himself some wine as he waited. Finally he heard a sad sigh as she addressed him, her voice softly-spoken yet echoing in his mind.

'Does it matter, Guillaume of Normandy? You are already powerful enough to take your heart's desire. With the power and shock of the new weaponry, you will be unstoppable.'

He found comfort in her words, for Cecilie did not lie. The loss of Hereward was not the disaster he had perceived it to be. For one thing, a lone Saxon had no chance of evading the Bretons. They may even offer him back to Guillaume as part of a treaty. And if Hereward did manage to reach the sanctuary of England, so what? The seer was right. No matter how hard England prepared against invasion, there was nothing they could do against his steam-powered arsenal.

'Is there nothing that can prevent me from taking England?'

Again, the eerie delay in answering that so infuriated Guillaume, but one he had to endure.

'No, my lord. Not even an act of God can stop you.'

29

Brittany

Hereward's limbs were stiff and weak from his lengthy imprisonment. How long had he been incarcerated? Weeks? Months? He now measured the passing of time in beatings and foul treatment, in the ever-increasing rat and cockroach populations in his rancid cell.

He could do nothing but allow himself to be dragged from the cell as silent, rough-handed guards grabbed him and brought him out into the daylight. Accustomed to gloom and darkness, he felt the sun's rays sliced through his eyes like knives, forcing him to keep them shut until he had time to adjust. They took him to a small courtyard close to the stables of what appeared to be a stone-built fortress. There they unceremoniously stripped him naked, and giggling servants poured buckets of boiling hot soapy water over his head. One old matron shushed them away, then set upon him with a rough scrubbing brush, sparing him no dignity as she cleaned every inch and crevice of his body. Once he was dried, the crone did her best to treat his wounds with pungent but soothing herbal salves. Hereward murmured his gratitude in English but she shrugged off his words with a muttered curse and stomped away, her duty done.

Hope rose in his heart. They would not clean up a man doomed to be tortured and executed, would they? His knowledge of Breton customs and manners was non-existent. What he had experienced so far had not impressed him.

He was thrown a bundle of clean clothes in the Breton style, and when he saw they were well made in fine wool and linen, his optimism grew stronger. A group of warriors approached him leading saddled horses. One handed Hereward the reins of a ribby ram-headed chestnut gelding and signalled he must mount up. A journey? But to where? Hereward took comfort that there was no sign of his odious captor Duke Hoel, who surely would want to gloat at any forthcoming execution. There was no way of finding out where they were taking him, with no indication that anyone in this party could speak English or French. It would be a journey in silence to some unknown fate. Wonderful! Could his life get any worse? Hereward briefly considered the odds of escape, taking his escort by surprise and galloping out of the castle on the bony nag. They were not good. The others were on fine-bred, fit horses and had bows and spears. Archers stood on the battlements, and every Breton would be his enemy. Hereward had no choice but to climb into the saddle and ride out of the castle with the mainly silent warriors.

The pace was leisurely and Hereward began to enjoy the freedom of the open countryside as they clattered through the craggy landscape of Brittany, his senses assailed with fresh air and the sounds of nature. It was good to see wild birds on the wing and the white flags of fleeing deer; wholesome creatures that gladdened the heart. He hoped never to see another filthy rat or cockroach again. It was an ancient, untamed landscape, scoured by harsh Atlantic winds and fiercely proud of its pagan heritage. He had never seen so many rows of menhirs and hilltop dolmens. There were more sacred stones here than around England's one-time pagan capital, Glastonbury.

After such a long confinement, his muscles ached and he was struck by regular painful cramps in his legs and feet, especially his soles where they rested on the stirrup irons. The guards were patient, resting when he needed and plying him with plentiful water and food. That they were polite, respectful, tending to his needs and not tying him up, even when they camped overnight, led Hereward to believe Hoel had received proof he was a noble-born Saxon of an important and powerful Earldom. A faint spark of hope flared. Maybe he was going home?

Five days' journey brought them to another coastal castle, this one far finer and grander in scale that Hoel's stronghold. Proud banners of black and white stripes fluttered from its battlements and a large, prosperous and well-built town surrounded it. A royal town, the seat of King Blaez? He would not have to wait long to find out; the castle was their destination. Similar in design to the Norman strongholds, there was nothing in England to match the grandeur and strength of the stone battlements.

A reception party clattered over the drawbridge across a wide moat, green with algae and bobbing with water fowl. Well mounted and dressed in fine garb, Hereward realised he was being greeted by a royal party. His fears finally began to ease: this had to be good news. Why would a King ride out to meet a foreign felon?

Elderly but tall, upright and noble in bearing, the man that Hereward rightly assumed to be the Breton King moved away from the others to ride up to him. To the Saxon's astonishment, he addressed him in good if heavily accented English.

'Lord Hereward, I hope you can forgive the inhospitality of some of my subjects. You escaped from the clutches of the Bastard of Normandy to find the sanctuary of my realm, and instead have been sorely misused.'

Hereward dismounted and dropped to one knee, bowing his head low in respect.

'My Lord King, your people have no love for Saxons. I could not expect anything more.'

Blaez signalled for the young man to stand up and remount his horse.

'Is there not an old saying, that your enemy is also my enemy? The centuries-old grievance between our countries will not disappear, but I believe we must put that to one side. What we both face is too terrible to confront alone.'

Hereward nodded, remembering he too had recently used that old saying. The extent of the Norman Duke's ambition had shocked him. He doubted Guillaume would stop until he had the whole of France and the British Isles under his brutal rule.

'Indeed, my lord King. The Norman Duke harbours ambitions for both our countries. United, we can defeat him, drive the upstart Norsemen out of France and back to their origins … as scattered, thieving sea wolves.'

He looked up to see the Breton studying him with an expression of curiosity.

'You do not know, do you?' Blaez murmured. 'The Bastard has kept secrets from you too, as he has from his duchess and people.'

He signalled for the Saxon to ride alongside him, making Hereward's heart soar with renewed hope. The King would not accord such a position of privilege to a condemned prisoner, to an enemy.

'I will return you to your homeland and family, young Saxon, with honour and gifts. But not before I show you proof of Guillaume's terrifying power. When the great raven flies over the carnage to come, it will be the Bastard of Normandy that has caused it. This we know for certain.'

Hereward shuddered. So the Duke's wife had been right: he was not alone in enduring the terrible vision of the blood-drenched battlefield and the monstrous raven. A nightmare shared by Norman nuns, Breton pagans and one lone Saxon so far from home. A vision this powerful must be heeded, urgent preparations made to defend their lands … Hereward said a prayer under his breath, for the Virgin to intercede for his swift, safe return to England. Not for his sake – his crimes in Normandy made him unworthy of Her pity – but for the people of England now under threat. It did not matter who the English eventually chose to be their King on Edward's death … Guillaume coveted the crown and was prepared to slaughter all who stood in his way.

To Hereward's frustration, the Bretons seemed in no haste to send their Saxon guest home. The hospitality and generosity of his hosts amazed him after the brutality of his earlier imprisonment. Despite his impatience, he had no choice but to accept their generosity, and he settled into his own area in the stronghold for sleep and privacy. Small and cramped compared with a Norman castle, but far more welcome. The King was a genial host compared with the volatile and dangerous Guillaume of Normandy. There was no guile in the continued stay, and at no point did he feel a hostage … The coastline of Brittany was rugged, frequently lashed by violent storms and high waves. Such storms battered the coast now. It could be weeks before the sea settled enough for fair sailing.

Hereward had received a full set of clean, new clothing and the gift of a young dun mare, smaller and more stolid than the Norman warhorses but a comfortable and forward-going, obedient ride.

It was on this good horse that Hereward rode beside the King, who was anxious to show him evidence of a new horror coming from Normandy. The Saxon had no choice but to accompany him, but his unease grew with every mile closer to the border, closer to the nightmare of being recaptured by the Normans. The presence of a large party of Breton warriors was of little comfort. Hereward knew the brutal power of their mutual enemy; he felt he had no need of any reminder. Within a few more hours of travelling, he discovered how wrong a man could be.

The smell hit him first, the sickly stench of dried blood, entrails, decay – horribly familiar to any warrior – but something more … an acrid, metallic smell over that of burnt flesh. Hereward's heart hammered, and he instinctively reined in the dun mare. Whatever they were about to see, he didn't want to face. The Breton king was resolute, pushing his uneasy troops into passing through a thick stand of wind-warped pine trees out into a cleared valley from hell.

There had once been a large, prosperous village in the clearing, but this was not apparent from the evidence left behind. No buildings remained standing … all that was left of homes and storehouses were shattered charred beams and ash. Living things had also been reduced to broken shards of burnt bone and ash. Whole families, from courageous defenders to new born infants, horses, cattle and poultry had all shared the same fate … their remains drifting and merging in a slight breeze. The next high wind would obliterate all that ever lived in Sains. Hereward felt the bile rise in his gorge. This was not warfare … this was genocide.

He felt a comforting hand on his shoulder. King Blaez addressed him in a voice trembling with his own turbulent emotions of shock and fury. 'I make no apologies for forcing you to witness this vile carnage of innocent lives. This is what my nation faces … oblivion. Our lives and ancient, proud heritage obliterated by the ambition and hell-spawned weapons of the Norman madman,'

'But he isn't insane,' Hereward murmured. 'That is what makes this nightmare all the more terrible. Guillaume is merely being practical. Wipe your enemies off the face of God's earth and take over their lands with no cost to your own army. Practical and efficient … that's the Bastard of Normandy.'

'I must show you more,' insisted the King, riding beyond the pitiful remains of Sains to a clearing on the edge of the pine forest. 'Not all the villagers were incinerated.'

Hereward bit down hard on a knuckle to force back the scream rising from his soul. Three rows of putrefying bloated human bodies lay in mute witness to Guillaume's brutality. Slaughtered swine, cattle and horses made up another pile. Again, Blaez put his hand on the young Saxon's shoulder. 'We will honour our dead with suitable reverence now they have had a witness. You must return to your land and warn your King of what we all face.'

As the lightning strike of first shock subsided, Hereward realised why he had had to see this nightmare for himself. No tale from a messenger could have conveyed the reality before his eyes. These people were not the victims of a massacre fuelled by sadistic spite, they were intended as mute yet eloquent examples to show the world the devastating effect of Guillaume's power. A warning to all that stood in his way that surrender was the only sane option.

Closer inspection brought fresh horror. The victims had not died of sword or arrow wounds. Steel-tipped javelins impaled their bodies … What sort of weapon could drive a lance clean through a human body? Straight through an ox's body? Not one wielded by a man. An army of demons? Were the outlandish rumours about the Duke of Normandy's pact with the Devil actually based in reality? It seemed so. What other answer could there be to this unnatural slaughter?

'The Norman Bastard has the power to obliterate all opposition to his might,' said Blaez. 'His greed and ambition condemn us all to death or slavery. You must convince your King to forgo the enmity of faith, young Hereward. We must all come together in a pact … no nation can withstand this alone.'

Hereward nodded, unable to find the words as the full power of his vision came back to haunt him. Now he knew. It was Guillaume who would bring the carnage, bring the spectre of the great raven down on them all.

30

Wales

Alban Arthan, the joyous mid-winter festival of the sun's return, had passed the occupants of the village of the witches in a blur. As had the new hope of *Gwyl Forwyn,* when snowdrops pushed through a hard crust of snow, the blooms so fragile yet so determined. The time of the Maiden had arrived, and soon the balmy days of spring would bless the land. This year, the miracle of rebirth was tainted by sorrow. This year, there were no ewes and new lambs on the pasture.

Nothing could ever be the same since the gwiber attack on the village. When the dragon swooped down on its vast wings, it had concentrated its predation on their sheep, easy targets penned up for the winter. Devouring many in single gulps, it had rendered others into bloody, torn pieces before devouring them, relishing the taste of hot flesh and blood in its fearsome jaws. While it feasted at a leisurely pace, smug with the luxury of invulnerability, Rhan and the other elders had gathered up their young charges and fled into the woods. All the novice witches and villagers except for Ffion, who had refused to leave her pony behind, thus dooming her to be the gwiber's last meal of the day.

Seren had pushed aside the terrible memories as best she could. One innocent life lost was one too many, but the carnage could have been so much worse. If Vanora had been behind the creature's attack, summoning it must have exhausted the witch, for no other evil had befallen the village. Seren was not complacent – the new season could restore the woman's strength – and the village remained vigilant.

There was no choice but to savour the life the Goddess had blessed her with. Any other choice would be an insult to Her gift of life. She could hear the Maiden's promise carried by the joyful carillon of bird song that woke her every morning, by the first touch of warm air on her face. She breathed in the sweet scent of daffodils, felt the living snow of blackthorn blossom in her hands while remaining aware of the sloe tree's vicious thorns.

Her stubborn heart stayed sad and not just for the loss of Ffion. Every day had been a test of Seren's willpower as she tried not to let her mind wander to the track leading into the village, to stop herself listening out for the approach of horses bringing visitors, foolishly imagining that at last Adwen had chosen to visit her.

That he could have lost his life in the battle with the Saxons was a thought she could not bear to tolerate. She told herself that she would know if he had died, that the bond between them was strong enough. She knew deep down that was wishful thinking, showing her tender years with a naïve dream. Reality was she had only known the Cornish druid for a few days. He was older than her and lived in another country. He was nothing more than her first infatuation.

One thing that kept her sane was an overwhelming compulsion to learn how to play the Irish bard's harp. She did not know why, it just seemed to be the right thing to do, that it was somehow important. Every moment when not at her studies, Seren would pester old Garnoc, the village musician, for lessons. He had never known such an avid and driven pupil. The girl would play until her fingers bled, repeating a difficult passage over and over again until she had perfected it.

At first she had used one of her tutor's harps, offering the excuse that Brandan's was too heavy for her to play. In truth she was as scared of the gilded instrument as she was of its owner. She kept it safe in its leather wraps, a supposedly mute object hidden in her home. But though she could not see it, the harp always reminded her of its presence. She was certain it had some sort of life of its own. There were times when it was silent yet aware, waiting like her for its beloved to return. Other times, she was convinced she heard a sad sigh of strings. A distant sound of otherworldly weeping. The sound was so unnerving, she wanted to be rid of the thing, perhaps to give it to Garnoc to care for.

Why had she made the promise to the Irishman? Had she been spellbound by his charm or acted out of fear? Maybe it had not been such a huge favour at the time, a simple gesture to help a brave warrior off to battle. It was only a harp after all. Who was she fooling? Seren had known there was something mystical about the instrument from the moment she had first heard it sing across the courtyard at Rhuddlan. It had such an ethereal yet seductive tone, an allure created by magic … fairy magic? That would explain her nervousness around it. It did not belong in this world.

How had Brandan obtained such a marvel? He was human – Seren could detect nothing of the Sidhe in him – and the Shining Ones did not give away their precious things. Yet another dark mystery surrounding the Irish warrior.

'Seren … where are you Seren? You are needed.'

Delyth's voice called across the village. Seren's heart leapt. Was her friend announcing a visitor?

'Maredud is calling for you … It is her time, and she wants only you at her side during the birth.'

Sighing, the blind girl swallowed back her disappointment and picked up her stick. She quickly made her way across the village with the confidence of familiarity to seek out the birthing house. With the Mother's consent, the gift of a new life would soon bless the village. This was what was important, not her foolish mooning over a man she hardly knew. One who could already be married for all she knew.

Maredud's fine, strong son announced his arrival with such hearty cries that, unanimously, mother and birth attendants named him *Croch* … loud and vigorous. Seren congratulated the anxious first-time father pacing outside the house.

'Ah, Pryderi, I hope you have plenty of Beltane-blessed mead put by to wet the baby's head. The whole valley will know this one has been born and will want to join the party.'

The young man had laughed, 'I suspect they heard him on the other side of Moel Pen-y-bryn.'

Seren left the celebrations and sought out the privacy of her favourite spot. It was a sheltered mossy bank within a short, safe walk of the village. Here she could be seen by everyone, but there was an unspoken rule that she was to be left alone while sat there. Her gift favoured solitude.

Seren sighed. Though it was still early in the new season, the afternoon sun was warm, a taste of what was to come. How could she be gloomy with the hardships of winter finally gone from the land?

She lay back on the dry moss and listened to the gurgle and splash of the stream; water melted snow from Snowdonia's high peaks. It was good to close her eyes and allow any dream to take her away. The horrific visions of the raven and the battlefield had ceased after she had left Rhuddlan. Nor had she been given any bad portents of Adwen's fate, and that alone had sustained her through the winter.

A familiar swish of linen robes, the tinkle of charms and the sweet scent of elderflowers forewarned Seren that her mentor was approaching. She sat up straight, brushing the hazel pollen from the overhead catkins from her robes, preparing to rise to her feet to greet Rhan.

'Please, child, stay where you are. I will join you on the grass. This blessed gift of early warmth must be enjoyed.'

Seren's heart beat faster. The revered head of the village would not come to her like this without a serious reason to talk. Seren was attuned to the most subtle nuance of voice and tone, so Rhan could not hide the tension in her voice.

'It is a beautiful day, though one so early is also cause for concern,' Seren ventured. 'Living things are stirring too early, and April can unleash a savage bite.'

'And yet enough will survive to carry on their line,' Rhan countered with a gentle smile. 'It is the way of the Goddess, ensuring only the strongest live on.'

'It seems so harsh.'

'Harsh but wise, Seren. All the beauty and life around us has prospered from this plan since the beginning of creation. It cannot be changed or always understood but it must be accepted.'

Seren raised her face to the sun, loving its caress. By summer it would be too strong and burn her moon-pale skin.

'*Mamau*, you have not come here to discuss the plight of over-eager butterflies, have you …?'

Sighing, Rhan took her hand and gave it a gentle squeeze.

'Nothing gets past you, little star. I would be a fool to try. I have been aware for some time that you have brought some affliction back from Rhuddlan. Don't look alarmed, not a sickness in the usual sense of the word. And it doesn't take a witch's intuition to watch your hopes rise and get cruelly dashed with every new arrival to our village.'

Seren did not answer but found herself twiddling with the charms on her belt in agitation, not certain she wanted the older woman to continue this chain of thought. Rhan was wise and perceptive. How did she expect her foolish lovelorn pining not to be noticed?

'Normally this would be your business,' Rhan continued, 'but a missive I received this morning from your guardian has made this lovesick yearning impossible.'

For Seren the sun became an orb of ice freezing time … This must be bad news, it must be. She gripped one belt charm so tightly, the silver star crumpled in her fingers, cutting her. She did not notice the warm trickle of blood down her wrist, too seized with dread for what Rhan would say next.

'Who is this man that has taken your heart, Seren?'

In a voice little more than a whisper, Seren told her teacher of her meeting with a Cornish druid, Adwen, who had gone to war against the Saxons, and of her great love for him. Rhan sighed with deep sadness; nothing was as painful and heart-breaking as first love. This was a youthful infatuation with no future, triggered by the man's chivalrous protection when Seren was under threat. Somehow knowing this made her difficult task easier.

'Seren, I must tell you that your guardian has found a suitable match for you. You are to be married to Daned, the son of Prince Adwr of Elfael.'

With her world spinning in shock, Seren dropped her head into her hands, weeping. She had always known that someday the Prince would arrange a marriage, that his paternal love for her would make sure it was not a disagreeable one to someone old or cruel. But meeting Adwen and knowing the pangs of love had driven that from her mind. Her throat constricted with sorrow, barely able to whisper, 'When?'

Rhan held her tight, letting the girl rest her head on her shoulder, a mother's role she was only too happy to fulfil.

'It is too late to organise the wedding for the most auspicious day, *Calan Mai* – the festival of union and fertility. So it will have to be *Alban Hefin*.'

Summer. Her freedom would end in the warm month of the summer solstice. A crazy thought broke through her misery: there was still time for Adwen to return and claim her. As if reading her mind, Rhan reminded her of the consequences of not accepting the match.

'Your guardian has found the son of a great Prince to be your husband, guaranteeing your future. To refuse would cause so much offence it could trigger a war. Many good men of the Teulu, including your brothers, could be killed over such a slight.'

Seren nodded. Of course she could not refuse. For her, there had never really been any choice, and leaving would divert away from the village the ever-present danger of an attack by Vanora. It was time to grow up and accept her duty.

31

Cornwall

Ladling a watery hare stew into a roughly-carved small bowl, Brandan approached the figure lying on a makeshift bed of furs. With one hand he supported the man's head, with the other he did his best to pour the warm liquid into the unresponsive mouth.

'Come on, my friend, do not make this difficult for me … Just one sip … good. How about another?'

When he thought he had done all he could, Brandan put down the bowl and wiped the man's face with a clean rag. Adwen breathed, his heart beat and blood flowed through his veins, but beyond that he was no more than a *puipead* – a marionette with its strings cut, unable to do anything for himself. Brandan fed him, kept him clean and watched over him, unable to leave him alone for long. Adwen could not help himself if in danger; he was at risk of choking on his own vomit and was totally helpless from attack by roaming predators, whether human or beast.

Brandan had lost track of how long he had stayed in this remote and primitive bothy, every day spent trying to keep the physical body of the Cornish druid alive. Adwen's mind and soul were trapped in another world, torn away from his body by the violent power he had summoned to dam then release the Tamar to flood the Saxon fortifications.

The Irish warrior had found him lying in a sacred circle of bluestone built high above the Tamar valley. Motionless, face ghostly pale and cold as stone, Adwen had at first appeared dead. Indeed anyone less familiar with the Veil between worlds would have had the body burnt or buried without hesitation. Brandan had lifted the man onto his mare and sought out the nearest shelter; riding back to the Cornish army would have taken too long. Adwen's hold on life was hanging on a spider web of frailty.

A rough shepherd's bothy, abandoned on the arrival of the Saxons, had given the two men some shelter. Unable to leave the druid for long enough to seek help, Brandan had done his best to fix up the near ruin and make it habitable. He had hunted close to the hovel for pigeon and hare … anything that could make nutritional broths to build Adwen's physical strength. Only then could he seek a way of bringing the druid back.

Brandan had no idea how to reunite the man, but he knew something that could. Magic.

In the long hours keeping watch, Brandan did his best to fashion a rough harp using a piece of fallen oak timber from the bothy roof and strung with sheep-gut gleaned from a rotting carcass on the mountainside. He also carved tuning pegs from the fallen sheep's bones. A crude instrument compared with his beautiful gilded harp but, as shown when his fingers played a glissando along the strings for the first time, an effective one as a useable instrument. That it had no special abilities like his golden harp was another problem to overcome. This time he would have to rely on the beauty of his playing. It was said back home in Ireland that he could charm birds to fly down from the sky to land on his hand – and make any high-born lady make room in their bed and open her legs for him. But whether this could tempt an otherworldly being to cross the Veil was another question, with no answer … as yet.

Next came the more dangerous question of who or what would answer his call for aid. Brandan needed to summon an entity familiar with crossing the Veil. At home and in Wales, he could summon the Fairy Folk, but he had no idea what existed in Cornwall. The only one who could readily explain this to him lay prone on the other side of the bothy, dead to this world and soon to be dead in both if Brandan failed.

The thought of riding away and leaving the silent and motionless Adwen to the wolves and rats had crossed his mind many times. Who would know? He had no bond with this man, had hardly spoken to him when they were together in Rhuddlan. That they had both fleetingly known the blind witch Seren was nothing to tie them together in any form of friendship. Abandoning him would not trouble his conscience, nothing ever did for long.

The answer must have lain deeper in his subconscious, that fate was telling Brandan that in the future this man would be needed to help him. With all the Celtic realms in the throes of portents and visions, Brandan decided it was wise to listen to his inner voice for once. Ignoring it in the past has led to many misadventures and scrapes. He bore enough scars to be mute witness to his past narrow escapes.

If there were anything living beyond the Veil in this ancient and mystical land of Kernow, did they speak the same language common to the Irish- and Welsh-dwelling Sidhe, or the *Tylwith Teg* as they named them? For all he knew, the Cornish dwellers beyond the Veil could be ravenous, mindless monsters, who once summoned would be set free to ravage the human world. Or sophisticated beings that hated humans and would relish prolonging the druid's suffering. They might be enraged by music. There was so much he did not know, and could not know, stuck up a mountain alone with a living corpse.

Brandan had searched the druid's few belongings for clues, some grimoire or Book of Shadows depicting the spirit folk of his country, but found nothing but a willow wand and a handful of scrying runes; a completely useless haul of geegaws.

He glanced at Adwen's features. Every day his face grew more grey and sunken, more like the cadaver of an elderly man and not the vibrant young druid who dared to control a river and had succeed with spectacular results. For good or ill, Brandan couldn't wait any longer. It was time to play his harp and summon whatever came across the Veil.

He could not try the circle of stones, which clearly had some deep spiritual resonance for the druid; it was too far. Nor were there the sacred groves beloved of the Fae on this storm-blasted moorland. Brandan's only hope was a clear pool fed by a lively spring surrounded by wind-contorted young alder saplings. The only place of potential magic close to hand.

Making the stricken Adwen as comfortable as possible and doing his best to block the door to predators – human or beast – Brandan strode to the alder pool, his sword in one hand, the makeshift harp in the other. He chose twilight, a time when the Veil was at its most fragile, and sat on a log preparing himself for an encounter with the unknown, and most likely dangerous, Fae of this land. Once composed, Brandan began to play, choosing the lilting reels that the Irish Shining Ones had always enjoyed.

Brandan lost all sense of time but darkness had fallen, one thankfully blessed with a quarter moon. He heard rustling many times as he played, the natural movement of fox and deer. The heavier bustle and grunt of a family of badgers. At one point, a barn owl paused from its nightly hunt and perched in the upper branches of an alder, its ghost face glimmering white in the moonshine. Worrying about leaving Adwen too long, the bard decided to stop playing. He had entertained the Cornish wildlife long enough.

Agitated movement at the periphery of his vision warned Brandan he was no longer alone. He knew if he turned his head, he would see nothing. Something from beyond the Veil was fascinated by his music. Remaining focused, Brandan continued to play a lively medley of jigs and reels. He heard the rapid, jerky movements split into many as, seemingly emboldened, several hidden figures crept closer to him. Difficult though it was to ignore his visitors, he played on, head down as if lost in the music.

As they buzzed around him with a high pitched sound like wasps and whispered to each other, Brandan recognised the language, close enough to that of the Irish Sidhe for him to understand. 'Kill?' … 'Capture?' …

'Torment?'

Brandan faced a dilemma. If he spoke to them in their own tongue, it would reveal his location to the Irish Sidhe … and to *her*. If he spoke in Irish and they didn't understand, or chose not to understand, they would leave and the druid lose his mute fight for life. He finished playing and put down the harp. It was a gamble, and Brandan half expect the darting figures to disappear, but they remained. Obscure, spiky shapes caught briefly in the moonlight, appearing to change size, not only keeping to ground level but also flitting around his head with a strong aura of malevolence.

'Do you want me to play more?' Brandan spoke quietly in Irish; this caused a bristle of angry agitation in the figures. He sighed; if he wanted them to stay he had to speak to them in their own language, with all the danger to his life this would entail. He repeated the question in the strange speech of the Sidhe.

As a cloud moved away from the moon, Brandan could finally see his audience, a gathering of small figures stood before him in the silver light. Any resemblance to humans was fleeting, and their angular faces with sharply feral all black eyes peered back at him with equal curiosity. Sometimes they were hairless, sexless and naked, skin hues of blue and green, then in a flicker of agitated air they became pretty golden-haired children with shimmering wings and clothed in silken raiment. Brandan averted his gaze and viewed them from the edge of his vision. An array of nebulous dark and ill-formed shapes betrayed their truer appearance.

Not wanting them to leave, Brandan began to play again, and was rewarded by their capering dance around him. Their shapes never remained constant, sometimes appearing to blend, creating new forms, their high, tinny voices gibbering in manic glee.

As their dance reached a giddy whirl, Brandan sat up and stopped playing. He had expected their furious reaction but not the depth of malevolence he detected. Fingers elongated and became sharp talons. Mouths thinned and widened, displaying a bristling array of needle-sharp fangs. They attempted to attack him, clawing and biting, but he was able to fend them away with his sword and fast reflexes.

'Calm down, my friends. I will play again for you, but not without a price.'

One stepped forward, appearing as an enchanting girl child, though malice marred her illusion of youthful beauty. 'We demand more music! The price for your refusal is your soul.'

Brandan adjusted his cloak as if preparing to leave and shrugged. 'I cannot trade with what no longer belongs to me. My soul was already long ago bartered away and lost.'

This produced a furious debate among the creatures, then another stepped forward, a male in illusory appearance. 'Then we will take your life!'

The warrior stood up and gave a nonchalant grin. 'You are welcome to it … I am of Na Fianna, death has no fear for me.'

Picking up his harp, Brandan began to walk away from the pool, gambling that the creatures would not let go of the music – or him – so lightly. They surrounded him in a bristling whirl of furious barbed wings, their talons and teeth sniping away at his clothing and flesh. Using his sword, he batted them away, fully prepared to go through with his bluff. The harp had worked; he could summon up more cooperative Fae …

'Wait, you have not named your price,' a voice squealed in indignation.

Brandan hid his triumph and feigned a weary reluctance. 'I will play again for you, but my price is your aid. I need your kind wisdom and advice on a matter of magic.'

Their curiosity aroused, they listened as Brandan told them of the druid's plight, though not of his whereabouts. The little female appeared before him again with an illusion of even greater ethereal beauty. Her manner was no longer spiteful but openly flirtatious. She sat at his feet and wrapped one thin arm tightly around his leg. The feel of her touch was nothing he could name but some curious sensation not of this Earth, a fright made flesh.

'This is deep, dark earth magic, far greater than that of us Spriggans. You must seek the Stone Maidens and play for their dance in the moonlight. It is they who spin with the threads of life and the fabric of time, the deepest, oldest magic in Kernow.'

The stone circle, it always seemed to came back to that. Brandan thanked the Spriggans and, keeping his bargain, began to play again. Though they appeared insatiable in their need to dance and sing, as the grey light of approaching dawn lit the horizon, one by one the creatures returned behind the Veil. The last one to leave was the apparently female creature, who rose up to human height and kissed Brandan on the lips with a whispered, '*Go raibh mile maith agat.*' Bemused, the warrior arose to find his way back to the bothy. *Iontach!* Unbelievable … not only had he made another conquest, but the little Spriggan bitch had had knowledge of Irish all along!

32

Normandy

What an object! Guillaume examined the weapon closely, marvelling at its precision. Cold brass smoothly merged with iron and wood, all beautifully fashioned.

'Once again, you have surpassed yourself, Master Ferro.'

The Duke smiled with a boyish enthusiasm at his most ingenious craftsman as he examined the latest and, by necessity, the last version of the steam-propelled weapon. It felt good in his hands, heavy enough to be powerful, light enough to carry and aim with ease, with a broad leather strap across the bearer's shoulders. What was now named the dracon had been improved beyond all recognition from the clumsy device that had killed Guy de Pas de Caux.

The wiry little Moor from Al Andaluz was the leading genius among his team of talented artisans and smiths. Ferro was a treasure, loyal, hardworking and inspirational to the others at Falaise. No other lord would ever have the man in his employ; Guillaume had made sure that would never happen. If he did not serve the Duke of Normandy, he would serve no man.

'How many have the smiths produced of this version?'

The Duke could not hide the curt impatience in his voice, and the Spaniard knew why. It was no longer possible to keep this vast project secret; rumours had flooded Normandy and crossed the border into the Breton lands. He had no doubt both the Kings of France and England would have received worrying reports by now of monstrous objects being wrought by the devil's minions deep in the forests surrounding Falaise.

The lighter, more efficient design that now fired javelins was in full production. More workshops had been built, more craftsmen employed to turn out as many dracons as was humanly possible, enough to arm a conquering army. So many more potential loose lips and paid spies amongst them.

Ferro replied with the comfort of bearing good news, 'My Lord, we produced one hundred of the old design. We now have one thousand of the new.'

His news was rewarded with the gleam of astonishment and relief in the Bastard's cold, slate eyes. Impatience ran through Guillaume's veins in a prickling constant torment. It seemed as if England's old King had spent the year dying; the messengers and spies had foretold his imminent demise many times. There was no word of Edward's announcement of an official successor, and that ambitious upstart Godwin of Wessex was ruling the country in all but name.

'I would be a fool not to be impressed at such success. I am of course delighted.'

'Furthermore,' Ferro risked an interruption,' I have constructed thirty of the flying boats, again with an improved and more stable design.'

Guillaume slapped the wiry Moor across the back. 'You are indeed a wonder of the modern world, my friend. Become a Christian and I will give you a title, lands and the highest-born, most comely virgin as your wife.'

He stepped away, paused before slapping Ferro again. 'By God's holy bones, man. Become a Christian and you can have one of my own daughters in marriage. I have a plentiful supply of them, and my wife has just been delivered of another!'

The Spaniard bowed low in thanks to hide his expression, unsure if Guillaume was jesting. With his own wives and sons slain and the Muslim world barred to him, converting to the Christian faith was a tempting plan. His future lay in Europe now. Whether the Duke was serious or not, Ferro agreed with convincing enthusiasm.

'Could this day get any better?' Guillaume laughed. 'All I need now is to hear that Edward of England has finally got his heavenly reward. And that you can make me a thousand more dracons.'

Ferro bowed low. 'The dracons I can promise, the rest is in the hands of Allah … Almighty God.'

If he had noticed the Moor's slip of the tongue, Guillaume did not show it. He left the man's company to stride around the big workshops and adjoining forges, breathing in the acrid smoke and tang of metal that permanently tainted the air. Marvelling at the skill of the smiths and artisans and revelling in their cheers of support as he moved among them, Guillaume realised he loved this place, was addicted to the stench of power and progress. The frantic industry around him, all these clever men working for him, was exhilarating. Guillaume decided to remain there at Falaise until the inevitable conflict. There was nothing to interest him now at Caen, where he had left his wife busy with the new baby and the rest of his growing brood.

This was the time to spend with men who would help shape his destiny, his engineers and the warlord barons, with the occasional brief bedding of a doxie to slate his insatiable lust. The only quiet, contemplative time he needed would be to spend with Cecelie in her rooms. She was the only one never to flatter or lie to him

Brittany

Frustration and delays dogged Hereward's every attempt to return to England. The seas around the Breton coast were notorious for their strength and ferocity; the bones of far too many valiant seafarers scattered the ocean floor. He had no choice but to wait for calm seas, knowing each day turning to each week brought growing power to the enemy.

He stood on a wind-lashed bluff overlooking the ocean's assault on the land, positioning himself far closer than was deemed safe. His hair and clothing were sodden to the skin from the freezing, turbulent water, his face whipped and stung by the lashing salt. Watching wave after wave rise and hammer down onto the rocks, Hereward stood in awe of nature's power, so unfocused, raw and untameable.

Only a force as powerful as nature itself could hope to defeat the Norman threat. Such a force did not exist … apart from God Himself of course. A deity invoked by kings before battle for hundreds of years … but had He ever listened to their pleas? Were the pious defeated out of His favour? And why did so many godless evil tyrants succeed? Such thoughts were heresy, never to be spoken out loud, even in the sanctuary of the confessional.

Hereward remained watching the storm-driven sea for many hours until fatigue and hunger turned him away from his naïve hopes of a glimpse of home and the miracle of calm returning to still the waves. If Guillaume was in league with Satan, then the evil one's power was strong. Strong enough to keep the Saxon lordling stranded in Brittany.

His lone wanderings had not gone unnoticed. Concerned members of the King's household ushered Hereward into the King's presence, where attendants fetched heated mead and gave him a heavy woollen cloak lined in coney fur. Once again, the Breton generous hospitality shamed him. How often had he mocked these people as hag-worshipping savages when carousing with Guillaume and his barons?

'This delay is troublesome for us both, Saxon,' sighed the King, joining him by the wide, well stocked hearth. Hereward felt the heat of the dancing flames on his skin but his soul remained cold. His heart had been frozen in horror ever since witnessing the Norman carnage in Brittany, with its chilling connection with his vision of hell on Earth and the raven.

'I wish I had more confidence your King will believe you and act swiftly,' Blaez said, gazing into the flames as if looking for portents of the destruction to come. 'Had you come to me before the Bastard's attack on my people, I am not sure *I* would have. There have never been weapons of such power and ferocity in the world of men before.'

Hereward could not answer. Such worrying thoughts had troubled his own mind on the long wait to return to England.

'If it helps your cause,' Blaez continued, 'I will send some of my men with you, to speak as witnesses to your King.'

The Saxon shook his head. 'I would be honoured, but though I can give a solemn and sincere oath on my faith they would not be harmed on my account, I cannot speak for my countrymen. I am so sorry.'

The Breton King nodded, understanding the complexity and fickle nature of trust. His reign over a land under constant threat from Normandy and the rest of Christian France could never be a tranquil one. His every decision was under intense scrutiny from advisors among his holy folk and nobles. Indeed, his decision to spare this young Saxon and send him safely back to England had met with much anger and dissent. Many wanted Blaez to keep him as a hostage, to gain some financial or political advantage. Others were furious with their King for trying to warn the English of the threat from the Bastard of Normandy, believing that while Guillaume crushed the Saxons, he would be no threat to Brittany.

They were wrong, Blaez had to believe, thinking of the longer game and gain. Once Guillaume had wealthy and settled England broken under his heel with the blessing of their holy man in distant Rome, he would have the manpower and horrific weapons to finally exterminate the last pagan kingdoms. A forewarned England was a small hope, but it was all he had to offer his people.

Hereward could see his host grow more sombre by the minute, gazing into the blazing hearth, eyes haunted by anxiety. He poured Blaez another goblet of spiced mead and handed it to him. The Saxon paused, uncertain if he should pose his next question, but it was one that had played on his mind since his arrival at the Breton royal household.

'There is something I have wanted to ask you, your grace, but have held back for fear of seeming addled by some malady of the mind. 'You have my permission to speak freely, young man. Have we not enjoyed a full and open candour since our first meeting?'

Hereward nodded assent, took a deep. nerve-settling gulp of the strong mead and pressed on. 'You have many holy men and wise women in this land. Have any come to you with a strange and terrifying vision of the future?'

The King sat back in his high-backed wooden chair, closed his eyes as if to shut out the images as he described them. 'A daytime sky made night by clouds of foul smelling black smoke. A battlefield of burnt and brutalised corpses, human and horse alike, ripped apart and consumed by unnatural flames. Death and destruction on an unheard of scale. Whole nations broken by a terrifying scourge. And above this scene of hell on Earth flies a monstrous creature. A huge raven.'

Blaez could tell by the young man's reaction he had received the answer he sought.

No words were spoken, there was nothing more to say.

23

Cornwall

He had no choice. To save the druid, Brandan was forced to risk the stricken man's fast-ebbing life and take him slumped across Lia's back to the circle of stones. It had to be soon. Not only was Adwen's breathing becoming shallower, his heart beat slowing, but Brandan needed the moon and a clear night to summon the Stone Maidens. Tonight was perfect.

As ever, Brandan was pragmatic about the outcome. With two hours left of daylight for safe travel, he lifted Adwen onto his mare's sheepskin-covered saddle and prepared to travel to the circle of stones. If the druid died, Brandan would bury him within the circle and move on. He had done his best and would think no more about it. By the time he arrived, a low mist glowing from the rising moon encircled the hill on which the ancient, enigmatic stones were set. A more spiritual man than Brandan would have found the sight mysterious and proof of their enchantment. He was a warrior, first and last, his occasional prayer before battle to Morrigu merely a good luck habit, no more than kissing the hilt of his sword and whispering encouraging endearments to his mare.

Tethering Lia beneath a stand of trees with a good covering of frost-free grass, he lifted Adwen over his shoulder and began the climb. The druid was not a tall man to start with, and his body was pitifully light, so Brandan made the summit without difficulty. The climb was not entirely without incident, though, as a curious sound reached his ears. A wind song from a light breeze wafting through the stone circle, perhaps? But the air was still, not moving the ground-hugging mist. Brandan paused to listen. The sound was faint, as if coming from a long distance, and was not the random notes of a breeze. He could hear women's voices, lilting and eerie, rising and falling in the still night air.

Unsettled by the fairy song, Brandan completed his climb, taking comfort that the Spriggan female had not lied to him about the existence of Stone Maidens. Whether they could help or not was yet to be discovered, but he was relieved to know his time with the druid was almost at an end. Adwen's fate would be decided this night in this place.

The singing stopped abruptly on his arrival at the stone circle. To Brandan this was a good sign: the Maidens were aware of his presence. He made Adwen as comfortable as he could, using his tunic as a pillow and his cloak to keep the frail form as warm as possible on the cold, hard ground. Brandan decided not to risk speaking the Sidhe language; he had exposed himself to discovery already that night, and there was a limit to how much he would endanger himself for a foreign stranger. Instead he sat on the ground beyond the circle and began to play, a free-form melody based on the strange, sad song he'd heard on his ascent of the hill.

Nothing seemed to exist beyond the circle of tall moonlit stones. Time froze.

Brandan concentrated on getting the best out of his makeshift harp – a problem he never had with his gilded one, which virtually played itself. To his astonishment, the Stone Maidens accepted the tune from the crudely-hewn instrument. The singing began again, joining with his music in an eldritch harmony that grew steadily louder, clearer. Brandan fought against listening to their words; to interpret them in his music would betray his knowledge of the Sidhe tongue.

At first he thought his vision tricked him as the solidity of the stones began to waver, their weight and form growing indistinct. All around them, the air became charged with a multicoloured strangeness, fluxing and warping as everyday reality merged with otherworldliness. Perhaps his world appeared to resist the change at first, for with an ear-piercing screech, the dense weight and form of the stones returned. Their solidity lasted only a few moments before losing the conflict, the stones becoming as malleable as wet clay.

With a sigh as old as time, the stones collapsed into themselves to reform as nine tall, willowy young women. Their silver-grey bodies were naked, their long hair heavily dusted with sparkling gem dust. Their eyes were crystalline, catching diamond fire in the moonlight. Eyes that were as old and cold as the stones the figures had come from. Brandan addressed them in Irish, reasoning that if a lowly Spriggan could speak it, these ancient beings most certainly could.

'Beautiful maidens, if I play for your dance tonight, could I beg a favour from you?'

Gliding in a silent, sensuous motion, the spectral forms surrounded Adwen. One knelt beside him and began to weep crystal tears. 'This is Adwen, beloved of our kind. His spirit is with us now. Why should we help you return him to this sad, blood-stained world of men?'

Brandan had not expected this and was for once in his life was briefly lost for words before recovering his voice to plead. 'My lady, he is sorely needed. One day he will return to your gracious company but all that we love and cherish in this world is under terrible threat. We need Adwen's wisdom and guidance.'

'And who are you to beg for his life?' one of them queried, as she approached him in a silent glide. Brandan kept as still as he could as her cold form examined him, forcing himself not to shudder at her touch, which filled him with a brief sensation of the Stone Maiden's great age. She was a being so ancient that her existence had begun long before Dagda and Danu had made life appear on the land. She knelt down and peered into his eyes with her curious crystal gaze. Something was amiss; the diamonds in her eyes darkened and she leapt up in astonishment and confusion, rushing back to the others in obvious consternation. What had he done wrong?

The Maidens held hands, some sort of silent debate rippled through them before they broke away again. One turned to address him.

'Play for us, Brandan of the Golden Harp, play for our dance, and Adwen will be returned to you.'

Disturbed and puzzled by their reactions, Brandan forced himself to concentrate on his side of the bargain. This time he played a stately reel, a dance that flowed like streams tumbling through the mountains. One of the Maidens remained on the ground beside Adwen, cradling his head in her lap. The others circled her, picking up the rhythm of Brandan's harp song and dancing with silent grace. As he played on through the night, the immutable forces of time and matter became like skeins of wool in the tapestry of existence, their pattern rewoven by the Maidens as they danced.

He did not see the moment Adwen's soul reunited with his body but he heard the silver laughter and cries of delight from the Maidens and rewarded their success with a lively tune of merriment. The hill summit briefly lost its melancholic atmosphere and became the centre of a joyous celebration of life. All life, whether human, animal or fairy, seemed to join in the dance. A carefree wind whipped around the dancers, bringing festive wreaths of sparkling mist up from the valley below, pre-dawn birds added their lilting voices to the harp music. It was beautiful, wild and carefree … and ended abruptly as the first beams of the rising sun reached above the horizon.

Once more nine tall stones stood in a circle, life in all its familiarity returned as if it had never been breached by another world. Adwen sat up unsteadily and rubbed his eyes before staring around him, disorientated and confused. Brandan dug out a flagon of water and offered it to the druid. The man drank deeply, coughed up most of it, then drank again. Gradually, as his senses recovered, he became fully aware of Brandan beside him. Adwen shrank away, frowning at first, then shaking with a fearful expression. The same perturbed look Princess Kellan's holy man had given the warrior months before. By all the gods, what was the matter with these people?

Adwen appeared to recover his composure and attempted a smile of gratitude. 'I am not sure what I have done to deserve your courage and aid, but thank you, Irishman, you have saved my life.'

'Neither do I,' Brandan returned with a rueful grin and a nonchalant shrug, 'but can I have my cloak back? It's bloody freezing.'

The Cornish gods rewarded his benevolence toward their holy man by the gift of a fat young buck. That Brandan had aided the druid through a mixture of boredom and a lack of direction to his life did not seem to bother them. The two men sat around the smoky fire in the centre of the bothy with bellies full of roasted venison, their eyelids growing heavy with approaching sleep. Adwen's recovery was going well, the fresh meat would give him a much needed boost. Their conversation was easy-going and friendly, Adwen's gratitude evident with every word, but occasionally Brandan would catch the druid looking at him with a puzzled and fearful expression. He wondered whether or not he would get a straight answer if he demanded to know why.

'Where do you want to go when you are fully recovered?' he asked instead, after taking a swig of cold spring water to wash down the feast. The long stay in the primitive bothy had become increasingly irksome to him. He missed plentiful alcohol and the taste of fresh-baked bread … and the wild company of his warrior clan. Most of all he missed Donal with an aching yearning that refused to be denied. A knife wound would have been more bearable than this pain. He forced himself to focus on the druid and his plans.

'My people will have mourned and forgotten me by now. I could go anywhere, start my life afresh,' Adwen answered, his mood contemplative, gazing into the lively fire as if it held the answers.

'The pretty little witch?' Brandan grinned, remembering their time together at Rhuddlan.

Adwen shook his head sorrowfully. 'She has her life and duties in Wales. And is no doubt married off by now. We could not have a future together.'

'Why not?' Brandan replied with a shrug. 'You said it yourself, you are a free man now. Go and find her. Take what you want in this life before some bastard takes it from you.'

'The philosophy of a killer for hire? A man with no responsibilities except to himself? I cannot live that way, Brandan. I am a druid, initiated under the sacred oak and the sacred stones of Men Myghtern Doniert.'

Adwen picked up a stray twig and poked the fire with it. 'I am duty-bound to return to my people. My sojourn behind the Veil has given me greater insight to the danger we all face. A curse rather than a gift, for what I know now terrifies me.'

So, had the man been given a greater insight into this world? Brandan wondered. Was this the cause of the strange and unnerving glances? He could take no more of this mystery.

'Why do you look at me sometimes as if afraid, druid? Do not insult me by denying it. Did you learn something about me from beyond the Veil?'

Adwen took a long time to answer, keeping his head down, focusing on the blaze. When he did answer, he gazed directly into Brandan's eyes.

'If I understood what I saw, I would tell you. You found me and saved my life, for that you are owed my complete honesty. Sometimes when I look at you, all I see is an attractive young warrior. But at other times ...'

Brandan grew impatient. 'What do you see, man? Tell me straight. I have seen that look before from you casters of runestones and bones, of magic smoke and potions.'

'I see a black shadow, Brandan. I see you stood before me, but there is a dark shadow around you ... coming from deep within you.'

The warrior paused, thought, then laughed, a hollow sound devoid of humour. 'Is that all? I kill for gain and pleasure. Of course I have a dark shadow. The darkest possible, I suspect.'

As if for emphasis, Brandan picked up his sword and kissed its blade. 'If the shadow foretells my coming demise, again, so what? I have led Death a merry dance all my life, and all dances must end one day.'

Adwen searched the Irishman's lean features for any signs of face-saving bravado but saw none. Brandan's grim fatalism was as much a part of the warrior's being as his gifts of music and swordsmanship.

'So, holy man ... a battle looms on the horizon? I should be there at its heart. I will return to your King's court and offer him the use of my sword and horse.'

Adwen gave a wan smile of assent, glad that he would have the man's company on the long ride home yet unsure if he should be bringing this dark soul into the heart of the Cornish kingdom.

With the druid now strong enough to defend himself, Brandan risked leaving the bothy and headed out to find another horse. He had gold to trade, but the famine and recent war had devastated the land. Many fine and useful animals had died or been devoured by a people desperate enough to commit a heinous act of sacrilege – for the horse was sacred to all the Celtic peoples, a creature beloved of the goddesses Epona and Rhiannon.

Brandan found the nearest still-inhabited settlement and made it known he would pay well for a sound horse. As expected, word soon spread through the desperate, impoverished populace, and within a day, peasants and ruined nobility alike appeared with a sorry selection of broken-down beasts. The warrior settled for a sound but aged bay gelding; nothing else was likely to endure the journey to King Cadoc's stronghold on the other side of Cornwall.

Castle Dore, Fowey, Cornwall

Hearing the sound of approaching hooves through a pall of driving rain, a sharp-eared sentry shouted a warning challenge. The solid-seeming wall of water blurred vision and muffed sound, so the lone horse was beneath the wooden outer gates of the stronghold before anyone heard his alarm. Below the double banks of earth ramparts, a weary man on foot led a grey mare on which lay a slumped form, ominously still. Deciding these visitors were not much of a threat, the captain of the guard barked out an order, and the drawbridge was lowered to allow them in.

'Fetch your best healer!' Brandan's voice was harsh with fatigue. 'I return Adwen Men an Tol to his people.'

The druid's bay gelding had collapsed and died some four days past, its old heart giving way. Brandan had not even had the strength to check on the druid over the last few miles; any pause would have caused his limbs to give in to the arduous journey and seize up. The man could already be dead, his weakened form having succumbed to the rigours of their journey across Cornwall. Only now, within the safety of these mud walls, could Brandan risk coming to a standstill, fighting the urge to collapse there and then. A warrior who had nothing left but his sword and dignity.

Compared with the formidable stone castles of the Normans or the mighty strongholds of the Irish, King Cadoc's stronghold was a primitive affair, a central large round house surrounded by banked-up earth ramparts crested by a wall of long, sharpened spikes. But it teemed with people, many of whom crowded around Brandan with curiosity and concern. He gave into their ministrations, vaguely aware of people removing the druid gently from the horse, someone else throwing a dry cloak over his shoulders, leading him out of the rain ... Then he accepted the gift of darkness and silence.

Night had fallen by the time Brandan awoke. He found himself in comfort, lying naked beneath clean sheepskin covers. Flickering tallow candles illuminated an anxious attendant sat on the rush floor beside him. Surprisingly, it was a young man dressed in fine, expensively-dyed wools and wearing a finely-worked ornate gold torque. A noble? Seeing the Irishman stir, the man reached for a flagon of watery mead and offered it to him. Brandan sat up, his muscles stiff and aching from the journey, and accepted the drink with a grateful nod and smile.

'I am Prince Maeloc. My father, the King, bid me greet you. You have given the Kingdom of Kernow back its spiritual heart, its hope. We are all in your debt.'

Fine words, but Brandan doubted their sincerity. The Prince bristled with suspicion and distrust. A thin, nervous young man who looked as if he could no more wield a sword than lift a horse, Maeloc spoke Irish surprisingly well, though with a pronounced Cornish accent. No doubt that was why he had been chosen to attend the exhausted visitor, in preference to some commoner member of the household. Brandan handed back the flagon and sank back onto the bed, allowing himself to relax and rest. No matter what was bothering the young prince, this was a rare safe haven, and Brandan needed to recover his full strength.

'I apologise for my poor attempts to communicate with you,' the Cornish nobleman continued. 'My wife, Isolde, is an Irish princess, in case you need better help from someone who speaks your tongue.'

The bard could hear the unease and reluctance in Maeloc's voice. So that was the problem: the man was fuelled by distrust and jealousy ... Maybe Brandan's womanising reputation had preceded him. With one curse already hanging over his head like a sword held by gossamer, he had no intention of flirting with any living soul, and immediately put Maeloc at ease.

'My Prince, your knowledge of my language is excellent. There is no need to disturb your wife to aid a mere foreign warrior. Now that my duty to bring Adwen to safety with his people is fulfilled, I shall be leaving as soon as my strength allows,.'

Maeloc appeared to relax. 'You are of course free to go if you so wish. I must warn you, your presence here has divided opinion. Some say you are nothing but a bloodthirsty Irish mercenary, here to collect a high reward for returning our beloved druid. Others that you are a hero sent by the gods to return our honour as a nation.'

Groaning, Brandan closed his eyes. He needed more sleep. 'Does it matter? You have Adwen back.'

Maeloc then excused himself and, finally left alone, the warrior sank back onto the soft sheepskins and considered his next move. Looking after the stricken druid had taken up all of his focus and energy – a deficit that would take more than that watery bee piss to rectify. At least the long journey had kept homesick thoughts of Ireland and Donal at bay. Certainly the journey across the Irish Sea had stopped the mysterious persecution, but would it begin again should he return home? As his eyelids became leaden, he resolved to discuss this with Adwen. The man was powerful enough to summon a flood and return to life from beyond the Veil. If the druid could not help him, who on this Earth could?

24

Wales

'Shall I pack the holly green gown?' Delyth asked her friend, who sat by the door of her home, needing to feel the cool air from the mountain on her face. 'You look so beautiful in that and with the sun so hot …' Her words trailed off, her efforts to sound cheerful and positive failing miserably.

Seren nodded with indifference. What did it matter? Her guardian, Prince Gwion, would give her a dowry chest of beautiful clothes, jewelled fine linens fit for a new princess. None of which she wanted, preferring the humble wool of her everyday garb of her life here in the village. Everything and everyone she loved was there or at Gwion's fortress. Her new life as a married woman would be spent among strangers. She was the first of her friends to leave, but all would soon. They were witches, seers, and all would one day depart from the village to follow a destiny of their own among the communities of their birthplaces. They had always known this would happen; the carefree time of their training had flown past so quickly … New girls would arrive soon to take their places and the cycle would continue.

The date and setting for her wedding were now agreed but, at her guardian's insistence, at least it was not to be at Rhuddlan. Seren sought any comfort she could in her plight, and this was good news. With Lady Vanora holding onto her position with the Welsh king by her long talons, Seren believed there could never be enough distance between them. No doubt the witch would curse Seren's union.

Instead she was to travel with her oldest brother and a sizeable number of the Teulu to Prince Adwr's stronghold at Elfael for the wedding. Seren knew she would stay there until her marriage to Prince Daned. She would never see Rhan, Delyth and Ceinwen again. Or Adwen.

'What about the Irishman's harp?' Delyth's voice cut through her self-pitying gloom. Seren sighed; the wretched haunted thing was a burden she would prefer to leave there in the village.

Seren glanced at the gilded instrument. Without its owner it exuded a melancholy that matched her own. How could she add to its abandonment?

'Yes, *cariad*, we will pack the harp.'

A joyful carillon of birdsong woke Seren from her first night in her new home. She arose from her bed and sought out sensations to tell her about the world surrounding the fortress at Elfael. What could the day tell her about this land? The first rosy beams of sunlight shone unseen by her on a mountainous region encircling steep foothills, but Seren knew they were there by the feel of the colder air swept down from peaks still capped with snow. She could smell the lush grass around the fortress and hear the bleat of many sheep and their well-grown lambs as they peacefully grazed around the stronghold. She had the strong sense it was a spectacular landscape, more dramatic than the gentler forests and hills of her home. Though it was dawn, the warmth from the rising sun was already strong against her face. Reluctantly, she would have to wear a veil when walking or riding outside today; a ruddy or tanned face was the sign of a peasant, not a high-born lady.

The fortress stood massive and brutal on the edge of the Brecons. She had been well received when her party had arrived late the night before, and had it not been for her hopeless love for Adwen, she could have accepted her fate with better spirits. A household servant brought her a simple breakfast of warm bread, honey and fresh spring water and helped her dress. Seren learnt what she could about the woman, finding out she was a homely, honest widow approaching thirty summers old.

'What is your name, my new friend?'

Seren could hear the confusion and fluster in the maid's voice as she answered. 'My lady? Can you not see I am just a serving woman?'

'I cannot,' Seren answered, with a reassuring smile, 'but I am still interested in knowing your name. I am alone in the darkness in this strange place; I need someone to be my friend and my eyes.'

Seren waited until the woman had recovered from the embarrassment of her mistake. The sparkling clarity of her witch eyes made it easy for people to forget she was blind. 'My name is Rhosyn, my lady. I was picked to serve you. Normally I work in the kitchens here in Elfael.'

'From now, "Fair Rose", you will remain with me as my companion. If that is all right with you?'

Astonished and delighted at her sudden elevation in status, the woman dropped to the floor in gratitude and kissed the hem of Seren's garb.

'Your first task, Rhosyn, is to choose a dress for yourself from my garments. It will be something that won't stink of cooking fat. The second is to describe what manner of man I will be marrying ... and please be honest.'

Seren patted the bed to encourage the woman to sit beside her and braced herself to learn what her future as a bride would be.

Later that morning, Rhosyn helped her new mistress take a stroll around the inner courts of the fortress. She guided her to a little haven of peace, a wooden bench surrounded by a few slender apple trees growing from a lawn of mossy grass. Wild flowers grew beneath and around the trees; flowers that were encouraged to grow there. Clearly there had once been a lady's hand working her influence on this dwelling-place of warriors, although Seren's future father-in-law had sired no daughters. Across the courtyard, men at arms were sparring, their bellows of encouragement and taunting banter rising above the clash of metal against metal.

Despite this noisy mock warfare, Seren could hear the flitter and tweet of small birds in the branches, smell the delicate fragrance of the blooms. A group of men walked close by, nobles judging by the swish of their long cloaks of fine fabric. They rudely ignored Seren's presence, but her sharper-than-normal hearing caught much of what they said. It was not good.

'Why should I accept a feeble-witted cripple?' The man sounded young, petulant. 'I don't care how good her bloodlines are. I will not accept this outrage.'

Another, slightly older man answered, his tone mocking. 'Calm down, brother. At least the wench is pretty and beddable ... It could have been much worse, Daned. Look at the fat hag poor Ceredig was forced to wed to gain land and a fortress in Powys.'

Someone else joined in the banter. 'And you can do whatever you like in front of her; your bride won't be able to see you.'

'At least Ceredig ended up with worthwhile property,' Seren's future husband sneered. 'All I get from the bitch's household is a trunkful of gold and trinkets and some nags. No doubt worn out and lame.'

Seren's eyes filled with tears. So that was what they thought of her, a sightless burden. And had they not been told she was also a witch? One that could be summoned to serve the King of Cymru? Unaware of the conversation amongst the young nobles, Rhosyn leapt to her feet as her young mistress tried to rush away in distress. The lady had not brought her stick and was in danger in an unfamiliar environment.

'Take me back to my quarters,' Seren demanded, 'by some route away from the men of the royal Teulu.'

The maid did her best, but seeing the two women hurriedly skirting the courtyard, the young nobles crossed to intercept their escape.

'Brother, I do believe your lovely young bride is here in person.'

Burning with shame at the open scorn in the man's voice, Seren kept her head down. She was thankful none of Prince Gwion's Teulu was within earshot; wars between royal households had been started with less provocation. To add to the insult, a callused hand reached out to raise her head.

'See Daned, the little star from the north is not just pretty, she is slender and beautiful. And she will never see what an ugly, under-endowed bastard you are when you screw her.'

'This is no way to talk to a high-born lady,' Rhosyn countered with great courage. 'Your father, Prince Adwr, would be shamed by your insolence.'

'Silence, woman,' Daned snarled, 'or you will be tending pigs instead of a sightless, fatherless discard.'

Seren stood tall, gathering up her tattered dignity as she fought back any sign of weakness and tears. 'Believe me, the prospect of being joined in wedlock with a spoilt boor of a younger princeling is hardly enticing. A chinless, beardless little wretch, the runt of Adwr's litter. But this union is desired by your father and by my guardian, and unless you want a war between the two principalities, I would suggest you shut up and put up with the situation.'

Daned answered her spirited defiance with a churlish spit at the ground by her feet. 'A war would be preferable to taking you. I wouldn't ride a blind horse, keep a sightless hound or pay a defective whore to service me.'

Seren heard the young Prince turn on his heel and storm off across the courtyard, his furious pace accompanied by the creak of leather and the jingle of spurs – long, rowelled spurs. It seemed that Daned was as cruel to his horses as he was to women. What had she done to deserve this? No-one could be as faithful a servant to the gods as she.

25

Brittany

An urgent tug at his bed coverings awoke Hereward with a start from a deep, dreamless sleep. The first good night's rest he'd enjoyed since fleeing Normandy. Despite the deep frustration of being stuck at Blaez's court, confounded by the long run of bad weather, the genuine warmth and hospitality of the Bretons had given Hereward a much needed, thorough rest.

'My lord,' whispered a servant, 'please make haste. The seas are calm and a fast, sound ship is leaving for Kernow this morning.'

Hereward tempered his excitement with anxiety. Cornwall? Another hostile Celtic nation. Perhaps he could persuade the captain to make a detour and drop him off on the English coast. But a fine day and a ship represented too good an opportunity to pass by, with the nightmare-inducing thought of Guillaume and his hell-spawned weapons gaining in strength every passing day.

He dressed quickly and, bundling up his new belongings, sought out audience with the King to thank him and take his leave.

He found Blaez in the courtyard, already mounted, with a servant holding a horse ready saddled for Hereward. The King's generosity extended to escorting him to the dockside. Hereward realised he would miss Blaez, who had become something of a wise father figure.

'Young man, I do not envy you the task ahead. Could any man believe the reality of the threat from Normandy without seeing the evidence for himself? Here is a scroll bearing my seal to give you protection in Kernow. King Cadoc and I are good allies, as close as blood brothers. You will come to no harm there.'

The King passed over the ornate gold-bound scroll with its large red wax seal then signalled forward a warrior bearing a large leather-bound bundle.

'And some hard evidence your King can see and touch for himself. One of the Norman lances ... the one found piercing right through the stout barrel of a full-grown ox bull. See, it is stained by the beast's blood.'

Hereward took possession of the objects with a respectful bow but dared to question his benefactor. 'My lord King, I have no wish to show ingratitude or lack of faith, but is there any way I can be taken to an English shore?'

Blaez smiled with understanding as he nudged forward his horse to head to the harbour. 'Of course the captain will try, Hereward. Your urgent mission will be best served by landing on Saxon soil. But there can be no guarantee … You are always at the mercy of the winds and tides.'

Bowing in acceptance and farewell, Hereward began to thank the King but was stopped by Blaez's raised hand.

'I have enjoyed your company, young Saxon. You are a good man despite your lineage and demanding faith that will bear no others. I have placed a heavier burden than maybe you can carry by sending you home. You may find yourself cursing my interference before long.'

Within the hour, Hereward was at sea, stood at the bow of stout cargo ship, single-masted, built of overlapping pitch-painted oak planks. A slow vessel with its one rectangular yellow sail and no added power from rows of men and oars. A clumsy tub compared with the sleek, swift Norman and Viking long ships that ruled these waters. Hereward did not care about the vessel's shortcomings or its reeking cargo of untanned cattle skins to trade, only that the ship dipped and soared across the rare benign waves, glassy and glimmering with morning sunshine. The rugged Breton coastline soon was lost to sight and Hereward's gaze turned to the approaching British Isles and to England.

Such good fortune was not to last; such was the fickle, cruel nature of the seas around his home isles. A strengthening wind raised the waves and tore at the single sail, forcing the captain to change direction rather than risk the ship blowing over and capsizing. Hereward watched the nearing English coast disappear behind brown, foam-crested waves and dark, lowering cloud. His eyes were seared by a flash of lightning. A storm. He saw the anxiety spread among captain and crew … They had no choice but to attempt to outrun the tempest and make land wherever they could.

At first Hereward made himself useful, helping the crew secure their cargo, marvelling at how surefooted the mariners were despite waves crashing across the deck threatening to wash all overboard. As the fury of the waves grew, Hereward realised the fear of the seafarers had focused on him; he'd picked up enough Breton to make out their curses. They bellowed above the howling winds, demanding their captain throw the foreigner overboard as a placatory sacrifice to their dark god Melegant. Heroically, the captain refused, but with their terror increasing with every lashing assault by wind-crazed waves, Hereward was all too aware that a lethal mutiny could break out at any minute. He found a defendable space by the stern and, grabbing his sword, prepared to fight for his life.

The captain used all his strength and a lifetime's worth of skill to keep the ungainly old ship ahead of the turbulent winds, moving ever further away from their destination but keeping afloat. Great swathes of freezing seawater dashed against its sides but the ship merely groaned with the assault on its oak planks and stubbornly rode out the monstrous waves, rising until almost upright in the water and crashing down with the bow disappearing beneath the roiling seas. The mariners had to concentrate on staying secure: any attempt to move across the decks could have led to their instant death, washed overboard. This bought Hereward more time, but even half blinded by stinging salt spray, clinging to the rigging for his life, the Saxon stayed alert for any moves against him.

An excited cry rang out across the deck as the raging tempest began to abate and someone caught a glimpse of land. Gradually, the valiant little ship pulled clear of the storm and into calmer seas bathed in strange, washed out yellow light from the setting sun. Even so, it was not the best of news: the landscape was a jagged mass of cliffs and rock formations, foaming as the waves crashed ashore. There was nowhere to land. With none of the mariners willing to look Hereward in the eye after their murderous outburst, he stood by the Captain, whose strong arms still held tight at the helm despite the exhausting battle with the storm. Though they were in calmer seas, the surf crashing against the cliffs held danger of its own.

'I fear we are far from our destination, my lord,' the Captain murmured in apology.

A smiling Hereward clapped the man on the shoulder. 'We are safe, alive, thanks only to your superb seamanship. That is all that matters'.

The Saxon looked out across the darkening landscape, knowing they would be in danger from hidden rocks and unlit promontories if they didn't make landfall soon … wherever in the known worlds that was. Realising the folly of staying close to such a treacherous shore after nightfall, the Captain slewed the vessel away and headed out to open water. A wise move rewarded by calming sea and clearing sky. Before long, there were stars to navigate by and a westerly breeze to fill the sail.

Within three hours of fair sailing, the crew were cheering at the sight of landing lights flickering in a distant harbour. Hereward's heart raced with a thrill of excitement. Landfall at last, and by God's grace, it would be on English soil.

26

Lyonesse

Hereward did his best to hide an overwhelming surge of disappointment as the ship made safe anchor at a small harbour of piled stone, lit by a circle of pitch torches. He could see straightaway that this was a town that had no fear of visitors from the seas. By that alone, he knew he was not home; England's coastline was on constant alert to the danger from marauding Norse and Danish seawolves.

He discovered that the Captain had skilfully steered the storm-beaten vessel to a group of islands off the Cornish coast. To the Bretons, it was the Land of Ys; to the Celts it was Lyonesse, a land of mystery and ancient legend; and to the Vikings the isles were called Syllingar. Hereward knew them as the Isles of Scilly. A fiercely independent and peaceful, safe haven, but still far from home. He barely took in his surroundings in the crowded dockside inn where the crew took refuge, sinking onto a musty but clean sacking pallet stuffed with straw and fleabane herb, and falling into a deep, dreamless sleep.

At dawn, he awoke to the tantalising aroma of fresh bread cooking and the sound of cheerful, hearty voices outside the inn. He quickly reached inside his tunic, and gave a gasp of relief: the oilskin-wrapped missive from King Blaez and the pouch of coin he had strapped to his chest were still there. His exhaustion the night before had been so complete, anyone could have robbed him with ease.

Stumbling outside to a bright dawn and pleasing early warmth, Hereward discovered his first clues as to why these isles remained so curiously free from strife. Arranged around a dockside cobbled square were stalls manned by people of many origins. He saw tall Vikings striding past Saxons with no enmity, traders from many Celtic lands, and evidence of descendants from the original denizens of the British Isles, small in stature, swarthy, dark-eyed people, as mysterious as their ancient language and origins.

Hereward began to relax. He could not remember a time since first leaving England when he had been able to walk freely with no sense of hostility or danger. Here, no-one seemed to care who or what he was, the only approach was from the traders hawking their wares, addressing him in good English. It had been a long time since he had heard his own language spoken without an accompanying curse or undertone of contempt.

He bought some bacon and fresh bread and a flagon of light beer and decided to break his fast sitting on some flat rocks by the beach, an expanse of silver sand over which small waves from a now benign, turquoise sea broke in ripples of rustling foam. As he finished the simple but delicious fare, he became aware of a young woman approaching him across the sand. She walked confidently, her head held high, a slight smile lighting up her features. Even from a distance, Hereward could make out a challenging twinkle in her cornflower-blue eyes.

Saxon by her garb, she was not beautiful in the conventional reasoning of the Saxon courts, but Hereward found her looks fascinating. And sadly, by the evidence of her tawny hair hidden by a headdress, she was married.

'You have chosen a pleasant spot to welcome in the new day, my lord.'

Startled, he rose to leave, but her smile disarmed him with its candour. 'Please, there is no need for alarm. Everyone knows by your garb and manner that you are a Saxon of noble birth. These are very small isles and word spreads faster than a cormorant diving for fish.' She gave an impudent curtsey. 'My name is Elgitha, by the way, and I am a denizen of Lyonesse. Welcome to the enchanted isles.'

Hereward bowed his head and smiled. 'Are they enchanted? Certainly the light seems to have a strange bright glow, and this peaceful community of erstwhile sworn enemies is hard to comprehend.'

'The ruling council is drawn from all the peoples who have chosen to settle here, all races are equal and no brawling is allowed. That is why we love it here.' Elgitha reached down and picked up a large seashell, the complex inner spiral a delicate shade of almond pink. She handed it to Hereward as if a great prize. 'There was once a great and prosperous kingdom here. The original Lyonesse. One day the sea arose and swallowed most of the land, drowning whole towns and many people. Some even say,' she continued, her voice lowering to a mysterious tone, 'on certain moonlit nights around Samhain, those who were lost return to wander around their drowned homes. Lamenting …' She laughed. 'But you know what those Celts are like for a good spooky story!'

Hereward smiled, nodding in agreement, having spent the last October in Brittany and experienced their enthusiastic celebration of Samhain. He bowed, ready to take his leave. The peace he had found was too great a blessing to lose by getting into a brawl with some jealous husband. Two young people in deep conversation on an empty beach would take some explaining.

'Mistress, I must take my leave of you … lest your spouse thinks something is amiss.'

A fleeting cloud passed over the young woman's deep blue eyes. 'My husband has passed onward to the Summerlands, leaving me here on these isles alone without even the comfort of his child.'

Puzzled, Hereward pondered on her use of a pagan term for the afterlife. Surely every Christian would speak of a soul ascending to Heaven? Clearly she was used to this confusion.

'I ran away to marry a Cornish man, a visiting young trader to Tyneham,' she explained. 'We were very much in love but obviously this did not sit well with my family. They pursued us, and my Gawan was wounded in a fight with my brothers. We escaped to Lyonesse but my brave husband died of his wounds three weeks after our arrival.'

A sorry tale of doomed romance and exile in one so young. So intriguing. He was not that naïve, of course. He realised it could all be a lie to seek the favour of a wealthy stranger. Somehow, he did not care if it was. His heart opened to the young woman, and his chivalrous, romantic nature inclined him to want to protect her.

'My name is Hereward of Mercia. I am seeking urgent passage home to England. Come back with me. It would be an honour to provide safe sanctuary in my home lands.'

Elgitha laughed and span around, arms wide to the skies. 'Lord Hereward … I know who you are. As I said, your arrival is the talk of the Saxon community here. But why should I leave this place? For damp and gloomy Mercia? It is temperate and beautiful all through the year in Lyonesse. There is peace and respect here for all, regardless of what god you worship, what language you speak.'

Hereward's mood darkened. If he failed to stir his homeland into action against the Norman nightmare, these uniquely peaceful isles would fall within hours and this lovely, spirited young woman would not be safe. He decided to confide in her; what harm could it do? These islands deserved to be forewarned about the danger too.

'My mission is of the utmost importance. We are all in grave danger from the Duke of Normandy. I must tell as many important people as I can, especially our English King. Come with me, Elgitha. You can help me warn the Cornish.'

Elgitha stepped away from him and walked a few paces onto the dry, pale sand. She span around, arms wide as if in offering to the cloudless sky, her features lit by a bitter-sweet smile that made her seem less comely and more beautiful.

'My lord, you cannot appreciate how much freedom means to one such as me. The dutiful daughter of a wealthy villein, promised since childhood to be the handfast wife to a powerful lord – an old man who already had a church-blessed but barren wife. He wanted me too, young enough to bear him heirs and pretty enough for him to enjoy the begetting … That was all I was to him, a healthy brood mare of good Saxon stock.'

She could no longer maintain the smile. 'Then I met Gawan and knew the true meaning of love. So, you can see, Hereward of Mercia. Only on these enchanted isles can I be truly free. Maybe find love again one day, and it will not matter here if he is Christian or Pagan, Viking or Breton. I can follow my heart in Lyonesse.'

Hereward sighed. She was right of course. But the freedom of these lovely, fragile isles was only an illusion, a temporary blessing that would one day fall to a determined conqueror; if not Guillaume, then another.

'I wish your charmed life here could continue forever. Really, Elgitha, I do with all my heart.'

Hereward stepped down from the rock to take her hands in his, all too aware of a thrill coursing through him from her touch. Was it so crazy to think about love at such a short encounter, to believe that this was the woman he wanted as his wife, to bear his sons? Or was it some enchantment at work from the deep, old magic of Lyonesse? He had to continue, to let her understand the danger she was in.

'I told you I am on a mission to warn our own people and also the Celts of the terrible danger we all face from the Bastard of Normandy. Nowhere is more vulnerable to his hell-spawned weapons and mighty army than these islands. I need your help. The people of Lyonesse need your help.'

Hereward paused, composing himself before venturing into dangerous territory: the world of nightmare visions and the threat of demons.

'Tell me truthfully, Elgitha, has anyone had a terrible vision … of a battlefield soaked in blood and piled high with corpses?'

'And a huge, eerie raven flying over the death and destruction?' Elgitha continued, eyes widening in fear and wonder. 'Yes. Old Mistress Trethweryth has had such nightmares many times. But we dismissed them as signs of the cruelty of old age, that she was losing her mind.' Elgitha fixed him with her candid gaze. 'But she isn't crazy, is she?'

The young woman began to walk back along the sands toward the town, halted, then returned to Hereward. 'I think you will need more than one voice to spread this message. Let me take you to the Wise Council. Maybe they can find a way to help.'

27

Cornwall

The wise men of Lyonesse had listened to and believed Hereward; well, at least, they had trusted the missive from Blaez of Brittany and the words of their own ancient seer. Within a day and a night of his addressing the Council – a gathering of respected men of every race on the Isles, who sat around a large circular slab of polished granite – Hereward was granted the help he needed. They gave him safe passage on a good, fast Viking merchant ship with an assembly of several volunteers: brave men who could see the urgency of the young Saxon's mission and wanted to help – or else to have an adventure. Either way, Hereward was grateful for their company.

As he stepped on board the ship, Hereward could see the familiar red-gold of Elgitha's long tresses, caught by the brisk wind and dancing like a fiery pennant. Steadying herself on some strong, tarred rigging, she stood at the bow, looking out toward England and the heartache she'd fled from.

'It was kind of you to come to wish me farewell, Mistress Gawan.'

Elgitha laughed. 'My Lord Hereward, if you want me to leave this ship, you must throw me into the sea. I am joining your mission.'

Hereward could not hide his delight to have her with him, despite the dangers they faced back in England. If her murderous family discovered Elgitha had returned, would they still pursue her despite her being under the protection of an Earl's son? He doubted it. Especially if he made her his lawful wife under God.

The ship cast off and made good progress across a choppy sea, with a steady wind in her sails. The sky remained a cloudless canopy of azure, like the Virgin's cloak, and Hereward said a prayer of gratitude to the Blessed Lady, the Star of the Sea, for her benevolence for granting him safe passage. Later, as he watched the approaching landfall grow ever closer on the horizon, he felt Elgitha's arm interlink with his.

'Will they believe us?' she asked him. 'You are the only one with status and a letter from a King. We are just a rag taggle group of unwelcome exiles from Lyonesse.'

Hereward sighed. He had thought the same thing many times during the voyage.

'Maybe our people will not. But that must not stop us from trying. If we fail, we must ride to Cornwall and Wales and hope they will listen. We cannot allow Guillaume to take one inch of British soil.'

Brave words that did not convince even himself. If the Duke of Normandy invaded these lands, could anything beyond divine intervention stop him? A wiser man than Hereward would not have returned to England but taken this lovely woman and fled to somewhere beyond the Bastard's reach. Perhaps to seek sanctuary with the powerful Scottish King, whose reign was blessed by the Pope and whom Guillaume could attack only if he was willing to damn his immortal soul with excommunication, and even risk intervention by a Papal army drawn from every Christian kingdom in Europe. Scotland would be the last safe haven. But Hereward was not that wise a man. He could not live under the shadow of cowardice and treachery.

He would live or die serving King Harold on English soil.

28

Wales

The forbidding high walls of the fortress at Elfael were hung with garlands of meadow flowers, though the blooms did nothing to soften the structure's brute design. Banners hung proclaiming the emblem of the noble house of Adwr, a fierce black boar with large, blood-stained tusks on a white background. Seren's blindness hid the cruel truth, that as she was only a ward of Prince Gwion, his banners were not hung in her honour. No-one had bothered to seek out her real father's lordly emblem of a silver star and stooping falcon against a background of deep blue. This omission was sufficiently offensive to trigger a blood feud, but with hopes of a successful marriage and no taste for another internal war, it was ignored by Gwion's party and no mention made to the bride.

The courtyards filled with arriving guests, greeted by an air heavy with the mixed aromas of preparation for a great feast, one to be enjoyed by noble and peasant alike. Everyone except the unhappy bride and groom. To their despair, the betrothal was binding: both Princes had insisted upon the union and there was to be no war.

Seren stood by her high window, as sorrowful as a wild bird trapped in a cage, unable to alter her fate. The heady scents of the flowers combining with those of the cooking made her queasy, and she yearned for the freshness of the air high up the mountains encircling the stronghold. Down in this valley, the summer heat rendered the air hot and stifling, a pall as heavy as the bridal gown she was forced to wear that day. The gown belonged to Daned's family, and all house of Adwr brides wore it. A monstrosity of heavy yellow linen encrusted with gold embroidery and jewels. A matching veil attached to a gold crown awaited her, the weight threatening to crush her skull.

Her own adoptive family had arrived earlier that morning but she had not spoken to them yet. She counted this a blessing, unsure whether or not she could hide her distress from people so familiar and so loved.

'Drink this, my lady.' Her maid pressed a silver goblet into her hand. 'It will help.'

'If will help only if it is poison, Rhosyn,'

The maid sighed, distressed by her mistress's deep sorrow. Her own wedding had been a love match, a cause for genuine celebration. There was something unnatural, something cursed by so much ceremony, feasting and festivity arranged for the unwilling union of two people who clearly despised each other, but such were the ways of the nobles. Not for the first time Rhosyn was grateful to the gods that she was born a commoner.

'Just cool, fresh spring water, drawn from a deep well.'

She waited until Seren had finished, hating to hurry her, but it was almost time. As was their custom, the wedding would take place at the great circle of stones where the gods had blessed young couples for countless centuries. But first there were old traditions to endure. Prince Gwion and a captain of his Teulu entered the chamber, armed with wooden swords, while Rhosyn threw an old peasant cloak over the bride – but not before the old man had wiped a tear from his eye at her delicate beauty and the loss of one he thought of as a daughter.

Meanwhile the Bidder or *Gwahoddwr* went around the stronghold and surrounding settlement inviting guests to the wedding. He carried a staff of stripped willow brightly decorated with coloured ribbon, which he used to rap on closed doors. Some of the peasants hid, pretending to be out in fields, for although the wedding meant plenty of free good food, custom also required giving the bride and groom a gift of coin, despite the wealth of the royal couple.

What should have been a merry, boisterous cavalcade of the groom and his supporters arriving at the bride's quarters to 'kidnap' her and take her to the great stones, became an ugly distortion of the start of the wedding rituals. Seren gave a little shriek of alarm at thunderous pounding and kicking against the heavy oak door. The men were already drunk, their demands littered with lewd language. Gwion held on to his ward's hand, sorrow and regret sinking deep into his soul … What had he done? Was it too late to stop this travesty of a wedding? By rights, he could fight them, refuse to let them take her away. With his Teulu, battle their way from the stronghold and take Seren back to the safety of his lands. They were of course greatly outnumbered and would not succeed, but that would surely be more honourable than to give Seren up to these beasts.

Seren felt the emotion surging through her guardian and knew she had to act fast; the door would soon yield to the bludgeoning. She could not allow her wedding to turn to tragedy and bloodshed. As the hammering increased in volume, the banter becoming still more menacing, Seren turned her head to her guardian. 'My Lord, do not consider resisting. I do not want bloodshed to stain my soul for eternity. I accept this union freely. It is my free choice to wed Daned today. Please, open the door.'

Rhosyn shook her head in sorrow, unable to look the girl's noble guardian in the eye. Could ever a young bride have walked so unwillingly yet with such great courage toward a groom who loathed and had rejected her already?

Seren, clad in a gauzy nightgown, lay on the bridal bed and awaited her fate. Her husband of ten hours was taking his time over consummating the union; Daned was still down in the feasting hall, carousing with his brothers and other members of the Adwr Teulu. Prince Gwion and her family had already begun the long journey home, having witnessed that the wedding held beneath the hawthorns beloved of the Great Mother had been correctly conducted. Once vows had been made and Seren and Daned had held hands to leap over the ceremonial fire, there was nothing more to be done. They had stayed for some of the seemingly endless wedding feast and then gone. There had been no reason to linger; Seren belonged to the House of Adwr now.

As a witch and midwife, Seren knew all about the stark facts of procreation and had helped bring the products of such couplings safely into the world. What it felt like to have the hidden centre of her womanhood penetrated by a man was a mystery. Rhosyn and the other married serving women had done their best to prepare her, giggling as they advised her to drink plenty of mead during the wedding feast, then to relax and allow her husband to force his way into her without a struggle. It would hurt but not for long – then the pleasure would begin. They did not add that the pleasure would depend on a considerate and loving partner, something in their minds Daned clearly was not.

Seren had followed their advice and was sleepy with a surfeit of good wedding mead. Maybe she could sleep through the whole act? She doubted Daned would notice or care. His duty began and ended in getting her pregnant with another noble-born son to fight for the House of Adwr.

Someone burst into the room unannounced and blew out the candles. She only knew they were no longer lit by the sudden acrid smell and the lack of their comforting warmth. The man undressed quickly without speaking a word. As he grabbed her, she could smell the reek of ale and mead on his breath, the sweat of desire on his naked body, the heat of lust emanating from his loins.

Something was wrong. This was not the wiry frame of the young prince but a heavier man, skin lax with folds and wrinkles. It was not her husband! Before she could protest, she was roughly thrown onto her back, her nightgown torn off. The man forced her legs apart and, holding tightly onto her wrists, pinning them to the bed, began to probe her small mound with his engorged member.

Outrage and fear spurred Seren on. Though held tight by the man's lust-emboldened strength, she did her best to struggle and scream for help. Puzzled by the reaction of the hitherto compliant young bride, her assailant loosened his grip long enough for Seren to push herself free.

'Who are you? How dare you try to violate me? I am the bride of Prince Daned.'

Scornful laughter met her protests, and a deep voice answered, needing no identification. It was her father-in-law, Prince Adwr.

'My son is not man enough for this bedding. My seed will be far better, of purer royal blood.'

Trapped in the room with the powerful old warlord, Seren prayed for protection to Morgan, the fearsome goddess of vengeance and men's destruction.

'And don't try any witch tricks on me, Seren. I have a powerful talisman of binding and protection made by my chief druid. Relax, girl, this will be far more pleasurable for you then a swift, reluctant tupping by that young ram. My greater skill and experience will bring you the reward of enjoyment and gratification.'

'My lord Prince, you dishonour me with this insult, this crime. At my wedding, you agreed to become my father in every way, to respect and protect me. That is why my guardian chose you, for your reputation of being an honourable man.'

Pinning her down on the bed again, this time entering her in one well-practised thrust, Adwr gave a grunt of pleasure as he broke through her maidenhead. He whispered in her ear, 'Don't you realise, child, I am honouring you. That over-indulged brat of a son of mine would never touch you, sweet Seren. You would become a rejected, barren outcast. A pitiful life, unable to return to your family. Once your belly is filled with child, you can live in luxury, unbothered by any man's unwanted touch. No one but us will know.'

His hips began to rock in a steady rhythm, as a threatening tone entered his voice. 'In fact, no-one must know. Say one word of this to anyone and you and your serving wench will die, your bodies thrown to the pigs.'

Trapped by the Prince's weight, impaled by his forceful, painful assault, and with the talisman stifling her powers, there was nothing Seren could do but endure with tears of shame and humiliation coursing down her face. Despite the illusion of freedom at the witches' village, her life had always been under the control of powerful men. The gods had turned their faces away from her. Even the harp propped up in the corner remained mute. She was alone.

29

Wales, Summer 1065

Maybe the gods had not deserted her after all, though their aid for Seren was subtle and long-term. Despite the frequent sexual assaults by her father-in-law, she had not become pregnant. The thought of carrying the Prince's child filled her with revulsion, and as months passed without her missing her menses, Seren realised her prayers had been answered. Prince Adwr took out his disappointment with increasingly aggressive and frequent coupling. Her husband Daned avoided her completely, which was some faint comfort in an intolerable situation. The atmosphere among the Adwr royal Teulu was claustrophobic and dysfunctional bordering on insane. Ambition to become Prince fuelled all the sons and poisoned their minds toward each other and their father. With their mother long in her grave and no daughters still living, Seren had no allies at court beyond the ever faithful Rhosyn.

Seren's virtual imprisonment at Elfael was worsened by a dreadful winter, so wet and cold that people were nostalgic for the iron-hard frosts of the year before. Driving horizontal sheets of rain battered the fortress, the surrounding land became sodden and every track became an impassable nightmare of deep, slippery mud. Rainwater ran down the sides of the fortress in a steady stream for weeks on end, seeping through thatch and windows. Dry tinder became hard to acquire, every room and hall stayed steamy and damp and sickness spread through man and beast alike. This at least gave Seren a purpose: she kept herself busy preparing remedies, and her healing gifts made her popular with the ordinary people of Elfael.

He was with her again. Deep in her again, making her scream inside with repulsion and humiliation. Seren had learnt not to fight back, because that excited him, increased his pleasure and the time he took with her. She lay still, impassive, silent, her face turned to the window, imagining leaping from it and flying away from this torment.

Eventually Adwr pulled out of her with a grunt, wiping himself on her robe and dressing quickly. 'The fault must be with you, witch. I have sired seven healthy brats in wedlock and lost count of how many out of it.'

Seren could not bear to touch her now soiled, torn robe, but pulling a woollen bed cover around her, rose to her feet and holding her head high, stared straight up into his mean little eyes. 'Father, have you not realised the gods are punishing you for this crime? How could our Blessed Mother Modron bless any child born of a cursed union of violence, shame and lies?'

Adwr slapped her face so hard that she fell to the ground, but she got back to her feet straightaway.

'You speak of a curse?' he snarled. 'If you have cursed this household we can get rid of you with no loss of face or honour.'

Seren's mind raced; this was dangerous. They would not let her live to go home and tell her guardian of this terrible and cruel ordeal.

'There is no curse, Father.' She used that familial term as her only weapon to shame him. 'This torment you force me to endure will end with the arrival of a child. It is in my best interest to conceive as soon as possible.'

Adwr laughed and threw off his clothing again. 'Perhaps you should relax more and learn to enjoy the experience. I can give you great pleasure if you allow me to. My wife cheerfully embraced my advances and was blessed with ten children.'

No doubt she died in childbirth, worn out beyond her years, ridden with grief over the children that had not survived, Seren thought, with the bitter taste of contempt. Seren despised Adwr. He had stolen the precious gift she had wanted to save for Adwen, a gift of innocence and pure love. For that and the betrayal of trust and honour, she could never forgive him.

Already nearly spent, the Prince was finished this time after a few rough thrusts.

'I have done my best for you, girl. Do not let your witchcraft interfere with nature. Let a baby grow within you and your life here will become far more pleasant.'

The Prince sauntered out, grinning to himself. His treacherous sons thought he was so old? Ready for the grave? He was more hearty and virile than any of those whining milksops! In truth he was enjoying the onerous burden of helping his daughter in law conceive. With his wife long gone, Seren's tender young body was a delight. Nor would it stop when the longed-for child was born, One heir was never enough. Not with his own sons ready to tear out each other's throats like a pack of leaderless wolves over an inheritance he intended to make them wait a long time for. A very long time. Seren came from excellent high-born warrior stock, better than that of his dead wife. And it was known the King of Cymru favoured this girl for her witch's wisdom. He could use her to find favour with Llewelyn. Adwr now planned that the blind witch's son would be the next Prince, and not his strutting, hate-filled brats.

Hidden in the shadows, seething with hatred, Rhosyn waited until the loathsome Adwr was out of earshot before rushing into the bedchamber to tend to her mistress. She carried a pitcher of hot water heavily infused with aromatic flowers and sweet smelling herbs to do all she could to clean Seren's skin of the stench of that man.

Seren smiled with gratitude as she stood on a towel and let Rhosyn tend to her. The bathing was soothing. But nothing could remove the vile feeling of that man's hands and reeking sweat on her body. Sweet water could not undo the violation of her inner being. She also braced herself for the plaintive tirade she knew would come with the maid's attendance.

'Princess, you could stop this nightmare if you wanted to. You are a witch. Put some hex on that animal, shrivel up his pizzle.'

And yet again, Seren had to sigh and explain that she was bound to do no harm, that any vengeful action she took against Adwr would rebound manifold.

'It would be worth it, my lady. Teach me and I will turn that old ram into a useless wether.'

With a soft cloth, Rhosyn gently dried Seren, taking care where the Princess's soft skin was bruised and chaffed by Adwr's assault.

'At least Modron has blessed you with no child. The Divine Mother favours you as an innocent victim of that old man's lust.'

Seren sighed as her maid dressed her. 'But at the cost of my life. Adwr will not accept he has failed, and will never allow me to return home. Unless a child is conceived, I suspect I will meet with an unfortunate accident very soon.'

Shocked, Rhosyn grabbed her mistress by the hands. 'Lady, we must flee this terrible place. Get as far away from these animals as we can.'

Seren's voice echoed her hopelessness. 'Where to, sweet rose? I could not go home without bringing shame and warfare to my guardian's household.'

Rhosyn did not let go of Seren's hands. This plan to escape was their only chance to have a future. She was a stubborn woman with a courageous soul and a strong sense of justice. She was even prepared to poison the foul old goat of a Prince to protect her beautiful, vulnerable Princess.

'Where would your heart tell you to go?' she asked.

Without hesitation, Seren answered, 'Cornwall.'

'Perfect.' Rhosyn danced around a startled Princess. 'So perfect. We will be far beyond their reach, and no blame could be placed on Gwion's Teulu. We will live simply, just quiet, happy lives as new dwellers in the magical land of Kernow.'

A dream. The reality was two vulnerable women trapped in the fortress of a Prince with a powerful and loyal Teulu at his command. How on earth could they escape? Seren was never without an armed escort, even for the simplest journey to gather healing herbs and roots. Complacency on the sentinels' part and the advantage of surprise were their only hopes. She needed time to make a plan. One that had to succeed, for the consequences of being caught would be severe and fatal.

'Rhosyn, when my next gift from the moon is due, I want you to spread the word that I am with child. That should buy us some time and keep that monster from my bedchamber.'

The maid's eyes grew wide. Princess Seren was taking her seriously – they really were going to flee! Rhosyn's heart hammered fit to burst out of her chest as the consequences sank in. Of course she would flee with her young mistress. There could be no turning back.

'In the meantime,' Seren continued, 'I need you to be as sharp-eyed as a hawk to discover when the fortress sentinels are at their most lax, to discreetly find the best route to Kernow. Work out the fastest horses to steal.'

Seren reached out to find the maid's hand. 'But most of all, you must not share this with anyone. Do you understand, Rhosyn? Not a single living soul must know what we are planning.'

40

Opportunity finally arrived with preparations for the *Gwyl Awst* fair, a joyous event celebrating summer, which brought in to Elfael people from all over the neighbouring lands. The area surrounding Adwr's stronghold would throng with many strangers and their beasts of burden. A chaos so distracting, Seren was convinced two women dressed as peasants could slip through unnoticed. From their boasting, Seren took comfort that the royal men and their followers would revel in free-flowing mead and beer and the arrival of many fresh faced women from the country: new young flesh to debauch.

With time to prepare, Rhosyn hid malodorous peasant garb in her mistress's chambers, keeping the tell-tale smell from Adwr by sweetening it with a liberal sprinkling of lavender water. Between them, the women stitched coin and jewels into the hems to sustain them on the long journey to Cornwall. Unknown to her gentle mistress, Rhosyn also hid small but sharp daggers within her garb, praying there would be no need to use them. Though gelding that old bastard would have given her much satisfaction.

Despite Seren's announcement of being with child, a delighted Adwr continued his foul visits, though he tempered his assaults with a new tenderness and care. Seren feared that her time-gaining ruse would fail and the nightmare would never end. The women knew they had no choice but to seize the opportunity of *Gwyl Awst* and flee for their lives.

The wait for the feast day was long and torturous. Both Seren and her maid became exhausted with the effort of keeping up the pretence that nothing was afoot. Seren was at least able to use the excuse of her pregnancy to cover any signs of anxiety.

On the morn of festival eve, Seren stood by her bedchamber window, her heart racing. 'Not long now, she whispered, holding her silver triple moon talisman in a tight grip. 'Please Great Mother ... deliver us safely from this prison.'

Her heart lay beyond the noisy bustle of new arrivals setting up camp in the valley below Elfael's ramparts. The newcomers had been coming in a steady stream since daybreak, and already the pastures had a merry air from laughter and many musicians. Seren's fearful mind though was focused to the south, to Cornwall, which seemed as far and unreachable as *Ynis Gwydrin*, the Isle of Enchantment.

The festival morning finally dawned. Both determined but also frightened, Seren and Rhosyn prepared by pulling their normal clothes over the peasant garb. This was a wise precaution, for a messenger from Adwr arrived as they finished a small taste of their breakfast, the rest hidden away for the journey. He announced in cold, officious tones that the Prince had commanded the Lady Seren to remain in her quarters during the fair. This was ostensibly out of fatherly concern for her supposed condition; the fair brought strangers, and strangers often brought illness. That the fair also would have given her a chance to send word of her ill treatment had not been overlooked by the Princess.

The women accepted the order with good grace and no sign of peevish disappointment. The man found nothing suspicious and returned to his master with Seren's message in reply: that her condition left her so nauseous and weak that she was grateful for the kindness shown and would prefer to spend the festival time confined to her quarters.

Nerves frayed, the women waited until midday to leave the castle. At that time the summer fair was at its height, cheers and screams of mock terror rising from the audience as they watched a troupe of myth dancers on a makeshift dais. The beat and jangle of roving musicians mingled with laughter and general uproar from the happy crowds. Peasantry and nobles alike treasured the diversion from their daily toil and woes. Too much so to notice two particular peasant women strolling through the crowds, carrying bundles on their backs from their journey to Elfael. Only the journey they were taking was actually as far away from the stronghold as possible.

The nervous escapees were forced to remain at the fair for most of the morning; two women leaving alone at the height of the festivities might have aroused curiosity. The only advantage to this was that it gave them a much-needed opportunity to stock up on things they would need for the journey. Rhosyn bought a scraggy mountain pony, aged, foul-tempered but sound enough to travel, and loaded him up with supplies and blankets and the well-disguised gilded harp, cleverly dodging the snapping yellow teeth of the pony's displeasure.

Just after midday, some of the local women, all heavily pregnant and with tired youngsters tugging at their skirts, began to wander home. Unable to bear another terrifying moment fearing discovery, Seren and Rhosyn took their chance and wandered in their wake, tugging at the reins of the reluctant pony. Every yard they walked away from the fair without someone raising a hue and cry was a blessing from the Great Mother. But although their hearts were hammering, they could not break into a run, not within eyesight of the stronghold. Only once they had passed through the surrounding valley and put a solid stand of old oaks behind them could the women think about increasing their pace.

The burden of navigating was heavy on Rhosyn. It was important for them to take the swiftest route down to Cornwall; any delay could be fatal. Seren was gambling that if Adwr tried to track them down– and his pride would make that inevitable – the searching party would head first toward her home. They would push fast, determined to capture her before she could reach the sanctuary of Prince Gwion's borders. But this was just a hope; there was no room for complacency.

With her servant stepping ahead, leading the pony, Seren held on to a harness strap and, walking close to the animal's shoulder, relied on its eyes to guide her across the rough, unknown terrain. Despite her fear, there was pleasure too, in the feel of springy grass beneath her feet after the cold stone of the stronghold; in the sensation of warm, clean air on her face after the stifling, smoke-clogged atmosphere of Elfael; in the peeping sound of swifts hunting above her head. Freedom. Even if it were for only a few, snatched hours, she would revel in every moment of her escape from the cruelty and oppression of Adwr and his verminous family.

Thankfully, the summer fair at Elfael had left the countryside empty of most of its scattered population; the fleeing women skirted all hamlets and villages, all remote farmhouses, eager to avoid being spotted. The locals were loyal to their Prince, and the two escapees would get no succour or protection in this land. Having been cooped up for so long in the stronghold, Seren soon began to tire, but her companion was loath to stop ... not yet. They needed far more miles between them and any pursuers, and the welcome cover of darkness was still many hours away.

Rhosyn made a rudimentary back harness from Alder saplings and loaded herself up with as much as she could carry comfortably. Then she helped her mistress up to sit on the pony. Seren was feather light and far less of a burden than their supplies, and to Rhosyn's delight, the little animal stepped out with a quicker pace and less sullen disposition. And with each sprightly hoof beat, Rhosyn felt a renewed flicker of reborn hope ...

41

Seren and Rhosyn had expected betrayal, recapture and death in their flight from Elfael and the baleful family that ruled it. They had not expected that they would reach the *Afon Hafren* – the wide, turbulent stretch of water that separated them from the sanctuary of Cornwall – and that when they did so, they would have to remain there for many months …

With a blind girl and an elderly pony, they had made such slow, cautious progress across the rugged countryside of their homeland that summer had gone and the mist-garbed time of early autumn had reclaimed the land. Avoiding villages and towns whenever possible, living off the land and sleeping rough, the two women had felt the stress of their flight take its toll on them. They were now gaunt, and dark shadows rimmed their eyes. Their once spry pony now showed its age with every step and struggled to travel many miles each day.

Many times, Rhosyn tried to lighten the animal's burden by removing and discarding the harp while Seren slept, but the instrument was an enchanted, unearthly thing that stung her hand like an enraged hornet. Both women hated the unwanted harp, but it seemed they were stuck with it until it was reclaimed by the Irish bard.

If the Teulu of Prince Adwr still sought them, there was no sign of it, yet the two woman dared not slow their pace to freedom or risk communication with anyone they encountered on their journey. With such a large area to search, no doubt Adwr would pay well for any information about a young blind woman and her maid travelling alone.

One morning, they rose at first light and finally pushed on toward the coast and the last hurdle to overcome … safe passage across the Severn to Cornwall. Serenaded by a carillon of birdsong, the women made their way down a well-worn track toward the busy port of Aberthaw. The sight of the low morning sun glinting on the river on its way to becoming an estuary and then open sea, filled their hearts with hope.

But as their steps quickened, the feeling of elation gave way to hesitancy and unease. Aberthaw was the biggest town they'd encountered in their flight. By now they should be able to see smoke from breakfast fires snaking into the sky. Hear voices raised in greeting and laughter. The silence was wrong, very wrong. As they drew closer at a slower, more hesitant pace, a breeze wafting from the river toward the land brought a warning taint of decay and the stench of lime pits from the town. Sickness or warfare had brought death to Aberthaw.

Rhosyn turned the pony's head, grabbed her mistress's arm and tried to turn her away from their destination. 'We must hurry, before the poison in the air reaches us.'

Gently shaking herself free, Seren refused to change her course. 'Find yourself somewhere safe and wait for me. If there is sickness or wounded to tend, then I must go down and help. It is my duty.'

'A duty that will kill us both!' The sharpness in Rhosyn's voice betrayed her desperation; she was so tired, worn out by constant fear, lack of food, the arduous journey and the weight of responsibility looking after her blind noble-born charge. And now this, just as freedom sparkled on the waves before them ... so close.

'I have come all this way,' she went on, 'turned my back on my family, my village ... everything I have known ... just to lose my life to pestilence?'

She sighed, knowing all protest was futile, knowing Seren would bravely walk down to the town on her own. 'As if I could turn away from you now ...'

Seren felt a deep wave of guilt envelop her. She had been so wrapped up in her own misery and need to escape that she had given little thought to her companion. 'I am so sorry ... I did not know. You never mentioned a family.'

'Why should you?' Rhosyn replied with resignation. 'You are a lady. The lives of your servants are of no concern to the high-born.'

'But I am not like that ... at least I thought I wasn't.' Hot tears of shame rolled down Seren's cheeks. 'Because you thought up and organised this flight from Adwr ... I assumed there was no-one waiting for you in the valley. How callous and selfish of me ... Can you ever forgive me?'

'Well, there is no one *close*.' Rhosyn's voice assumed a hard tone to hide old sorrow. 'Not now. And that bastard would not allow the only witness to his crime against you to live. What choice did I have but to protect the only living person I care about?'

Seren reached out and found her, enveloping her in a tight embrace of love and gratitude.

'I owe my life to you, Rhosyn. And remember, I am no longer a lady. In Cornwall, we will be equals, both refugees. Hopefully both friends.'

'If we ever get there,' Rhosyn muttered. 'I know it would be easier to change the direction of the Severn than to stop you marching into that town. Let's get this over with.'

So began their extended stay in Aberthaw, whose population was stricken by the bloody flux. The feared pestilence had already claimed many lives including that of their only physician. Grateful for the arrival of a healing witch who was unafraid of the disease, the despairing town elders gave the women comfortable lodgings in the town's best tavern. Seren wasted no time preparing tinctures from her own bag of remedies and sent some of the last able-bodied townsfolk to search for a certain type of tree bark in the surrounding countryside. The rest she set to work boiling water for all the citizens to drink; Seren knew the flux was spread through filthy water, not carried on the air. Somewhere near the town was a malign source of the flux, and it would be her task to find it.

As the health of the town improved, so word of a witch healer spread. Anxious families took Seren to women in the throes of a difficult labour; to children stricken with the croup. And as her workload grew, so did the danger from Adwr's spies, who would be eager to hear news of a beautiful blind witch in Aberthaw.

As winter drew in, any hope of escape across the river seemed increasingly slim. Storms lashed the wide stretch of water, creating waves of a size normally seen only on the ocean. It was only a matter of time before Adwr's forces came to the port to seize their runaways. Rhosyn made sure the town's grateful elders knew of the danger and sacrifice made by their healer, reminded them that nobody had died of the bloody flux since the day Seren walked into town, so that they would not forget it was their duty to keep her safe, to ensure she could escape at first sign of danger.

Rhosyn made sure all that dwelled in Aberthaw knew, 'Lady Seren is blessed by the Goddess with her healing gift ... betray her and you will bring down the wrath of the Dark Mother herself!' A warning that held even more resonance at this time of Ceridwen.

Inevitably, it was not long before the town was put to the test. A family from a village beyond Aberthaw, travelling to visit relations in central Wales, joyfully relayed to anyone who would listen on their journey, how their daughter was safely delivered of a healthy baby boy despite his bad presentation in the womb. The saviour had been a slender, beautiful but blind witch. Word soon spread to reach the ears of a well-paid spy, a retired warrior from Prince Adwr's Teulu. Seren's freedom and possibly her life span now could be counted by hoof beats, dependent on the speed and stamina of the Prince's horses as a group of warriors led by Daned rode out from Elfael.

Of all things to help her, it was the baleful harp that gave Seren the first alarm of impending danger. Its occasional wistful song of longing had ceased on the day the women had arrived in Aberthaw. It had appeared to pause, as if hesitant and excited by the closeness of Cornwall. Seren was certain the Irish bard was alive and somewhere over the Severn, and with that knowledge came hope that Adwen was alive as well. Seren could never forget that day when she had said farewell to her beloved druid as he rode out to war with Brandan at his side. How she prayed the Irish warrior's prowess in battle would keep Adwen safe.

Were the two men still together? Some strange, deep instinct told her this was so. As the harp pined to be reunited with Brandan, so she yearned to be with Adwen. Somehow she knew that he would not reject the fleeing wife of an odious fool, that her lost honour would be of no importance to him.

Seren was wandering through the busy throng of a frost fair in the town when she heard the harp's shrill cry of alarm from her lodgings. She held out her long stick before her and ran along the mud- and dung-covered street, ignoring the hazards as she slipped on discarded rubbish and bumped into passers-by. Thinking someone was stealing the harp, she forced her way through the crowds in a panic. She could not lose it now she was convinced the instrument would lead her to Brandan and therefore also to Adwen. Her heart threatening to burst through her chest with exertion, she fell through the tavern door into the arms of a worried Rhosyn.

'The wretched thing has started to caterwaul,' said the woman. 'It is frightening the wits out of me!'

Helping Seren to a seat, Rhosyn then fetched her a goblet of mead.

'Drink this, you look pale as a ghost.'

Seren took a small sip of the strong brew then sighed. The harp was still there and its cry was one of impending danger.

'We must go. Now. Find some seafarer brave enough to risk the waves. That sound is a warning. Adwr has found us.'

From their quarters, the golden harp's cry grew louder and more insistent. Seren shuddered. She could almost feel the hot, laboured breath of Adwr's warhorses bearing down on the town.

'Grab the harp, Rhosyn ... we must run to the harbour and beg for passage from Aberthaw. We have no more time ...'

Witnessing her terror, the tavern-owner shouted orders to all within hearing, calling for food and clean blankets for the women. Within minutes, though reluctant to let their healer go, the townsfolk had rallied around to help the girl who had saved them from the bloody flux. Anything less they felt would be to risk the fury of Ceridwen; Rhosyn's stern warnings had done their task well.

Rhosyn carried their bundles under her strong arms and Seren brought the screaming harp. With the help of the townsfolk, they ran to the harbour and called out for anyone able to set sail immediately. At first, they were met with a wall of sullen silence. None could look the terrified women in the eyes. Though it was still early morning, the horizon was obscured by darkness, a line of storm clouds heading toward the mainland. No sane sailor would risk a crossing, despite the desperate pleading of the townsfolk. Someone shouted for horses, good fast horses, to let the women flee along the coastline. Their beasts would be fresher than those of the pursuers.

The sense of time running out coursed like ice water through Seren's veins, and she prayed out loud: 'Cerridwen ... please ... It will be these good people who will suffer from Adwr's wrath for sheltering us ... Let us get away from the town.'

The distant sound of a horse's high whinny came from beyond the valley, followed by the faint but gaining thunder of hoof beats. Adwr.

Hearing her prayer and understanding the immediate danger, an experienced old sailor named Dwl nodded a curt assent to the women and held out his hand to help the blind girl board first. His was a small fishing vessel, tough and weatherworn like its captain. With no time for farewells, Dwl cast off and trimmed his sails to move away from the dockside.

Seren sat on a bench in the centre of the vessel, hugging the now quiet harp and fretting over the punishment the town risked reaping for harbouring her. She whispered another prayer to the Dark Mother for the town to be spared Adwr's wrath. As Rhosyn joined her after stowing away their few belongings, it was clear she felt the same.

'There is nothing we can do, Seren. We offered them help and they accepted it. They could have driven us away with stones and curses or betrayed us to Adwr. May the Goddess grant them protection for their kindness and loyalty.'

Rhosyn glanced back to the town, already nearly lost to the choppy, high waves. An eerie low mist was rising from the sea, at odds with the wind and the storm in the distance. It moved away from the wind, not with it, thickening and roiling toward the land. Within minutes she could see nothing of the harbour or the town, shrouded by the strange mist.

The impenetrable mist drifted inland, beyond the town and into the surrounding hills.

Enveloped by the sudden and uncanny fog, Prince Daned and his hard-riding warriors did not see the edge of a sharp decline until their horses suddenly jinked and shied away. Still drunk and disorientated from the previous night's revelling, Daned lost his balance, unsettling his horse, which spun and dropped a shoulder, tipping the young man into a ravine to his death.

Shocked at the loss of the princeling they were honour bound to protect, the others retrieved the broken body.

'What will we do?' asked one of the soldiers as he draped the body over his horse.

'Return to Elfael. What else?' said their captain. So they turned tail and headed back home.

As they approached the borders of the house of Awdr, the captain ordered a halt.

''Twas nothing more than an accident,' he said.

The men did not mention the fog, but nodded silent agreement that they would never tell the truth of what had occurred. For they had already decided on the way home that the mist had been supernatural in origin. This thought had haunted them all and made them feel under a curse for pursuing a blind girl who had the favour of the King of Cymru.

When the body of Daned was placed before the throne, Adwr said nothing. He merely raised a tired hand to have his son removed and interred.

Although the flames remained unfanned by the silent tongues of those that had witnessed the young Prince's death, a dark discontent and fear took the occupants of the kingdom. Deep down, Awdr knew that some other force had intervened to spare the witch from his wrath. Now she was a widow, there was little point in continuing to pursue her.

Seren and Rhosyn would have been relieved to know that no-one from Adwr's Teulu ever returned to threaten Aberthaw and its people.

PART TWO

1066

1

Cornwall, January 1066

A strengthening ice-barbed wind buffeted the Irish warrior's face as he rode to the summit of an exposed tor. Patrolling the borders between the Celtic world and the enemy Saxon territory was a tedious occupation at any time of year, and traversing the harsh moorland uplands of Cornwall in the depths of winter was not Brandan's first choice of occupation. But it had to be done. He had chosen to stay and fight for the Cornish King, reasoning it was no different from his mercenary life as Na Fianna back home ... though could he ever call Ireland home again? He doubted it.

At least patrolling the borders kept him away from Castle Dore – not that there was anything wrong with the stronghold, beyond it being overcrowded and smoke-filled, or with his fair treatment by his new master, the Cornish King. Any discomfort came from close proximity to Prince Maeloc and his pretty Irish wife. No wonder the man was suspicious, constantly looking for signs of betrayal. Isolde's green eyes sparkled with mischief, and many times she had attempted to flirt openly with Brandan. There had been a time when he would have relished such a dangerous, secret coupling, but not now. A safe haven in winter in a foreign country was not something to risk on a dangerous dalliance; besides which, one curse already upon his head was one too many.

Remaining in Cornwall had been Adwen's firm advice to him. Unless Brandan could find the source of the malevolence back home, his life would remain in danger. The druid had made a pact with him: if Brandan served on the frontline against Cornwall's enemies until the danger was past, Adwen would then accompany him back to Lismore and deal with the threat himself. It was a good deal, one that the bard had accepted eagerly. Adwen was the most powerful druid in the known world, the best man to have on your side against malign supernatural forces.

Brandan had seen little action since his decision to remain at Castle Dore; the enemy army had long withdrawn far from the borders, no doubt still licking their wounds after the calamitous defeat on the banks of the River Tamar. The only occasional skirmish was against outlaw bands – desperate men on the run from their own people's justice. The scraps of information coming from spies within England explained the lack of interest in further attacks on the Celts: sickly for some time, King Edward had fallen into a deep sleep, a living death from which he was not expected to recover. All focus in England was on the succession.

The English expected Harold to become King, as their Witan's preferred choice. Ambitious enemies surrounded England; this was not the time for a mewling boy or some unwanted distant foreign relation. If Harold did gain the crown, then the bordering Celtic countries could expect trouble. The new King would have the whole of England to call on for men and arms, not just those from his Wessex earldom. Brandan was convinced the Saxon monarch would burn with desire for revenge for two ignominious defeats by the Celts. Maybe the great war all feared would be one of attrition and conquest, possibly genocide? The vision of the great raven was one of terrible slaughter beyond normal warfare. He shivered again, this time not from the cold wind but with a sense of foreboding.

Brandan pushed his new mount down the hill to ride closer to the border. It was a good-quality dark bay moorland pony – shaggy, strong and swift – though no match for the peerless Lia, who was taking a well-earned rest. Nor was the new harp he'd fashioned comparable to his gilded instrument in the safekeeping of that little Welsh witch. Would her Craft tell her its true origins? That it was not of human construct but stolen from the Sidhe, and contained the cursed and trapped spirit of a fairy? All he knew was that it was safe, and that it mourned him and called out to him in his sleep – yet another thing in his life that loved him and had had to be abandoned.

The pony's ears pricked sharply forward, its gaze fixed intently on a stand of wind-warped woodland below them. It could be just the wind moving a branch, or a herd of red deer – or a party of Saxon raiders. Brandan gathered up his party of Cornish warriors and, risking a gallop down the rock-strewn hill, headed for the woodland. Whether he brought back fresh venison or enemy heads, it was worth checking out.

With his usual fearless ferocity, he led the way down the hill, hoping for a violent skirmish with enemies … His sword was as hungry for blood as he was for action. As his pony breasted a thick swathe of ferns at the edge of the woods, a discordant yet joyful cry filled his soul. Startled, he sat back hard in the saddle, hauled in the animal's headlong charge. How could this be? It sounded like the ethereal, fairy voice of his haunted harp. Raising his sword arm, he shouted a command for the others to stop. If magic was in these woods, these ordinary warriors could be in danger – he too, of course, but Brandan was at least well versed in the ways of supernatural forces.

'There is something otherworldly in these woods,' he warned. 'I will investigate on my own.'

The thought of encountering bucca or spriggan was enough to silence any dissent among the other warriors: the Cornish preferred to keep a healthy distance from the Fae. Brandan dismounted and handed his pony's reins to one of the warriors. He'd decided to proceed on foot after seeing the deep tangle of vicious, barbed blackthorn in the woods. There was no need to injure a good pony.

Using his sword to cut a way through, Brandan entered the foliage. He was all too aware that the siren call may have been a trick from his unknown tormenter, that the power of the magic had finally tracked him down beyond Irish soil to lure him to his death. He was sick to his soul of running, of living his life as a fugitive. If he had to face his enemy as a cowardly shadow in these foreign woods, so be it.

As he stood in a clearing, he noticed an unnatural quiet: there was no bird song, no rustle of forest creature, so common before a visitation from beyond the Veil. Then a brace of pheasant broke cover in a flurry of wings and panicked clutter. Brandan shook his head. What an idiot he was. His arrival among the trees was the reason for the forest hush. He pressed on through the tangle, and soon the spirit voice began again, this time more lyrical, louder ... closer. It was his harp; what else could it be?

The warrior focused on the harp's song, plaintive, calling out for him, wanting his long fingers to caress its strings again. It could be a Sidhe trick. Maybe *she*, the Sidhe Queen, had finally tracked him down, luring him to eternal doom in revenge for escaping from her obsessive, lethal infatuation – and stealing her enchanted harp. the eternal love song of the   All that remained of the dead Fae who had loved him, at the cost of her life. He could never abandon the harp.

The instrument's lament became so loud, so strident, that no human could keep it from him, and as he prepared to rescue it from the presumed possession of some miscreants, his sword ready to slash throats and sever limbs, he discovered instead two terrified women attempting to hide in a thick clump of holly bushes. One gave a yelp of horror at the sight of the wild-haired warrior standing over them, sword in hand. The other's elfin face broke into a wide smile of recognition and relief ... despite her sightless gaze. Seren? Attempting to soothe her companion, the witch rose to her feet, holding out her hand to the other woman.

'Rhosyn, *cariad*. We are safe now. This fine Na Fianna warrior is Brandan of the Golden Harp, and he will protect us.'

Brandan wanted to take the blind girl into his arms in a welcoming embrace but sensed her continuing, curious fear of him still dwelling beneath the surface, despite her words of delight and welcome.

'My lady, I cannot express my astonishment at finding you here in a tangled wood in Cornwall. But then you are remarkable – why else would I have entrusted my precious harp to you?'

'I will be only too happy to return the wretched thing, Brandan. It has been pining from the minute you left for war … when you rode off with …'

Brandan smiled and gave Seren's hand a gentle squeeze.

'With Adwen, who is alive and hearty and dwells in a nearby castle.'

For the first time, the girl relaxed in his company. He could feel her exhilaration and joy welling up within her. She was as in love with the druid, as Adwen was with her. Despite having no supernatural ability himself, Brandan had always known of the druid's yearning for Seren. There were things in life so obvious, there was no need for the Sight.

He took back his harp, holding it tight to his chest as its loving spirit flowed into his in a river of wild music and exaltation. With the harp back in his possession, he felt complete again … well, nearly. If only Donal was with him, Brandan's joy would be total. But a wide sea and the bane of a deadly curse separated them, and maybe always would.

As he led the two women out of the gloom-laden woods into the light, Brandan was shocked to see their condition. He recognised the signs of starvation, the eyes sunk back in their sockets, the raw-boned, grey and emaciated features. They had suffered greatly on their long journey from Wales. He doubted they would be able to make the long trek across the moors on horseback and ordered the warriors to make camp, while sending a party back to the castle to fetch food, blankets and a carriage to get the women back. In the meantime, he did what he could to make them comfortable.

2

England, January 1066

Harold leaned out of a narrow window, allowing the freezing wind to batter his face. He needed fresh air. Throughout the night, brutal ice storms had swept through London's crowded streets, and all had sought shelter, however meagre, from the vicious onslaught. In contrast, the atmosphere of the court within Westminster's Palace was as febrile as that of King Edward's bedchamber. Harold had already spent many days in the overheated room that stank of death, though a coma-bound Edward still drew shallow breath. The King could not last for much longer; his flesh had shrunk, giving him a skull-like appearance, and each breath was laboured and increasingly weak.

The Earl left behind in the room a skulk of solemn clergymen keeping close watch and fervently praying for Edward's soul, no longer pleading with God for the pious King's life. Edward had fallen into this death-like state some weeks earlier, though he had awaken briefly to urge Harold to take care of England. At least, that was what the Earl claimed, with Queen Edith his only witness. Both of them Godwin siblings.

The next days would be tumultuous. Finally, after many months of serious ill health, the old man was dying heirless, and the seething ambition of England's powerful earls was now breaking to the surface. Harold knew speculation raged as to who was to succeed to the throne, and wild rumours rippled through the land. The dying King's nearest blood relation was Edgar Aethling, a boy of 14. Nobody wanted the lad to succeed. The spectre of Norman ambition had badly unsettled the population, and only a charismatic warlord would do as the new King.

The obvious choice was himself. Harold knew he was popular with the people and the Witan, but not with other ambitious nobles who harboured long grudges against Godwin power and ambition.

By the hour, they gathered at court, the news about Edward's decline carrying across the realm on the winter storm wind faster than any messengers on fleet horses. The Earls of Mercia, East Anglia and distant Northumberland had ridden hard through the ice-bound landscape to discover to their fury that he, Harold of Wessex, was already there at the dying King's bedside – as was his sister Queen Edith. The new arrivals gathered outside the King's chambers. Resentment was festering into dangerous rebellion. So deep were they in furtive debate, huddled together, heads down, that they did not see Harold approaching.

'The Godwin jackals are tearing at the carcass,' muttered Edwin, the new Earl of Mercia, 'even before the old stag is dead.'

Nodding in terse agreement, Osulf, another new Earl of the wild and restless land beyond the Tees, instinctively reached for his sword. He felt nothing but loathing for the Godwins – Harold's brother Tostig had once held the earldom of his region. Unlike Harold, this Godwin son had been unpopular with the people, raising high taxes and murdering local noblemen. To keep the fragile peace, King Edward had exiled Tostig to Wiltshire – a travesty of justice, Osulf thought, as the bastard had deserved to hang and be left for the crows.

'And you good gentlemen are not also jackals?' Harold questioned, enjoying their startled discomfort. He stood, arms folded, and waited for their response.

'We desire only a strong and just King,' Osulf replied, with a bold stare directly into Harold's pale blue eyes. 'One able to keep the Normans and Danes from our shores and the pagans in their place.' He did not mention the Earl's humiliating defeat by the Cornish; there was no need. The man's smirk and mocking stance said it all.

'Then we are of one mind, Earl Osulf,' Harold smiled, a fierce, challenging gesture with no more warmth than the icy wind whistling around the palace. Such was the tension between the noblemen, the sudden flinging open of the King's chamber doors startled them. The Queen, surrounded by her protective retinue, strode swiftly from the room, a kerchief hiding her face. The King was dead. Harold knew she did not weep for her husband, but for her own precarious position in court now she was a widow with no heir. If, by God's Grace, he became King, he would immediately exile his sister to a nunnery as a gesture of good will to the other powerful earldoms. He had no need of her meddling in what would be a troubled reign. Not all of England's enemies were from foreign shores.

Normandy

Echoing through the torch-lit corridors, Guillaume's bellows of rage sent serfs and hounds alike scattering for any hiding place from their master's wrath. The Duke liked to find a physical focus to vent his rage on. What was the loss of a serf's life against abating the fury of the Bastard? Nothing – less than a hunting dog's. There had been little warning of the tempest to come. A group of riders, messengers from a coastal Barony, had approached Caen that evening, their manner deceptively leisurely, their intent to speak in person with the Duke.

Their message had lit the firestorm of Guillaume's wrath: the Godwin usurper, Harold, was King of England. Given the dying King's blessing, chosen by their witan of nobles and hailed a hero of the English people. How could this have happened? Edward had promised the throne to him. To him! This was an outrage; one that must be paid for in blood. Treacherous Saxon blood. Needing solitude, Guillaume wrapped himself in a heavy fur cloak and sought out the peace of a high battlement.

Damn the woman, Guillaume's secret oracle had told him the throne of England would be his but warned it would have to be taken by force. She was right, damn her soul, she was always right. The Duke's impetuous heart demanded action straightaway, but he knew his army was not ready, and winter held his land in an iron grip. Moving against Harold now would be costly in men, horses and arms. Patience would give him the righteous power of a blessing from the papacy, for that feeble, pious fool Edward had sworn an oath on the Bible that England would be Guillaume's. Patience would give him his terrifying army of steam and might; one that would be invincible. Patience would give him total victory.

Frustration twisted in his gut. His castle at Caen had become an intolerable prison, a mausoleum to his past and the indignities he'd endured to become Duke. He decided that a soon as travel was even vaguely possible he would go to Falaise and remain there until his army was ready. With no distractions from his wife and family, he would be able to supervise the building of Ferro's awesome airship fleet, watch over and spur on the manufacture of hundreds of fire-spitting steam dragons. To get his own hands dirty with coal dust and burnt with sparks of molten metal. To become as one with the new weaponry as he had once bonded with his sword.

Guillaume glanced up to the brooding night sky, muttering a dark curse on the soul of King Edward of England. He hoped the knife-sharp wind would carry his message upwards to the angels too seek justice against Edward, the man his misguided, deluded people demanded be made a saint.

'You weak old fool. All the death to come is your fault. If you think you can hide in heaven, you are mistaken. The agonised cries of the dying and brave Saxon blood will stain your soul and send you down to the hell you truly deserve.'

As his rage cooled, reason took over. God's will was on his side. Edward's craven betrayal had come at a bad time for war, but Guillaume's hissing, spitting dracons were ready in their thousands, his fleet of air-born death growing larger by the week. The Duke could wait until he had the full sanction of the Holy Father in Rome to strengthen his cause. He could wait until fair weather and calm seas favoured his ships both on water and in the air. Waiting would not change the outcome, he would crush the Saxons and their usurper King like ants beneath his heel. England was already his.

3

Cornwall. Summer 1066

Adwen had never questioned his calling, accepting it was the decision of the gods to grant him the gift/curse of Sight, the courage of a warrior and the imagination of a poet. How could he question, when they had also given him love, their greatest blessing of all, in the form of Seren? The druid sat crossed legged, in the centre of a circle of sacred stones, waiting for the power of a full moon to aid his trance journey across the Veil. Something he now dreaded with every visit, knowing the darkness of ever-looming evil would attempt to taint his soul and haunt his mind. For the first time, he doubted the gods' wisdom in granting him such powers. For the first time, he felt inadequate to the duties they assigned him in his visions. For the first time, he wanted to walk away, return down the hillside and attempt to live an ordinary life.

He tried to concentrate on remembering good times, like the extraordinary day that winter past when his beloved little star had travelled back into his life, sitting out the uncomfortable shake and lurch of a swaying pony cart. Seren had been waif-like, starving, exhausted. But her beautiful, sightless eyes had brimmed with tears of joy and love for him as he had helped her down from the cart into his arms. There had been no need for her to tell him of the cruelties she had endured, or the risks she had taken fleeing from Wales. The whole shocking story had flooded into his mind as they kissed. He had vowed there and then that Seren would never know anything but love and devotion and respect in her life from that point on.

The joy-filled days since her arrival at the castle had sped past. Watching her recover her strength and blossom in the peace of the hospitable Cornish court had given Adwen great satisfaction. Though they were openly affectionate in each other's company, Adwen had given the Welsh girl time and space to recover from her ordeal. The touch of a man would bring back terrible memories … so much so, she might never accept intimacy again. That he would accept and understand, but it would not lessen his love, nor his determination to spend the rest of his life with her.

In the early days, inevitably, the warrior within him had urged retribution for Prince Adwr's heinous crimes against this vulnerable young woman – a thought shared by Brandan, who would have happily taken on a suicidal mission of bloody revenge. Sensing Adwen's simmering anger, Seren had pleaded with him not to raise a hand against the Welsh prince.

'The Goddess will deal with him in Her own time,' Seren said. 'The law of return will bring down Adwr, there is no need for revenge. Unity at this time of threat is far too important to jeopardise.'

Despite his violent, blood-soaked nature, Brandan had reluctantly agreed with her and, thus outvoted, Adwen had capitulated.

Once again, Adwen realised he owed the Irishman a debt of honour. He shuddered as if touched by ice, despite the humid pall of a pre-storm summer evening. What was the secret locked deep inside the warrior? It was hidden behind a mystical wall so impenetrable that Brandan himself was unaware of it. But he, Adwen, with his strong druidic power, could feel the wrongness emanating from beneath the handsome exterior. The druid's only comfort was that Brandan of the Golden Harp was on their side. At least, for now.

Such dark thoughts intruding on those of joy and love from Seren's presence in his life brought him back to the present. To the strident call from the gods to enter behind the Veil and search for more knowledge. The increased frequency of these unwanted, but necessary, visits gave one clear message. Time was running out.

Still at some distance and below him, the rugged moorland landscape glowed with an unsettling, green-yellow light as the setting sun competed with a wide band of encircling storm clouds, which were rumbling and flashing ominously. Adwen pulled his cloak around him, knowing he had to wait out the storm, hoping it would clear before the full moon rose and set in the night sky to come. Nothing had so much spiritual energy as the moon at its fullest; to waste an Esbat night would be to waste the whole month.

As the sun set, the slow progress of the coming storm augured only ill. Such a tempest would be large, violent and long-lasting. Adwen wished he could be back in the safety of Castle Dore, sat by the hearthside with Seren. By the gods, he'd even endure trying to ignore the dangerous, flirtatious glances of that princeling's Irish wife to be out of the storm. Adwen marvelled at the willpower of that charmer of a bard to keep away from her mischievous wiles. Even if it did mean long weeks away on border patrol. When he had first known Brandan, the handsome warrior had made no secret of his shameless womanising past as they chatted on their trek to safety. The Irishman had needed to unburden his past, seeking answers to the curse that had sent him in exile from his homeland.

It was Brandan's future, not his past, that concerned the druid more.

The moon was rising; Adwen felt the familiar, uncomfortable feeling building in his chest, the pressure tightening at the base of his skull. Those who waxed lyrical of the moon's great beauty had not experienced the pain its full force had on a receptive human body and mind, especially at a full moon. He had no choice but to force himself to relax, allow the waves of celestial energy to envelop and possess him, give himself to the great gift of the Goddess without question or complaint. He stood boldly in the centre of the circle of stones, knowing they would amplify the power enough to tear his soul from his body and send it beyond the Veil. An increasingly brutal process as the darkness of coming evil grew unabated.

Seren watched from the shelter of wind-warped gorse, her alarm growing with every moment Adwen stood in a vulnerable state of trance within the circle of stones. The combination of a great storm approaching and a full moon was too dangerous for a druid. Only the female power of a witch could withstand such a merging of old earth, fire and spirit magic. What had driven Adwen to take such a risk? He was no novice in the ways of elemental forces.

Her hand tightened on Brandan's arm; she had pleaded with the warrior to take her to this high tor and, alarmed at her insistence, he had conceded without much argument. 'If I need to help him, guide me to his side,' Seren murmured, knowing the courage of the Irishman would not falter.

As they approached the circle of stones, Seren paused. An image of an ethereal creature entered her inner vision, one she had never encountered before. As insubstantial in form as a morning mist, yet with a powerful aura announcing her as a being from the time when the old earth magic was new-born. Her long crystal hair flowed around her, as fluid as a mountain stream and as sparkling, dancing with rainbow light. She was garbed in silver mist that rippled as if driven by the same unknown celestial breeze that made her hair dance. Her eyes were pools of darkness, inlaid with sparks of dazzling light, like the night sky.

As she neared Seren, her beauty and wisdom were those of ancient mystery and imaginings, fey yet powerful. She was a complex goddess made from contradiction, darkness and light, kindness and cruelty, all things in balance. Seren knew her name: this was Creide, the rarely-seen Goddess of magic and the Fae. Astonished and honoured, she attempted to bow, but unaware of her trance state, the warrior supported her, held her upright in his strong grip.

Creide was such an unexpected visitation. Until now, Seren had never been approached directly by her deities, who had always sent emissaries. What message could Creide possibly bring? The Goddess did not speak, but held out something to the young witch: a silver chain bearing a stone that burned from within with powerful magic. Creide laid it on the rock-strewn ground and then simply disappeared, with no words or change in enigmatic expression. Seren reached down and picked up the necklace, but with the vision over, her eyes had returned to darkness. The stone felt rough-edged, cold and without a single trace of magic, but any gift from a goddess, however enigmatic, could not be discarded lightly, and Seren placed it around her neck.

She put the gift from her mind as deep rumbles from the oncoming storm grew in intensity and frequency. There was little time before it would cover the sky and engulf the tor. Yet Adwen was so far away, wandering through a land so different from theirs. His empty body stood resting on his staff, his eyes open but glazed. The air crackled and fizzled with the storm's close proximity. Blue fire danced along the druid's staff, attracted to the iron sickle-and-moon ornament at the top.

Brandan swore. His friend was at the highest point in the landscape, an easy target for the lightning. He ran to snatch Adwen to safety, but Seren cried above breaking thunder, 'Lead me to him but stand well away. This is a task for witches not warriors. If you break the trance by force, you will strand his soul beyond the Veil.'

Though unconvinced, the Irishman complied, holding Seren tightly as the first whiplashing of wind-driven rain reached the tor. A bolt of lightning hit a tree in the valley below with a searing flash and deafening explosion of sound. Closer, it was getting closer ... Brandan and the witch reached Adwen just as the buffeting of wind and rain grew to full storm force. With great gentleness, Seren tried to prise the staff from Adwen's hand, but his grip was like iron, locked onto the wood as if in the rigor of death. Taking his ice-cold face in her hands, she began to chant, her words lost to the wind's *Ban Sidhe* howl. But not lost to Adwen's heart. 'Please ... listen to me ...' she pleaded in Welsh and Cornish. 'Come back to the living land now. Back to me, who loves you beyond all others.'

With the brutal, unstoppable force of a vast hammer, all three were hurled to the ground as lightning hit Adwen's staff in a blast of searing light and crushing sound. They lay as dead until the storm had passed, leaving only surly reminders of its anger grumbling on the horizon. Now bathed in serene moonlight, Seren was the first to recover. Soaked to the skin, her head spinning, she frantically reached out and crawled along the ground until she found the others. Her hands searched their prone bodies for signs of life. All common sense screamed they couldn't be alive, yet how did she herself still live after taking the full force of a direct lightning strike? She had no immunity from nature's violent forces.

Her fingers traced the familiar, beloved line of Adwen's strong features, so cold. She felt for a pulse in his neck and, with a whimper of astonished relief, found it, strong and regular. Satisfied the druid was safe, she continued her search along the ground, her wet garb now torn and muddy.

She reached another prone form on the ground, even colder than Adwen. It had to be Brandan, but a deep-rooted instinctive sense made her hesitate. She did not want to touch him, nor did she want to find him still alive. Why had she thought that? She felt a sob of sorrow and guilt rise in her throat.

Let the Goddess strike her down now for such a terrible notion, she thought. She deserved it. How could she feel that way about the courageous foreigner who had saved Adwen's life? Haunted by remorse, she shook off the unwanted, treacherous thoughts and reached out to find the warrior. He too was lying as still and cold as stone, but his heart beat with a healthy rhythm.

By some extraordinary miracle or the grace of the Mother Goddess, Seren herself was completely unharmed – no burns, no injury at all – and, to her relief, so were the others. She sat back down, the sodden warm ground creating a steamy mist rising with the perfumed scent of the washed earth. Her hand reached for her new talisman around her neck but it was still nothing but an inert stone. Adwen recovered next, his eyes wide and haunted. He held Seren in a tight embrace and instinctively moved away from the still form on the ground.

He had been given two vivid visions in the Beyond … one showing the arrival of a young, flaxen-haired hero who would aid them, the other giving a terrifying glimpse of Brandan's true nature. Adwen dearly loved the Irish warrior as a friend; he owed him his life, his future with Seren. But hating himself for thinking it, he prayed with all his heart and soul that the warrior would not recover from the lightning strike. Adwen even considered picking up a nearby rock and bringing this wrongness of a life to an end by his own hand. He could leave Brandan resting for eternity in a grave in the centre of this hallowed place, a place of binding for all restless, eldritch spirits.

Adwen glanced across at the witch, lit by the full glow of moonlight, and saw the shadow of knowledge and shared guilt in her face. What was happening to them? Why had they turned into such vile monsters? Was it a corruption reaching out from the growing sense of evil to turn them against a brave and loyal ally? Their friend?

Whatever the answer, Brandan's stirring chased away all thoughts of murder, dispelling them from their hearts like the fading memories of bad dreams. The warrior sat up and shook his head with a rueful, puzzled expression. 'What the fuck happened? I feel like I've been trampled by a herd of wild horses.'

4

Cornwall

Whirling high above him and calling to each other in their harsh voices, the large black birds were the sacred symbol of Cornwall. Hereward paused to watch the pair of courting choughs ride the balmy air, equally at home in England as across the border in Cornwall. How he wished he had the same ease of passage over the often invisible borders that divided men.

On the far banks of the Tamar, the wild, wind-buffeted Cornish countryside echoed that of Brittany: rugged, rocky and with plentiful ancient standing stones and sacred circles. A land of mystery, ancient beliefs and the stubborn pride of its people to survive separate and sovereign from neighbouring England.

Hereward had no idea what reception he'd encounter across the river. He was a despised enemy of the Cornish, and in many Saxon eyes, he would become a traitor the moment his horse's hooves touched the rich, red soil. Hereward was fiercely loyal to his own people. This mission had one aim – to ensure the future of a free England – but he doubted many would see it that way. Most certainly, he felt his own heavy burden of guilt. Had he not seen the horrors Guillaume had inflicted on that Breton town, he would not have been there that day. It was the greatest gamble of his young life. No wonder his hesitation had transferred to his nervous mount.

He turned to Elgitha, riding behind him on a feisty chestnut pony mare, alongside his stalwart new friends from the Scilly Isles and Wessex. They believed in the truth of his warning; they believed in him. To turn away would be cowardice, a betrayal of their trust. Hereward had to ride on and bring the bad news to Cornwall. Otherwise any peace he found at home in Mercia would be short-lived. The fens would run red with innocent blood, the skyline be black and roiling from a burning land. He had seen this future so many times now in his haunted dreams.

As spring had given way to a hot, dry June , the vision of bloodshed and the raven had grown in intensity across pagan and Christian lands alike. The nightmare vision worried gentle nuns closeted in meditative convents, it disturbed the dreams of many children, awakening their households with their screams of terror, and it infiltrated the visions of druids and wise women. All this mounting awareness of doom-laden omens was a gift in disguise for Hereward and his growing band of supporters. He had travelled from the Scilly Isles with a handful of Bretons and Saxons and a Dane, all convinced the danger was real. Others had joined him as he had travelled, eager to spread the ill tidings and give warning. Their only hope was to be prepared, to find a way to avert the coming catastrophe that was so real in their visions.

With Elgitha riding at his back, he had travelled across Wessex to give his warning, expecting hostility but finding ears only too willing to listen, frightened people who now saw malign shadows and darkness despite the long days of summer sun and plenty.

His only failure had been the most serious. His message had been rejected by England's new King. Supported by the senior clergy, Harold was convinced there was nothing the Norman Duke could send over the Channel that he and the English fyrd could not defeat. He believed all the dreams and visions were the work of the Devil, sent to weaken English resolve, evoked by spells and sent by the pagan lands. Even the evidence of the steam-powered lance had done nothing to change his mind, while the story of the pierced barrel of the ox had been dismissed as a foolish, exaggerated tale, nothing more than mischief-making from the Breton King.

Humiliated and disheartened, Hereward had left Wessex to travel to the first of the Celtic lands to give them his warning. Whether he accepted it or not, Harold would need allies when the first Norman dracons launched their fire-spitting lances on English soil.

Making certain the Cornish could see the banners of the Goddess flying at the head of his entourage from Lyonesse, Hereward once more urged his reluctant horse to walk into the Tamar to swim across the summer-low river crossing. Elgitha's mount was braver, and with a giggle she kicked on her little mare, giving a little scream of delight as it plunged into the river, sending a splash of cold water over Hereward. Hereward saw Elgitha through the curtain of sparkling rainbow water, his heart beating faster with love for the brave young woman who had risked returning to Wessex just to be with him.

Word of their mission must have sped ahead on the swift wings of the wind: before they had ridden many miles into Cornwall, well-armed riders intercepted them in a thunder of many hooves. A war party? How could it not be, so close to the border. Hereward urged his supporters to stay calm, keep their weapons sheathed, allow themselves to be taken prisoner if need be. He would not allow this fateful encounter to turn into a bloodbath.

As they approached, the riders reined back into a relaxed walk. That at least was a good sign. At the head of the group, riding under the banners both of the Goddess and of Cornwall, a young man sat tall in the saddle. His high status was evident in the gold circlet on his head and the elegant, twisted gold torque around his neck. Beside him rode a holy man, a warrior druid … whose charisma was as apparent as the striking streak of pure silver in his dark hair. In amongst the Cornish warriors, slouching, one leg cocked over the front of his saddle, was every Saxon's nightmare of a heathen warrior. Naked but for plaid trews, his tightly muscled body shone berry-brown from the summer sun. An intricate, coiled tattoo of a raven was emblazoned across his chest, and his long black hair was braided back, revealing a handsome face lit by ferocious, intelligent dark eyes like obsidian orbs – and as cold.

'Welcome,' the druid addressed their visitors with a smile of genuine warmth. His young yet wise grey-eyed gaze fixed on Hereward. He spoke in passable, heavily accented English. 'Thank you for helping the flaxen-haired warrior, the young hero of my Goddess-given vision, to arrive safely in our land. On behalf of Cadoc, my King and his sons Maeloc and Berwin, and the people of Kernow and Cymru, once again, welcome.'

Hereward dismounted and bowed low in respect to the Cornish Prince and his druid advisor. His elation knew no bounds. At least in this hostile enemy land he would be treated well, his message accepted and acted upon. His decision to cross the Tamar was vindicated; whether or not his own people would allow him to return was yet to be discovered. The two groups merged and headed further inland, where open, gorse-studded and rocky landscape was bathed in sunshine and a warm breeze carried from the sea.

On their arrival in the valley below Castle Dore, the visitors received an unexpected, warm greeting from the peasants toiling in the hay fields, despite the inevitable hostile glare directed at Hereward himself and the other Saxons among his group. Many of these locals were probably survivors of the frequent bloody skirmishes with the invaders from Wessex. Hereward, though relieved by the reception, was also perturbed. So, according to that druid, he was believed by these people to be the subject of a vision? But what if he was not the right young Saxon? What if another, true hero was out there? Hereward did not feel like a champion; he was just one ordinary young man swept along by the winds of circumstance, doing his best to stay alive. He prayed they were wrong, that the whole warning of coming carnage was wrong, that it was what King Harold and the priests believed: a shared vision created by devilry to weaken the moral of Guillaume's enemies in the battle for England's crown.

Surrounded by farm dwellings with well-tended arable fields and paddocks with fine cattle and sheep, the large, imposing central fortress rose above an inner circle of dwellings, all built behind a high, wide earth rampart bristling with sharply-pointed stakes. Good protection against any army. That is, any *normal* army, thought Hereward with a shudder of foreboding: Castle Dore's defences would be no match for what awaited them across the Channel.

Once they drew close to the wooden gates of the inner courtyard, the Cornish King himself appeared with an escort of warriors and noblemen. Younger in summers than the Breton ruler, Kind Cadoc looked prematurely aged by warfare and the burden of responsibility. Living within striking distance of Wessex had taken a toll on his peace of mind. Nothing Hereward brought to his court would do anything to alleviate his disquiet. Members of the King's household arrived behind him to take the visitors' horses. Once dismounted, Hereward took Elgitha's hand in his with an encouraging squeeze, bowed low and prepared to deliver news far worse than of a Saxon incursion across the Tamar.

Elgitha sighed with pleasure as she felt her face, now blessed with clean, soft and perfumed skin. Anything that made her more attractive to Hereward was welcome to her. On arrival at what the Cornish optimistically called a castle, she had willingly accepted the fuss from a giggling group of castle serving women under the direction of an attractive young woman who she discovered was Prince Maeloc's Irish-born wife. Elgitha had let them help her clean away the grime from the journey from Wessex with a bronze bowl of warm, sweet scented, water, and had gratefully accepted a clean, embroidered linen robe in a pretty shade of pale green. She was also thankful for a goblet of strong, quality mead and a plateful of bread and cold mutton. The rations of hard, stale bread on their journey staved off the clutching talons of hunger but nothing more. It was good to experience pleasure again.

Once Elgitha was refreshed and made comfortable, the Princess dismissed the serving women and introduced her to another guest at the castle: another Princess, from Wales. How strange and unpredictable her life had become since meeting Hereward. Here she was, the exiled and disgraced daughter of a humble villein, keeping company with two Celtic Princesses. Within a few moments, Elgitha realised the Welsh girl was blind; and though an attentive servant, Rhosyn, remained at her side, Seren appeared relaxed and confident despite her difficulty.

'About time I had some new merry company,' Isolde announced with a giggle. She spoke the language of her adopted country with a delightful Irish lilt that complemented her flirty manner. Prince Maeloc had his hands full with this one, thought Elgitha.

'The court has been so full of doom and gloom since our druid Adwen returned to us with that handsome rogue of an Irish warrior at his side,' the princess continued.

Isolde was beautiful in a ripe, comely and wayward manner. Her pale skin was flawless, her large amber eyes sparkled with life, her smile was full of mischief and sexual allure. Elgitha felt sure it would take more of a man than that pinch-faced Cornish princeling to satisfy this woman's needs in the bed and beyond. Isolde was cursed with a soul born for adventure, not for raising a brood of puling babes within the smoky confines of a stone and mud round-house. Elgitha did not envy the woman's life of duty and privilege.

Isolde glanced at Elgitha, and with her head tilted slightly to one side in mischief, continued, 'And what a novelty to have a dashing Saxon nobleman in our court ... How I would love to run my fingers through that long, golden hair. Unless he is already taken?'

Was he? Elgitha was not sure. Hereward had been attentive and chivalrous toward her on their odyssey across Britain but had not made any attempt at intimacy. Maybe because she was only a commoner and he the son of a great Earl, one with the power of a king in his own lands. Indeed there was a time when Mercia, like Wessex, had been a separate Saxon kingdom.

No novice in the ways of the heart, Isolde saw a cloud of hurt and uncertainty in the Saxon woman's dark blue eyes. Another heart-lorn woman in her court. 'Well, what a sorry brood of womenfolk! There's me, married to a jealous, ridiculously under-endowed man whose bedroom endeavours consist of few feeble pokes and he is finished. My body aches for that wild Irish warrior, but he would rather stay out on the moors than risk a tumble with me. I must be the only willing female that notorious womaniser, Brandan of the Golden Harp, has never bedded. Yet. I do not take no for an answer.'

The princess was clearly enjoying the intakes of scandalised breath from the other women, and did not appear to fear her words carrying back to her husband from some prying servant or slave. She continued, 'It is obvious to anyone with even half a mind that Seren and her druid are in love with each other but doing nothing about it, torturing each other with noble celibate misery.'

Isolde turned to the new arrival, 'And now there is you, the lovely Elgitha, hopelessly mooning over that Saxon nobleman. What is the matter with you, ladies? We are on the brink of a terrible war, according to all these awful prophesies. What are you waiting for? We have but one chance of life and love on this side of the Veil.'

For all her impish ways, Isolde seemed genuine in her concern for the other women. 'Hard as I try, it seems I cannot have my wicked way with that dark and dangerous Brandan, but what is stopping you two from following your heart's desire?'

What indeed? Seren did not speak. This light-hearted, candid banter was uncomfortable to her, as she sensed it was for the Saxon woman. Seren loved Adwen, but the druid understood what she had endured at Elfael, that she had known the intimate touch of a man only as a cause of pain and humiliation, a brutal assault on her inner being, both in body and soul. Surely Adwen was showing his respect for her by giving her time to heal … as much time as she needed. She doubted the wanton Isolde would ever know what a true act of love that was.

5

Cornwall, September 1066

The time had come. There could be no doubt the waiting was over, and the illusion of peace and summer serenity gave way to a growing dark shadow casting coldness and fear across the land. King Cadoc's well-placed spies in England had reported back to him that Harold was preoccupied with a treacherous brother and with an incursion in the north of the country from ambitious Viking sea wolves. The King had taken his attention away from Normandy … a grave mistake that would prove costly. To them all.

Hereward walked with Elgitha through a shaded grove of mature willows, the graceful boughs of which reached down to touch a sun-dappled river. They found a tree trunk by the clear water and sat watching the tumbling, comical antics of a family of otters, but without any joy. He could sense her apprehension. This was not a lover's tryst, and she knew it. Hereward had wanted somewhere quiet to break bad news to her. That he could no longer stay in exile when England was in danger, he had to return to Mercia, to fight alongside his father and brother. Leaving her behind in Cornwall under the protection of King Cadoc.

His hand reached out to gently push a stray lock of red-gold hair from her face. She took his hand in hers as the first of many tears rolled down her cheek. 'I know you are leaving, Hereward. You are too loyal, too courageous not to fight for Mercia. But must you abandon me here?'

Hereward's heart twisted with uncertainty. He loved Elgitha, thought he could keep her safe by having her remain in Cornwall. But he could not bear the distress in her eyes.

'I plan to return, beloved. Once the danger is defeated, to bring you back to Mercia to be my wife. I want our union blessed by God in a Cathedral and witnessed by my family, by Earls and the King.'

He could see surprise and great joy spread through Elgitha's being. Did she not realise that he loved her? That he was keeping himself pure until their wedding night, both as a mark of respect to his future bride and in penance for his crimes against women in Normandy? Of course she didn't; the poor woman was not a reader of minds. He was such a fool.

Hereward quickly explained to Elgitha why he had kept his distance and how much he loved her. Her answer was to gather him in a tight embrace, her lovely eyes shining with more tears, but this time of joy.

'You wonderful, noble but foolish man. I have travelled so many arduous miles since leaving Lyonesse to be with you. I have loved you from the moment we first met on those sands. But I thought you could not care for me … as a commoner and the widow of an enemy.'

'There is but one enemy now,' Hereward replied, stroking her hair, 'the one I must face protecting my own people.'

Elgitha took his face in her hands and kissed him, not in a chaste gesture of affection but with such deep longing it took his breath away.

'We both know the horrors you will face in battle,' she said, 'and that you might not return to me. How can we put off sharing our love, our bodies? From this moment I can be your handfast wife in heart and soul … let me also be your true wife in body. Hereward … please. Love me now.'

His need growing, Hereward groaned; she was right. Much as he wanted his marriage sanctioned in church under God, there might never be another time in this world where they could be together. So they made their handfast vows in the solemn way of their ancestors, witnessed by the otters and the sun, and consummated their union there behind a curtain of swaying green willow.

Though Hereward could never erase the memories of those innocents he'd taken by force – nor would he want to, in respect for their pain and in self-punishment for his crimes against them – he was granted this precious, brief time of peace. Enough to take Elgitha as his wife with mutual joy, pleasure, heartbreak and passion blending in one overwhelming emotion as their bodies became as one.

The morning had given way to midday, and Hereward knew the other Saxons would be waiting in the castle courtyard, already on horseback, readying themselves for the journey to join with the English King's hard-pressed army. His heart twisted in pain as his new bride clung to his waist while he dressed, her tears hot against his skin. There were no words that could offer hope or comfort to Elgitha, no promise he was sure he could keep. He removed his gold crucifix from around his neck, kissed it, then fastened it about hers.

'Pray for me, beloved, pray to God and the Blessed Virgin every day for my safe return.'

Elgitha rummaged in her clothes and brought out a small, well-worn leather pouch. Inside was an old beaten brass medallion with the crudely-etched image of the Virgin and Child. She pressed it into Hereward's hand, with such despairing fervour that the thin metal dug into his flesh, drawing a fine line of blood. He did not flinch or complain.

'This sacred talisman, blessed by Saint Alban himself, has kept my family safe for centuries,' she told him. 'Keep it close to your heart, day and night, I implore you.'

His eyes blurred with tears, Hereward nodded in solemn agreement. He stood up abruptly and strode away from their leafy grove, unwilling to prolong the agony of their leave-taking. He would not change his mind and stay in Cornwall. Loyalty and obligation as the son of an Earl had to take precedence over his desires as a husband when all they held dear was under such terrible threat. He was certain Elgitha understood this, though her heartrending weeping remained in his heart even when he was well beyond earshot.

Back at the castle, a small gathering waited to say farewell to the first of their company preparing to engage with the enemy directly. It was a bitter loss. The Cornish had sheltered these men, born of their old enemy, and seen them for what they were: ordinary, brave men who wanted nothing more than to raise their families and crops in peace and security … The Saxons' needs were identical to theirs. They were joined only against a common enemy, and there could come a time when they would have to fight each other again, but not today.

King Cadoc and his sons were amongst the gathering, their eyes already shadowed, haunted by what was to come for them and their people. The Tamar would not be respected as a border by the brute force of the Norman army.

'Your courage will never be forgotten by my people,' announced the Cornish King, presenting a generous bag of locally mined gold to buy supplies along their journey across England. 'Our poets will sing of the golden-haired young man who braved such danger and hostility to bring us warning.'

Hereward dropped to his knees in respect and gratitude. Then, standing once more, he climbed up onto his horse. He turned its head and trotted out of the stronghold as the head of the Saxon exiles, his eyes resolutely focused to the east and England. He was unaware of two people missing from his leave-;taking, they were of no importance, not with his beloved and desolate Elgitha stood on a hilltop as he passed by, her arms gripped around a sturdy oak sapling for support as she wept.

'You should not be here,' Brandan growled, keeping his back turned to the bewitching woman who had followed him to a meadow outside the castle. 'You will get me hanged and yourself thrown into disgrace and slavery.'

He continued to wipe down his horse with handfuls of dried grass. A morning spent schooling the mare in the heat of the late summer sun, sharpening her up for battle, had left them both sweat-drenched and weary. He had returned to the shelter and shade of a small stand of willows beside a stream of fresh spring water, the ideal place for his camp, close enough to the castle but free of the bustle and intrigue of such a crowded dwelling. Isolde bent down and pulled up some more parched grass and took it to the warrior.

'Are you not leaving soon? Off to fight a battle few will survive? Can I not give you a farewell gift in gratitude for your valour?'

She let her hand brush his as she passed him the skein of dried grass. 'Nobody knows I am here. Nobody cares I am here. Not even my husband, who has not visited me for many moons.'

'Be careful what you ask for, Princess.' Brandan turned to face her, his resolve weakening. By all the gods, she was desirable! Her deep blue gown was laced tight, barely hiding the creamy swell of her breasts. Her lips were full and moist and the sun lit red and gold glints in her lustrous dark hair. She stared at him, her eyes gleaming with longing. She gave a sultry smile of triumph as she glanced down to admire the hardening effect she'd had on the warrior.

'I do not play games of courtly love,' Brandan continued, his voice slurring with lust. Celibacy did not come naturally to him, and the past months in Isolde's beguiling presence had been torture. 'Nor will I sneak into your chambers like a thief in the night. If you want me to take you now, here on the earth, ridden hard like a common slattern, then so be it. If not, return to your husband, Princess Isolde.'

'Out here, in this meadow, there are no princesses, warriors or slatterns.' Isolde's hand teasingly stroked the raven tattoo on his naked chest, then traced a slow path down to his stomach. He grabbed her hand before she could move lower. 'Brandan,' she insisted, 'there is just a man and a woman who both want pleasure. Nothing more.'

Brandan's already weakening resistance collapsed. He pulled her down to the ground and, releasing himself, threw back her gown. Eager, she parted her thighs wide, raised her hips to take him. Brandan slammed into her with full force, rewarded with her tightening around him, taking him in deeper and deeper into the inner core of her being.

Isolde bit her lip then gasped in erotic pleasure. Everything she'd fantasised about since the warrior's arrival at court was at last happening. He was so strong, so big, pounding into her with a steady, relentless rhythm, filling her completely. Every part of her body thrilled, quivering with excitement until the focus of the inner heat became so intense, so unbearable that she sought and gave way to an explosive release, her body bucking and shuddering beneath his. But he was not finished with her. As she relaxed, whimpering with the echoing delights of her climax, Brandan pulled out of her, only to turn her around and enter her from behind.

Horrified at first at the indignity of being mounted like a rutting beast, Isolde tried her best to pull away. But the warrior held her hips in a tight grip, his thrusts losing none of their power, until she submitted to the pleasure and began to ride another, more overwhelming tidal wave of rising exhilaration. This time it was even better, even more intense. She threw back her head and screamed as she came, and Brandan climaxed at the same time with his own roar of triumph, pumping her full of his essence. They fell back onto the hot, dry earth, the warrior still deep inside her, both panting and laughing in the sated aftermath.

'That was unbelievable,' Isolde murmured, groaning in disappointment as he withdrew from her. 'What fools we have both been. All those wasted months we could have been doing this.'

Brandan shook his head as he lay back on the ground and said, with a rueful grin, 'Doing this every day would have led to inevitable discovery and disaster. A stray remark, a servant with a loose tongue. You might have developed feelings for me, hastening that inevitable conclusion.'

'Feelings for you? Do not flatter yourself, warrior.' Isolde's voice developed an icy edge. 'You are nothing more to me than a large, hard cock. I'll admit, one well-wielded though.'

She rose to her feet, dusted down her gown and pinned up her hair. Then she walking away with a regal air, as if but moments before she had not been on her knees on the dry earth, mewling and imploring the warrior to thrust ever harder and deeper into her.

Brandan did not answer. He'd known such contempt many times from high-born women after pleasuring them. It mattered not, and he had the satisfaction of knowing that he could have sired a future king of Cornwall that afternoon. There was more than one Irish heir born with his dark good looks.

Ignoring the haughty Isolde's swift departure, he lay back on the dry, hard earth of late summer, in no hurry to return to the cramped and busy castle: for warriors, indoors was only for harsh winters. Walls of earth and stone were as claustrophobic as a grave. At first the sun caressed his face like a lover, but soon it was eclipsed by a dark shadow. A stray cloud in an otherwise all azure sky? Brandan opened his eyes to see a now familiar sight, the large raven circling above him, as if he was already carrion.

'What are you trying to tell me, lady?' Brandan addressed the fearsome Goddess of war through her messenger. 'Have I not done all you have ever wanted? Taken so many lives in battle with your name on my lips? Served you with devotion all my life? If this creature is a portent of my death, I do not need it. I know what is to come.'

The raven descended and alighted on a nearby oak stump, cocked its head at a sharp angle as bird and man observed each other in an uneasy silence. The raven's plumage was unlike that of ordinary birds, it did not have the usual blue-green shine on glossy black feathers. Instead it had down of deepest black, as if it had been hatched in a world without light, a place where no sun, moon or stars had ever shone. Only the bright, ruthless eyes had a sparkle and gleam, an intelligence beyond that of any Earth-born corvid. Brandan was again tempted to lob a stone, send the bird back to whatever dark realm it had come from, but he could not help reason that this raven belonged to Morrigu herself. With the greatest battle of his life in his near future, this was not a time to enrage her, his only true protection in combat.

'What do you want of me, lady?' Again he addressed the raven as her messenger. 'I need more than a visit from this silent creature.'

Enigmatic as in all their past encounters, the raven returned to the skies. This time it flew toward the Cornish coastline and out to sea, heading perhaps across the Channel, where Guillaume the Bastard built up his army in readiness for a massive invasion, one the foolhardy English King refused to believe in. As Brandan watched the raven grow ever smaller in the firmament, a shadow of blackness darker than the night sky, he felt an unnatural cold envelop him. With no cloak, he endured the ice touch on his bare skin as the horizon itself darkened, as if a violent storm brewed across the sea. But there was no storm. The pitch–hued shadow vanished, as did the unnatural cold, and the horizon returned to hazy blue. A premonition?

Whatever was going to happen, it would be soon.

6

Normandy, September 1066

The Duchess Matilda gathered her children closer to her as from a higher vantage point she watched the Norman army gathering in the flat fields surrounding Caen. With most of her personal household joining her family, arriving in a cavalcade of carriages, the atmosphere was one of a feast day, but there was nothing festive in Matilda's demeanour. Many of the men gathering below them would not return to their families, leaving them only memories of this last day together.

The late summer sun shone brightly, making the polished metal of Guillaume's new arsenal dazzle, hurting the eyes of onlookers and warriors alike. With no prior warning of their existence, the fiendish weapons had come as a shock, silencing the crowd of onlookers, not least the Duchess. So, *that* was the reason for her husband's foul moods and unusual secrecy over the past year. She had suspected a mistress; if only it been something so human, so expected. This was more akin to devilry, to defying the natural order of God's work on Earth.

How could such death-bringers shine like the trumpets of the angelic host of Heaven? wondered the Duchess as the unfamiliarity of the new weapons, their strange design and size, sent a shudder of unease through her body. She had waited to wave off the Duke as he prepared to claim his rightful inheritance, the throne of England, with an army of noblemen and their powerful warhorses, skilled archers and commoner pikemen. Had it not been for the sight of the fearsome arsenal at his disposal, his wife would have been fearful she would never see her beloved Guillaume again. But what could the Saxons do against this? What could any army in the known world do?

Her eldest son, Robert, stood apart from his younger siblings, his fists tightly clenched. Despite his tender years, he was already a tall, stocky figure. His fierce devotion to his mother had grown even more fervent since seeing Guillaume violently threaten her. Matilda sighed, her heart sorrowful, knowing how much the boy now hated his father. How could she make a child … no … a young man now at 15, understand how much she loved the badly damaged but brilliant man that was Guillaume of Normandy?

Their attention was drawn by a roar from the crowd, rising from the castle gates and spreading through the army gathering below in the fields. The sound announced Duke Guillaume riding across the drawbridge over the wide moat, preparing to take his place at the head of his army. He sat straight-backed on his favourite black Friesian stallion, and his polished chain mail competed with the copper and bronze of his new weapons for eye-catching dazzle.

Matilda heard her son swear under his breath at the sight of his father in all his warlord glory.

'The Duke's strength keeps us safe and secure, my children,' she chided, showing the steel within her. 'Must I remind you again that our marriage was built not just on a political alliance but on love? I expect you all to love your father as much as I do.'

'And we must be grateful to him for a loving home and the royal blood of France in our veins?' Robert turned to his mother. His eyes had the same flinty determination as his father's but were brimming with a child's tears of fury. 'How many times have we heard this? How many times have we been told about his terrible childhood? Enough!'

If Robert carried on like this, Matilda felt, she would have failed as a mother of a future Duke of Normandy. Perhaps even, God willing, a future King of England. Bitterness and hate would consume him, make him cruel and greedy for power like Guillaume. What mother would not want her child to have a future of long years of peace and prosperity?

The boy had not finished but walked away from the spectacle of the Norman army moving away from Caen, turning his back and focusing on the castle, his inheritance.

'How can you talk of loving a man who dishonours you every day with filthy country women, with *putains!*'

Matilda sighed. 'You are far too young to understand. A man of your father's energy needs his appetites sated beyond what one woman can fulfil.' She smiled and patted her swollen belly. 'A woman with child.'

The Duchess did her best to sound light-hearted, hiding the knife of pain and betrayal turning in her heart. 'These women are not important, just vessels for his passing desires. They mean nothing to your father or to me.'

Robert turned back to face his mother, the anger in his eyes glowing with renewed fire. 'So, how can you explain the royal-born lady he keeps in her own luxurious chambers at Falaise?'

Her eyes widening with shock, all colour drained from Matilda's face. She fled to the carriage, needing to sit down as her world span. How could this be true? Guillaume had pledged his fidelity to her, to love only her. And how did a child know about this betrayal?

'I am a man now,' Robert went on, 'with my father out of the country. I will ride to Falaise and see for myself if the rumour is true.'

Matilda nodded, watching furious energy and determination flare in her son's eyes; the same look she'd known so well in his father's. She could not stop him, nor would she try. It was time to cut the apron strings, for if, God forbid, misfortune struck Guillaume in England, then this boy would be Duke. A case of history repeating itself from father to son. She gave Rollo – her gentle, respectful name for Robert – a tight, loving hug, knowing such tender intimacy between mother and child would soon be a thing of the past. One day Robert would be Duke of Normandy, though she prayed this day would be in the distant, not the near, future. At least they could not curse him with the hated title of Bastard.

Robert's army escort accompanying him to Falaise consisted of old retired soldiers and raw boys untested in war, many no older than himself. He was unconcerned. Any powerful, ambitious baron who might have wished him harm was safely with his father in England.

As planned, his arrival at the castle was unexpected, sending the household into a flurry of temporary disarray. Used to Guillaume's sudden, impulsive visits, the major domo set recovery in motion with a few snapped commands while Robert remained mounted. Bowing low with genuine respect, the head of the Duke's household at Falaise approached his son and waited to be addressed.

Robert's voice assumed the clipped, impatient manner of his father. 'My visit will be a short one,' he stated. 'I need my men fed and rested. The horses too must be given excellent care. Feed them, check their shoes, treat any cuts or bruises from the journey. I have but one reason to be here, to speak to my father's high-bred whore.'

The man blanched, genuinely puzzled. 'My lord Robert, I wish I knew of whom you speak. My place is to serve you with as much diligence and loyalty as I do your father, but to my knowledge no highborn lady dwells at Falaise.'

Robert's face purpled in fury. 'My informant from this castle was insistent. The whore is kept locked in a tower. I will not be denied!'

Wringing his hands, fearful of the boy's temper, the wretched major domo's mind raced. Any female of interest to the Duke, highborn or otherwise, could not dwell within this place of warriors unnoticed.

'My Lord, in truth, I know not of whom you speak. But your father has a place of spiritual refuge and private contemplation in the southern turret. It is kept locked; no-one is allowed to enter on pain of death.'

His voice wavering, desperate to defuse the young lord's anger, he continued, 'Is it possible that your informant saw the Duke enter his private rooms and wrongly assumed their purpose?'

Leaping from his horse and not waiting for an attendant to grab the reins, Robert gripped the hapless man's shoulder, oblivious to his wince of pain. 'Take me there, now.'

As they approached the foot of the turret and the iron-reinforced oak door barring their way, an old woman rushed from the shadows to intercept them. Her grey hair was a tangled bird's nest of disarray, her yellowed eyes wide and wild with dementia. She stood against the door, oblivious to the danger to herself.

'Go away. You cannot come in, by order of the Duke himself.'

Robert's hand covered his nose as the stench of old, unwashed flesh and stale urine assailed him. What madness was this? Who was this vile harridan?

'Move, hag, or you will meet your maker unshriven.'

'I will not disobey my Duke,' the woman screeched, unafraid. 'Nobody disturbs the lady. Nobody!'

Robert glared at the major domo. 'You lied.'

The man fell heavily to his knees, mumbling a hasty last prayer of forgiveness. 'Lord Robert, I beseech you, there has been no mention to me, no knowledge of a lady kept here. Your father told us it was his private chapel, a holy place. This must be no more than the crazed rantings of an old woman. Her mind is addled.'

Ignoring him, Robert shouted for men to break down the door. He had no intention of negotiating with a madwoman for the key. As the guard approached, the woman began to screech in fury, throwing herself against the door to bar their assault. 'Kill her,' Robert ordered, too impatient to prolong this bizarre and unseemly delay. The first death at his command. He was surprise how easy it had been.

Once the door yielded to a battering ram, Robert decided to go into the tower alone. There was something wrong about all this; a locked tower, a crazy old woman guarding it. What manner of foul secret was his father hiding here? The air within was stale, dry, more tomblike than a dwelling place, and his heart beat faster as his suspicions rose. Had his own father gone insane, like the hag whose bloodied corpse lay outside? He paused at the foot of the steps, listening for the sounds of surprised distress above him, but there was only silence and a darkness no candle had lit for many a month. He pressed on, not waiting for a torch, using his hands on the walls to guide him up a winding stair.

Another door barred his way at the top, but this yielded to him, unlocked. Inside was set of well-appointed rooms, well lit by the southern aspect, but the air was musty with a sickly sweet taint of decay. Robert became fearful, the sense of wrongness spreading like ice through his veins. Were the rumours of his father's devilry true? Had he done more than build superior weapons in league with Satan himself?

Sword in hand, Robert slowly pressed on, now expecting an assault by demons, but he saw nothing other than rooms furnished for a woman of high birth. Fine but dusty tapestries softened the stone walls, clean but old herbs and rushes were strewn on the floor. The rushes were desiccated by age, crumbling beneath each footstep, creating a cloud of dust to rise above his feet, giving off a faint ghost of their former heady scents. A gilded goblet filled to the brim with stale wine remained untouched on a table, its companion empty, with just a few dried dregs of wine at the bottom.

Then he saw her.

Robert's heart froze. A woman sat by a window, clad in a sumptuous gown of fine green wool covered by a coating of grey dust and cobwebs. He could not see her face. Her head was turned to gaze out of the window and rested on the wall, her blonde hair hanging loose down her slender back. So still. Robert did not address her, instinct screaming that there would be no point. He wanted to turn and hurry away, back down the stairs, back to Caen. Order that Falaise be razed to the ground, burnt, purged of his father's madness.

But the all-too-human instinct of curiosity spurred him on to approach the woman with faltering, hesitant steps. There was no peril to his life here, only to his soul, for he knew that whatever he saw would remain seared there for eternity. As he moved to confront the still form, his hand sped to his mouth to stifle a scream. A large spider ran onto the woman's hand and paused there; no instinctive movement from the figure flicked the creature away. His father's supposed mistress had been dead for a long time, preserved and desiccated by the dry air of the locked tower. A beauty once, perhaps. Her skin was now fragile yellow parchment, her eyes long sunk away to nothing. On her slender neck, he saw the telltale cause of her demise: purple-black bruises around her throat in the shape of two broad hands. His father's hands.

7

Ireland

The clean, earthy aroma of the outer peat walls could not disguise the stench infesting the hovel's fetid interior. Holding a lavender posy tightly to her nose, the young woman hesitated at the goatskin flap that served as a door, dreading the encounter to come. Desperation had driven her every step deep into the wild countryside; there was no way she would turn and leave now. She heard a greeting in a thin, wavery voice. Mistress Bronagh, the hag whose aid she sought, already knew she was there.

She ducked her head beneath the low entrance and entered slowly, her knees buckling as the reek assaulted her like a guard dog. The smell was strong enough to stop a warrior dead in his tracks. fighting but losing her instinct to retch, she felt the bile rose high in her gorge as she faced the squalor within.

'Back to see me so soon, *stóirín?*'

Swallowing back the nausea, she found the hag rustling through a pile of malodorous animal skins. The old woman's hovel was packed with foul-smelling herbs, scraps of unrecognisable dead animals hung festering from the roof, the earth floor was littered with bones and filth. A thick haze of oily smoke tainted all that entered the single room. She shuddered, contaminated by its touch.

'I did what you wanted. Is not all well with you now?'

The old woman, a chaotic assemble of tattered robes and yellowed grey hair, beckoned her visitor to sit on a crude seat made of a log stump set beside an equally rough-hewn table. She would have preferred to stand but was unwilling to upset the witch and so, doing her best not to soil her fine embroidered linen garb, did what she was bidden. Bronagh sat opposite her and, rummaging through her robes, produced a leather pouch, spilling the contents onto the table. A weasel skull, some dried rat embryos, shards of rose quartz, owl feathers and a clear vial of fresh blood. She waited for her young visitor to speak first.

'All is not well. The curse drove him from these shores and the sea has kept them apart, but now there is this great battle looming. My husband has gone to Wales and will be with him again.'

Sharply intelligent blue eyes, too young for the rest of her form, peered from beneath the unruly chaos of Bronagh's hair, eyes that studied the child-woman before her with piercing insight. The visitor's elfin beauty and guileless face hid a raging jealousy and overwhelming need to be adored, bordering on madness.

'Is it not normal for a healthy young man to slake his needs where he can when so far from his wife?'

The woman's face contorted with scorn. 'Would I be here in this dreadful place if he was just bedding some local slatterns? This is far worse. He loves that bastard. Adores him with all his heart. I am no more than a brood mare to him.'

The hag nodded with understanding. This was a difficult situation for a woman of such pride and powerful desires. It was not her fault she had been married off to a man whose true passion and love lay with one of the same sex.

'For my magic to be strong enough to cross the sea, I will require a high price.'

'Name it, woman.'

Smiling, Bronagh reshuffled her talismans. 'My price will not be of gold but of living flesh and bone. Are you still so willing?'

Without a flicker of hesitation – a lack of compunction that even the practitioner of dark magic found chilling – the woman nodded. 'Yes.'

'If it involves your son?'

Again, she agreed with no pause or uncertainty. 'The loss of my son will force my husband to lie with me again to produce another heir. Bringing him new life is something his accursed lover could never do.'

The witch sighed and recast the talismans. 'Unlike you, lady, I have no taste for the death of an infant. But I do want the boy in payment, to raise as my own.'

'In this vile dump?'

So she objected to how the child would live but not to his death. And they called old Bronagh evil …

'Do not be fooled by this shell, my outward appearance. Illusions spun to protect me. My real home is elsewhere, one far finer than the mud and stone palace you call home.'

The young woman stood up abruptly. 'I have no home until my husband lies with me and the other is destroyed. Do what you have to do to make this happen. I must plan a way to get the child to you without any blame falling on me.'

In a swift movement, Bronagh grabbed her hand, held it in a painful, strong grip. 'Not so fast, *a chara*. What you have asked me to give him is not something trivial like a curse of the hard word. A pact of dark magic this powerful must be sealed in blood.'

The hag held up a thin, sharp knife and, ignoring her visitor's struggles to pull free, made a small cut into the girl's wrist, letting a trickle of blood fall into another clear vial. 'Have you forgotten the last time so quickly? I exact a high price, but I always deliver what you ask of me.'

Pulling back her arm and cursing under her breath, the child/woman flashed the hag a look of sheer hatred as she rose to her feet. She pulled out a linen kerchief and bound the wound on her wrist.

'No more torture. This time finish him off. Besotted fool that Donal is, even my husband would not be desperate enough to bed a corpse.'

Bronagh watched in silence as her visitor pulled the hood of a peasant's grey wool cloak over her head. Such malice and soul-deep hatred in one so young. Had she not learned that most men of great power and responsibilities needed their dalliances yet still honoured their wives? Especially ones proven to produce healthy sons. None of this meant anything to her; humans were there only to exploit for their greed and folly. Bronagh would have a new child to love and raise and her customer would learn a harsh lesson by her grim actions. One paid for in far more blood than that one small vial. Bronagh could foresee a tidal wave of it. And very soon.

8

England, September 1066

Driving rain and a brisk autumnal squall battered trees, making the old Roman road slick with wet leaves. A force of mounted house carls and fighting men on foot tramped on, heads down against the wind, too tired to think of what lay ahead or dwell on their recent resounding victory against the Norwegians at Stamford Bridge. There was no time to rest or celebrate: exhausted messengers had brought them grim news. The Norman army had landed on English soil.

A collective groan of relief echoed through the ranks as King Harold ordered a brief halt to rest, with men collapsing on the road where they stood. The King used the time to accept an audience with Leofric's younger son, Hereward. The lad had grown since the Godwins had skilfully manipulated the old King and engineered Hereward's long mission, or more accurately banishment, to Normandy. His imprisonment by the Bretons had been an extra bonus to their plan to weaken the House of Mercia before the tussle for succession on King Edward's death. It had been a plan Harold himself had had no part in, for all his ambition. He had no time for political manoeuvring. There was nothing noble or valiant in such machinations. His honour and integrity were things he held dear.

'The wanderer has finally returned from the pagan lands,' he noted. 'You look well, young man. Considering.'

Harold sat on his horse, too tired to dismount without giving in to his fatigue, and gestured for his visitor to do the same to they could talk eye to eye.

'Your timing is perfect, Hereward. An extra sword is much needed to defend our lands. I am sure your brother Edwin, the new Earl, will be delighted. The Mercian forces suffered badly at the hands of Hardrada and his band of Viking cutthroats until we arrived to save them.'

Hereward nodded, unconcerned at the unsubtle slight; the bitter old rivalry between Mercia and Wessex was so petty and pointless now.

Nothing mattered beyond being prepared for what was to come. He had not rested since landing on English soil, and all thoughts of his own comforts had long gone. He had 'rested' long enough chained to a damp Breton dungeon wall.

'Do you believe me now, my lord King? Have you heard what the Bastard has brought to our shores? Terrible weapons that make our swords and spears appear like children's playthings – as effective as wet reeds.'

Harold shrugged. Not this again! The boy was obsessed with phantoms, foolish old wives' tales around the hearthside. He had more immediate concerns; he urgently needed to piss, to have some food and to find a place to let his horse graze. Since the Confessor's death in January, wild rumours about the Normans' weaponry had flooded the land, each more bizarre and unbelievable than the last. Harold had dismissed them, as he had Hereward's warning and talk of a missive from some pagan tribal leader. What more could this beardless youth now add to this ongoing nonsense?

The Mercian rummaged through his robes and produced a vellum scroll, handing it to Harold.

'We have so little time left to save England. This was written by me in our language, but the terms were dictated to me by King Blaez of Brittany himself, who set me free and sent me home to fight against the Norman threat that endangers us all.'

Harold took the missive and threw it unread to the ground in contempt, moving his horse forward to trample it under its hooves.

'No heathen comes to me with "terms". His quarrel with a Christian Duke is not my concern. Nor should it be yours, Hereward.'

Shocked by his contemptuous response, Hereward could not understand the King's refusal to speak to the pagans. What the hell did religion matter when they all faced annihilation?

'They can help us by strength of numbers,' he argued. 'Any old hostility and grudges can be sorted out later, but if we let Guillaume move further into England there will be no later. My lord, I have seen what these weapons can do. I am a witness to the truth.'

Hereward could see the King was on the edge of physical and emotional collapse. The forced march from victory against the Norsemen and the treachery of his own brother had taken a hard toll. His slumped shoulders bore the weight of responsibility for England's future and freedom. The Mercian sighed. It was a big thing to ask of a man shamed by the pagans twice in the last year: humiliated first by the Welsh, then by the Cornish. Hereward did not want to state the demoralising obvious, but Harold faced a third and catastrophic defeat now.

'I will not allow one painted heathen to set foot on English soil,' Harold insisted, fixing the Earl of Mercia's upstart brother with a determined glare that briefly brought light and life flaring to his deep-shadowed eyes.

Close to tears in desperation, Hereward was forced to press on, whatever the consequences to himself. Harold was a just and fair ruler but these were distressing times; the King could imprison him or worse.

'My King, I beg you to reconsider. On my knees if you want, and in the name of all we hold holy. We must protect the future of Saxon England. We cannot prevail alone against these demonic weapons.'

Harold nudged on his bone-weary horse to push past the younger man's mount.

'We can – and if they do exist, then by God's good grace, we will.'

Hereward pulled back. There was clearly no reasoning with the King. But how could he, as a loyal Saxon subject, allow Harold's pride to end in the inevitable massacre to come? With Hereward's older brother now Earl of their fenland domain, he was free to travel, to ride to Wales and petition the Celts himself. But how could he turn his horse away from Harold's army … be branded a deserter, a coward? He could not. Hereward dismounted and retrieved the treaty from the ground where the Breton monarch had thrown it, before it could be torn and trampled by many more hooves and feet. Dusting it off, he tucked it into his jerkin. It might yet be needed, if he survived the battle to come.

9

England, October 1066

Battle nr Hastings

Senlac Hill. Little more than a steep rise in the ground above a wooded region with an area of bog at its base. Harold had the advantage, resting the exhausted fyrd on the summit of the hill, which was now bathed in an early morning autumn mist glowing in the sunrise. A beautiful sight that for many would be their last.

Down below, the Normans were well established. They had had enough time to build fortifications and raid the countryside for supplies. Their warriors were well fed and well rested, and as the Saxons would soon find out, far more than well armed.

'They've let us hold the best position on high ground,' Earl Edwin exclaimed. 'Are these jumped up Vikings really such fools?' He reined in his horse and turned to address to his younger brother, Hereward.

'They don't need the advantage,' Hereward muttered, his spirits at an all-time low, 'not with the weapons they have. It will be a massacre.'

'Nonsense,' Edwin snarled, 'You are bringing shame on our house with these fairy tales. Your time among the Breton savages has addled your brain.'

'By the Blessed Virgin, I wish that were true. I want to be wrong, my brother. So wrong.' Hereward's voice was dulled by resignation. 'I'd far rather be derided as a crazed fool than be right.'

When would they realise what hell the Bastard was ready to unleash on brave men fighting for their freedom, their homeland? When it was too late, when the bodies lay in row after row of splintered bone and flayed flesh, staining the soil crimson with life-blood?

'What is the King waiting for?' Edwin was impatient for action; the Normans were so close. 'Those bastards have been on English soil for too long. Time to drive them back into the sea.'

Hereward did not answer. Had his message to Harold finally sunk in and persuaded him to wait for reinforcements with the arrival of the Army of the Goddess?

The sun warmed his face. The morning mist was already evaporating and the day dazzled. The trees had not yet lost their leaf canopy but were a glory of russets, golds and rich browns. The *ki, ki, ki* of a soaring hawk made him raise his eyes to an azure sky uncluttered by clouds. Beautiful.

A messenger from the King galloped behind the Mercian ranks to seek out the Earl. With a savage grin, Edwin stood up in the stirrups and waved his sword in assent.

'Let's ride, brother. We will be first to strike the Normans.'

At his command, the standards of Mercia – bearing the blue and yellow cross of St Alban – were raised high to wave defiantly in the morning air. The Earl himself carried his personal ensign, a brave act that would make him a trophy for an enemy archer.

So, this was where and when his life could end? So be it. Hereward took in a deep lungful of fresh air and nodded to the encircling hawk, wondering if it would peck out his eyes later on the battlefield. Driving his heels into his horse's sides, he galloped alongside his brother and the howling throng of the Mercians. Life became nothing else but the drumming of hooves, flying divots of mud and the ever-nearing line of the enemy. Some watched the skies for a swift moving cloud, but no arrows flew from the eerily silent Norman ranks.

His heart hammering, Hereward focused on a group of the enemy and, tightening his grip on his sword, urged his horse to greater speed. A noise, harsher and louder than thunder followed by a high-pitched whine, exploded from the Norman ranks. Startled, Hereward's horse tried to shy away in mid gallop and fell heavily, trapping him beneath its thrashing body. Around him, men and horses screamed in agony, pierced through with burning javelins. A nightmare of pain, blood and the stench of burning flesh as the Bastard's weaponry took a vicious toll of the Mercian warriors.

In anguish, Hereward looked for his brother's distinctive red roan charger and found it lying dead nearby with a javelin pierced through its head and neck. Edwin lay behind it, hit by another through his chest, impaling him to the blood-soaked ground. As his own horse thrashed in a dangerous flail of hooves, Hereward pulled himself free and crawled along the ground to reach his brother. He beat out the flames and tried to free Edwin from the nightmarish weapon, but it had driven too deeply into the ground. There was nothing he could do but cradle Edwin's body in his arms. The javelin had pierced Edwin's heart; a swift death, faint comfort for the new Earl of Mercia.

Shocked into silence, King Harold's army watched the slaughter of the Mercian cavalry in appalled disbelief. This could not be real, this was a nightmare that would dissolve in the light of day.

One horse struggled and rose to its feet, then another, both turning to gallop back to the Saxon lines through the oily, foul-smelling smoke. Somehow the sight of those brave beasts running back toward them snapped the watchers out of their fear-crazed stupor, and a great cheer of encouragement spread through the ranks, urging the horses on to safety.

Men also began to stir amid the burning carnage, but survivors fallen from stricken horses made easy targets for the enemy dracon spears. A defiant cry echoed across the silence of the battlefield. A Saxon rider galloped in front of the Norman lines, proudly bearing the double-headed eagle standard of the Mercian earldom, deliberately drawing attention away from the fleeing survivors. This courageous, foolhardy move triggered more rousing cheers of support from Harold's men ... and the hiss of more Norman weapons preparing for deployment.

'Ride, Hereward, ride for your life,' urged the King. 'Dear God in heaven protect him.'

Maybe divine intervention aided Hereward's flight from the Norman killing field, or maybe it was the complacency of the enemy after their successful rout. Certainly the thick smoke hanging like a baleful curtain hampered their view of the vulnerable survivors. With no further casualties, both the new Earl and the men on foot reached the fragile safety of the Saxon lines.

It would be the last quarter ever given by Guillaume.

'Do you believe me now, Sire?' Hereward gasped, fighting for breath, tears stinging his eyes from the death of his brother and of so many brave men cut down by the cowardly rain of fire. 'Is this still a foolish fairytale told by old women?' His face contorted with disgust, Hereward used his cloak to wipe away the oily black dust covering his face and hands ... soot made of burning human flesh. He threw the cloak onto the ground; there was nothing on this Earth that would make that garment clean again.

Ashen faced, the King nodded a curt assent. His mind raced. What defence could men use against such foul devilry? The clergy? Maybe the Normans' unnatural weaponry would melt to nothing when fervent prayer from pure souls and holy water were pitched against them. Harold sent word that there would be no more attacks on the Norman defences until the monks from nearby Battle Abbey were summoned to the battleground. All previous fierce eagerness to engage the enemy had evaporated with the first Saxon warrior impaled on a flaming javelin. None was a coward or short on valour, but in the face of this insanity, Harold's army as one were content to hold back.

The morning's sky of unbroken blue was now tainted with the foul smoke of burning corpses of man and beast. No carrion birds yet flew above the silent battlefield, but a flotilla of brown and yellow clouds did;, low clouds that billowed toward the Saxon lines. The horses saw them first, raising their heads sharply at the sound of flaming braziers in the sky. Panicked, they whirled and bolted, bringing down riders and trampling foot soldiers. As the clouds neared, Harold's men could see wooden boats slung beneath them, carrying Norman troops. Many of the fyrd turned and fled; those who remained aimed their bows at the sky.

As the sky ships flew above the disarray of the Saxon army, their sailors tipped flaming balls of burning pitch down upon their heads.

'Retreat,' Harold bellowed, appalled at the sight of his men burning alive. 'Sound the bloody retreat!'

Damn him, young Hereward had been right. This was a battle no one nation could win.

From his vantage point above the Norman camp, Guillaume raised his sword and slashed at the air above his head in triumph. Rank after rank of Norman knights and fighting men cheered as one as the defenders broke rank and fled. There was nothing that could stop his rightful claim to the throne of England now, not one force of man or nature could prevent his army rolling across the landscape in an unstoppable tidal wave of brute power. Lady Cecelie had been right; she always was.

He glanced to his right, to his half-brother Bishop Odo of Bayeux, and saw the shock and conflict in the man's eyes. It had been his first sight of Guillaume's awesome weaponry in action, and the reality was brutal and terrifying.

'Fear not, brother. You will soon be the most powerful holy man in this realm, an appointment to high office sanctioned by the Holy Father himself.'

'The Pope supported your claim to the English crown, but had he known about all this ...'

Odo's voice trailed off, unable to express his full horror of the carnage. It was as if Guillaume had opened the gates of hell and unleashed fire and brimstone over the Saxon fyrd. This would not be seen anywhere in Christendom as the work of a godly man. The frightening prospect loomed of excommunication from the Mother Church for allowing this nightmare to exist; a punishment that could threaten not just the Duke but every Norman soul – himself included.

Ignoring the ambitious but pious fool, Guillaume spurred on his stallion and rode down to rejoice with his army. With the Saxon army in chaotic flight, there was no reason not to rest and celebrate their easy victory. All would bow down before him in surrender as his army of metal and steam continued with the conquest. First England, then one by one he would pick off the Celtic realms. Only Scotland would be left, and that strong, remote and staunchly Christian kingdom would also one day fall. Might was the only thing any populace would respect and obey. Who in all the world was mightier than he?

10

Like shepherds rounding up a panicked flock, Earl Hereward and the other English warlords did their best to rally and reassemble the scattered fyrd. It would have been easier to hold a handful of snow in midsummer.

Hereward reined in his spent horse and signalled his huscarls and thegns to rest. They had ridden hard all day across a frightened land, discovering many deserted villages, some abandoned so quickly their livestock remained untended. Easy pickings for the fast-approaching Norman army from hell. Hereward could understand the peasants' fear ... it was based on fact. Guillaume was moving to claim England for his own with a brutal, heartless but effective strategy. The denizens of each town and village in his way faced the same stark choice. Those who surrendered and swore a sacred oath of fealty to him were spared. Sometimes. The Norman Bastard's moods were as dark as his damned soul. More often than not, all men and boys were slaughtered, buildings and crops burnt to cinders, leaving nothing but scorched earth and wailing, grieving survivors.

The new Earl's gaze inevitably looked south. The sky was clear and larks rose in joyous chorus above the sea of yellowed grass on the ancient downland. Warm days were precious this late into autumn and the birds celebrated with the beauty of their song. A light breeze carried the sweet smell of gorse flowers, but for Hereward the afternoon air was tainted with acrid smoke. The sun-hazed horizon was dark with fast approaching doom. He would go to his grave with the smell of his brother's burning flesh forever scorched into his senses. Who would stand against the Bastard's war machines? Who could? Hereward remembered his last encounter with the King as he had sent his surviving nobles away from the carnage of Senlac Hill to muster another army. His face had been gaunt from lack of sleep, his eyes shock-glazed and deep-shadowed. Yet his courage had not faltered.

'If we sought sanctuary,' the King had said, 'we would need to flee to Scotland and beg for King Malcolm's aid. We would never reach the Wall; the Norman Bastard has the wind from hell itself at his summoning, guiding his death clouds.'

The King had sighed, feeling the full weight of responsibility for a kingdom and the fate of its people resting on his shoulders. Refugees from the Norman destruction had told of Guillaume's open threat to kill every Saxon in England and repopulate the country with Normans if they did not yield to his rule. Harold had no doubt he would carry this through, far easier than subduing a conquered people.

'If we are to make a last stand against such monstrous evil then we must be as close to God as we can be.'

He had reached across and clasped Hereward's hand in a firm grip. 'Ride, my young friend, hard and fast, and gather all who can fight. The young, the old, the walking sick ... women. Anyone that can hold a weapon, be it sword or hay rake.

'We will meet at Glaston, where Joseph of Arimathea brought the precious blood of Christ to this blessed land and founded the first church.'

Hereward had nodded a bleak assent. He did not share his King's faith in divine intervention, but he could see some logic in the choice of location. Harold's seat at Winchester was too heavily populated; defending it against such a foe would leave a bloodbath for which no man, King or usurper, would ever be forgiven. Furthermore, Glaston was close enough to the pagan realms to call on their help. Harold might resist, but his back was against the wall, and desperation makes for tough choices.

The King had commanded that he seek out help, more men at arms. There was only one place Hereward could rally such aid. He must return to Cornwall.

Glaston Tor

A convoy of wagons bearing weary and injured warriors trundled across the rolling downs of Somerset. They travelled across a hidden land, shrouded in a dense grey pall; the sun had risen but could not win against the all-pervading gloom. Beneath their hooves, a night frost had hardened the going for the draught horses, creating a bone-jarring journey for the passengers as the wagons bumped over deep, iron-hard ruts. New volunteers on foot followed behind, glad of the leisurely pace of the heavy-set animals, as were the defeated warriors from the Senlac carnage, who shuffled along bleak-eyed like living ghosts.

Hereward rode away alone from what remained of the Mercian fyrd, seeking the highest ground to get above the fog. He paused on a hilltop and sighed in wonder. Rising above the sea of shape-shifting grey, their destination gleamed vivid green in the morning sunshine. A great man-made mound, the seat of the Mother Goddess ... a mighty spiral of grassed-over earthen banks built by an ancient people who had left no record of their lives beyond their awesome and mysterious sacred places. Though he could not see it from his vantage point, an expanse of still water surrounded what was known by some as the Isle of Avalon.

But to Hereward, this was Glaston, the holiest place in England, where the flame of their Christian faith was first lit. Christ himself was said to have visited here as a child with his uncle Joseph of Arimathea. Wise men said that after the Lord's death and resurrection, Joseph had brought the chalice that held Christ's blood, the Holy Grail, to this site. The saint had also driven his wooden staff into the rich Somerset soil, where it had sprung into life as a thorn tree: one that still blossomed every Christmas and Easter and thrived so far from its home in the distant Holy Land. A faith-confirming miracle that made Glaston so precious to the English.

The exiled pagans in Wales and Cornwall knew this place as Ynys Wytryn – the Isle of Glass. The Saxons, by conquering the earthly representation of their Great Mother, had crushed their morale; so much so, the Tor's loss had festered over the centuries, the distress becoming no less for the passage of time. Hereward had to forget this possible barrier to a truce and pray the threat from a terrifying mutual enemy would be enough to bury such deep wounds, so many old grievances.

Whether this was the best choice for the last defendable place in England or a trap, only time would tell, but Hereward worried about how much faith the King had placed in help from God. The Normans marched across England under the official sanction of the Holy Father in Rome, God's representative on Earth. Did that not mean the Saxons should renounce their King and bow to the Bastard to save their immortal souls?

A voice cut through any more pondering over these dilemmas. Wirt, Hereward's trusted huscarl, bellowed above the sound of hooves and slow, rolling wagons.

'My Lord, how much further? The beasts are faltering and in need of rest.'

So close, no more than a half a day's ride, but Hereward could see no point in pushing the men and beasts beyond recovery. Guillaume was fully occupied consolidating his success across the south and east of the country. His greedy eyes would turn to the west soon enough; his needed to kill Harold if he was to crush the tattered remnants of Saxon resistance. Yes, the Bastard of Normandy would turn west, but maybe not yet. Please not yet.

He dropped the reins lightly onto his horse's neck to let it rest and frantically graze. His gaze wandered once more to the landmark rising from the flat plains below. After his first sight of the Tor had filled him with wonder, further study of it had made him feel a deep and primal instinct of unease. The stone church built at its summit seemed too fragile a barrier against the old ways of this ancient island. Just a few centuries past, his Saxon forebears and their faith had been newcomers, arriving first as bold

Germanic and pagan raiders then later as peaceful settlers, bringing their own culture and embracing a faith not born of this green land. Isles that had been once inhabited by a different race of men for countless thousands of years.

The more Hereward surveyed the mist-wreathed Isle of Avalon, the more he became convinced it did not belong to the Saxons, however many new myths were accredited to its enigmatic form. The story of the saint's visit with the holy chalice was appealing, but it was a story that relied on faith. What if the Christian God was not there? Could the great battle be lost already? Hereward glanced down to the shadowy forms of his warriors in the valley below. Such defeatist thoughts were dangerous, weakening his sword hand and infecting these brave, good men with fear and despair. He was the Earl of Mercia, by the grace of God, heir of a proud, courageous and powerful lineage.

Hereward sat up taller in the saddle and gathered up the reins with renewed purpose. These men deserved better than a leader with doubts and a crisis of faith in his King and his God. Hereward signalled assent to his huscarl; there was a good, clear view across the landscape here and a plentiful supply of firewood and fresh water

'You are right. Man and beast must rest. We will make camp at the first good place we reach, my friend. This fog will burn off soon and it will be pleasant to rest today with warm sun on our faces and backs.'

11

This time, Seren did not remain behind like the other women of Castle Dore, nor did she need to argue her case with Adwen or the Cornish King. The druid's last, terrifying spirit journey during the lightning storm had given him knowledge that every holy man and wise woman would be needed in the war to come. As his control over the Tamar had proved, not all battles were won by swords and spears.

Seren sat astride a sturdy brown moorland pony, one from a race that had dwelt on these islands from before the arrival of men, its instinctive understanding of the difficult landscape giving her confidence. She needed all the strength she could muster; for the first time in her young life she was riding to war. A war that could be the appalling carnage of her visions. Could be? Seren was now certain that it was. Messengers from the now Earl Hereward had confirmed their worst fears: that the invaders from across the Channel did indeed have terrible weapons, some that reined fiery death from the sky and others that hissed like dragons and spat spears that could pierce through a solid wooden wagon. Seren shuddered at the thought of what such a thing could do to a man.

The ever-loyal Rhosyn rode with her, refusing to remain behind at Castle Dore, as she had told her mistress, 'Not with Elgitha returning to England with her Hereward and that wanton Isolde's belly swelling by the day. I do not want to be there when she births a babe with black hair and eyes!'

Seren smiled at the memory as she rode at her beloved Adwen's side. No more separation from him. No more fear of reprisals from Prince Adwr for, however long her life would be, it would be spent in her newly-adopted land of Cornwall. Under the protection of the Cornish King and his powerful druid. Seren did not dread an encounter with the Welsh nobility, who were also believed to be on their way to fight under the banner of the Goddess. There was a solemn truce on all blood feuds between tribes and noble houses across all the pagan kingdoms. So she could now tell the truth to her guardian about what had happened to her, and there was nothing Prince Gwion could do about it.

The long journey to the rallying point on the outskirts of the small town of Cerden passed without incident but with a growing sense of unease badly affecting morale. The usual banter and bawdy songs from a marching army fell to silence as messengers sent by Earl Hereward arrived from England. These men, all foreign mercenaries unafraid of entering pagan lands, spoke of dark and terrible acts of slaughter, of towns burnt to cinders, of hundreds of acres of crops scorched to ashes and livestock found as charred and twisted carcasses. Human corpses dangled from trees by the hundreds, with nothing to attend them but winged seekers of carrion.

There was hardly a man among the Cornish throng who had not left behind a home or farm, leaving the very old and the very young to help the women gather in the harvest and prepare for winter. The ruthless spectre of death stalked England and soon its skull-like head would set sightless orbs toward the west. The knowledge there was so little a small army of ordinary men could do in the face of such power added leaden weight to their every footstep, an extra burden of fearfulness onto every ridden beast.

By the time they arrived at Cerden, the already dark mood had deepened and they made camp in near silence broken only by the whinnying of the army horses calling out to those from the town and the barking of local stray dogs at the newcomers. This time the next day, the war party would cross onto English soil – at least, that was what the Saxons called it. To the Celts it would always be Ynysoedd Prydain, the British Isles. It would be a curious sensation, crossing far more than a mere boundary and openly entering a land that had been forbidden to them for so many centuries. A journey into the heartland of the enemy, with no guarantee of a safe reception.

Nobody barred their way or challenged their arrival. The land seemed empty; cultivated fields abandoned; stray livestock left unattended. Fear of the Norman army had emptied the countryside, left villages and hamlets deserted. So different from the wild moors of Kernow, this cultivated region was a landscape of ghosts. With no opposition, the Cornish war party made speedy progress, following well-made roads and tracks that did not hinder or tire men or beasts. A day's unremarkable travelling into England brought no ambushes, no hostility, indeed not one sighting of any local Saxons. It made for an eerie journey, so much so that few were able to rest when they made camp just a few hours' ride from Glaston.

The next morning dawned fair again as the Cornish and their Irish mercenary warriors set forth for their appointment with death. Seren felt the landscape change again around her, from the scents of cultivated fields, red soil rich with pungent fertilisers to the sweet smell of open sward, a sea of rolling grassland. She could hear the bleat of flocks of sheep and the high-pitched call of kite and buzzard above her. A feeling grew within her; a primal connection to the landscape, though she was Welsh born and bred. Maybe her distant ancestors once lived there? It was a curious sensation that did not diminish as she neared Glaston and the great Tor.

The feeling grew stronger with every hoof beat, the music of a gentle four time rhythm of striding horses bringing Seren ever closer to Ynys Wytryn. A deep, old earth magic power stirred her blood like no standing stone or circle had ever done. This place was more than sacred to the Welsh and Cornish, it was the most precious site in the entire Brythonic world. Its grievous loss was mourned every Samhain. Now Seren could understand why. She felt her whole body thrill, surging with powerful echoes of the ethereal energy of the universe.

Adwen felt it too, bringing his horse next to her pony, reaching out to hold her hand in comfort and support. Emotions among the wise ones would run high as they neared this stolen place, so beloved of their ancestors. The ancient spiral structure was the earthly representation of the Great Mother of All, said in legend to be fiercely guarded by Gwyn ap Nudd, King of the Fae. The first Saxons had been pagan, had respected and protected the site, but when they had converted to the new faith sweeping Europe, the site had been desecrated with a Christian holy place of dead stone built at its summit, preventing the healing energy of the Goddess from rising and blessing the land.

Adwen tried to catch a glimpse of this violating abomination as they approached the Tor, but a dense spectral mist hid the summit from prying human eyes as if covering the sacred hill's shame. How wise was it to make a stand against the Normans at Ynys Wytryn? A place the Saxons called Glaston, revered by them as holy, a rallying point for their own faith. Defeat here would send spiritual shockwaves through pagan and Christian alike, laying all their realms open to conquest by Guillaume's relentless army. The druid sighed. There was nothing he could do to change the course of fate; this was the place kings and princes had chosen to make their stand. No-one would find him lacking in courage.

With but an hour left before sunset, the Cornish army halted to make camp. The Tor was so close now that, though she could not see it, Seren's mind reached out toward it, felt the pain of its abandonment and disfigurement as if the earth itself was weeping. As the warriors dealt with the horses, camp fire and sleeping arrangements, Seren risked wandering away from the noise and bustle and found a small grove of willow, the winter-bare boughs gracefully bending over a stream. Back home, this would be a place of old earth and water magic, somewhere she could expect an encounter with the Fae. There was nothing here now but that which she could touch and smell. Or hear – the gurgle of water eddying around stones, the rustle of night creatures stirring. A sad sigh of a breeze through the willows. The trees were alive but, like so much of the animal and plant life this close to the Tor, merely living and not thriving, vulnerable to disease and blights. Was this how it would be everywhere if the Normans succeeded: all the magic places lost under all-conquering stone and a faith that denied their existence?

The task before them seemed too great, and what use was she? A witch who could summon up a wind and face down spectral snakes, against weapons that tore apart men and beasts with iron and fire. She knelt down and prayed, but in this spiritually muted place, found no solace.

12

Hereward had done all he could. The headlong clandestine ride across the Tamar to seek the aid of the Cornish King and his army could have condemned the young Saxon as a traitor. He was beyond caring. What was one man's life compared to an entire kingdom?

His mission bore greater fruit than he could ever have imagined. On a wide plain near the coast, Hereward found far more than Cadoc's troops and his friends, Seren and the druid Adwen. Word of the Norman invasion had spread like the wildfires the invaders had created, and the Cornish army was now united with those of Kings from Ireland and Princes from Wales, with hope of more on their way. Never before had the Celtic nations gathered together in this way or marched as one under the banner of the Goddess, old blood feuds and grudges buried in a mutual amnesty. Hereward's mind reeled with astonishment. These people respected the visions of their holy men and women, listened and acted on the warning, unlike Harold and his advisors, blinded by their faith and fear of the unknown.

Though he encountered considerable reluctance and resistance, Hereward finally persuaded the Celtic leaders to ride to Glaston to parley with King Harold of the English. He knew these warlords would do far more than talk. Like a great tidal wave surging across the land, what they had started could not be held back. It was no love of the Saxons that had brought the army of the Goddess to ride across the border. It was the prospect of avenging an old outrage and taking back from Norman and Saxon possession alike the most precious religious site for their peoples.

It would be a bitter price to pay, but as Hereward rode back across the Tamar alongside King Cadoc at the head of a great army, the leaden sense of burden lifted from his soul. He had fulfilled his duty; fate's future direction would be decided by Kings and Princes ... and by God. He could not turn back the clock and be nothing more than the younger son of a Saxon Earl. He ruled – at least, he was meant to rule – the wild lands of his native Mercia as its Earl, and with that came great responsibilities … Fate had thrown him in the deep end and he had to learn how to swim.

A King's desperation brought them to the meeting place, mutual loathing barely hidden as they gathered in a glade, under a broad stand of mature oaks. Harold of the Saxons stood across the glade from three Welsh Princes, two Irish Kings and Cadoc of Cornwall. Accompanying the rulers were noble-born warlords, Christian bishops and pagan druids and one young, blind witch.

The night air blowing through the bare branches was tainted with the stench of ash and death; the future carried on the wind toward Glastonbury. The pitch torches staked out to light the glade struggled against the wind; many were extinguished and refused to relight, doing nothing to lift the dour mood. Harold was a ghost of his former vigour, a man with the courageous spirit slowly being crushed out of him by defeat and loss. His beloved kingdom and people were dying under Guillaume's brutal fist.

Harold turned to the man who had brokered this meeting, Earl Hereward, speaking quietly as the others sought advantageous places to stand according to their rank.

'This is insanity. What motive have these godless barbarians to help us?' Sighing, he continued, 'They would gladly celebrate a defeated England. Wait until we are destroyed, then drive out the Normans, and these lands would be theirs again. Christ will turn his head away from England and weep as stone circles return to replace our holy churches.'

How could Hereward answer this? The King was probably right. His words in return now seemed feeble: 'But if there is any chance, however slim, we must ask for the Celtic lands to help us. They are under as much threat as us. Look at the size of the army they have brought to England; can we truly afford to turn away such help in this, our darkest hour as a nation?'

The Cornish King finished his own discussion with his fellow pagan rulers and stepped forward to address Harold in fluent English, his voice strong and commanding. 'So, you reject our aide? So be it. How are your difficulties our problem? Was not this Norman lord named rightful heir by the dead Saxon King and by your holy man in Rome?

Hereward swore under his breath. The future hung on a knife-edge. There needed to be a diplomat, someone who could rise above the pride of kings, knock some sense into these hostile, sparring rulers. He instinctively looked to the druid and Seren. Their courage and wisdom had brought the Celts together. Could they broker an alliance now?

It was Seren who first stepped forward to the centre of the oak glade, silencing the warriors with the sight of her willowy form and beautiful eyes that seemed to glow with an inner light. Curses broke the silence. 'A witch!' One of the bishops strode forward, crucifix raised as a weapon to prevent her from addressing the summit, expecting her to cringe away and flee back to her people at its holy, sanctifying touch.

'Let her be, I implore you,' shouted Hereward above the hostile clamour. 'She knows what we all must face, or die with our lands undefended. Let her speak.'

To his relief, a Saxon earl held back the bishop, clearly eager to hear what the young woman was going to say.

Seren fought back her anxiety. How could she address these powerful men? Her only language was Welsh, tempered with a little Cornish. Her mind guided her to the rainbow stone, the sliver of sparkling quartz that had been given to her within the circle of stones. She remembered it now, from that meeting beyond the Veil that would have felt more like a dream had it not been for the evidence of the rainbow quartz. It had been a parting gift from Creide, the elusive Goddess of fairies and magic. Seren wore the stone on its silver chain around her neck and thought no more of it than a pretty trinket. The whirl of dancing colours trapped within the clear quartz she could not see, except in her dreams. She had thought it simply a symbol of light to give her hope. Now, as she faced a hostile group of her people's enemies, she knew it was far more. Holding the crystal tightly, Seren spoke with as much authority as she could muster,

'There will always be bloodshed and enmity between our peoples. We will continue to fight over land and faith for many centuries to come. But there will also be times of peace and plenty.'

From their reactions, Seren knew they had somehow all understood her, though she had addressed them in Welsh. Creide's stone had granted them comprehension of her words through her magic. She continued, ignoring the growing fear-driven rage among the Saxon holy men, who gripped their talismans of the dead man like the drowning clutch at anything within their desperate grasp.

'But none of this will come to pass if Guillaume succeeds,' Seren told them. 'He brings to these shores weapons that cannot be beaten by swords and bows or by the valour of our warriors. United we may stand a chance, however slim, of holding his onslaught back.'

One of the bishops pushed roughly through the throng of noblemen, using his crozier as a staff to clear a path through to the witch. 'If our weapons cannot withstand the Duke's army, what can?'

Seren could feel his rancid, wine-tainted breath close to her face, sense his outrage and hatred, a deeper fear and loathing of all women coming to the surface of his being. She heard Adwen's shout of warning as the bishop raised his crozier as if to strike her. Seren quelled his anxiety with a raised hand and a gentle smile. 'This man will not hurt me. He follows a creed that says "Thou shalt not kill". Is that not so?'

The bishop's hostility had not abated, but he lowered the crozier. 'Witchcraft and devilry. Is that how you plan to fight the Norman Bastard?'

Seren smiled, although she realised that this man was dangerous: fear of loss of power had him murderous, despite his status as a Christian holy man. And why not? Did not the druids of her own people also fight alongside the warriors?

'Devilry? We have no knowledge of this term. There are no devils in our lands, in our beliefs. But I and the other wise ones will invoke old, deep earth magic to defend ourselves … defend your people too, if you allow us.'

'Never!' bellowed the bishop.

His hasty response did not find universal favour among the Saxon contingent nor with their monarch. King Harold was too worn down by failure to argue. His words ended the meeting.

'I cannot sanction witchcraft. My warriors will fight under the Cross of Christ. But neither will I sacrifice my people to the fiery death of the Norman demon weapons by turning away any help. Fight alongside us, brave warriors of Ireland, Wales and Cornwall. Fight alongside us with my full blessing and deepest gratitude.'

Adwen ran to catch Seren before she fainted, the effort of communicating through magic having weakened her. 'Beloved, you did it!' he murmured, as he cradled her slender form in his arms and kissed her forehead. 'You bloody did it! You are a marvel … Who else could bend so many hostile hearts to their will?'

'Less a marvel than someone who needs to sit down,' Seren whispered, smiling, 'somewhere quiet. And perhaps a goblet of mead to steady my nerves?'

13

Brandan took his horse up one of the few hills in the landscape of open fields and scattered woodland. This was a gentle terrain, grazed down by centuries of sheep flocks, a land tamed by early peoples whose names and history were long forgotten. But they had left a magnificent monument to their beliefs and labour in the Tor.

He was not alone. Others had ridden to the summit, some to gaze in awe at the Isle of Glass, others to search the horizon for the first glimpse of the Norman army. They acknowledged the wild Irishman with a nod, before returning to their own thoughts. Brandan was grateful for this. He wanted time to contemplate, to study the lie of the land, looking for any place of surprise and ambush to undermine the enemy's swagger and might.

Down below in the marshalling fields, warriors on foot and mounted on sturdy local ponies arrived by the hour. Many came on their own or in tribal groups, but there were no great armies from Ireland or Wales; that would have been folly. If, or more likely when, the Norman invaders turned with their conquering greed toward those Celtic kingdoms, the armies would be needed there to defend them. These new arrivals were brave souls volunteering, all driven by the vision so many had shared. Brandan sighed, confused. Was he the only one who suffered no dread dreams of destruction and despair? Why had he been spared these nightmares? His own sleep was dreamless and deep.

Further inland, word had spread of an ever greater host of Saxons gathering around their King. These were desperate men with nothing to lose, survivors of Guillaume's scorched earth barbarity. Sighing again at the futility of the coming battle, in which they had no hope of a tactical advantage, Brandan returned to the camp. It was dragons and gwiber that were needed here to combat the Norman death machines, not brave men and women armed with swords and spears.

No less desolate in their thoughts, all the druids and witches drawn to the last stand beneath the Tor had also sought a high view of the green fields that would soon run with red blood. Early arrivals had discovered the sad remains of a once proud circle of stones, many of which had gone or been smashed and desecrated. Only one pair with a lintel stone in place remained in mute defiance.

Beneath this one arch, they stood at first in contemplative silence until the sound of hoof beats announced new arrivals on the hillside. Seren held onto Adwen's arm with a tight grip, alarmed at the muted power-waves emanating from one of the newcomers. Adwen's protective arm around her shoulder strengthened as he recognised the Lady Vanora in a group of warriors from Wales, sent from the King's own Teulu.

'The woman has much changed,' he related to Seren in a low murmur. 'She has aged beyond her natural years and looks haggard and drawn.'

'One cannot summon a gwiber and not be affected; she sacrificed her youth and vanity to kill me and my sisters.' Seren did not hide the bitterness in her voice. Why should she?

To Seren's discomfort, Vanora approached her, halting her horse in front of her as if to block the view over the Tor – a pointless gesture and a hostile one. Remaining on her tall horse to look down on the younger woman was another deliberate act of contempt.

'So, it seems the child witch was right, the visions do appear to be cloaked in truth. But I see no reason for your presence here. You despoil this holy site as a runaway traitor. Maybe something even worse.'

Seren could feel the druid tense with anger and she stilled him with a gentle touch. 'An abused and much wronged wife, my lady. And as we are all here under one banner, hardly a traitor. At least I am not a murderess. I do not have the blood of an innocent child on my hands.'

'Nor do I,' Vanora replied with a smirk. 'How could I? My total dedication to serving the Welsh King has left me tied to the court at Rhuddlan ...'

She pulled her horse around in a tight half circle with cruel tugs on the bit, sending up a flurry of small stones and clods of grass to fly up and hit Seren.

'You are a widow now, made so under dark circumstances, and I would advise you to remain in exile. For your own safety, of course.'

Vanora kicked on her horse to gallop away with her followers.

'She is a nothing, a spent force, Adwen,' murmured Seren to calm his anger, 'and she knows it. All she has left is her spite.'

But Vanora's diatribe had served one useful purpose: it had revealed to Seren that her husband was dead. So at least she knew she was free from the hateful house of Adwr forever, free to be with Adwen for as long as the gods allowed.

'Brandan? Brandan!'

The warrior turned sharply at the sound of his name carrying across the night air. His heart twisted with astonishment and delight as a familiar form broke away from his escort and ran to greet him. Brandan attempted to bow low in respect to King Donal. But the man was not wasting time with the usual show of respect. He grabbed Brandan in a fierce embrace and kissed him openly on the mouth, to the ribald cheers of the Irish and the shocked indignation of the Saxons.

'The Goddess has blessed our love and brought us back together. Even if it is just for one last night.'

Overjoyed, Brandan beamed in delight at the King's words. The long time apart had clearly done nothing to destroy Donal's love for him, and his unexpected arrival at the head of a battalion of Irish warriors meant Brandan could fight alongside his countrymen again, be once more proudly Na Fianna.

'I will ride under your banner, my Lord King,' Brandan announced, his heart beating faster with longing for time alone with Donal, 'but first I must take my leave of King Cadoc, out of respect and gratitude for the hospitality of the Cornish people.'

'Especially their women,' Donal laughed, as he granted the warrior permission to leave his presence.

As dawn approached, King Donal lay on a makeshift bed of sheepskins over the rough earth and watched his lover slumber, his naked body lit from the warm glow of a dying fire. How Brandan could sleep so deeply on the eve of such a battle was a mystery. After they had made passionate love, Donal had spent the rest of the night in a fretful and failed attempt at rest. He'd left his tent and exchanged bravado-laden banter with his men. Paced the lines of horses, calming the fractious ones with a soothing word and pat on the neck. Checked his weapons and armour over and over again, polishing the chain mail, iron buckles and bronze and garnet decorations himself, not trusting an aide. His life could depend on these trappings of war not failing in the heat of battle.

With daybreak now upon them, it was time to rouse Brandan from his sleep. With one finger, he lightly traced the intricate curved lines of the large blue tattoo on his lover's chest. Donal knew and loved every inch of the complex pattern, had done this journey many times in the past, but never with such a sense of impending heartbreak. The chances of either of them surviving the next few hours were slim to nil. Brandan's tattoo was the stylised pattern of a raven, no doubt to show his devotion to Morrigu, a wise choice of deity for a warrior. Donal had the sun sign of the great god Lugh, son of Dagda, displayed on his own chest, a majestic and natural choice for a King.

As Brandan stirred and awoke, the King saw a change in his eyes. Donal had known them flash with cold fury, smoulder with lust and become smoky with satiated hedonism, but now they were the blackest he'd ever seen them. He had never witnessed Brandan's eyes sparkle with real emotion before, not with the love that shone from them now. He reached down and took Brandan's face in his hands. 'I love you, my warrior. Heart and soul. If we should both be sent Beyond today, I will find you. I swear on all the gods, we will ride through the Summerlands together for all eternity.'

Brandan did not share his certainty; he suspected that Donal, as a good man and a just King, would have a more exalted position in the afterlife than one with a lifetime tally of lies, murders and adultery. But he knew it would be cruel and unwise to mention this: a weakening doubt would take power from Donal's sword-arm in battle.

'Just ride?' Brandan replied with a knowing grin. 'In that case, we had better enjoy these last moments of life.'

He pulled Donal down on top of him, kissing him with the fierce hunger of need and love. There was no point in holding back now, not with Death's shadow hovering above them. Brandan knew he would love only once in his life, and this man was the one his heart, body and soul craved. A locked place in his soul sprang free as he finally, openly declared his adoration for the King, and found himself exhilarated by the liberating feeling of joy it brought. No other human born had ever claimed his heart, and Donal owned it completely.

The King's hands felt the scars on the warrior's battle-torn body. So many old wounds … Every expanse of summer-tanned, hard-muscled flesh bore silent reminders of the brutal reality of Brandan's life. It was a miracle that, having survived assaults by axe and sword, he had not succumbed to a lingering death from infection. Donal loved the scars; they symbolised that the warrior had survived and healed many times to be with him now. Now, in these last moments, this intimate and precious time alone with Brandan was perfect. And perfection was always doomed.

A shadowy figure waited outside the King of Lismore's battle tent, using the cover of a glade of thickly-tangled holly bushes. Neither corporeal nor ghost, it was a shape-shifting entity created by dark magic. It had dark spaces for eyes, but someone else saw through them, far away in distant Ireland. As it observed two fire-lit shadows become one and heard groans and murmurs, the sounds of pleasure and roughly-sated male desire, it smirked in triumph.

'Such powerful love makes a weakling of the strongest warrior,' the being jeered, speaking another's thoughts yet without a mouth of its own. 'And love will slay Brandan today, not some enemy sword.'

The dawning light warmed the flat landscape, raising a spectral mist over the still waters of Avalon. A beautiful sight that became soiled and shattered at the approach of the Norman army. And what an army it was: thousands of well-armed men in a tight, disciplined formation that would have made the Roman legions appear an uncontrolled rabble. They halted in an area favourable to them and waited for the last opposition to bring the combat to them. Only it would be not a battle but a massacre.

As war horns rallied the army of the Goddess, Brandan and the King parted without a word. They had said all that they needed to in their time alone. Donal jammed down his helm and rode to assemble his forces, while Brandan sought out the company of the Na Fianna, his comrades in life and death. To have fought alongside each other would have been a dangerous distraction for both men, especially now the emotional barrier between them had gone.

As Brandan cantered along the still-lush grass, he felt a curious feeling build within him, pushing aside the pleasure aftershocks and warm glow of the morning's last, frantic, farewell lovemaking. A growl built in his throat as the agitation grew focused to an intense bloodlust and fury. It was something he always felt in the heat of pitched battle, but never so soon before. He halted the mare and tore off his cloak, chain mail, trews and tunic, exposing his hard-muscled torso and raven tattoo. Freed his hair from its braids and leather binding. He was not surprised when a near-naked and painted Tailte found him and, without a word, handed him her pouch of war paint, the blue and black of the old ways.

This felt right, a primeval return to when warriors became more than human, when they represented Death incarnate to the enemy. There would be no tactics, no quarter given. Brandan would become mayhem and slaughter until he himself was killed. Coldness gripped his heart, crushing out the heat of love, the life-affirming graces of compassion and mercy.

'You'd think the bastards would wait until there were some deaths,' a Na Fianna warrior grumbled, alarmed by the sight of an unusual number of gore crows gathering in the bare branches of a nearby stand of trees. Brandan agreed. The scavengers were attracted to the smell of death; a battleground was easy pickings, with eyes the first to be devoured. But the battle had not yet started, so why were they here now? Were these enchanted birds of ill omen? His hand reached out to touch the raven talisman around his neck. Never had he needed Morrigu's protection so badly. Like a whisper insinuating past his lifelong fatalism, Donal's love had weakened his usual resignation to death, and for the first time he wanted to survive a conflict. How insane was that, when the odds had never been so stacked against him?

The whir of many wings announced more arrivals, this time rooks, jackdaws and crows. Then came the flash of colour magpies and jays, adding further to the avian throng. All corvids. Not one red kite or buzzard joined the gathering of scavengers. Clearly this was some dark magic at work, but for which side in the conflict? Normally all raucous, quarrelsome birds, the avian spectators roosted in eerie silence on every available branch. More unnerving still was the way their black, glassy eyes appeared to focus on one man: on Brandan.

'Your namesakes are here to cheer you on, my friend,' murmured a deeply unsettled Tailte. 'You are the "Raven" after all …'

'It is just a name,' Brandan growled, 'nothing more than that, and given to many dark-haired boys.'

In truth, the sight of so many carrion birds, drawn to the scene of impending slaughter, unnerved him badly. The strangeness of the turmoil building within him was somehow connected to their arrival, but he could not explain exactly how. He just knew it on some deep, primal level. He forced himself to make the most of it, for the sake of the morale of his fellow warriors. He halted his horse, stood up on the animal's narrow back – a considerable feat of balance and horsemanship – and called out to the other riders.

'This is a wondrous omen, my brothers and sisters of Na Fianna! These are messengers from Morrigu herself, our beloved dark goddess, our blessed champion in battle. They have come to feast on our enemies!'

Uncertainty and unease rippled through the ranks. The warriors knew that the birds had no loyalty to any side in the aftermath of battle, feasting off friend and foe with equal relish and appetite. Brandan grimaced: this was not the reaction he had hoped for. Such hesitation meant the battle was already lost. Not for the first time, but maybe the last, he made a whispered, desperate plea for courage from the Goddess.

As if in answer, a dark shadow crossed the sky and the air reverberated with slow, loud wing beats that echoed in the warriors' souls. It was a sensation of dread, yet thrilling too, filling their hearts with ice fire. As one, the warriors gazed upwards. Brandan recognised the creature at once. It was the spectral raven, the larger-than-normal, unnatural creature he believed came from the other world: not the world of Man or Sidhe, but that of the Goddess of battle.

'Give me your strength, Morrigu,' he roared to the heavens. 'Let me honour you today with the heads of our enemies.'

Tailte joined his declaration with the *Diord Fionn,* her proud war cry, which was then taken up by the others and rippled along the Na Fianna lines until the many voices were one.

Guillaume sneered with contempt as he heard the Irish war cries echo across the open plains, clearly audible despite loud hisses of building steam rising from his formidable arsenal. The Irish were such barbarians. A dying race of painted savages, they would feel the brutal crush of Norman might far harder than the Christian Saxons. The Duke wanted to rule the Saxons; he wanted to exterminate the Irish and Welsh. To wipe their memory from the face of the Earth. Their demonic pagan ways were too enmeshed in their wild souls for him to let them live. Their empty lands would be home to generations of Anglo/Norman settlers.

Peace and prosperity would reign under his iron grip. Guillaume would build like no King had before – magnificent cathedrals, prosperous monasteries, mighty castles of stone – so that no man could doubt who ruled the lands. Vast new forests would cover areas of now peasant-infested scrubland to give him sport ...

His reverie was abruptly broken by a hard-pressed messenger. What was left of the Saxon defending army had begun its assault. At last, the final battle for England had begun.

The Duke stood up in his stirrups to get a better view of his army. And what an army! His men stood still, with heads held proud, confident in their untouchable power and loyalty to the Duke. His vision had become theirs. The conquest of these isles would see them rewarded with land and a life of peace and plenty. With virtually no losses to their number since landing on this soil, nothing had stopped their relentless advance across their new lands. Guillaume of Normandy was now King of England, by conquest and by the blessing of Rome. All that was needed was to crush these last, pathetic pockets of futile resistance.

The sun glared off polished chain mail, helm and weaponry, making a dazzling display of superior technology. A gilded army, rank after rank of iron-clad warriors, disciplined and determined. Over a hundred of them held steam dracons in their arms. The fearsome devices hissed with eager menace, primed and ready to unleash their death bolts. Behind them, poised and awaiting Guillaume's signal, gangs of strong men held the tethers of the flying boats, ready to launch and soar high above the enemy lines, from where they would terrify both men and horses and release burning hell down upon their defenceless heads. Invincible, the day and England were already his. He could see victory shining in the eyes of his soldiers, and for the first time, nothing but respect and obedience from all his barons.

The defending force had no strategy against the Normans' devil weapons, just their ferocity and courage, the strength of their sword-arms and the agility and speed of their horses. Brandan rode at the head of the Irish warriors, pushing down toward the enemy lines at a flat-out gallop. The thundering of many hooves arriving to his left made him snap his head around, puzzled. A helmed warrior with familiar white gold-hair streaming behind him like a pennant led a group of hard-riding horsemen. Hereward. The Mercians were joining forces with their pagan foes, a plan created by Harold of England. Brandan gave a nod of respect and a broad, fierce smile as the Saxon brought his horse to ride alongside his, a gesture of solidarity that raised a cheer from both forces.

With a low hiss and scream, the enemy unleashed the first barrage of dracon-powered javelins, piercing men and horses with their ruthless precision. Many fell, but with nothing to lose, the cavalry pressed on, preparing to rush the Norman lines at high speed, whatever the cost.

To the west, Harold and some of his thegns brought the battle to another front in the hope of distracting and splitting the Norman assault, allowing the bulk of his army to make a slow and stealthy progress to get behind the enemy lines and thus surround them. A desperate plan, but there could be no other when valour and skill at arms meant nothing.

Guillaume could not believe his enemies' suicidal tactics. He soon realised it was a waste of valuable resources picking off the horsemen as they charged, regrouped and charged again. Harold's army on another front was a larger threat, and after defeating them, he would still have the rest of England to subdue. Already the Scandinavian sea wolves were reported to have taken advantage of Harold's earlier defeat and were moving their forces back into the north of the country, damn them! He ordered his dracon-bearers to cease fire and sent in a battalion of infantry backed up with cavalry, all armed with traditional weapons of sword and bow.

This added fuel to the Celt and Mercian ferocity; they relished a battle in terms they could understand. The Normans had seriously underestimated their courage and determination, and the defenders fought back hard, pushing the Duke's forces further and further back.

Guillaume had no choice but to redeploy the steam-powered arsenal. What he had first thought an undisciplined, impetuous charge was in fact a clever tactic, drawing out and depleting the invaders' resources before they faced the determined remnants of the English army.

Brandan even through his bloodlust became aware of a figure gliding through the battlefield toward him. Glowing eyes burning into his despite the distance between them. Instinct told him this apparition was not human, and neither was it Sidhe. What manner of illusion was this? Brandan dismissed it as some witch's trick, maybe from his unknown tormenter. He had no time for this nonsense in the heat of pitched battle and pulled Lia's head around to gallop away. At least, that was his plan. There was something sickeningly familiar carried in the apparition's hand, something he needed to ignore but was compelled to turn and stare at.

The figure approached on foot at unnatural speed, unseen by any battling warrior around it. Dressed as a Norman fighter, it had in one hand a blood- and gore-stained sword and in the other a human head, which it was carrying by its long, dark russet hair. When close to Brandan, it raised the severed head high with a malicious, mocking laugh. Brandan's world collapsed in horror and anguish. 'Nooooo … It can't be … Not Donal …'

Dangerously weakened by his grief, Brandan lost focus on the battle; the Normans' advance with their fearsome weapons had not been slowed down for long by the brave assault by the mounted defenders. The hissing dracons brought down wave after wave of horses and men with their high-powered flaming javelins. Acrid black smoke obscured the rolling downs, with only the summit of the Tor rising above the stinking carnage. Brandan looked around wildly for the Norman taunting him with Donal's head but could see nothing beyond the nightmare of dying beasts and warriors. A javelin hissed toward him, too fast for him to avoid it impaling Lia through the chest. Cursing, Brandan leapt clear of his stricken horse. More grief. He had nothing left to lose. Waving his sword high above his head, he charged toward the advancing Normans, leaping over the dead and screaming the war cry *'Diord Fiann!'*

He became death incarnate, hacking and slashing at the empty air, but it was a futile attack: the soldier with his lover's severed head had disappeared as if the apparition had never existed. The other Norman attackers stayed safe behind their solid wall of metal weapons and spitting fire. Brandan's brave stance and loud cries of grief-fuelled defiance made him an easy target. Volleys of fiery javelins spat and flared by him within a hair's breadth of his body, yet he remained unharmed. From their separate vantage points, both Harold and Guillaume became aware of the blood-stained Irishman moving away from the carcass of his dead mount and trying to take on the might of the Norman army singlehanded.

Harold shivered with dawning recognition. Could this be the same man who had taunted the Saxon defences in Cornwall before they were swept away by the raging Tamar? Impossible. Maybe this was something supernatural; he had been warned to expect the use of pagan magic in this battle. Could the rider of the dappled grey horse could be a premonition of Saxon success … or a warning of failure? Harold tried to force such foolish thoughts aside. Reason told him this warrior was just a man, insane with suicidal bloodlust. But his heart hoped otherwise.

'Give that crazy Irish bastard some cover!' Harold commanded, erring on the side of good omen. When faced with such overwhelming odds, he was prepared to seize on any sliver of hope, however faint. Indeed, the Na Fianna warrior's refusal to back down to Norman might had raised spirits; battle cries from all the gathered nations rang out, joining the eerie howl of the Celtic wind horns. Saxon swords beat upon shields in a defiant rhythm.

Across the battlefield, Guillaume was unperturbed by the revival of the enemy forces, seeing it as akin to nothing more than the last pathetic bellows of a dying stag. But the naked Irish warrior intrigued him. What madness or courage spurred the young man on? To be so vulnerable, with no armour against the entire might of his army? Guillaume drove his horse hard to gallop through the disciplined ranks of his army, refusing an offer of a dracon from a startled soldier. This was to be settled in the old way, by sword. The battles across England had been too easy, boring to a warrior such as he, like shooting arrows into rats trapped in a deep barrel. The Duke intended to have some sport with the crazed, painted barbarian before crushing Harold and his mismatched allies once and for all.

The defending force looked on as a breach appeared in the front line of the Norman advance and a rider on a big Friesian stallion galloped through it. A tall man, barrel-chested and bearing a sword, rode toward the Irishman and circled him, holding his horse in a tight hand canter. A red tunic resplendent with two gold lions proclaimed the rider's identity. Duke Guillaume of Normandy had personal plans to kill the unlikely symbol of defiance.

This did not please Harold. What if the pagan warrior overcame Guillaume by some great skill of arms or madness-fuelled freak occurrence? The King would be robbed of his right, of his victory. Guillaume was his. Any hope the man would be cut down in a hail of javelins from his own side ended when the dracons became still, all the Normans pausing to watch the outcome of the one-to-one combat. The heady war cries of the Saxon and pagan army fell silent as they too became engrossed in the mismatched skirmish.

A treacherous thought briefly flitted across the English King's mind, to bring down the madman with a well-aimed arrow, leaving Guillaume for himself. Shocked at his own crass selfishness, Harold prayed for forgiveness.. The chances of the Irish warrior surviving his battle with Guillaume were in any case too slim to merit a wager. If God willed it, Harold would have his time confronting the Bastard of Normandy.

Brandan stood tall and firm at the galloping approach of the Norman leader. The invader had a strong, obedient horse beneath him, but Brandan had his agility, skill at arms and the power of the dark fury building up inside him. Brandan's sword Fiacre felt light and alive in his hand, eager to taste more flesh and blood. The Irish warrior remained calm and poised as Guillaume circled the black stallion close around him. The iron-clad hooves threw up clods of earth and the animal's snorting hot breath sent flecks of spume through the air as the horse champed at the bit. Brandan followed the steed's progress, knowing at any minute Guillaume would wrench it around tightly and charge straight at him.

The horse circled even closer then whipped around, but its high, showy action made it slow, and Brandan was ready. Guillaume leant down and took a slice at the warrior but found only air. Growling in frustration, the Duke brutally hauled his horse to a sudden halt, quelling its answering rearing rebellion with a vicious dig of his spurs before driving it on for another head-on charge. Again, Guillaume's slashing sword found no target, it was as if he was attacking smoke.

His frayed patience evaporating into outrage, Guillaume whirled the horse around in another tight circle. The Irish warrior stood with his head high, a mocking grin on his handsome face, beckoning to his adversary to attack again. His impudence and courage provoked renewed cheering from the defenders and jeers at the Duke's inability to bring him down.

An ugly sneer contorted Guillaume's face. This painted heathen would not mock him. He attempted another charge, this time at an even slower pace. Taking a brutal hold of the reins yet still spurring on, he forced his stallion into a high-stepping agitated trot. The animal shook its long mane with frustration and discomfort. Guillaume waited until he was close enough to reach down and touch the warrior, then threw his weight to one side, forcing the horse to swing sideways. With both hands on the hilt, the Duke cleaved the air with his sword, expecting to connect with flesh, sinew, bone and blood.

Laughter greeted him, echoing across the smoke landscape from the enemy. The Irishman had the brazen nerve to give a cheeky bow to his supporters. Yet again his agility and fast reflexes had saved him.

Enough of this! Guillaume rode back to his troops and grabbed a loaded dracon. The Devil take chivalry and honour. This was war. This move silenced both armies as it appeared the duel was to become nothing but unequal slaughter. The Irish warrior did not change his provocative mocking stance but stood facing with fatalistic courage the hissing death to come. He kissed his sword and held it in front of him with both hands. The shocked silence broke into howls of outrage from the defenders and cheers of encouragement from the invaders. The Irishman could possibly avoid one steam-powered javelin but not a barrage. Guillaume halted his stallion and took careful aim - this nonsense was now over.

A quiver of many wings broke his concentration as, seemingly from nowhere, a flock of rooks hampered his view in a flurry of black feathers and raucous cries. Guillaume swore, trying to keep the warrior in sight, finding himself suddenly vulnerable to attack. In desperation, the Duke shouted at the flying vermin to try to disperse them, but the air became more agitated with the arrival of yet more birds – a mass of magpies, crows, choughs and jackdaws. Circling Guillaume in a malevolent dark cloud, they pecked at any exposed flesh they could find. His horse, uncontrollable with panic, reared upright to rid itself of its brutal rider. Unbalanced by the heavy weapon and unable to keep his seat, Guillaume kicked his feet clear of the stirrups and landed heavily as his mount galloped back to the Norman lines.

Guillaume desperately swatted away the birds with the dracon, struggling to focus on his enemy through the whirlwind of feathers and sharp beaks. The Irish warrior had not moved but stood glaring at him with eyes as baleful and black as the birds'. The Duke's face ran with rivulets of blood from the bird strikes, despite the protection of his helm. There was no time to waste; one well-aimed strike from a beak could take out an eye at any moment. Guillaume fired the dracon.

Time froze. Brandan stopped dead in his tracks, chest heaving with exertion, while all around him remained still as statues with weapons uplifted, horses poised mid-rear, warriors' mouths open in silent bellows of defiance. His assailant lay on the ground on his back, the heavy weapon thrown to one side, his arms raised to protect his eyes from the birds. What madness was this? Was he dead and this his last dream before departing beyond the Veil?

A woman's voice surrounded him, overwhelming his senses; a voice so powerful, so unearthly, that Brandan instinctively dropped to his knees and crouched low to the ground, hiding his face from the awesome presence. Darkness enveloped him, not from any lack of light but from the shadow of immense black wings. The air crackled, charged with an immense cold force, so very old, from a time before the sun and moon were created.

Reality screamed as a rent tore through it in a whirlwind of ancient, unearthly energy. Brandan finally found the courage to glance up as a tall figure stood before him, robed in flame, her radiant beauty terrible in its war-like glory and far beyond that of any mortal ever born. Morrigu. Once more the Goddess walked upon the Earth. Her eyes blazed with fierce pride and a love that enveloped the warrior in an embrace of such power it could have wiped out whole armies of men. An all-devouring selfish love that could never soften to forgiveness or to sacrifice. A love lesser than that known by humans, for all its passion.

Brandan's whole being convulsed. His back contorted with spine-snapping spasms and a scream began deep inside his soul, rising in volume and intensity before exploding from his lungs to echo across the time-frozen battlefield. He lost control of his senses and collapsed, lying still and death-like on the ground.

'Arise, my beloved son. The time of your destiny has arrived.'

Brandan tried to speak, but was so overcome that his words came out in a hoarse whisper. 'Who are you? What do you want of me?'

Laughter, humourless, imperious, deafened him, causing him to cower even lower to the ground.

'My son, you know who I am now. The answer has always been there, locked deep in your soul. I have protected you since birth by the gift of forgetfulness. Now it is time to remember who you are. You are the human-born son of Morrigu. You are my Prince of Ravens. My living weapon against the ambitions and pride of human men. Created to protect my people against a seemingly unbeatable foe.'

A flare of blue fire blazed out from the outstretched hands of the Goddess, surrounding Brandan. He stood in the centre of the fiery whirlwind for a last few seconds of human existence before the vortex entered his body to transform him to something terrifying. Awareness of his being as a lowly warrior bard faded to nothing as he became a new form of preternatural life, his body now invincible, immune to any weapon forged by Man. His skin colour changed to a glossy blue-black. His eyes lost all white pigment, becoming cold and glistening shards of polished jet. Vast wings of iridescent black feathers grew between his shoulders, allowing him to rise above the battleground and soar across the smoke-acrid sky.

Time once more regained its relentless momentum.

Cries of horror rose above the battlefield as Guillaume's forces discovered their leader slain. Killed by the flying vermin, his face pecked to a fleshless skull, the Norman invader had fallen to a cruel end. Now the invaders' cries turned to screams as the first wing-beats of the newly-born creature sent shock waves across the battlefield, sending men and horses crashing to the ground.

Revelling in his power and speed, the Prince of Ravens flew above both armies, gaining in strength and murderous purpose with every wing-beat.

His eyes had become weapons, flashing with cold blue flames. All that Brandan had been now lost, he became a fury, a whirling, lashing, living rage of destruction, one that was beyond discriminating between friend and foe. Unknowingly, the Goddess had created a flawed being, one that should have had no understanding of human emotions. She had not calculated that her monstrous son would retain feelings. The creature that had once been Brandan was consumed with grief and anger over the loss of his beloved soul mate. The Prince of Ravens knew not why it was so furious; it lived only to kill and kill again.

A black bolt of feathered doom, it scorched its way above the Norman lines, weaving a deadly path, incinerating men to ash and melting their fearsome new weapons into molten pools. Men by their hundreds died defenceless against the unearthly blue fire. Leaving only silence in its wake, the creature soared back into the sky, where it had some sport with the Duke's flying ships, sending them crashing into each other by its powerful wing-beats. With their hot air–filled canopies collapsing, the flying ships tumbled from the sky. Some of their helpless sailors were tipped out to fall to their doom, others were burned alive by their own barrels of blazing pitch. In a few seconds, the entire fleet had been destroyed.

The Prince of Ravens had defeated the foreign invaders, but it was not enough. The fierce joy of destruction had become all that it was, a bloodlust that needed more fuel to sate its appetite. It flew high above the Saxon and pagan armies, becoming a vengeful black cloud against the grey skies as it decided which one to devastate first.

Adwen turned his horse away from the Cornish cavalry in full retreat and galloped back to the high point where Seren and the other mystics waited at the circle of stones. Many were keening and wailing, so distraught were they at the carnage, their terrible visions finally coming to fulfilment. The stench of burnt flesh and bone hung in the air, carried by a pall of black smoke on the wind created by the Raven's wings. It settled on the living in a greasy miasma. On reaching his beloved little star, Adwen leapt from his horse, allowing it to gallop to any safety it could find, and swept Seren into his arms for what could be their last moments together this side of the Veil.

'What can we do?' Seren wept, her blindness no comfort against the assault on her senses, the terrible aftermath of the burning that all were forced to breath in, the cries of terror, the screams of the agonised dying men and horses.

Adwen had no answer, beyond accepting they had lost Brandan to the hidden reality within him, to the horror that was the Prince of Ravens. The druid's vision quests had come to realisation. Why hadn't he listened to the warnings? Killed Brandan when he was a mere mortal? Frozen in horror and tormented guilt, how could he find some inner reserve of strength? What could stop the deadly Prince of Ravens before it ravaged all the world of men, left the entire Earth scorched in its primal rage?

The hilltop became crowded as desperate warriors from all the armies that had fought under the banner of the Goddess inevitably returned to their spiritual leaders. They all pleaded with the mystics, with Seren and the druid, for help. Warriors wide-eyed with shock, many with terrible burns, knew this was no longer the time for fighting men; it was the time for skilled wielders of the old, deep magic of the earth. Their expectation only fuelled Adwen's despair. Turning to the witch, he cried, 'How can any mortal defeat the son of a Goddess?'

'We have to try, beloved,' Seren said, reaching up to touch the druid's face, saddened by the river of tears she felt running down it. Had he given up hope? If his strength failed, would hers be enough?

'I can stop this!' she insisted.

A shout from an unexpected arrival astonished those gathered on the hillside. The Irish King, Donal, had galloped hard to join the mystics at the circle of stone. Reining back to a sudden halt, he leapt off his mount – a wretched, wounded beast exhausted to the point of collapse – and strode to the centre of the stones.

The King was alive. Brandan had been pushed over the edge of reason by an anger and grief borne of an illusion, a cruel hoax from the warrior's unknown enemy that had now damned them all. Donal took the blind witch's hands in his, to convince her of his determination and sincerity.

'I am the only one the human heart within Brandan has ever loved,' he said. 'I must try to summon back that man of flesh, blood and desire. Free him from the curse of the Raven.'

Seren's sightless eyes widened at this announcement. Was this a tiny ember of hope, when all the terror of her visions had now become brutal reality.. She reached out for the King's hand, found it wet with fresh blood from the battle. 'It is too late, my lord King. The warrior is no longer human. Brandan is now the Prince of Ravens, an abomination, one that will destroy all human life.'

'I know why,' Donal replied, his face deathly pale. 'One of the Na Fianna, a warrior called Tailte, saw a spectral form in the guise of a Norman soldier approach Brandan, bearing my severed head. This foul lie is what triggered the Raven hidden within him to such an excess of destruction, of this I am certain. The human within is seeking vengeance, so maybe that human is still there.'

Donal was speaking with great urgency, convinced there was a slender chance he could reach any remaining spark of humanity and emotion hidden deep within the Raven. He could see the doubt in the mystics' eyes, but what other hope was there? With no other answers, Adwen and Seren gave their blessing and support. The young King stood alone under the last tall stones. It was a precarious place, beneath the heavy lintel of rough granite, buffeted by the storm force of the Raven Prince's flight. Donal ignored his own wavering balance and, summoning up all the power and passion of his emotions, called out to the baleful creature circling high above the scorched and burning battlefield.

'I call out for Brandan of the Golden Harp. I call for my beloved to return to me. My only love, which my heart and soul will hold forever.'

None believed the creature could hear or heed the man's cries, yet the Prince of Ravens swooped dangerously low, forcing Donal to drop to his knees to keep his balance. He flinched with every battering downbeat of the creature's great wings, the blows bruising him as if he was being beaten by many men with hammers. Any closer and the creature would break every bone in his body.

'He is in grave trouble, the next assault could kill him,' growled Adwen, grabbing Seren's hand. Maybe their combined magic could fend off the Raven long enough to buy Donal more time?

'Brandan. You were lied to … See for yourself, I am alive. Alive!'

Despite the pain, Donal gathered his resolve and returned to his feet, stood his ground, tall and proud, head high. The next attack could be the last, and he would die not on his knees but as a King.

Urged on by some deep instinct, Seren let go of Adwen's hand. 'Help me reach my pony,' she said.

Adwen led her out beyond the circle of stones to where the animal was tethered. The wretched creature was terrified beyond belief. It pawed at the tree trunk that held it captive. At Seren's calming hand, the beast ceased it's struggle. She ran her palm over its head and down its back. Then she retrieved the golden harp from one of its saddlebags.

Pleading with the haunted instrument for help, Seren played a few chords, the gentle sound making a stark contrast to the death-bringing downbeat of the Raven's wings.

'Louder!' urged Adwen. Fate had given the harp to this girl, wisdom had made her learn to play it, and the trapped soul of the dead fairy who loved Brandan would surely help her.

As the Raven Prince plummeted toward the ground, a spectral wind howling with ferocity, Seren played an Irish love song. She had no idea how she knew the words or the melody; the music just flowed through her body and into her slender fingers. The river of beautiful sound, amplified by Cerise's magic talisman, rose louder and louder above the thunderous beat of the Raven's wings. The enchanted song entered one by one the hearts of first the Irish, then the Cornish and the Welsh, and their voices joined with that of the harp. The song was carried on the burning wind and reached the Saxon army, and they too began to sing. Each joined in with their own language, yet there was no discordant noise; the song became blended into a magical harmony of great power. Yet again Cerise's blessed gift of the rainbow stone had come to help them.

Confused at first by the beautiful sound ascending, the Raven halted in mid-plummet and rose higher in the sky to avoid it. Once again Donal cried out to the monstrous being: '*A rún mo chroí*. I love you, Brandan of the Golden Harp. I love you.'

The black cloud of rage borne on supernatural wings grew briefly fainter, a frantic blur of confusion and doubt. Hating the feeling of weakness, the Raven reacted with a yet greater anger, one needing instant gratification. Its obsidian gaze caught by the obscenity of dead stone crowning the Tor, the Raven plummeted toward it, blasting it with cold fire, pulverising the building completely, sending nothing more than dust flying across the landscape. As the Raven soared high again, the heartbeat of the Tor stirred from its centuries of enforced slumber. The ground beneath the watching humans' feet reverberated with movement from deep within, the sound growing to a deafening rumble of released energy.

Though all felt the surging power erupt from the Tor's summit, few understood it. In a shimmering ripple of mystic colours, the Mother's healing energy surged down the hillside and undulated across the battlefield, instantly healing the wounded, however grievous their injuries, before fusing back deep into the landscape where it belonged. Confused and buffeted by the shockwave of benign energy that drained its deadly anger, the Raven soared yet higher to try to escape it. It circled high above the battleground, seeking its former malign purpose and fury-driven power, looking for more victims to slaughter.

Seren could tell from the muted sound of its wing-beats that the Raven had flown dangerously high, but the threat it posed to the world was too great for her to stop the music now. Boosted by the miraculous gift of beneficent energy from the Tor, Seren poured all her being into her playing, helping the Sidhe spirit's song to soar higher and louder into the sky. Beside her Adwen sang, his voice deep and melodious, redolent with his own formidable druidic power.

The being that was the Prince of Ravens flailed and span as it fought to assert itself over the human soul lost at its heart. Explosions of lethal power flashed out from its body, causing bolts of blue flame to strike the ground below. Trees groaned and came crashing down. Rivers burst their banks. People were thrown from their feet to cower desperate for purchase on the unstable earth.

Did Brandan win his battle for his humanity or did Morrigu simply abandon her horrific son? Whatever triggered the change, it was as sudden as a lightning strike. The Raven lost its power, its wings, and reverted to an all-too-human body, plummeting toward the ground. But as Donal's horrified cry rose toward it, the body's fall began to slow. A new sound replaced the harp music and the human song: a chilling, heart-stopping buzzing like that of a huge swarm of bees. It erupted above the battlefield and rose up to meet Brandan, who was then swathed in a protective cloud of glittering gold.

The Sidhe.

One by one, a group of the Shining Ones materialised through a portal from their unearthly realm. An array of fairy folk in their many guises had flown into the air and surrounded Brandan, and now they gently eased him back onto the ground.

Donal tried to run to his lover, but Adwen was stronger and able to hold the distraught man fast. The Sidhe would destroy any human who approached them unbidden.

Brandan's face was ashen, his head lolled back at an alarming angle. One of the Sidhe wept, cradling his lifeless body in her arms. It was Queen Leanan herself, the golden-haired one who sought out human lovers among the poets and bards, whose jealous desires would drain and steal their lives as well as their souls. The Fairy Queen who had once fallen in love with Brandan. He alone had escaped her deadly embrace, stealing the haunted golden harp as he fled her lethal jealousy. The same jealousy that had killed the fairy and trapped her soul in the harp for the crime of also loving Brandan.

'He cannot be healed or exist in your world,' the Sidhe said, addressing Donal and Adwen; her voice rang clear and beautiful but cold as a glacier.

'If he is lost to this world, he will also die in yours,' the King replied, his voice bitter and cracking with emotion. 'We know of your ways, Leanan of the Sidhe.'

The Sidhe female laughed, her cruel nature revealed, her indifference to all feelings but her own.

'But you are wrong, human. Even I cannot harm the son of a Goddess. Morrigu's anger is as lethal to us as it is to humans. I make this solemn vow before Men and Sidhe, before the Goddess herself. Brandan of the Golden Harp will live on, honoured and safe in our realm.'

Beyond care for his own life, Donal refused to accept he was losing the warrior forever. He had to act fast. 'At least let me say my farewell, lady … Even you could not be so cruel as to deny me that.'

Leanan cut off his words with a ferocious growl, for a few seconds reverting to her true form, a terrible beauty normally not seen by any human or Sidhe except at their deaths. 'And allow him to remember? To have memories of your pathetic, feeble human love fester within him, tempting him to try to escape again? That will never happen. Never.'

Her arms tightened around Brandan's body with a possessive gesture. She was once more a golden-haired fey beauty, but the cruel gleam in her eyes had not softened. 'He is mine again and now will always be.'

The rest of the Sidhe surrounded Leanan, shielding her with their flowing robes or wings, bathed in shimmering golden light, and the air vibrated with deafening humming. With a thunderous bellow, the portal between two worlds reopened and the Sidhe returned to their realm taking Brandan with them, lost forever from the world of men.

On the blood-soaked ground, forgotten in the drama, lay Brandan's golden harp, its strings vibrating with a heart-rending fairy lament and the silver sound of unearthly and invisible falling tears.

14

Aftermath: England, 1067

Could one live as a man without a heart and with a gutted soul? A hollow man on a throne of straw? King Harold of England paced the floor of his audience chambers at his palace in Winchester. Petitioners addressed him, but their words were lost in meaningless babble to his unease. The crown felt heavy, uncomfortable, as if made of base metal rather than its actual pure, beaten gold.

He was now the undefeated and undisputed sovereign of the Saxons. The would-be usurper, William the Bastard, was dead and his arsenal of devil-spawned weaponry destroyed. Even the age-old menace from the north had gone for now: England's Norse enemies had slunk back to their fjords, broken and humiliated. So why was he not elated? Why had he not enjoyed the recent merriment and feasting to celebrate the wedding of the noble, heroic and steadfastly loyal Earl Hereward and his pretty bride, Elgitha?

The truth … that was what burnt out the King's heart and haunted his every waking hour of life. What did it matter that his brave army had once again trounced the latest Norse threat? It was not he who had defeated the Norman invaders, protected his throne: accursed pagan magic had. The Celtic realms were stronger than ever, and his tenuous rule of England depended on their good favour. If they decided to reclaim England for their own, he would not be able to stop them. He wore a debased crown of humility and dependence, a craven treaty with the Celtic realms having been signed with reluctance on the battlefield. A treaty that stipulated no Christian church should ever again be built on top of Glaston Tor. This enforced meekness and betrayal of his faith burned like acid through his being.

He needed to find a way of fighting back, a way of destroying all magic once and for all, so that earthly power was held only by those of strong sword bearing arms and pure Christian hearts. But in God's holy name … how?

Ireland

Queen Liadan watched as her husband paced the battlements, head down, arms holding himself tightly in an embrace of unstoppable sorrow. It had been the same routine every night since his arrival back at Lismore. Donal had returned from the triumphant rout of the Norman invasion a broken man. She had expected some short phase of passing grief for his slain lover but not this endless, destructive mourning. She told herself, time and time again, that it would pass, that her successful plan to destroy Brandan would bear the fruit she had desired, and her husband would love her again. Only her. So far there was no sign of that happening.

She knew also that his anguish would soon become more terrible when that witch Varnora took away their son. But that too would pass when he would have to come to her bed to sire another heir. Perhaps the old hag could make him a potion of forgetfulness? Something that would eradicate all memory of that warrior from his mind, take away all knowledge that he had once proudly held a treasured boy child in his arms. The Queen decided that must be so, even at the cost of her own soul or the lives of the people she ruled at her husband's side. Liadan had no regrets, not even at the terrible cost of her pact. Donal was hers … *hers* … no-one else would share his bed and live.

Darkness hugged the walls and shadows flitted across the floor of the hallway, luring her forward to the battlements of a stronghold haunted now by cruel secrets and darkest magic, all instigated by her hand. She paused, put on an expression of innocence and loving concern, perfect for the supportive, devoted wife Donal needed to reign this quarrelsome land. Soon the dead warrior would be not even a fading memory, it would be as if Brandan of the Golden Harp had never existed. Liadan would pay any price to make it so.

Normandy

Leaving his shocked and sorrowing mother and younger siblings at Caen, the 15-year-old boy who was now Duke of a broken land rode to Falaise, his seat of power. Unlike his family, Robert did not mourn, shed not one tear for the man who had sired him. Only the knowledge that his veins ran with the blood of the French royal house sustained his pride, gave him the inner strength to rule. Indeed, if he could find a way of purging all the Norseman blood that came from the Bastard, he would.

His father had been a cruel man in league with the devil, at least in his dark heart if not in reality. The crushing defeat of Norman power had left their lands lawless and vulnerable. It was time to let the people know they had a leader, give out a strong warning to their enemies.

Robert had chosen a pure white stallion, a Percheron war horse bred in

Normandy; a breed belonging to this land, unlike his father's favoured Dutch horses. The magnificent beast was too much horse for him, and he struggled to control its restless energy, but he wanted the animal to be symbolic. He could not help being his father's son, but he was also his own man, one born of Normandy and of France.

Robert's household guard consisted of the men too old to have gone to England and the youngest sons of barons lost to the disaster. He needed every one of their swords. A generation of men had been wiped out in a foreign land, sacrificed to ambition and pride. Guillaume's name was cursed by the people and denounced from every church pulpit. To have had those terrible weapons was unnatural, the work of the devil and his demon craftsmen. Guillaume must have traded his immortal soul to have obtained them. Robert knew those who said this were fools. His father had simply harnessed the brilliance and hard work of clever men, and the knowledge of the weapons was now his inheritance. He wanted them. He needed them.

Robert saw the hatred and rebellion in the eyes of every serf his cavalcade passed. To them he was the spawn of Satan's minion. There was justifiable fear, with Normandy on its knees under the rule of a child; every enemy with a past grudge would be preparing to strike. And there were so many enemies: the Bretons, the King of France, Norman noble families in exile …

His own father had known such hatred as a child, and living in fear of his life had forged him into the indomitable force that Robert had hatred. And yes, now he was dead, the son admitted, had loved in equal measure. Robert had inherited a bitter legacy of blood, but he would not yield one inch of his demesne to his enemies. They would underestimate the young Duke of Normandy at their peril.

Bent double, Ferro worked alongside his companions in a field of peas. Dressed in workmanlike peasant garb, he looked like any hard-toiling local, his once immaculately-manicured hands now callused and ingrained with soil. He had shaved off his neatly-trimmed beard and cut his long hair to mimic the severe style of Norman men. With luck, any pursuers would pass him by without a second glance. The inventor's change of fortune had happened so quickly. Guillaume had insisted the Moor was too valuable to risk taking to England until after it had been conquered and subdued. Ferro had not argued but instead had continued to develop his ideas at the Falaise workshops.

When news of the disaster had reached the castle, the Spaniard had panicked, destroying his workshops, burning all his diagrams and books in an inferno of desperation. What did they matter? The information was still in his mind. With Guillaume gone and a child now Duke, all protection had disappeared, and the Spaniard had fled Falaise with the other inventors and artisans.

With nowhere to go, he now dwelt in a remote abandoned hamlet on the furthest edge of Normandy. The disappearance of the original inhabitants was a mystery; perhaps they had paid the ultimate price if their lord and master had fallen foul of Guillaume's rage? It would not have been the first time something like that had happened. It would not be long before another baron took the land for himself, but until then Ferro remained there with a handful of the fugitive artisans. They lived like peasants, foraged for food from the abandoned fields and lay low.

With one of the others keeping watch, the Spaniard took a break, collapsing on the sun-cracked earth and sharing bread made from stale flour with the others.

The events in England had left Ferro badly shaken. What kind of force could totally obliterate so much power and metal within minutes? The few pitiful, broken survivors who had returned to Normandy had spoken of an attack by some awesome supernatural force, conjured by the pagans. Nonsense of course, but what else could have caused such catastrophic destruction? A great wind? An earthquake? He was beyond caring now. The safe sanctuary of Falaise was gone with the death of his protector, and Ferro faced an uncertain future.

Cornwall

Salt spray from the rolling surf bathed Seren's face, and she laughed. She had heard the wave's approach but been unprepared for the cold shock and power of its touch. She had previously known only still lakes, tumbling streams and the meander of wide, dignified rivers. She strolled barefoot along a beach for the first time, her arm locked securely around that of her husband: Adwen, the chief druid of all Kernow. He paused briefly to stoop down and pick up a large scallop shell still warm from the summer sun baking the beach. He pressed it into her hand, loving her smile of delight at the feel of a new treasure.

They continued to walk, revelling in the sunshine and the heady breeze blowing in from the ocean on which seabirds rode on still wings above them. The hardships of winter and the nightmare of battle seemed a distant dream now. Reality was soft, warm sand under their feet and the caressing heat of the sun. Reality was being together, joined in love. Reality was the gentle rise of Seren's swelling belly and the promise of new life. Adwen's child, one who would be raised in joy and love.

Earlier that morning they had revisited the fairy grove where they had left the haunted harp after the battle. The Sidhe soul trapped by Leanan's curse within the instrument had been inconsolable after the battle, grieving in glissandos of tormented strings that nothing could sooth or quieten. With no human magic able to break the curse and give the fairy peace, Seren and her husband had had no choice but to give her back to the Sidhe, and had buried the harp beneath a weeping willow by a sparkling stream. Today they had discovered the harp gone and wild roses growing over the spot: a good sign perhaps that the instrument might not have been dug up and stolen by human thieves but taken to the fairy realm, and maybe back to her beloved Brandan. Sadly, Seren had to accept that was unlikely, given the Side's Queen's legendary jealousy.

The walk along the sunlit beach with the warm southerly breeze buffeting them as if playful, helped relieve their sense of melancholy from the morning's duty.

'It is finally over now, isn't it?' Seren halted and gazed up. 'The Prince of Ravens destroyed all the Norman hissing dracons and flying ships, and the seers' dreams of future carnage have stopped. We are safe now.'

Adwen sighed inwardly as he watched the tide roll in and crash along the wide beach; such great power, far beyond that of Man. He did not share his wife's optimism. The Duke of Normandy had been just one ambitious man with the courage to grasp and utilise new knowledge from the east. With the help of Morrigu and her fearsome son, the Celtic realms had won an important battle, but the real war had not yet started. One by one, lands across the known world had fallen by the sword to worshipping that broken figure, that one jealous god who would tolerate no others.

The pagan lands were now on the twilight of existence, caught between a mainly Christian Europe and the wide ocean from the edge of the world, the waves of which now rose like mountains and pounded against these western shores. There was nowhere else to go, nor would he ever leave this land steeped in thousands of years of his people's heritage. The gods, the landscape and the people were intrinsically linked, part of the ageless circle of life combining the elements of fire, air, water, earth and spirit. Destroy that link and his people would perish or become the slaves of an alien faith.

Seren felt her husband's mood change, become pensive and anxious. Her own optimism was purely self-defence; she had this chance for happiness with Adwen and would cherish every moment in the sunshine of tranquillity. She shivered as a cloud passed over the sun, as if in warning; fleeting, but enough to remind her how fragile this time of peace was.

Adwen held her closer, wrapped his cloak around her slender shoulders. Her tremble could not have been from cold; the sun was strong and the wind warm. Was it a reaction to a fearful premonition? Despite her blindness, she had glanced up sharply. Adwen followed the direction of her sightless eyes, but there was nothing to mar the perfection of a cloudless azure sky. Even the gliding sea birds had gone.

Had it been a shadow of ill omen, another warning? Adwen shielded his eyes against the sun with one hand and scoured the sky again for some natural explanation. There was none.

The spirit form of the Raven, wrenched from its earthly incarnation, returned to the Beyond behind the Veil and to its resting place in the cold and darkness. There it waited with infinite patience for a summons to return …

ABOUT THE AUTHOR

Raven Dane is an award-winning fantasy author based in the UK. Her published works include the highly acclaimed *Legacy of the Dark Kind* series of dark fantasy/sci-fi crossover novels (*Blood Tears, Blood Lament* and *Blood Alliance*).

However, Raven's skills in fiction don't end there. Her comedy fantasy *The Unwise Woman of Fuggis Mire* - a scurrilous spoof of high fantasy clichés – was met with great enthusiasm by the reading public. In more recent years Raven has met with critical acclaim for her steampunk/occult adventures *Cyrus Darian and the Technomicron* and *Cyrus Darian and the Ghastly Horde*.

Cyrus Darian and the Technomicron was the winner of the best novel award at the inaugural Victorian Steampunk Society awards 2012.

Raven also has many short stories published in anthologies including one in *Full Fathom Forty*, a celebration of 40 years of the British Fantasy Society, and the first annual of ghost stories from Spectral Press, called the *13 Ghosts of Christmas*.

Further works include poetry, published in an anthology of pagan verse.

Her third Cyrus Darian novel was published in 2014.

OTHER TELOS TITLES

HORROR/FANTASY

RAVEN DANE
ABSINTHE & ARSENIC

DAVID J HOWE
TALESPINNING

SHROUDED BY DARKNESS: TALES OF TERROR
edited by ALISON L R DAVIES
An anthology of tales guaranteed to bring a chill to the spine. This collection has been published to raise money for DebRA, a national charity working on behalf of people with the genetic skin blistering condition, Epidermolysis Bullosa (EB). Featuring stories by: Debbie Bennett, Poppy Z Brite, Simon Clark, Storm Constantine, Peter Crowther, Alison L R Davies, Paul Finch, Christopher Fowler, Neil Gaiman, Gary Greenwood, David J Howe, Dawn Knox, Tim Lebbon, Charles de Lint, Steven Lockley & Paul Lewis, James Lovegrove, Graham Masterton, Richard Christian Matheson, Justina Robson, Mark Samuels, Darren Shan and Michael Marshall Smith. With a frontispiece by Clive Barker and a foreword by Stephen Jones. Deluxe hardback cover by Simon Marsden.

URBAN GOTHIC: LACUNA AND OTHER TRIPS
edited by DAVID J HOWE
Tales of horror from and inspired by the *Urban Gothic* television series. Contributors: Graham Masterton, Christopher Fowler, Simon Clark, Steve Lockley & Paul Lewis, Paul Finch and Debbie Bennett.

HELEN MCCABE

THE PIPER TRILOGY
PIPER
THE PIERCING
CODEX (Autumn 2015)

SIMON CLARK
HUMPTY'S BONES
THE FALL

GRAHAM MASTERTON
RULES OF DUEL
THE DJINN

SAM STONE

THE JINX CHRONICLES
1: JINX TOWN
2: JINX MAGIC (Autumn 2015)
3: JINX BOUND (Autumn 2016)

KAT LIGHTFOOT MYSTERIES
1: ZOMBIES AT TIFFANY'S
2: KAT ON A HOT TIN AIRSHIP
3: WHAT'S DEAD PUSSYKAT
4: KAT OF GREEN TENTACLES (Autumn 2015)

THE DARKNESS WITHIN: FINAL CUT
ZOMBIES IN NEW YORK AND OTHER BLOODY JOTTINGS

KING OF ALL THE DEAD by STEVE LOCKLEY & PAUL LEWIS

THE HUMAN ABSTRACT by GEORGE MANN

BREATHE by CHRISTOPHER FOWLER
The Office meets *Night of the Living Dead.*

HOUDINI'S LAST ILLUSION by STEVE SAVILE

ALICE'S JOURNEY BEYOND THE MOON by R J CARTER

APPROACHING OMEGA by ERIC BROWN

VALLEY OF LIGHTS by STEPHEN GALLAGHER

PRETTY YOUNG THINGS by DOMINIC MCDONAGH

A MANHATTAN GHOST STORY by T M WRIGHT

FORCE MAJEURE by DANIEL O'MAHONY

BLACK TIDE by DEL STONE JR

DOCTOR TRIPPS: KAIJU COCKTAIL by KIT COX

SPECTRE by STEPHEN LAWS

CAPTAINS STUPENDOUS by RHYS HUGHES

TELOS PUBLISHING
Email: orders@telos.co.uk
Web: www.telos.co.uk

To order copies of any Telos books, please visit our website where there
are full details of all titles and facilities for worldwide credit card online
ordering, as well as occasional special offers.

www.ingramcontent.com/pod-product-compliance
Lightning Source LLC
Chambersburg PA
CBHW070611170726
48291CB00003B/772